SWEET MISS HONEYWELL'S
REVENGE

OTHER HARCOURT NOVELS BY KATHRYN REISS

Paint by Magic

PaperQuake: A Puzzle

Pale Phoenix

Dreadful Sorry

The Glass House People

Time Windows

SWEET MISS HONEYWELL'S
REVENGE

A Ghost Story

KATHRYN REISS

Harcourt, Inc.

ORLANDO   AUSTIN   NEW YORK

SAN DIEGO   TORONTO   LONDON

www.HarcourtBooks.com

Sweet Miss Honeywell's Revenge is based on the stories *Dollhouse of the Dead, The Headless Bride,* and *Rest in Peace,* written by Kathryn Reiss.

Library of Congress Cataloging-in-Publication Data
Reiss, Kathryn.
Sweet Miss Honeywell's revenge: a ghost story/Kathryn Reiss.
p. cm.
Summary: Just before her mother is to remarry and her stepfamily is set to move in, twelve-year-old Zibby gradually realizes that her antique dollhouse is haunted by ghosts, one of whom is out for revenge.
[1. Dollhouses—Fiction. 2. Ghosts—Fiction.
3. Supernatural—Fiction. 4. Stepfamilies—Fiction.] I. Title.
PZ7.R2776Sw 2004
[Fic]—dc22 2003018699
ISBN 0-15-216574-6

Text set in Granjon
Designed by Cathy Riggs

First edition
C E G H F D B

Printed in the United States of America

Heartfelt thanks to my husband, Tom, for reading
this manuscript countless times and for understanding
the psychology of ghosts. This book is dedicated to him,
and to our five spirited children:
Nicholas, Daniel, Angie, Alexandra, and Isabel.

We cherish the memory of Jan Strychacz—father,
father-in-law, grandfather—who moved on peacefully
as I finished writing this story.

From ghoulies and ghosties
And long-leggety beasties
And things that go bump in the night,
Good Lord, deliver us!

—Scottish prayer

PROLOGUE

ONCE UPON A TIME there were four ghosts, but not enough room for all.

Not enough rooms in the whole little house.

Four ghosts:
One sat quietly, watching.
One was desperate, gathering energy.
One just wanted very much to play.
And the last grew greedy and wild, anticipating change…

Bent on revenge.

CHAPTER 1

"But you promised." Zibby glared at her mom.

"Ten more minutes, Zib. Then we'll go home."

"Not home! You said we could go to Sportsmart."

"We will, we will. That's what I meant." Nell Thorne was distracted, glancing around the large convention hall at all the booths and displays. "Now wait here like a good, sweet, wonderful girl for just ten more minutes, and then I promise I'll be ready to go." She gave Zibby a bright smile and dived back into the crowds of people.

Zibby glowered after her. She gave a swift, backward kick to the wall she was leaning against. Charlotte, at Zibby's side, threw her a scornful glance.

"You baby," said Charlotte. "Now that you're twelve, do you think maybe you could *not* have tantrums in public? It's so embarrassing." Charlotte, Zibby's cousin, was twelve, too, but acted like she was about twenty-five.

"I just want to get my Rollerblades." This was so stupid—having to hang out here while her mom moseyed around looking at dollhouses. "You'd think getting my birthday present would be more important than some dumb doll show."

"It's a miniatures convention," Charlotte corrected Zibby. "And it comes only once a year, so give your mom a break. Anyway, I don't think you're having such a bad day just because of some Rollerblades. I bet you're upset about the wedding—and Ned."

"That's *stupid*," Zibby retorted, her voice rising. "And *so* totally not true." She kicked the wall again, really hard this time, then jumped back when a bell started ringing somewhere nearby. Sort of a clanging handbell. As if her kicking the wall had set off an alarm or something.

She closed her eyes to blot out her cousin's disapproving face. She wished she could just blot out this whole day. Charlotte was right about one thing: Zibby *was* having a really bad day. Today was August 30, her twelfth birthday, the day she had been waiting for all summer—but there were three things wrong, and she couldn't change any of them. She was furious and getting more furious by the minute.

First of all, the special plan for this birthday to go camping with Amy, her best friend in the whole world since they were three years old, had fizzled into nothingness with the shocking news that Amy's family was moving away—immediately—because Amy's parents had great new jobs in Cleveland and had to start working as soon as they got there. Which was last week.

Second of all, Zibby's mom, Nell, had planned a birthday dinner at Zibby's favorite restaurant—the Fat Lady— for a special treat. Normally, that would be a good thing—

and Grammy and Gramps were invited, too, and Aunt Linnea and Uncle David with Zibby's cousins Charlotte and Owen, and of course her mom's fiancé, Ned Shimizu. But then Nell had insisted on inviting Ned's two bratty kids, Laura-Jane and Brady. Zibby liked Ned well enough, but his kids were horrible. It was a good thing they would keep living with their mother over in Fennel Grove even after the wedding. The wedding was happening in about two and a half weeks, but the birthday dinner at the Fat Lady was happening tonight. Zibby wasn't looking forward to either.

Third on the birthday-disaster list—and the most pressing right now—was the fact that Nell had promised Zibby they could go to Sportsmart to buy Rollerblades. Zibby had saved her allowance for months, helped out with her mom's catering company, and pulled a million weeds in Gramps's vegetable garden. Now, with the added birthday money from her dad, who lived in Italy, Zibby had one hundred and eighty-six dollars in her pocket—more money than she'd ever had before. More than enough for the coolest royal blue and silver Zingers and a matching helmet. Her mom insisted Zibby also get new, thick knee pads and wrist guards, but at least Nell was going to pay for those. *If* they ever got to Sportsmart.

The problem was that just before they left the house, Aunt Linnea phoned to tell Nell about the miniatures convention down in Columbus—the nearest big city to their small town of Carroway, Ohio—and then Nell had dragged Zibby to this convention first, promising they'd stop at Sportsmart *afterward*.

Well, Zibby was still waiting for *afterward*. Before they'd arrived at the place, Zibby hadn't even known what a minia-tures show was, though Aunt Linnea talked about them often. Now she knew more than she ever wanted to know. This miniature world was not for kids—*adults* were the ones milling about by the hundreds. Everybody was so ex-cited about looking at dolls and doll furniture, and even the miniature stuff people used to build the dollhouses: shingles and bricks and stones and boards. Zibby loved building things and was a very good carpenter, but she didn't have a dollhouse and didn't want one. She wanted royal blue and silver Zingers.

The bell was still clanging, giving Zibby a terrible headache. Plus now her foot hurt from kicking the wall. It was a sweltering end-of-summer day, and even though the convention center was air-conditioned, the heat seemed to seep inside anyway. Zibby felt sweaty and flushed. She edged away from Charlotte and headed toward the snack bar to get a soda.

Charlotte followed her but kept gazing around the con-vention hall, probably looking for her own mother, Zibby supposed, who was somewhere in the middle of this crowd and loving every second of it. Aunt Linnea's hobby was col-lecting exquisitely handcrafted furnishings for her doll-house, a replica of a famous stately English home called Blickling Hall, which took up one full corner of their for-mal dining room. Aunt Linnea went to miniatures conven-tions like this one all around the country, and now Zibby's mom was catching the miniatures bug, too. Nell was talking about building her own dollhouse. The two sisters could easily be here browsing and buying until midnight. And Sportsmart closed at nine. Summer was all but over, and school was starting soon, and Zibby needed her blue Zingers. She needed Nell to be done with dollhouses.

Zibby sipped her soda and checked her watch. "Ten minutes are up," she said over the sound of the insistent bell. "So where *are* they? I'm surprised your mom hasn't run out of money already. Have you seen the prices on the things she's got in those shopping bags?" She shook her head. "Must be nice to be rich."

"You're just being a pain because your precious Amy is gone," hissed Charlotte. "But I don't see why you should say mean things about my mom. I don't say mean things about *yours*."

Zibby flushed. "Sorry."

She really didn't mean to be rude. Aunt Linnea and Uncle David were both kind and generous people, and they had been especially helpful to Nell and Zibby when Zibby's dad moved out two years ago. At first he was just going on a monthlong business trip to Italy to help his company set up a new office there. But one month had turned into six, and the plan for Nell and Zibby to join him had come to nothing once he'd met an Italian woman named Sofia and fallen in love. Zibby couldn't believe it for a long time, not even last summer when his weekly postcard announced that he and Sofia were getting married and would Zibby fly over and be their bridesmaid? She couldn't believe her mom's reaction to the postcard, either. Nell had just read it and shrugged her shoulders. "Don't look so surprised, honey," was all she said. "I saw this coming for a long time. Even before your dad went to Italy in the first place. You'll enjoy visiting Italy, getting to know another country. Don't blame Sofia."

But Zibby had seen nothing coming, and *no way* was

she going to the wedding, and she *did* blame the unknown Sofia. She had been waiting for them to be a family again, and now they wouldn't be. It had to be someone's fault. That postcard had gone the way of all the others—into her bottom desk drawer, unanswered.

Zibby drained her plastic cup of soda and tossed it toward a trash bin. She missed, and the cup bounced to the floor. *Figures,* thought Zibby, stooping to pick it up. She felt hot and dizzy, and her hands were tingling, and there was still that stupid clanging bell....The room seemed to turn in a fuzzy whirl. She staggered, clutching at Charlotte for support.

Then the room steadied and the bell stopped ringing. Zibby blinked in the welcome silence, and discovered it wasn't Charlotte's arm she was holding but the arm of a tall woman in a long gray dress. Charlotte was sitting by the snack bar.

"Oh—I'm sorry—," Zibby began, but the woman took Zibby's hand tightly in hers and swept down the closest aisle, with Zibby stumbling along at her side, trying to keep up. She glanced up at the woman and saw dark eyes, like coals, glittering back at her from a long narrow face. The woman released Zibby's hand, but still Zibby's feet hurried her along at the side of this woman in gray. Zibby felt as if she were still being pulled, though the woman no longer held her hand.

They walked up aisles where craftsmen were displaying miniature furniture. They walked down aisles where vendors were offering porcelain doll families, tiny cases of plastic food, and microscopic household goods of every kind—from umbrellas to hammers to lamps that really lit up. The noise level in the convention hall was deafening. Zibby knew she should be back with Charlotte at the snack bar, but she also felt exhilarated and wanted nothing in the world more than to be following this strange woman.

Zibby found herself glancing purposefully around her as she walked, as if she were looking for something—but she didn't know what. The woman in the gray dress seemed to have disappeared into the crowd, but Zibby didn't need her now. She looked right, she looked left, she was searching and searching…and then she saw it, there at the end of the aisle.

Just what she had been looking for…wasn't it?

Yes—just *exactly* what she had always been longing for! They had come to the antique dollhouse section, and there, right in front of Zibby, was an old dollhouse. It was half as tall as Zibby herself, and brown shingled, with two brick chimneys and a front porch and a front door with a dusty panel of real stained glass. There were three stories and a tower. Unlike the other dollhouses on display, this one was covered with dust, but Zibby didn't mind.

It was absolutely beautiful. It was *perfect*. Zibby reached out a tentative finger and touched one of the little tower windows. Her finger came away grimy. She looked closer. For a second it seemed as if something had moved on the other side of the window, something gray. A mouse? Something flickered briefly at another window—but the little windows were all so dirty it was impossible to see through them. And what did it matter? The whole house was wonderful, clean or dirty, with or without mice.

She knew she absolutely had to buy it, had to *own* it. Panic stabbed her: Aunt Linnea had told her that antique dollhouses could cost thousands of dollars! How would she ever afford this house? Yet she had to have it! It *had* to be hers, forever and ever, no matter what the cost.

In a daze, she reached for the price tag looped over one of the chimneys. She turned the tag over. In shaky handwriting the sign announced:

Dollhouse, circa 1915. As is.
Contents Included.
No refunds, no returns!

Only $186.73

"It's a real bargain, dearie," said a cracked, raspy voice, and Zibby looked around, startled, to find an elderly woman with snow-white hair and bright, eager blue eyes, sitting on a wooden chair behind the dollhouse.

"Oh, yes, it is!" Zibby agreed. Only one hundred eighty-six dollars—and such a coincidence! That was exactly how much Zibby had in her pocket, saved for her Rollerblades! If only she had the seventy-three cents, too. Well, she could borrow that small amount from Charlotte. But wait...Zibby rooted deep in the pockets of her jeans and came up with two quarters, two dimes, and three pennies she didn't even know she'd had. Seventy-three cents!

"I've got the money!" Zibby told the woman, grinning wildly. "I've got *exactly* the right amount—down to the penny. Isn't that amazing?" She felt jittery, thrilled to the core to be making this perfect purchase.

"Amazing, dearie!" The woman rubbed her wrinkled hands together, watching eagerly while Zibby counted out the money.

"I love this house," Zibby replied, handing over her pile of bills and the coins. "It's perfectly perfect. I think I've wanted it forever."

The woman scribbled a receipt. "And now it is all yours."

"Oh, yes! It's my birthday present to myself!"

"You understand there can be no refunds?" pressed the old woman, regarding Zibby with sharp blue eyes. "Absolutely no returns?" She pointed out the words she had written in the same shaky hand on a slip of paper:

Purchased—one dollhouse.
$186.73 exactly.
Absolutely no refunds.
Absolutely no returns.

"Do you see this? Do you agree to our transaction?"

"Yes, yes, I see it," said Zibby impatiently. "I agree."

"Then sign here, please, stating you understand the nature of this sale. Your legal name." She turned the paper over and showed Zibby what was written on the back:

I understand that I am now the new owner of this dollhouse. I take full responsibility for the house and all its contents. It is now 100% mine and belongs to no one else on this earth.

"Do you understand?" asked the woman, leaning so close that Zibby could smell her hot, minty breath. "Is it clear enough?"

"Totally." Zibby took the proffered pen and signed on the line: *Isabel Thorne.*

The old woman rubbed her hands together again and an expression of relief flickered across her lined face. "Good," she said. "Very good."

"Zibby!" cried a familiar voice, and there was Zibby's mom, with Aunt Linnea and Charlotte, all hurrying toward her.

"Look!" she shouted. "Look what I've bought!" She turned back to the woman, saying, "I can't wait to show them!" but then blinked in surprise because the chair the woman had been sitting in was empty. The woman had vanished into the crowds.

"Zibby, we've been looking all over for you! I thought you'd be out in the parking lot, you were that much in a hurry to get to Sportsmart." Nell shook her head. "And now here we find you right in the thick of things." She paused and looked at the big dollhouse. "This is a gorgeous— Linnea, look at this old house."

"It's mine, Mom! I bought it!"

"You bought it?" Aunt Linnea laughed. "With what? Houses like this cost the earth." She looked at the receipt Zibby held out, and raised her eyebrows. "Only $186.73? That's incredible."

"I had exactly enough money, Mom. It was so lucky."

"And you don't even like dollhouses!" Charlotte sniffed. "What about your Rollerblades?"

Nell looked very pleased. "What a great buy," she said, hugging Zibby. "Much better value than Rollerblades. And we can work on it together," she added. "A real mother-daughter project, if you want. You do all the structural repairs, and I'll help you buy the furnishings—or we can make a lot of them. It's an astonishing bargain, Zib. A marvelous investment."

Their voices breezed around Zibby like a warm wind. Nothing anyone was saying seemed to reach her. She couldn't hear very well because the clanging bell had started up again. Nell was saying something about how they should leave now because if they weren't going to Sportsmart after all, then she could stop by the florist's shop to check on the flowers for the wedding bouquets.... The bell tolled louder while Aunt Linnea arranged to borrow a dolly to wheel the dollhouse out to her van. It clanged ever more jarringly as Zibby left the convention hall, keeping both hands firmly on the dollhouse so that it would not fall as Nell pushed the trolley across the parking lot. Charlotte was asking when she'd be able to see the wedding dress Nell had chosen, but Zibby couldn't hear her mom's answer. When they reached the van, the ringing of the bell was louder than ever. Zibby put her hands to her ears. "I'm getting such a headache from that bell," she moaned.

"What bell?" asked Charlotte.

Nell and Aunt Linnea looked perplexed. "I don't hear anything," said Nell.

Zibby stared at them, incredulous. Were they all deaf? She shook her head, and the clanging seemed to wobble a bit, too. Could the ringing be *inside* her head?

The dollhouse just fit into the van. "There! Now to get it home." Aunt Linnea slammed the door with satisfaction.

The slamming of the door somehow cut off the noise of the bell. Silence fell around Zibby like a cloak, and she shook her head again to clear it. She felt strange and heavy and very, very tired. She felt as if something had happened. As if something had changed.

"Home?" she asked. "But—what about Sportsmart?"

"You've spent all your money, Zib," Nell reminded her.

"Spent all my money? But..." Just then the fog that had cloaked her for the last half hour suddenly lifted. She had indeed handed all her money—every penny of it—to the white-haired woman. She had purchased the big dollhouse they had just loaded into Aunt Linnea's van.

"But—but wait a sec." Zibby jammed her hands into her pockets. She couldn't believe this. She felt numb from the shock of seeing her precious birthday money transformed into this monstrosity of a dollhouse.

"I don't want it!" she yelled at her mom, jerking her hands out of her pockets. "I don't know how it happened—but I don't want this stupid house. Take it back!"

A piece of paper had flown out of her pocket and was drifting slowly to the asphalt. Nell picked it up. She glanced down at it. "We can't take the dollhouse back." She handed the paper to Zibby. "You know that."

Zibby stared at the piece of paper in surprise.

Purchased—one dollhouse.
$186.73 exactly.
Absolutely no refunds.
Absolutely no returns.
I understand that I am now the new owner of this dollhouse.
I take full responsibility for the house and all its contents.
It is now 100% mine and belongs to no one else on this earth.
Agreed to by: Isabel Thorne.

"Sorry, Zib. But it seems pretty clear. You've got yourself a dollhouse." Nell opened the door of the van and climbed inside. Aunt Linnea already sat in the driver's seat. Charlotte waited in the back. Zibby stood in the parking lot, her head pounding.

The paper was signed by her, but she didn't remember signing it. Or did she? Maybe she remembered it—but only as a hazy dream.

She darted off across the parking lot, weaving in and out among the parked cars, narrowly missing a direct hit from a station wagon backing out of a parking place. A horn blared at her but she ignored it. She reached the convention hall and pulled open the double glass doors. She raced up one aisle and down the next, looking everywhere. But the old woman was nowhere to be found.

Absolutely no refunds. Absolutely no returns. Zibby was stuck.

How could she have willingly spent every cent of her Rollerblades money on a dollhouse she didn't want? She couldn't believe she had done it.

It was a trick! The thought stabbed her and she knew it was true.

But for the life of her, she couldn't explain who could have tricked her—or why.

CHAPTER 2

PRIMROSE 1919

Primrose Parson didn't hate her governess, not really. At least not enough to do something *truly* awful to her. At least not at first. But practical jokes were something else entirely. A good trick now and then made having to live with a governess like Miss Honeywell a bit more bearable.

"Poor Primrose Parson," the housemaids whispered to each other as they passed the schoolroom door. Poor little Primrose, who never had other children to play with anymore, though the neighborhood was full of children—for Miss Honeywell did not like going to the park. Poor Primrose, who never was allowed to buy sweets, though her parents were rich as kings—because Miss Honeywell did not believe children should waste time going to shops when they could be studying. And candy rotted their teeth, anyway.

Primrose's parents spent most of their time away from home, traveling the world. When they were at home in their Columbus, Ohio mansion, they were busy throwing or attending lavish parties. Their children rarely saw them—but this didn't bother them, because they were being raised by the loving Nanny Shanks. Until Miss Honeywell came and everything changed.

Before Miss Honeywell came, Primrose had worn her hair in two thick brown braids, always neatly tied with ribbons to match her dresses. Primrose's chubby body had glowed with health from playing out in the park with her friends, under the kindly eye of Nanny Shanks. Nanny always took Primrose along to the shops to buy sweets or ice cream, and Nanny enjoyed sipping cups of tea with the neighbors' nannies while Primrose played with the other children. Nanny always requested fresh bouquets of flowers for the nursery table. She was a gentle, loving soul, good-humored and quick-witted. She was all Primrose had ever had in the way of a proper parent, and was all Primrose needed.

But then, six months ago, on Primrose's eleventh birthday, her parents had returned home for a brief interlude. At Primrose's birthday dinner, they announced they had decided the time had come for their eldest child to receive a more formal education than the old nanny could give her. They acted as if this were *good* news. Exciting news. But it turned out to be horrible.

Primrose had been banished from the nursery, where dear Nanny Shanks remained to take care of the toddler twins. Lucky little twins! Peony and Basil, both fat and smiley, were getting to be more and more of a handful—two handfuls—and that meant Nanny Shanks needed the help of Bettie Sue, formerly one of the kitchen maids but now promoted to nursery maid. Nanny was no longer free to play with Primrose, or to take her on walks to the park or the zoo.

Now that Primrose had moved out of the nursery and into the schoolroom, she rarely saw her beloved Nanny Shanks or Bettie Sue anymore, or the little twins. She rarely saw anyone but Miss Honeywell and Mr. Pope, the new tutor.

Miss Calliope Honeywell was the governess her parents had hired before they resumed their travels. She was in charge of overseeing Primrose in the subjects of literature, geography, art, history, handwriting, and deportment. Twice a week there were also lessons in mathematics and science with the tutor Mr. Thaddeus Pope, a quiet, intense man, with a dark mop of unruly hair that he tried in vain to slick back with scented pomade. He loved his subjects with a passion and never noticed that Primrose didn't share his interest. But at least he never scolded her for daydreaming, the way Miss Honeywell did. And Miss Honeywell was a fine one to fuss about daydreaming—the hypocrite!—for Primrose had often seen the governess gazing dreamily at the tutor. Primrose suspected Miss Honeywell was sweet on Mr. Pope.

Now Primrose spent her days in the big drafty schoolroom at the top of the house, and her nights in the little bedroom off the schoolroom. Miss Honeywell slept in an even smaller room, next to Primrose's. Mr. Pope came only on Tuesdays and Thursdays, but Miss Honeywell was there all the time. Primrose learned to braid her own hair, though the bows on the ends of the braids were not as jaunty anymore, and often came untied. She grew thinner from long hours of study and infrequent snacks. There was hardly any time for play because Miss Honeywell didn't believe in playing. Most of the toys had been left in the nursery. Worst of all, her dollhouse had been left for the little ones to play with. It was just a small wooden cottage with painted walls and a cheerful family of little stuffed mice living inside, but Primrose had pretended it was a fine mansion, furnished with beautiful furniture just like the things in her own house. She had spent hours making up adventures for the mouse family. In the schoolroom, when daily lessons with Miss Honeywell were finally over, Primrose longed to lose herself in the dollhouse. But Nanny had wanted to keep the house for Basil and Peony, who also loved the mouse family. And Miss Honeywell said playtime was a frivolous waste of time, and Primrose, at eleven, was a young lady now and far too old for toys.

Primrose knew she wasn't too old at all. She knew having a doll family like the little mice would help her escape into the world of her imagination—away from Miss Honeywell. She wrote letters to her parents, begging for a dollhouse of her own, and smuggled the letters to the kitchen maid, who winked and whispered she would see they got sent. Miss Honeywell would never have allowed such letters to be sent; she always checked Primrose's letters for good penmanship and proper grammar, and besides, begging for things was unseemly. But a letter finally returned from Papa, promising that when he returned from abroad, he would see about getting Primrose a dollhouse.

But who knew when that would be?

Primrose lay awake nights, listening to Miss Honeywell snore and wishing her parents would come home. Nanny Shanks never snored. Nanny Shanks sang lullabies and told jokes and read stories, and she was always ready for a cuddle in the big rocking chair, even when Primrose was way too big to sit on anyone's lap anymore.

Miss Honeywell said she wanted to instill proper values in Primrose. She said she thought that Primrose was impudent and unlady-like, lacking in discipline, and needing to be taught manners. She said Primrose was a spoiled little rich girl who needed a firm hand. She said her own parents had taught her that singing was frivolous, joking was immoral, and the reading of novels was a waste of time. She didn't even have a lap, really. And who would want to sit on those unwelcoming bony knees, anyway?

It was Miss Honeywell's horrible loud snoring that prompted Primrose's first practical joke on the governess. One night the snoring was so loud, Primrose couldn't sleep. She tossed and turned in her narrow bed and then finally had an idea. She slid out of bed and very quietly tiptoed from her room. The schoolroom was dark, but she crossed it without lighting the lamp. She opened the door to the hall so slowly that it didn't even creak, and then she closed it behind her just as carefully. White nightdress billowing out around her, Primrose flew down the back stairs—down three flights on silent bare feet to the kitchen, then down yet another flight of stone steps to the big shadowy basement laundry room. Primrose crept in the near dark past the vast metal sinks and wooden wringers. The damp sheets hanging on the lines touched her face as she sidled up to the canvas bag hanging on the hook by the outside door. The bag contained clothespins. Primrose reached in and grabbed one.

She sprinted up the cold stone steps to the kitchen, then hesitated. She could return to the schoolroom the way she had come, of course—or she could go through the house and up the front staircase. With her parents gone from home so much, Primrose rarely saw her house anymore. She slipped through the butler's pantry to the dining room, then moved out into the large front hallway. The graceful curved staircase beckoned, but she wandered into the drawing room. She flitted around the room, fingertips brushing against the elegant chairs, the grand piano, the fringed settee adorned with silk pillows. She could almost see her mother sitting there, or at the piano—her father reading his newspaper in the leather armchair, or standing by the fireplace, poking up the blaze.

With a sigh Primrose returned to the hallway and started up the stairs. She hesitated a moment on the landing, debating whether to run down the hall to the nursery wing for a quick peek at the little twins, and maybe a hug from Nanny Shanks. But the sleeping house was cold, and her teeth were already chattering.

She continued up to the schoolroom and slipped into Miss Honeywell's bedroom. Miss Honeywell was a bony form on the bed, angular even under the puffy comforter. Her mouth hung open and the snores rattled her thin lips like the braying of a donkey. Her mouse-brown hair, which by day she wore coiled tightly in a bun at the back of her neck, rested on the white pillow in two thin braids. Primrose made a face at her.

Nasty old Honeywell. Maybe this will shut you up for a while.

Primrose slid the clothespin gently onto the governess's long nose, then pushed slightly harder to wedge it firmly in place. Abruptly the snoring ceased. For a second all was quiet, then Miss Honeywell gasped and coughed.

Primrose stifled a giggle. She scurried out of Miss Honeywell's bedroom. She leaped back into her own bed and drew the quilt up under her chin. Then she closed her eyes and pretended to be asleep. She tried to make herself breathe evenly as she heard the coughing from the other room continue. She counted slowly as she breathed—in, two three four; out, two three four—and heard the creak of the governess's bedsprings. She continued counting as she heard the soft pad of slippered feet crossing the floor, and then the creak of her own bedroom door as it opened. She forced herself to keep breathing, eyes closed, even when she sensed the governess standing right by her bed.

The loud clanging of Miss Honeywell's handbell rang next to Primrose's head. "All right, young miss!" shouted Miss Honeywell's voice.

Primrose opened her eyes as her covers were pulled off. "Oh, dear, can it be morning so soon?" she exclaimed innocently. "I was having such a pleasant dream!"

"Get out of bed this instant, you bad girl. I'll teach you about pleasant dreams!" Miss Honeywell fastened her bony hand on Primrose's arm and dragged her out of bed. The bell in Miss Honeywell's other hand jangled as they walked out of Primrose's bedroom and into Miss Honeywell's. "A taste of your own medicine is what will cure you."

She stood poor Primrose in the corner by the windows and wedged the clothespin onto Primrose's small nose. It was tighter than Primrose had thought, and pinched quite dreadfully.

Primrose reached up to pull it off.

"Oh, no, you don't, young miss," said the governess with spite in her voice. "You'll stand here for a full hour wearing that clip on your nose. While wearing it, you shall be thinking about your unlady-like deportment."

Primrose tried a smile, her most charming. "I was just trying to help you, Miss Honeywell. Your snores were so loud, I thought you might wake yourself up."

"Trying to help me, indeed!" Miss Honeywell slipped back into her warm bed. "I have never seen such a spoiled child in all my days. Now you stand there and think about your deplorable manners. Think about all the luxuries you have while children all around the world live in terrible poverty! Think of the children in countries torn by war! Think of the soldiers who fought and died trying to save them—"

Miss Honeywell often lectured on and on about the evils of war, and about her younger brother, Lester, whom she had raised after their parents died. Lester had been killed a year ago in the Great War, over in France. Primrose was sorry about that, but she didn't see why Miss Honeywell seemed to think it was all Primrose's fault. Primrose glared at her governess now but did not dare to reach up and remove the clothespin. She kicked at the wall in anger.

I'll take it off as soon as she goes to sleep, she thought. But Miss Honeywell did not go to sleep at all. Instead she lay there watching Primrose watching her. They watched each other for a full hour while Primrose's little nose ached and ached and finally grew numb. From time to time she kicked at the wall in frustration but didn't dare to speak. *Miss Honeywell is a horrid woman,* Primrose thought. *No wonder she has never married! Her brother Lester was probably happy to go off to war just to get away from her. Who would want to live with someone as mean as her? And who snores like a donkey besides?*

"Hee-haw! Hee-haw!" Primrose brayed under her breath.

"Pardon me?" snapped Miss Honeywell from the comfort of her bed.

"Nothing," muttered Primrose.

"Nothing?"

"Nothing, Miss Honeywell."

"That's *Sweet* Miss Honeywell to you."

"Nothing, Sweet Miss Honeywell," repeated Primrose dutifully, though it came out sounding more like "Sweed Biss Huddywell" because of the clothespin.

When the clock out on the landing chimed midnight, Miss Honeywell blew out her lamp and turned on her side at last.

"All right," she said, "you may go back to bed now if you have learned your lesson."

Primrose snatched the clothespin off her nose.

"Have you learned your lesson, Primrose?"

"Yes," hissed Primrose, longing to hurl the clothespin right into the governess's face. She added under her breath, "You old mule."

"Excuse me?" The governess's voice rose sharply.

"I said, yes, Sweet Miss Honeywell." Primrose left the clothespin on the windowsill and walked quietly out of the room, back to her own bed. She lay shivering under her quilt for a long time. Her nose throbbed.

Well, so much for that practical joke. But she would do better next time. It was time for some changes around here. No more meek and frightened Primrose Parson. Time for a change in the balance of power.

Primrose started making plans. Salt in *Sweet* Miss Honeywell's sugar bowl—for a start. Cockroaches in her coffee. Dry, grainy, itchy washing powder sprinkled in her undergarments—the possibilities were endless.

Primrose rubbed her nose and smiled in the dark. Oh, yes, it was time for a change.

CHAPTER 3

Zibby refused to have the dollhouse in her bedroom. Nell sighed and said she would gladly take it. The two of them lugged the house upstairs, resting halfway to catch their breath. It took up a whole corner of Nell's bedroom, sitting on the green carpet as if in a grassy field.

Aunt Linnea had wiped off most of the dust before putting the dollhouse into her minivan, but now Nell brought a washcloth from the bathroom and rubbed off the rest. "There," she said. "Now let's check out the rooms. Come on, Zib—you've got to be a *little* bit interested!" Nell stooped to unfasten the catch. With a creak, the front of the house swung open.

Despite herself, Zibby leaned forward to look. Inside the house were eight large rooms, four upstairs and four downstairs. And at the top of the house there was a single attic room, and two little rooms inside the tower. Zibby could see that the walls of all the rooms must once have been covered in delicately patterned wallpaper, but it was all so old and faded and peeling she could barely make out the colors. A thick layer of dust covered the little floorboards. There was a staircase in the front hallway leading up to the bedrooms, and then one more flight up to the attic. A few pieces of furniture tumbled across the floors. Nell set them up in the largest bedroom: a brass bed, a red velvet couch, a grand piano, a leather armchair, a little round table and two chairs—one with only three legs. The largest of the downstairs rooms was stuffed with a bundle of cloth. Zibby reached in and tugged it out.

It was a large pillowcase tied shut with a grimy yellow ribbon. Whatever was inside made bumps and bulges through the fabric. "More furniture, probably," said Zibby indifferently, handing the bundle to her mom.

Nell's fingers worked swiftly to untie several knots in the ribbon. "Not furniture, I bet—oh, Zib, if this is what I think it is…"

"What?" Zibby felt a thrill of excitement. In books and films kids were always finding hidden treasure. What if—what if there were *jewels* in this pillowcase? Precious jewels stashed away by some long-ago family—and where better to hide them than inside an old dollhouse, where no thief would ever think to look? Maybe her Rollerblades money had been well spent after all! Eagerly she leaned forward as Nell spilled the contents onto the green carpet.

But instead of a cascade of precious gems, a dozen or so small dolls dropped out. Zibby shook the bag, hoping for at least one jewel, and out came a few wads of folded doll-clothes. Then the pillowcase was empty.

Zibby sat back on her heels in disgust. But Nell was sorting through the dolls with a big smile on her face. "Oh, Zibby, look at these—each one would have cost big bucks at

the miniatures show. And now you've got a whole household of little people to live in your dollhouse! And even
some outfits for them...fashions of the nineteen-twenties, it
looks like." Nell was busily unfolding the wads of clothes.
"Here's a dress for a little girl doll. Let's see if we can find
one to wear it." Nell rummaged among the dolls and held
up one about four inches tall, with brown braids. "This one
looks cute. Let's dress her up."

"Oh, *Mom.*"

"Whoa—look at this one." Nell held up another doll—
this one scaled larger than the others on the floor. It was
about seven inches high and wore a long gray dress. Zibby
thought the expression on its porcelain face was extremely
unpleasant. This was not a doll she would ever choose to
play with—even if she liked to play with dolls.

Which she didn't. She stood up and, hands on hips,
watched as Nell sorted through the other dolls. There were
father and mother dolls, children dolls, baby dolls, and servant dolls. Nell exclaimed about the fine quality of work-
manship, but Zibby interrupted her. "I'm outta here."

She stomped downstairs and pulled her bike helmet and
old, too-small Rollerblades out of the closet, then sat on the
front-porch steps to put them on. *Stupid old skates, stupid
dollhouse, stupid birthday.* Everything was ruined.

She zipped along the sidewalk under a canopy of green
leaves. Oaktree Lane was narrow and winding, and ended at
a little park, where she and Amy had often played together.
Amy's house was the last house on the street, right next to
the park. Zibby moved toward it with a fast, swooping
rhythm, imagining that instead of these clunky old skates

she wore new royal blue and silver ones. Imagining Amy skating at her side.

Zibby couldn't imagine moving. She had lived in the house on Oaktree Lane her whole life. It was a shabby house, with peeling blue paint and a rickety front-porch railing, and a yard shaded with oak trees. But it was comfortable. It was the house her mom and Aunt Linnea had grown up in—though Aunt Linnea now lived in a grand house across town. Aunt Linnea and Nell's parents—Zibby's Gramps and Grammy—now lived in the new condos by the river. Zibby loved her house, but it felt too big for just her and her mother. Ned was spending more and more time at the house these days—even though he wasn't officially moving in until the wedding. Sometimes he stayed overnight, sleeping on the couch. Zibby didn't mind. Without her dad there, the rooms had seemed empty. Just as Oaktree Lane seemed empty without Amy.

Amy and Zibby—everything great from A to Z. This had been their motto. But now there was an unfamiliar dark green car in the driveway of Amy's house. It hurt Zibby's eyes to see it there. The real-estate sign in Amy's front yard now had a bold SOLD banner stretched across it. She noticed for the first time a big yellow moving van parked across the street from the house. She skated past it into the park.

Tree-lined bike lanes led through manicured beds of flowers and shrubs. There was a baseball diamond on the far edge of the park, and a soccer field in the middle. There were two playgrounds—one for the littlest children, with baby swings and tiny slides and lots of sand, and one for bigger children, with higher slides, swaying bridges, tire swings, and a delightfully inconsistent fountain that kids could wade in, which would now and then shoot up jets of water from different spouts. Toddlers played in the sand, and a group of six- or seven-year-old boys ran through the fountain, trying to escape the jets of water. It hadn't been very long since Zibby and Amy had played there.

"Oh, sorry!" Zibby cried, expertly dodging a man who, it seemed to her, suddenly materialized in the path right in front of her. She'd nearly hit him.

The man was thin and stooped, although not really very old. He had a shock of dark hair and wore a diamond-patterned vest and a heavy black coat—strange choices on such a warm day. He raised his head and peered at her, then smiled slowly as if smiling were a very great effort for him. "Have you seen her?" he asked vaguely, then dropped his head again and shuffled onward, very, very slowly.

Seen who? Zibby zipped along the path away from him, grateful for her young body, her strong legs. She drew in gulps of flower-scented summer air, and some of her anger dissolved. The day was not completely horrible after all. She was healthy, she was not tired, and she was a really good skater even on old Rollerblades. Today was her birthday, and she was not going to waste the rest of it feeling mad about the dollhouse.

Zibby circled around and headed back toward the entrance. The man was gone. She sped past the playgrounds, down the tree-lined path back toward Oaktree Lane. Then she heard a bell ringing, and her stomach clenched. She circled to a stop. But no—this bell was not in her head. This was a totally normal bell, and the sound was coming from Amy's driveway. Zibby looked over the bushes separating the park from Oaktree Lane and saw that the bell ringer was a girl about her own age, standing in Amy's driveway waving a large handbell. Zibby's heart leaped. Maybe Amy was back! Maybe her family had invited friends over for dinner or something. Maybe they had decided not to live in Cleveland after all.

"Penny!" the girl called. "Penny, it's dinnertime!" And in another second a smaller girl shot off the slide at the playground and raced past Zibby on the path out of the park. "Keep your shirt on!" the smaller girl yelled, and then she and the bell ringer disappeared inside Amy's house. Zibby skated slowly back down Oaktree Lane toward home, her heart heavy and sad.

Back at the house, Ned had arrived with his bratty kids, and they were all waiting to take Zibby out for her birthday dinner. *Can this day get any worse?* she thought, heading to her room to change into a dress for the restaurant.

As she stepped into her bedroom she frowned. The dollhouse stood right next to her desk. Its windows glinted in the early evening sun like eyes winking.

Mocking her.

"Mom!" she yelled, turning and thudding back down the stairs. "I told you I didn't want the dollhouse, and I don't! So you can just take it back to your room."

"It *is* in my room, Zibby," said Nell mildly from the foot of the stairs, but the look she shot at Zibby said, *Watch your tone of voice, young lady.*

Zibby didn't care. "Then what's it doing in my room?" she hissed at her mom as Nell started up the stairs. She led her mom down the hall to her bedroom. "See?"

Nell shook her head. "I didn't touch it," she said. "But

Laura-Jane came up to use the bathroom…She must have moved it—although it is pretty heavy…"

"She should stay out of my room!" Zibby snapped.

"And mine," Nell agreed. "But come on now, let's not have a big confrontation about it. We'll just move it back."

Together they slid the big dollhouse across the bedroom floor, out into the hallway, and back into Nell's bedroom. Then they went downstairs and everyone climbed into Ned's car. Zibby was crushed between six-year-old Brady and eleven-year-old Laura-Jane. Zibby elbowed Laura-Jane in the side. "Stay out of my room," she hissed.

Laura-Jane kicked her in the ankle.

Zibby had met Ned's kids only half a dozen times, and they had not improved upon acquaintance. Brady was cute but wild and loud. His head was topped with wiry black hair standing on end as if cut by a lawn mower. Laura-Jane looked very much like her dad and brother, with black hair and dark almond-shaped eyes—though her hair was straight, thick, and long, almost long enough to sit on. It was impossible to know whether Laura-Jane had the same wide smile as her dad and brother because she never smiled. At least not so Zibby could see.

They met Zibby's grandparents at the Fat Lady and sat at a large round table reserved for them, surrounded by potted fig trees. The soft light from old-fashioned brass lamps blanketed their corner of the restaurant in a warm glow. Glasses clinked around the room and waiters spoke in muted voices. In the background, soft music played. Zibby didn't know what it was, but it had a lilting beat that she thought might be Greek.

There were gifts to open while they waited for their food:

the new camera Zibby had been hoping for from Nell, with a pretty photo album to go along with it. A beautiful blue sweater from Aunt Linnea and Uncle David that would be perfect the first day of school. A matching hairband covered in blue cloth from Charlotte. And Charlotte's brother, fifteen-year-old Owen, gave her three paperback mysteries. Ned and his kids gave Zibby a fancy box of watercolors, brushes in all sizes, and a big block of paper. Zibby's dad and Sofia had sent a 1,000-piece puzzle—a scenic aerial photograph of Venice's Grand Canal and tiny winding waterways leading enticingly off it into the old city. The card said, "We'll take you on a gondola ride when you come to visit! Happy Birthday—love from Dad and Sofia." Zibby had zero plans to visit Italy, but her dad did not give up easily. The best present of all came from Grammy and Gramps, who waited eagerly while Zibby tore off the wrapping paper.

"Ooh!" said Brady. "A treasure chest!"

"I bet it's a jewelry box—or a makeup kit," said Charlotte. "Zibby, it's really time you started wearing some makeup."

Zibby shot her a withering look and ripped off the last of the paper to reveal a toolbox. Her own toolbox! Thrilled, she grinned across the table at Grammy and Gramps, and opened the clasps. The box was stocked full of real tools from the hardware store. Zibby's smile grew wider as she examined the hammer and screwdrivers, the hacksaw, the wrenches, pliers, and drill. Little plastic cases held screws, nails, nuts, and bolts.

She remembered how her dad had taught her to use his tools, and how together they had made the birdhouse that hung in the tree outside her bedroom window, the mailbox on their porch, and the spice rack in the kitchen. When she had wanted to move onto bigger projects like the new bookcase for her bedroom, her dad had encouraged her to do it all on her own. "You've got a touch of magic," he'd said. "Not everyone can work with wood."

The memory made her wistful. Was he teaching Sofia how to build their own gondola?

Grammy was looking anxiously at Zibby. Zibby pushed away the thoughts of her dad and smiled. "Thanks a zillion, Grammy and Gramps! This is *so* cool!"

Charlotte was shaking her head. "I don't get you, Zibby. You like the weirdest things."

And Laura-Jane rolled her eyes. "Totally," she agreed.

"Can I use those tools?" begged Brady, dipping into the box. "To build a spaceship?"

"Maybe sometime," Zibby said, hastily removing a hammer from his greedy paw.

"Every gal should have a good set of tools," Gramps said.

"And you can use them to repair your new dollhouse," suggested Nell.

Zibby changed the subject quickly.

They ate pasta and salad, and the talk was all about the upcoming wedding. Ned Shimizu had been Nell's boyfriend in high school. He had been a super baseball player for the school team, along with Uncle David. After high school, Ned had gone away to college, then married and moved to Fennel Grove—the town next to Carroway—and Nell had lost touch with him for years. But after his divorce, Ned moved back to town as the new editor of the *Carroway Gazette*. Nell's catering company, DaisyCakes, had been hired to prepare the welcoming luncheon held for Ned by the board of directors—and the two of them had found each other again and quickly renewed their friendship. Zibby watched her mom and Ned laughing over their dinners and knew they were very well suited. If only he didn't come as a package deal! Laura-Jane sat like a sullen lump next to Charlotte, and Brady leaped about like a firecracker, his eyes snapping with mischief. He couldn't sit still for two seconds.

Charlotte was seated between them at the table and was having a hard time, Zibby was amused to see, with Laura-Jane making snide remarks under her breath and Brady grabbing the fries off Charlotte's plate. Charlotte, who as usual was trying to act grown-up and gracious, looked sick of both kids. Zibby was glad she and Charlotte still had *something* in common, even though Charlotte was pretty much a pain these days.

When everyone had finished their meals, Nell signaled to the waiter, who carried out a beautiful chocolate layer cake from the kitchen. Everyone—except Laura-Jane—sang, "Happy Birthday, dear Zibby" in rousing voices. Zibby blushed when the manager of the restaurant came over and handed her a single red rose and everyone in the restaurant applauded.

Then Ned dropped his bombshell. His kids' mom, Zibby knew, often had to travel for her job, and now it turned out she had to leave for a long trip to Japan that would last more than a month. Laura-Jane and Brady would be moving in with Ned...which basically meant they'd be coming to live with Zibby and Nell for that time.

Brady hugged his dad, but Laura-Jane just sank lower in her seat and groaned. Zibby wanted to groan, too, but her mom's bright smile made her smile back at Ned and say, "How nice."

Grammy looked from one girl to the other, then patted Zibby's hand. "You and Laura-Jane will have time to help with wedding preparations, dear. Maybe the two of you can look through old yearbooks for photos of your mom and Ned when they were dating! Won't those be fun to display at the reception?"

Zibby winced as Laura-Jane shot Grammy a baleful look. "Maybe," Zibby said politely, but Laura-Jane just snorted and muttered something under her breath.

"That would be great," Ned said heartily, to cover Laura-Jane's rudeness. "A fine project for the girls to do together."

Then at last it was time to go home. Zibby gathered up her gifts, thanked everyone, and headed out to the car. It had been a long, weird day, and she was exhausted.

Home again, Zibby went straight upstairs to brush her teeth. Then she trudged down the hallway to her bedroom and collapsed on her bed. She saw the dollhouse sitting by her desk and sat up again as if shot out of a cannon: *How dare she!*

"Mom!" yelled Zibby, jumping off the bed and pelting to the stairs. "You can just come right up here and take it back! I told you I don't want it!"

Nell looked up from the couch. "What in the world?"

"The dollhouse! You put it in my room!"

"I most certainly did not." Nell looked annoyed. "How could I?"

Zibby took a deep breath and lowered her voice. "Well, someone came in here while we were at the restaurant and moved it."

"That's ridiculous," said Nell. But she got off the couch and started up the stairs.

"See?" demanded Zibby, pointing to the house in the corner by her desk.

"I do see, but you must have just brought it in here yourself," said Nell.

"I did not!"

"Hmm." Nell frowned, and Zibby could tell her mom didn't believe her. "Go to bed, Zib. It's been a long day."

"I didn't move it in here, Mom!"

Nell just shrugged her shoulders and looked impatient, and Zibby felt too unsettled to argue further. Together they slid the house back into Nell's bedroom. Then the doorbell rang, which meant Ned was back from taking Laura-Jane and Brady home to their mother, in Fennel Grove, and so Nell kissed Zibby good night and ran downstairs to let him in. Zibby curled up under her blanket and listened to the murmur of their voices.

She had not moved the dollhouse. So...who had?

She heard the sound of a car passing out in the street—maybe the dark green car belonging to the new neighbors in Amy's house. She heard tree frogs out in the yard. And then she heard—scratching.

Scratching? Yes—scratching and scraping. She sat up in bed, listening. It seemed to be coming from her mom's room across the hall. Mice in the walls?

Zibby slipped out of bed and tiptoed across the hall to peek into Nell's room. The dollhouse waited in the shadows, an unfamiliar bulk in the corner. There was that scraping sound again—and a movement inside one of the tower windows—and Zibby remembered the flicker she'd thought she'd seen at the miniatures show. But there had been no sign of a mouse when Nell opened the dollhouse. So what was going on? Zibby hesitated, staring at the house, but nothing else happened. She returned to bed and closed her eyes.

Her sleep was uneasy, full of twisting shapes and shadows, and a bell clanging over and over inside her head.

Zibby was right there in her bedroom, lying in her bed. The night outside was dark and still, but inside her room there was an orange glow and a strange crackling sound. She sat up slowly and saw that the dollhouse was there by the desk again. It was on fire. Flames leaped high from all the tiny windows and licked the legs of Zibby's desk. She knew she should run from the room and call for help, call the fire department, but—impossible!— now an arm was reaching out from behind the dollhouse. Not a doll-sized arm, but a man-sized arm, an arm with a groping hand...

Someone was there. Someone was in her room. Zibby squeezed her pillow in panic. She opened her mouth to call for help but no sound came out. She could see everything in sharp detail: the crumbling, blackened wood of the dollhouse, the falling miniature bricks from the chimney, and the arm...the hand! She could see that the hand was wearing a black glove. It was scrabbling around in the flaming wreckage, the fingers reaching, reaching toward Zibby—

Zibby jerked herself awake with a little shriek and sat up in her bed. It had all been a dream, of course, only a dream, and there was no smoke, no fire, no grasping hand in a black leather glove...but there *was* something—something looming in the shadows by her desk. She couldn't help it; she opened her mouth and screamed.

The dollhouse was back.

CHAPTER 4

"You must have been sleepwalking, Zib," said Nell soothingly, stroking Zibby's hair, "and moved the dollhouse into your room again. There's just no other explanation."

"Unless *you* were the one sleepwalking," countered Zibby, her voice trembling. "And *you* moved it." She sat cross-legged on her mom's bed. "Can I sleep in here?" She couldn't bear to see the dollhouse in her bedroom, and she was too tired to move it again.

Nell slid over and made room for Zibby in the big bed. "We'll figure it out in the morning," she said drowsily, tucking the sheet around Zibby.

But Zibby lay awake for a long time, listening, waiting, her eyes straining in the darkness. She half expected to see the big dollhouse gliding in through the doorway. But nothing happened, and finally she slept.

In the morning, Zibby found herself alone in the big bed. A note on Nell's pillow told her that her mom wouldn't be back until late afternoon—she was doing a big luncheon in Columbus. Nell's work often required her to be gone from home, but never before had Zibby felt so unsettled about being alone.

DaisyCakes had started as a part-time business but blossomed into Nell's full-time job after the divorce. DaisyCakes was immensely popular in Carroway and nearby Fennel Grove—and word kept spreading. The food was known for its simple elegance, fresh organic ingredients, and reasonable prices. Zibby was proud of DaisyCakes and sometimes worked with her mom on the weekends. It was fun to cook together in their large kitchen—an addition to the house, specially equipped with two stoves, two refrigerators, a pantry, and an extralarge freezer. It was fun, too, to help serve food at fancy parties or to be in charge of placing the last delicate fringes of cilantro on platters of delicious appetizers.

Zibby slid out of Nell's bed and walked to her own bedroom. Ignoring her uneasiness, she went directly to the dollhouse. The doll in the gray dress was perched on the roof, leaning against a chimney.

Mom must really be having fun, Zibby told herself. But it was unlike Nell to tease.

Zibby dressed quickly. She snatched the doll off the roof and stuffed it into the pillowcase with the other dolls. Latching the front of the house securely, she wrapped her arms around the structure and tried to lift it. Too heavy. She tried to push it, but it caught in the rug and wouldn't budge. She hesitated, then had the idea to work her quilt underneath the dollhouse. She could pull it along on top of the quilt.

It worked perfectly. The dollhouse slid along silently behind Zibby on the quilt as she pulled it back into her mom's bedroom. She left it in the corner, where it had been last night. Then she hurried downstairs, casting a backward glance over her shoulder.

On the table in the sunny kitchen, Zibby found another note from Nell, this one saying that Aunt Linnea had called to invite Zibby to lunch with Charlotte at noon. Nell and Aunt Linnea refused to believe that Zibby and Charlotte didn't really like hanging out with each other anymore.

At least there were still hours till noon. Zibby decided to skate over and see who those new neighbors were in Amy's yellow house.

The moving van was gone, but Zibby skated back and forth in front of the house, listening to banging sounds coming from the backyard. For a second she could almost believe it was Amy back there, working on the clubhouse they always intended to build. Amy was good with tools, too, and had once even used a power saw by herself.

Zibby skated down the driveway toward the sound. The girl called Penny was kneeling in the backyard beside the pile of boards Amy's dad had given them for their clubhouse. The girl was trying to hammer two of the boards together with wide, awkward swings of her arms. If she didn't watch out, she'd be banging her hand next.

It hurt Zibby to see the boards intended for the clubhouse being messed with, but Amy's parents had refused to take them along to Cleveland. Amy had said Zibby could have them, but without Amy, what was the point of having a clubhouse, anyway?

"Hello, Penny," Zibby said.

The girl turned, her dark eyes wide and startled. She looked about Zibby's age—or maybe a little younger. "Who are *you*? And how come you know my name?"

"I heard someone calling you when you were playing in the park yesterday."

"Oh." The girl tilted her head and her dozens of tiny black braids moved, the beads at the ends clicking prettily. "That must have been Jude, ringing me home for dinner."

Zibby nodded. "Is your sister inside?"

"Nope. Two nopes. Jude's not my sister, and she's not inside. She's out with my mom, buying stuff for the house. It's a lot of trouble to move."

"Where did you move here from?"

"Pennsylvania. And I wish we hadn't come."

"Me, too," said Zibby. Then, seeing the hurt expression flash across Penny's face, she tried to explain. "I mean, I wish my best friend hadn't moved away to Cleveland. This is her house. I mean, it *was*."

"Oh. That's too bad," said Penny. She looked as if she meant it, and Zibby felt friendlier. "So, what's *your* name?"

"Zibby Thorne." She wanted to ask more about the other girl, Jude, but Penny didn't give her the chance.

"Zibby's a funny name."

Zibby was used to having people comment on her unusual nickname. "My real name is Isabel. I'm twelve, as of yesterday. How old are you?"

Penny swung her hammer again and tried to hit the nail into the plank she was holding. Zibby winced. "I'm eleven," she said. "And my real name is Penelope, but thank goodness no one calls me that. I *hate* the name Penelope. Do you hate Isabel?"

"No, I like it. It's an old family name. But when I was

little, my cousin Charlotte—she's a couple months older than me and learned to talk first—couldn't pronounce it, and started calling me Zibby instead. And the name stuck." Zibby gestured toward the pile of boards. "What are you doing with these?"

"I'm trying to build a dollhouse. But it isn't working."

Dollhouses, again! Zibby shook her head. "Well, that's because these boards are too long and too thick for a doll-house." She frowned, picturing the clubhouse she and Amy had planned.

"Well, I have some smaller pieces from the wooden packing crates we used for moving," said Penny. "Do you think they would work?"

Zibby inspected the crates. "Maybe." She hesitated, then added, "I'm pretty good with tools. I could help you, if you want."

"Hey, that would be great!" Penny fished a piece of folded notepaper out of her back pocket. "Look, this is a sketch of the kind of house I want. A *troll-house.* I have a whole family of trolls."

"Pretty fancy," Zibby said. "And complicated. I don't think you can make this kind of house out of these crates. The wood is too rough—" She broke off as a wonderful idea popped into her head. "Wait, Penny! Would you like to have a *real* dollhouse? I mean an already-made one? It's an antique, and it comes with a whole bagful of dolls and some furniture. It only costs one hundred and eighty-six dollars." Zibby wouldn't charge Penny the extra seventy-three cents.

"I don't have that much money."

"I could lower the price," Zibby offered quickly. "My

mom says it's a really special old house. It would be perfect for your trolls. Maybe your parents will buy it for you."

Penny looked unconvinced. She picked up her sketch and looked down at the crates.

"Come on over to my house and see it, at least," pressed Zibby. It would be the perfect way to make everybody happy. Zibby would get the dollhouse out of her life—and get most of her money back. And this new neighbor girl would have her troll-house or whatever.

A green car turned into the driveway. "Okay, I'll ask my mom," said Penny.

The tall girl Zibby had seen the day before jumped out of the front passenger seat and stood in the driveway. She flashed Zibby a smile. "Hi," she called. "I'm Jude."

They've got to be sisters, thought Zibby, glancing from one girl to the other. *They're practically twins!* Penny had zillions of braids and Jude's hair was a short cap of tight black curls, but their heart-shaped faces, their warm brown eyes and dark skin, and their smiles were identical. "Hi," she replied. "I'm Zibby."

Penny's mother unfolded herself from the driver's seat. She was a tall, angular woman wearing loose white trousers and a baggy blue shirt. She had short, tightly curled black hair like Jude's and unwrinkled deep brown skin. She smiled at Zibby and shook her hand. "I'm Claudia Jefferson," she introduced herself. "How nice that there's someone in the neighborhood for the girls to play with. We were afraid they wouldn't meet anyone until school starts."

"Zibby lives up the street, and she's twelve just like Jude," Penny reported. "And her very best friend used to live here in our house."

"Oh, dear." Mrs. Jefferson looked sympathetic. "It's hard when friends move away."

"Yeah, but it's hard to be the ones moving, too," Penny said. "And Jude has had to move *twice,* remember—first from her house to ours, and now here to this new house."

"Penny says you're not her sister," Zibby said to Jude, "but that's hard to believe. Cousins?"

"Guess again," Penny said with a mischievous grin.

"Oh, Penny, don't always make it into such a big deal." Jude sounded embarrassed. "She's my aunt, that's all."

"Your *aunt?*" Zibby asked in astonishment.

"That's right," said Mrs. Jefferson smoothly. "Jude's daddy is Penny's big brother—my son, Malcolm. Jude's parents are out of the country this year, working at a hospital in Kenya. They're both doctors."

"So I came to live with my grandparents," added Jude. She poked Penny. "And my aunt Penelope."

Penny poked her back. "If you call me that again, I'll shave your head while you sleep."

Zibby was trying to figure it out. "You mean," she said to Penny, "your mom and dad are Jude's *grandparents?*"

"Yup," said Penny. "Isn't that totally weird?"

"You're what's weird around here," Jude told her. "Whoever heard of an eleven-year-old aunt?"

"If you're mean to me," Penny warned her, "I'll—"

"I know, I know." Jude sighed. "You'll shave my head while I sleep."

Then the two of them giggled, and Zibby realized they were friends as well as antagonists.

"But if you shave Jude's head," Mrs. Jefferson told her daughter, "then she'll be bald and silly-looking and still calling you *Aunt Penelope* every day of your life. You wouldn't like that."

"So watch yourself," added Jude. She and her grand-mother laughed together. Then Penny told them Zibby had a dollhouse she wanted to sell, and could she please go look at it?

"You can come, too," Zibby invited Jude.

"Run along, girls," said Mrs. Jefferson. "But be back for lunch."

Zibby skated slowly down the street with Jude and Penny walking along on either side. "I have Rollerblades, too," Jude told Zibby. "But they're packed in a box—like just about everything else."

"Well, when you find them, I can give you the grand tour of Carroway," Zibby offered, but her mind was on the dollhouse.

Penny was chattering a mile a minute about her troll family. Up ahead Zibby saw a girl on a bike who looked from the back like Charlotte, but then the girl turned the corner and disappeared. Zibby waved to Mr. Simms, their across-the-street neighbor, and introduced Jude and Penny. Then she turned into her own driveway and spun around neatly to sit on the porch steps to unbuckle her skates.

A flash of brown caught her eye. It was a man in a sol-dier's uniform, wearing a funny kind of helmet like ones she'd seen in old war movies. He was tall and thin, and marching along Oaktree Lane. He stopped directly across the street and stared at her. He seemed to be trying to speak to her—that is, his mouth was moving as if he were speak-ing—but she couldn't hear a word. "Look at that guy,"

Zibby said, turning to Jude and Penny. "Looks like he's ready for action! Should we salute, or what?"

"What guy?" asked Jude. But when Zibby turned back to point out the soldier, he was gone.

"Must've been in a hurry to get to his war," Zibby said, shrugging. She led Penny and Jude inside the house. With more care than usual, she stowed her skates and helmet in their proper places in the hallway closet, then she took a deep breath. "Upstairs," she said to her guests. "The doll-house is in my mom's room."

She led the way to Nell's room. "I'm sure your trolls will really like this house," she said to Penny over her shoulder. "It's got loads of space—" She broke off in the doorway. The dollhouse was not where she had left it by her mom's dresser.

She wheeled around and pushed past Penny and Jude to cross the hall to her own bedroom. She stopped at the door-way when she heard a bell ringing—the bell inside her head.

"What is it?" asked Penny, behind her. "Is something wrong?"

Holding her breath, Zibby peered into her bedroom. The dollhouse was back again, next to her desk. She let out her breath in a little sob. *Maybe Mom came home from work while I was out....* She tried desperately to think of logical reasons to explain what was happening. *Maybe Charlotte came in and moved the house—after all, I did see that girl on her bike....*

Slowly Zibby crossed the room to stand in front of the dollhouse. It was still latched, but the sack of dolls was lying open on the floor. The girl doll with the brown braids lay on the front porch. Zibby stared at the doll. It stared back blankly.

"What a cool dollhouse!" exclaimed Penny. "It's perfect!"

"But this is one ugly lady," said Jude, pointing to the doll in the gray dress perched on Zibby's pillow. "I'll sleep with my teddy any day."

Zibby walked over to her bed and frowned down at the doll. The stern painted mouth seemed to be turned down even further than before, and her painted eyes glared up at Zibby. "I *don't* sleep with it," muttered Zibby, reaching for the doll with distaste. "And I didn't put it there." She tossed the doll across the room to lie by the dollhouse, not caring in the least whether she cracked the little porcelain head or hands.

She stood by her bed, debating whether to tell Jude and Penny about what was going on. But what could she say that made any sense? What *was* going on, anyway?

While she lingered, Penny and Jude had turned to inspect the dollhouse. "This is fantastic," Penny gloated. "I love it! I'm definitely going to beg my parents to buy it for me. Even though it costs a lot."

"They'll get it for you," predicted Jude. "Tell them it can be your moving-in present." She rolled her eyes at Zibby. "Penny is spoiled rotten. I guess it's not totally her fault, but she gets away with murder. It's because her parents tried for years and years for a second child after my dad was born, and finally gave up. Then when my dad was all grown-up and married to my mom, and I was a brand-new baby, Nana got pregnant with Penny."

"She calls me her Miracle Dream Baby," Penny said importantly.

Jude made gagging sounds.

While Penny examined the dollhouse, Zibby sat down at

her desk. She resolutely turned her back on the house. She couldn't bear to look at it.

Talking to Jude, who sat cross-legged on Zibby's bed just as if she'd sat there before, wasn't like talking to Amy, of course, but Zibby and Jude found they had a lot in common. They were both twelve. They were both going to be in seventh grade when school started. They both had fathers living in foreign countries. They both had to deal with troublesome people in their families—Charlotte, in Zibby's case; and Penny, in Jude's case—though Zibby had to admit to Jude that she liked Penny and didn't see anything annoying about her. "Oh, you will," prophesied Jude. "Nothing in the world is worse than an eleven-year-old aunt!" But she smiled.

"A twelve-year-old cousin who thinks she's twenty-five is worse," Zibby insisted with a giggle. She felt so comfortable with Jude already, she could almost forget about the weirdness with the dollhouse. Almost, but not really.

Zibby told Jude she wanted to become a carpenter when she grew up, and Jude confided she planned to become an architect. She pointed to the dollhouse. "Somebody did an awesome job designing and building that," she said. "Why are you selling it?"

Zibby glanced over her shoulder at the dollhouse. Was it even *right* to sell the dollhouse, knowing that something was very strange about it? Yet she couldn't bear having it in her house. She couldn't stand to look at it, knowing it somehow traveled around, always back to her room...all by itself.

But if she told Jude the truth, this nice new girl would grab Penny and race for home. They'd both say Zibby was 100 percent crazy. Zibby *couldn't* tell Jude the truth, so she tried for a casual shrug. "I don't play with dolls much," she muttered. "I'd rather skate instead."

"I'll dig out our skates tonight," Jude promised.

Zibby nodded, pleased that the remaining days of summer vacation without Amy suddenly weren't going to be so empty. Then the doorbell pealed downstairs, and Zibby left the Jefferson girls in her bedroom and ran down to the front door. She could see Charlotte outside the screen.

"You're supposed to come over to my house for lunch," Charlotte announced. "Our moms arranged it. We can go on our bikes."

"You didn't need to come get me." Zibby's stomach felt too unsettled for lunch, anyway.

"Well, I was riding around, so I thought I'd just stop by." Charlotte reached back and lifted her curls off her shoulders. "It's so hot out here," she complained. "Hurry up and get your bike and let's go."

"Was it you, Char?" Zibby demanded suddenly. "Earlier—when you were riding your bike? Did you come into my house and move the dollhouse?"

"What are you talking about?" Of course, Charlotte always managed to sound innocent.

"I think you know perfectly well," Zibby snapped back—but deep inside she didn't really think Charlotte had been there already. She sighed and opened the door. "I'll be ready in a few minutes. I've got some friends over."

"What friends?" laughed Charlotte. "Your only friend in the world is in *Cleveland*."

Just then Penny appeared at the top of the stairs. "Oh, there you are," she said to Zibby.

"This is my cousin, Charlotte Wheeler," said Zibby grudgingly. "And this is Penny Jefferson. From Pennsylvania."

"Penny from Pennsylvania?" said Charlotte with a smirk. "Got a brother named George—from Georgia?" She giggled, pleased at her own wit.

"Don't be so stupid, Char," said Zibby.

"I've got a brother named Malcolm," Penny offered. "He's in Kenya. And a niece named Jude. She's upstairs."

"A niece?" queried Charlotte, and so Penny went into her long explanation about how she came to be Aunt Penny to Jude, and then of course Charlotte wanted to meet Jude. They all went to Zibby's bedroom.

Jude was sitting on the floor in front of the dollhouse. She'd started arranging the dolls in the dollhouse living room. She was walking a little girl doll with long blond hair up the little staircase. "This house is amazing," she said to Zibby without turning around. "Are you *really* sure you want to sell it? I'm not actually into dollhouses, but even *I* can see this is a special sort of dollhouse, not just a toy. A family heirloom sort of thing." She sat back on her heels and looked startled at the sight of Charlotte. "Oh—hi!"

Zibby introduced them. "I've got to go to Charlotte's house for lunch," she said. "But we can get together again later this afternoon."

"Why are you talking about selling the dollhouse?" demanded Charlotte. "You only just bought it yesterday!"

"I told you already. I don't even know why I bought it—and I *definitely* don't want it. I'm going to get those blue Zingers."

"I think you're crazy."

"Isn't this the coolest dollhouse?" Penny asked Charlotte eagerly. "I'm going to try to get my parents to buy it for me—like for an early birthday present. Then my trolls will have a real house! Do *you* have a dollhouse?"

"Yes, I do," Charlotte replied. "But," she hastened to add, "dollhouses are my *hobby*—decorating them, I mean. Not *playing* with them."

"Mademoiselle Charlotte is *far* too mature for dolls," Zibby informed Jude and Penny.

Jude laughed and held up the little blond doll. "This one looks like you, Charlotte."

Charlotte tossed back her long curls. "Whatever. Anyway, Zibby, let's get going."

Zibby took the blond doll from Jude with a mischievous smile. She walked it along the little hallway into the dollhouse bathroom. "Oh, wait a minute! I can't go out to lunch yet—I have to pee so desperately!" She perched the Charlotte doll on the tiny iron toilet.

Penny and Jude laughed.

"You are such a *child*," said Charlotte witheringly. She looked pityingly at Jude and Penny. "And now you've got her for a neighbor. Good luck!" She stood up abruptly, hands on hips. "So, are you coming or not, Zib? Last chance for lunch—or I'll just tell my mom you couldn't be bothered."

Zibby rolled her eyes at Jude. "Now you see what I meant about cousins being worse than aunts, right?" She pitched the blond doll headfirst into the little porcelain bathtub, and they all followed Charlotte downstairs.

When they reached the front porch, Zibby dashed back

upstairs. Once again she slid her quilt under the dollhouse and dragged it back across the hallway into her mother's bedroom.

"Now *stay there*," she hissed, and closed the bedroom door firmly behind her.

CHAPTER 5

Charlotte lived on the other side of Main Street, where streets were named after spices and herbs, and all the homes were historic, built by the first families to settle in Carroway. Large elm trees shaded the sidewalks. Zibby and Charlotte rode their bikes under a green canopy of leaves past Coriander, Sage, and Thyme, then turned onto Nutmeg and zoomed up Charlotte's driveway.

They ate egg-salad sandwiches in the shady gazebo near the fountain in Charlotte's garden. This wasn't unusual; it was where they often ate when Zibby stayed for lunch with her cousin. But in the past they had sat on the grass, gobbling sandwiches from plastic picnic plates and sucking drinks from juice boxes, then swinging on the rope swing dangling from the elm tree. Now they sat on ornate wrought-iron chairs at a table covered with a lace cloth. Their sandwiches were cut into dainty triangles and arranged on china plates. They drank juice from thin china teacups. The rope swing had been taken down a couple months ago, when Charlotte decided she was too grown-up for such childish things. Zibby missed it. Charlotte had packed away all her toys— except the dollhouse, which didn't count as a toy, she always explained defensively, because it was her hobby.

Thinking about Charlotte's hobby reminded Zibby of her own dollhouse. *Was* it right to sell it to Penny, even if the girl could come up with the money, knowing there was something really weird about it? Her head ached with indecision. She drained her juice and set the teacup back onto its saucer, pushed back her wrought-iron chair, and stood up. "Listen—I'm going home now," she said, interrupting Charlotte, who had been chattering on about a cute guy who was a friend of her brother Owen.

"What?" Charlotte stopped in mid-rave. "But my mom said you were going to be here for the afternoon. I got some new makeup and I wanted to try it on you—you know, fix you up a little. Like a makeover at a spa! Just mascara and blush. I mean, now that you're twelve…"

The last thing Zibby wanted was to smear makeup on her face. "No way," she said. "I've got things to do."

Charlotte shook her head as if Zibby were a grave disappointment. "Well, I guess people mature at different ages. At least that's what Mom says."

Zibby strode off to the house without another word. She wanted to just jump on her bike and ride straight home, but first she knew she had to tell Aunt Linnea she was leaving. Aunt Linnea looked surprised.

"I thought you'd stay until dinnertime, Zib. That's when I've arranged with your mom to bring Charlotte over to spend the night. Uncle David and I will be out late, and Owen has got plans already—so we thought you girls would enjoy a sleepover." Usually when Aunt Linnea and Uncle David were out late, Charlotte stayed home with her brother. Zibby knew her cousin would be furious not to be allowed to stay home alone. She was glad to be leaving now, before the fireworks when Charlotte heard about the arrangements.

"I've got plans with the new girls who moved into Amy's house," she improvised hastily. "But I'll be home in time for dinner, when Charlotte gets there."

"Well, all right, dear. See you later."

"Thanks for lunch, Aunt Linnea," Zibby said, and was off on her bike, hurrying back across town to Oaktree Lane. She decided she would go home first to check on the dollhouse. If it had moved, the sale was off. She just couldn't send something so weird over to Penny and Jude's house. If the dollhouse had not moved, then she would lower the price and hope that Mrs. Jefferson would agree to pay it right away and take the thing off her hands.

Zibby rode through the bustling town center, then along the bike path by the river. Carroway was an old Ohio town, settled by pioneers way back in the early 1800s—when Abe Lincoln was a boy, Grammy had told her. Carroway's Main Street stretched the entire length of town, with branching streets leading off into the wooded countryside. The town center was a square of buildings around a grassy green. There were three old churches—one where Ned and Nell would be marrying each other very soon—and a modern synagogue. There were four banks, an antique store, and the old town hall, which had become the Carroway Little Theater. Aunt Linnea and Uncle David often performed in local plays, and Owen had once been Peter Pan, hoisted high on wires and made to fly. The new town hall was on a side street, an awkward modern building of steel and concrete, and next to that was the old brick building that housed the *Carroway Gazette,* where Ned was working right now. He had often urged her to feel free to stop in and say hello and have a tour of the place, but she never had. She didn't have time now, either.

Zibby veered off the riverside bike path, turned the corner, and pedaled on to Oaktree Lane. Shuffling tiredly past her house was the man she'd seen the day before in the park. He moved with his shaggy head down, with the same weary gait. His diamond-patterned vest and black overcoat seemed too heavy for a summer day. It made Zibby feel hot and tired just to look at him. He lifted his head as she passed, but did not smile.

Zibby parked her bike and let herself in the front door with her key. The air was as humid outside as inside, and Zibby wished her house had central air-conditioning the way Charlotte's did. Only the bedrooms were air-conditioned at Zibby's house. She poured herself a glass of peach juice in the kitchen and took it upstairs. With each step her heart beat faster. The door to Nell's bedroom was closed, just as she had left it. She strode right into her own room, chin thrust out defiantly, heart beating hard.

There it was *again.*

Somehow... *there it was.*

The dollhouse. Right back by her desk as if she had never moved it. *It's almost enough to make you feel you're losing your mind,* she thought wildly. But she wasn't crazy. She took a deep breath and approached the dollhouse. All the dolls were as Jude had left them. The blond doll was upside down in the bathtub, too—just as Zibby had left her. Only the house had moved.

No, wait. Only the house—*and* the doll in the gray dress. This time she was perched atop Zibby's desk lamp.

Zibby heard a bell clanging faintly. The palms of her hands began to sting. She clenched her fists and ran from the bedroom, away from the clanging bell, down the stairs, and out of the house. She ran all the way to the Jeffersons' house. The sale was off.

But the Jeffersons' green car was not in the driveway, and no one answered the door when she knocked. Zibby walked back home and slumped into a kitchen chair. She picked up the phone, then realized she did not know the Jeffersons' phone number. Maybe it was the same as Amy's? She tried Amy's old number, but a recording said it was no longer in service. She remembered how her mom sometimes called Information for phone numbers that weren't listed, and she punched the buttons. She asked for the Jeffersons on Oaktree Lane and was rewarded with a new phone number, which she wrote on the noteboard next to the phone.

She called the new number, hoping for an answering machine. It would be a lot easier to break the news to a machine. After she listened to a man's deep voice speaking on the tape, sorry to say no one was there, and so on, Zibby took a deep breath and started talking fast.

"Hi, Penny, it's me, Zibby Thorne, from down the street. Well, I just have to tell you—um, I'm really sorry to have to tell you—but you can't buy my dollhouse after all. My mom said I couldn't sell it, not to you or to anybody. She said it's really old and special, a sort of heirloom thing, just like Jude said, and I mustn't sell it. But I thought maybe Jude could design a dollhouse for you, and I'll build it—if your parents will buy the right kind of wood and stuff. I can do all the work with my birthday tools. It will be fun. Okay? Call and let me know, and maybe we can bike over to this miniatures shop my mom goes to in Fennel Grove, and we can get some ideas from the other houses there, and, well...that's all. I mean, I'm really sorry, Penny, and I hope you're not too mad. Bye!"

Zibby hung up, out of breath and hoping she had sounded sincere. She didn't dare go back up to her bedroom, so she just sat in the kitchen trying to read one of her new mystery novels from Owen until her mom came home. Every noise distracted her: the hum of the refrigerator, the shouts of kids outside, the clink of the metal flap on the door when the mail was delivered.

When Nell finally arrived, she had Charlotte with her. Charlotte was frowning fiercely.

"Hello, sweetheart." Nell deposited the pile of mail and two bags of groceries on the counter. "Can you go get the last bag from the car? I stopped off at the store, and then picked up Charlotte. Aunt Linnea and Uncle David will be gone tonight so—"

"I know, Mom. I already heard." Zibby hugged her mom and pushed past Charlotte. She brought in the last bag of groceries and helped Nell put things away. Charlotte sat at the kitchen table, glowering.

"Here's your weekly mail," Nell said, sorting through the pile and handing Zibby a postcard. Zibby glanced at it— another scene of the waterways of Venice, this time in moonlight—and tossed it onto the table. She didn't need to read it, really. They all said the same thing: When will you come to Venice?

Nell took a pan of her homemade macaroni-and-cheese casserole out of the refrigerator and popped it into the microwave. Then she turned to gloomy Charlotte. "Come on, honey," Nell said comfortingly. "You and Zibby will have a nice evening together. It's not as if your parents have called in a babysitter for you."

"They might as well have," Charlotte said sulkily, "for all they trust me. I'm old enough to stay alone! But they treat me like an infant!"

"Maybe they thought you'd have more fun here," suggested Nell. She washed the salad greens and tossed them into the salad spinner to dry them. Deftly, she chopped a tomato and a cucumber for the salad. "Here, Zib—can you assemble the salad while I make up some dressing? Then we'll be ready to eat. And Char? How about if you set the table. It's only the three of us tonight."

"No Ned?" asked Zibby. "No Laura-Jane and Brady?"

"He's taking them to visit their grandparents, but we'll see them tomorrow," replied Nell. She handed the silverware to Charlotte, who remained slumped at the table. Nell put her hand on Charlotte's shoulder. "Come on, cheer up."

"It isn't fair," muttered Charlotte. "My friends can stay home alone. Or go out on dates."

"Dates?" Nell laughed. "In middle school?" She slid a plate of macaroni and salad in front of Charlotte. Charlotte pushed it away, burst into tears, and ran out of the room.

Nell and Zibby looked at each other. "Uh-oh, I can see the teenage years approaching," said Nell ruefully. "I hope Linnea and David have nerves of steel."

"Charlotte is a total pain," Zibby said, embarrassed by her cousin's behavior. She wished Charlotte had been allowed to stay home alone. Then Zibby and her mom could have dinner in peace—just the two of them. That was a rare occurrence these days, and now that Ned and his kids were moving in, would they ever get time together?

They heard the slam of a door upstairs. Then came a cry—abruptly silenced by a heavy thump.

She and Nell looked at each other, then both of them rushed for the stairs. A thin trickle of red seeped from under the closed bathroom door. Nell gasped. Zibby reached for the knob and pushed open the door.

There on the floor lay Charlotte, her forehead streaming blood.

CHAPTER 6

"Charlotte! Oh, no, Charlotte," cried Nell, kneeling on the tiled floor next to her unconscious niece.

Zibby stared in horror at the blood streaks on the side of the porcelain bathtub, then joined her mom at Charlotte's side. All of Zibby's annoyance had evaporated at the sight of her cousin lying bloody on the floor, with eyes closed and breath coming in shallow gasps. The gash on Charlotte's forehead was wide, the skin split, blood pulsing.

Swiftly, Nell pressed a clean towel to the wound. Zibby felt sick. She knew Charlotte must be feeling even worse. "Char? Char, can you hear me?" Nell asked urgently.

Zibby let out her breath in relief when, after another second, Charlotte opened her eyes and stared up at them, dazed.

"Who was it?" Charlotte whispered. She clung to Nell's arm.

"Don't move, darling," cautioned Nell as Charlotte

struggled to sit up. "You were out for a few seconds, and you may have a concussion. Can you tell me what happened?"

Charlotte closed her eyes a moment, as if talking were too difficult.

"Somebody pushed me!"

"That's impossible, honey. No one is here but us, and Zibby and I were in the kitchen."

"But I was standing at the sink," faltered Charlotte. "Looking in the mirror. And I saw someone come into the room behind me. It couldn't have been either of you because neither one of you is wearing gray... But, *someone* came in and... I don't know. I suddenly sort of tripped backward, falling toward the tub..." She put a hand tentatively to her head and moaned.

Somebody wearing gray pushed her? Zibby's heart thudded.

Nell helped Charlotte sit up. "You must have imagined the person in gray. Now you're going to need stitches, I'm afraid. Can you stand, honey? We need to get you to the hospital."

Zibby filled a cup with cold water from the sink. "Can you drink this?"

Charlotte reached out a hand, then dropped it again. "Oh—I'm so dizzy..."

Nell frowned. "Straight out to the car, Charlotte. Lean on me."

"Shouldn't I call an ambulance?" worried Zibby. On TV she'd seen people with lesser injuries than Charlotte's whisked away in ambulances, lights flashing.

"We'll get there faster if we leave right now in my car," said Nell. She and Zibby helped Charlotte down the hall, then down the stairs, one slow step at a time. Zibby felt helpless and miserable. She remembered the last time she'd felt this lurching sickness in her belly. It had been four or five years ago when her dad caught the tip of his big toe in the lawn mower. She hated when anyone in her family was sick or hurt.

Nell settled Charlotte in the car and gave her another clean towel to press against the gash. "Zibby, this might take a while in the emergency room," said Nell. "Can you stay alone? Or shall I call Grammy to come over?" She rooted around in her purse for her cell phone. "And I need to call Linnea and David and tell them we're going to the Car-roway Clinic…"

"I can stay here alone, Mom. You don't need to call Grammy."

"Well, okay, but call her if you want company." Nell looked distracted. "There's no answer from Linnea. I'll try again from the clinic." She glanced over at Charlotte, who sat silent and drooping. "We'd better get going."

Zibby waved until the car turned the corner, even though she knew neither of them was watching. Then she climbed the steps of the porch and sat down in the old rocking chair. *Charlotte saw somebody wearing gray.* That fact pounded in Zibby's head. *She thinks somebody pushed her.* What if Charlotte were right? What could it mean?

The summer evening was still. The people who had been mowing their lawns or watering their gardens had gone inside. Probably most families were finished eating dinner and were watching TV or putting their children to bed. The fireflies were just starting to come out. Zibby stood up and walked restlessly across the porch, then back inside the house. She left the front door open but locked the screen. She was drawn to the kitchen by the smell of their uneaten macaroni and cheese.

Nell had left the casserole cooling on the counter. Zibby spooned a large portion into a bowl, ignored the salad, and carried the bowl upstairs. When she reached the hallway, she thought she saw a flash of gray zip around the edge of the doorframe into her mom's bedroom. Zibby froze. Could there really be someone else in the house—some *intruder*?

Holding her breath, Zibby peeked around the door of Nell's room. The room seemed undisturbed, and the closet door stood open. No one was there. Zibby looked under the bed just to be sure. She checked the bathroom, too. Empty.

Then she edged carefully into her own bedroom and found that it, too, was empty. Relieved, she sat cross-legged on her bed and ate her dinner, glad for the cooling breeze through her bedroom windows. She heard the cars passing outside, the next-door neighbor calling her children in from playing, a dog barking. Then she tensed, listening—was that a bell? Yes, she could hear it, ringing softly. It didn't sound like the Jeffersons' dinner bell. It was higher in tone, more strident, and didn't really seem to be coming from outside the window at all; it was ringing inside the dollhouse.

Hesitantly, Zibby crossed to the dollhouse and knelt in front of it. With guilty recognition she saw the blond girl doll—the Charlotte doll—still lying upside down in the little bathtub where Zibby had tossed it that afternoon. Its little forehead lay against the cold porcelain. But now the doll in the gray dress stood leaning against the little bathroom sink.

Zibby snatched both dolls out of the dollhouse and dropped them to the floor.

Outside Zibby's bedroom window a soft rain began to fall. It was growing dark. The ringing bell grew louder and more strident, and Zibby realized it was the telephone. She ran to answer it in Nell's room. Nell was calling to say that Charlotte was going to have to stay overnight at the hospital for observation, and that Nell would remain with her until Aunt Linnea and Uncle David could get there.

"But will she be all right, Mom?" asked Zibby urgently.

"I'm sure she will," replied Nell. "But the gash was deeper than we thought, and the doctors want to keep an eye on her."

"Oh, Mom, tell her I'm really, really sorry. I feel terrible."

"We both do. It was a freak accident." Nell's voice was reassuring. "Now, sweetheart, I'll be home in another hour or so. Are you all right?"

The rain was now slashing like a scythe through the darkness. Zibby looked out the windows, feeling scared and unsettled, but she replied bravely, "I'm okay. See you later."

As soon as she hung up, a crash of thunder shook the house, and the lights went out. The lightning that split the night illuminated the bedroom. Zibby hugged herself. A power failure was nothing to be scared of.

From time to time the power would go out during a storm, but always her mom had been home, and her dad, too, and it was fun, an adventure. Her dad would light candles and Nell and Zibby would make popcorn the old-fashioned way, in a pot held over the flame of the gas stove. The three of them would sit together and eat popcorn, and her dad had been great at devising quizzes for Zibby and Nell. Name all the presidents. The state capitals. The rivers of South America. Five things you could eat that grew in the desert. It had been cozy and companionable in the dark.

But now Zibby was alone. She didn't know if she should try the switches in the fuse box on the kitchen wall. She wasn't even sure where the candles were. For a second Zibby missed her dad fiercely. But probably Ned Shimizu would take charge of things like fuse boxes and candles when he moved in, no problem. Too bad he was out of town tonight.

Zibby felt her way down the stairs and into the kitchen, waiting for flashes of lightning to light her way. She found a flashlight in one cupboard, but no batteries. She found a box of skinny little birthday cake candles and a box of matches. But she didn't have a cake to stick the candles in.

Her eye fell on the little jade plant on the windowsill above the kitchen sink. She lifted it down and stuck candles into the dirt. Then she struck a match and lit one. She used the lit candle to light the others, just as she'd seen her mom do on birthday cakes. The candles flickered in a circle around the jade plant. Now what? She couldn't watch TV or listen to music, or even read very well by such feeble light. And the little candles burned so fast, they'd be gone in minutes. She could go back upstairs...to the dollhouse.

She pushed away this unaccountable urge and reached across the table for the newspaper. She read the advice column and the comics.

Come upstairs! You have so much to learn.

The thought was like a whisper running through her head. Where did it come from? Zibby kept checking the lighted dial on her watch and listening for her mom's car in the driveway. But Nell did not return, and soon the skinny birthday candles had burned down to nubs of wax.

Now what? Zibby looked around the shadowed kitchen. Then she remembered the big red heart-shaped candle that Amy had given her as a going-away present, even though Amy herself was the one who was going away.

Come up! You must learn to mind your manners! This time the urge to go to the dollhouse was stronger, more insistent, but again Zibby tried to push it away. Almost against her will, Zibby groped for the handrail and started up the stairs. She hurried down the hall to her room. The house felt different in the dark. Bigger. Cold, even on a summer night.

Ignoring the dollhouse as it beckoned to her, Zibby found the heart candle on her bookcase. It sat on a thick round holder of glass. She hadn't intended to burn it at all, but this was an emergency. The first match she struck flickered out before it caught the wick, but the second burned brightly. Zibby lit the candle and set it on the glass holder atop her desk. Light!

And in the light, something awful.

All the little dolls were out of their pillowcase sack, lined up on the rug in front of the house. All except one. The doll in the iron-gray dress now sat up on the roof of the dollhouse, leaning back against the tiny brick chimney. Zibby's breath caught in her throat. No one could have moved the dolls. They had—impossibly—moved by themselves.

Zibby's hand trembled as she lifted the heart candle in its thick glass holder and approached the dollhouse. She plucked the grim-faced doll off the roof—and felt a stinging across her palm as if her hand had been struck. She dropped the doll and at the same time her hand gripping the glass candleholder dipped, toppling the red wax heart onto the pile of dolls on the floor.

The candle's flame caught the dry, aged fabric of one of the dresses and a little flame grew while Zibby rubbed her aching hand and stared at it. In a panic she snatched up the empty pillowcase and snapped it down hard onto the flame, extinguishing it. Then she edged over to the desk for the box of matches. She lit the red candle again and assessed the damage.

The frown-faced doll lay on the floor, the skirt of her long, gray dress askew. Thank goodness, Zibby noted, the flame had not damaged the rug. It had only singed the mother doll's green sleeve.

Then she froze. What was that noise downstairs? Was there a prowler in the house with her, after all? She gulped in a breath and held it, listening. Then with a quick puff she blew out the candle. She mustn't let him see the light.

Then the sound came again—the click of the front door—and her mom's welcome voice. "Zibby—I'm home!"

Abandoning the dolls, the dollhouse, the candle, and the fear of prowlers, Zibby tore downstairs into Nell's embrace. "Oh, Mom! I'm so glad you're here."

"Believe me, I'm very glad to be here." Nell tiredly shook back her wet ponytail. "Have you been sitting in the dark? Let's get some candles lit!"

"I looked, but all I could find were birthday candles."

"Poor Zib. You should have called Grammy and Gramps." Nell opened the cupboard next to the refrigerator and reached up high. "Here they are." She brought down two white tapers in brass holders. The rain beat down outside, drumming on the roof. The wind roared. Zibby was so glad to have her mom home that the fear she'd felt upstairs with the dollhouse receded, and the weird business with the doll in the gray dress seemed almost something she had imagined.

Nell crossed the room to the stove, turned on the gas, and held the candle to the flame. Then, without warning, the back door blew open in a gust of wet wind and the gas flame flared, singeing Nell's hand and wrist. She dropped the candle with a yelp of pain. Zibby flew to slam the back door, and then the electricity came back on. The kitchen light blazed overhead like a sunburst.

"Oh, Mom, are you okay?" cried Zibby.

Nell had rushed straight to the sink and was running cold water over the burn. She grimaced. "I'll live." She examined her reddened wrist. "It's certainly our night for accidents."

Zibby pictured the candle flame igniting the mother doll's sleeve. She thought about the doll who looked like Charlotte lying in the dollhouse bathtub. She remembered the flash of gray she'd seen going around the corner upstairs.

Accidents? Zibby didn't think so.

CHAPTER 7

PRIMROSE 1919

Up in the nursery there had been lots of toys for Primrose to play with: a rocking horse with a mane of real horsehair, shelves of puzzles, spinning tops, wooden animals, and fairy-tale books. There were building bricks and roller skates and games of checkers, jackstraw, and old maid. There were dolls—baby dolls in bibs, fine lady dolls in lacy dresses, and even a tiny doll from Japan, wearing a silk kimono. Her father and mother had brought that doll back from their last long trip. Best of all, there was the dollhouse. But now all playthings belonged to the twins.

In Miss Honeywell's schoolroom, there were very few toys. Primrose had brought the Japanese doll along to the schoolroom, and a few of her favorite games—though Miss Honeywell never wanted to play, and so the games gathered dust on the bottom shelf. Primrose had also brought her skates to the schoolroom, hoping that Miss Honeywell would take her out to the park, where she would be able to soar along the paths as she had on outings with Nanny

Shanks—but Miss Honeywell said that skating was not ladylike. The only time they went to the park together was when Miss Honeywell wanted Primrose to gather plant samplings for her botany scrapbook. Girls and boys her age on skates would whiz past Primrose, shouting and laughing while Primrose knelt resentfully by the bushes, collecting leaves.

Primrose was sitting at the table in the schoolroom, trying to memorize the major rivers of the world. She had a globe in front of her and was penciling the names of the rivers onto her blank map. Miss Honeywell sat across the table, writing a letter. Primrose used to think Miss Honeywell wrote regularly to an invalid relative or some such person, but in fact, Primrose had seen an envelope just the other day addressed to Mr. Pope! Miss Honeywell was sweet on the tutor, and now that Primrose was certain of this fact, she found it highly entertaining to watch Miss Honeywell gazing at him as he sat, oblivious, trying to teach Primrose about the marvels of electric currents. Miss Honeywell wrote him one letter each day. Her handwriting was sharp and clear, unlike Primrose's round, uneven script. Whenever Primrose's handwriting grew too uneven, Miss Honeywell smacked her palms with a ruler and made her write the whole page over again. Mr. Pope also fussed a bit about her messy handwriting and illegible numbers, but at least he only scolded, never hit. Miss Honeywell kept her temper in check on days when Mr. Pope came. Primrose suspected this was part of Miss Honeywell's plan to win his regard. She was probably hoping Mr. Pope would ask to marry her.

As if anyone would *ever* want to marry Old Sourpuss!

Now Primrose was trying hard to write the names of the

rivers clearly. She heard the clock on the landing chime ten and remembered wistfully how Nanny Shanks would always ring for milk and cinnamon toast to be brought to the nursery—or hot chocolate when the weather was cold—at this time of morning. Probably right now the twins were sitting in the cozy nursery at their little table, sipping hot chocolate and eating toast. While here she was, working hard, and no chance of a break until lunchtime. Two more hours of geography, and then after lunch there would be arithmetic and science with Mr. Pope—it was too much to bear.

Primrose's eyes filled with tears, but she dashed them away. Miss Honeywell hated tears. "If you want to cry, I'll give you something to cry about," she would say coolly, and out would come her ever-present ruler, ready to smack. "Young ladies must exhibit self-control."

Primrose sighed and glanced over at the windows yearningly—then drew in her breath. "Oh, look!" she cried before she could stop herself. "It's snowing!"

She shoved back her chair, but Miss Honeywell's voice—colder than snow—stopped her. "Sit down, young lady, until you have memorized the names and locations of the rivers."

"Oh, but—it's the first snow of the year!" Primrose gazed out at the fluffy flakes.

"That does not concern us." Miss Honeywell turned back to the letter she was writing.

Primrose frowned furiously and imagined the bookcase behind Miss Honeywell tipping forward, tipping...tipping... until—CRASH—it fell straight over onto Miss Honeywell, flattening her like a flounder.

Then she imagined the snow outside falling and falling

until a huge snowbank surrounded the house. Then, somehow, she would lure Miss Honeywell to the window—
how? Because a rare specimen of songbird had just perched
on the tree outside?—and then *WHAM!* One giant push
and down would go Miss Honeywell into the snow. Deep,
over her head, knocked out cold. No one would find her
body till spring. *Oh my goodness gracious,* Primrose imagined
herself saying. *So that's where she went off to? I'm afraid I
never noticed a thing. I was too busy memorizing all the rivers
of the world.*

These sorts of fantasies often helped to pass the long
hours of lessons. Primrose sighed and looked back down at
her map. But as soon as Miss Honeywell left the table and
went to her bedroom for another sheet of writing paper,
Primrose dashed to the window and stood, transfixed. She
unlatched the casement window and leaned out.

The snow was beautiful. It drifted silently, thickly, the
flakes looking heavy and soft. Already the ground was covered. She heard a shout, and there, around the side of the
house, came Nanny Shanks with the little twins. Peony was
tipping her face to the sky, grinning. Basil roared with
laughter, patting his little mittened hands together. Nanny
Shanks stopped and bent down to show the toddlers how to
make a snowball. Primrose longed to grab her coat and
gloves and run outside to join them.

A hand like a claw tightened on Primrose's shoulder and
spun her away from the window. "You have not finished
your map," Miss Honeywell said, and withdrew a ruler from
her skirt pocket. "You have much to learn, young lady, the
first being obedience. Hold out your hands."

Rebelliously Primrose put her hands behind her back.

"Hold out your hands," Miss Honeywell repeated implacably, "or it's into the closet with you." The governess never raised her voice, but it had the power of a shout.

The closet. That was where Miss Honeywell locked Primrose for bad behavior. The most recent time had been last week, after Primrose had poured a cup of cold water into the center of Miss Honeywell's bed, soaking her mattress. She had been in the closet for two hours that time, huddled in the dark among the coats.

She held out her hands, wincing as Miss Honeywell struck the ruler six times across her palms. "I hate you, old Honeywell," muttered Primrose, blinking back tears of pain and rage.

"That's *Sweet* Miss Honeywell to you," snapped the governess. "You shall learn to mind. There is never any excuse for disobedience. My brother, Lester, had to learn that the hard way, and you shall learn it, too. Now it's back to work with you, and no more interruptions—"

A clamor from the courtyard below stopped her, and this time Miss Honeywell was the one who peered out the window. Primrose edged over to look as well.

A long black shiny automobile had driven in, with the Parsons' chauffeur at the wheel. A dark-haired woman in an elegant red cape was helped out by the driver. A tall man in a black coat emerged next.

"It's Mama and Papa!" squealed Primrose. "I didn't know they were coming home today!" She glared at Miss Honeywell. "You might have told me, you know."

The governess pressed her lips together, frowning out the window. "I expected them later tonight, when you would be in bed. But I suppose they'll want to see you. So don't just stand there! Go at once to your room and put on a nice dress. Your green and blue silk."

For once Primrose and Miss Honeywell were in agreement. Primrose skipped into her room in delight, almost forgetting her still-stinging palms. The green and blue silk was a dress her father had bought on his last trip, and Primrose had not yet had any chance to wear it. Primrose changed swiftly from her brown woolen school dress. She jumped on one foot and then the other while Miss Honeywell buttoned the silk dress up the back.

"Hurry, hurry! I can't wait to see them!"

"Spoiled young girls must learn the virtue of patience." And it seemed to Primrose that the governess's fingers moved more slowly than ever along the row of buttons.

Primrose bit her lip. She resolved to tell her parents *everything*—about the closet, the ruler, the scoldings. About how *Sweet* Miss Honeywell acted perfectly horrid to Primrose, how she flirted with Mr. Pope and once even contrived to walk him all the way home—helping him to carry the electrical circuitry he had brought over in two large boxes to show Primrose—leaving Primrose locked alone in the schoolroom the whole time she was gone. How there was never any playtime. How Primrose never got to see Peony and Basil anymore. Her parents would send Miss Honeywell away forever and let Primrose go back to Nanny Shanks.

There came a tap on the schoolroom door, and Miss Honeywell opened it to the uniformed maid, who dropped a curtsy and said Captain and Mrs. Parsons would like to see Miss Primrose in the front parlor at once.

"Come along, Primrose." The governess took Primrose's hand in a tight, restraining grip.

"That's *Sweet* Primrose to you," hissed Primrose, snatching her hand away. She pushed Miss Honeywell aside. She darted past the maid and slid all the way down the banister to the grand entrance hall. Her feet raced across the marble floor to the parlor door. The door was closed.

Primrose straightened her skirts, took a deep breath, and tapped on the door. Then, as she heard Miss Honeywell's footsteps behind her, she flung the door wide. "Mama! Papa! I've missed you so much!"

CHAPTER 8

The next morning, Nell, her burnt wrist wrapped in gauze dressing, left early to meet Aunt Linnea and Uncle David at the hospital. Zibby sat at the kitchen table poking at her fried egg.

The phone rang and she snatched it up. "Mom?"

"No, it's me," said Penny's voice excitedly. "Zibby—wasn't that the best storm last night? You should see our backyard—the old elm tree crashed down and just missed the garage by inches! Come on over. I was thinking we could make a clubhouse in the branches—"

"I can't come," murmured Zibby, interrupting Penny's chatter.

"What's wrong?" asked Penny. "You don't sound very happy."

"I'm okay." Zibby hesitated, then told Penny what had happened to Charlotte the night before. Just the bare facts—nothing about the dollhouse.

"Oh, poor Charlotte," said Penny. "Well, listen, as soon as you can, come over to our house, okay? I was thinking that since your mom won't let you sell your dollhouse, then we could sort of have a club to build me one. A dollhouse club! Jude will draw up the plan, and you can build it with your new tools, like you said. And I'll make the furniture. What do you think?"

Zibby thought the last thing she wanted was to be in a *dollhouse* club. But she said that would be fine, and maybe they could get together later in the day. With a sigh, she hung up the phone and turned back to her egg—and screamed.

There on the kitchen table, leaning against Zibby's glass of orange juice, was the grim-faced doll in the gray dress. *You shall learn your manners.*

Zibby jumped away so fast that her chair tipped over and crashed to the floor. She leaped over to the sink and snatched the salad tongs out of the dish rack. Holding her breath, she used the tongs to pick up the doll. She carried it over to the trash bin in the corner and dropped the doll in as if it were a rancid piece of garbage. Swiftly she tied the plastic bag closed. But even that wasn't good enough. The doll was bad news, and she wanted it *gone.*

She carried the plastic bag outside into the yard and stuffed it deep into the trash container next to the recycling bins. She pressed down hard until the lid latched. "This is what I know about *manners,*" she said, her voice gritty and hoarse.

Zibby walked around the house to the front porch and sat there trying to read her mystery book. But the real mystery, the mystery of the dollhouse, clouded her mind and made concentration impossible. She just sat there in a fog until her mom drove into the driveway. Aunt Linnea drove in right behind her. Zibby ran to greet them.

Charlotte sat in the front seat of the van. Uncle David and Owen sat in back. Charlotte had a bandage on her head. She looked pale. "I had to have sixteen stitches," she announced through the open window. "That's more than when you cut your foot at the beach."

Zibby had had eleven stitches four years ago after gashing her foot on a piece of glass in the sand at Lake Pymatuning. It had been a happy vacation up to that point, and then the rush to the emergency room had cut the holiday short. Zibby's dad had held her on his lap the whole time the doctor was stitching the cut.

Zibby pushed the memory away. "You're definitely the gold-medal winner of stitches."

"The one with the most stitches gets the most ice cream after lunch," said Owen from the backseat. "Want to come over for lunch, Zib?"

"Not today," she replied. "Char can have my share— just this once. As extra pain relief."

"No thanks," Charlotte objected predictably. "And I think you really ought to cut down on ice cream yourself, Zibby. You've got to start thinking of your figure."

Zibby snorted. Before Charlotte had become so ladylike, she could dig into a gallon as well as anybody. "I'll let you think about it for me," said Zibby. "Saves me the trouble." But she was glad to hear Charlotte sounding like herself. That meant she hadn't been hurt *too* badly.

"We just wanted to pick up Charlotte's overnight things,"

Aunt Linnea explained, getting out of the van. "She's supposed to lie down for the rest of the day. Doctor's orders."

"And I've got to get to work," said Uncle David from the backseat.

"So do I," said Nell. "I'm catering a bridal-shower tea party."

"You'll soon be the bride," replied Aunt Linnea, returning to the van with Charlotte's overnight case. "We should be giving *you* a tea party or something."

"No, please don't bother." Nell shook her head. "There's enough going on as it is, trying to get everything ready for the wedding. Tonight Ned's taking Zibby and me out for dinner with his kids."

"We just went out to dinner with them," Zibby moaned. "How about I stay home?" But then she remembered the dollhouse and knew she didn't really want to be alone.

"I want you to come," said Nell, frowning at her. Then she turned back to say good-bye to Aunt Linnea, Uncle David, Owen, and Charlotte. "Get some rest, Char. Call us later, okay?"

Zibby waved good-bye and followed her mom into the house. She listened with one ear to Nell's lecture about how important it was to get to know Laura-Jane and Brady— but her other ear was listening to something else. A bell ringing—upstairs.

"Okay, okay," she muttered distractedly. "I'll come to dinner and be nice."

Dimly she heard Nell telling her that she was taking the DaisyCakes food to the tea party event, but she would come back home shortly.

Zibby said good-bye, but she could barely hear her own

voice over the peal of the bell. She could see that her mom heard nothing out of the ordinary. When Nell's car backed out of the driveway, Zibby strode up the stairs. As she reached the door to her bedroom, her palms started stinging. She clenched her hands into fists and stepped into the room.

There on her desk stood the doll in the gray dress.

Don't think you can get rid of me so easily, young miss. It seemed to gloat.

Zibby approached the doll warily. Gingerly lifting it by the hem of its gray skirt, she held it aloft between thumb and forefinger and carried it over to the dollhouse.

So your mother hopes to be a bride, does she? I'd rather hoped to be one myself.

Zibby tried to ignore the voice in her head as she shoved the doll into the dollhouse attic. She bundled up the whole sack of dolls and stuffed them into the house, too. She closed up the house and latched it securely. She hated to touch the dollhouse. It felt alive and malevolent to her.

She wrapped her quilt around and under the house, and dragged the whole thing out into the hallway. This time she did not take it back to Nell's room but instead bumped it down the stairs. She dragged the dollhouse through the dining room, through the kitchen, then out the back door. She thumped it roughly down the back steps. She tipped the house out of the quilt onto the flagstone patio. One little brick chimney broke off, but who cared?

She took a deep breath and folded the quilt carefully. She laid it on the back steps where it would be safe. When she turned back to the dollhouse, she saw a man standing just outside the backyard gate, watching her over the fence.

It was the same man she'd seen before, the tired-looking man. He ran his hand through his shaggy dark hair.

"Can I help you?" Zibby demanded.

"Have you seen my lamb?" he asked in a soft, choked voice, pointing to the dollhouse. Or at least that's what it sounded like he said. Zibby shook her head.

"I haven't seen it," she told him curtly. She hadn't known people could keep farm animals in this neighborhood.

The man hesitated, staring at the dollhouse as if he wanted to ask her something else, but then he lowered his shaggy head and shuffled away. Zibby waited, watching, until he had reached the street. Relieved, she turned back to the patio and the business at hand. But there was the soldier in uniform, the one she'd seen at the park. He was just standing there—by the back door.

"Where did you come from?" she asked him, her voice rising. "How did you get into our yard?" She had not seen him come in through the gate. She saw he was young— maybe still a teenager.

He opened his mouth as if to answer, but no sound came out. He moved his lips as if trying to speak, then finally found his voice. "I tried to get away," he said to her quietly. "Poor kid. I know what it's like…"

Why was she getting all these strange visitors just when she needed to be alone? Was this guy looking for the man who was looking for the sheep? Zibby ran to the fence to check for the shaggy-haired man, but no one was there. When she turned back to the young man, he was gone, too.

Zibby told herself he must have run out the back gate, but she felt uneasy all the same. She turned back to the dollhouse. The flagstone patio was choked with weeds. Gardening had been her dad's responsibility—a chore he'd enjoyed. With him gone, Zibby and Nell rarely remembered. Gramps came over occasionally to mow the grass. *Maybe Ned would like to do the gardening,* Zibby thought idly as she walked into the garage and returned with the can of lighter fluid that her mom used for the charcoal grill.

Zibby opened the nozzle and sprayed the fluid over the dollhouse, watching it sink into the old, dry, thirsty wood. She soaked it well, using the entire can. Then she ran back to the kitchen for the matches.

Never play with fire, Zibby thought grimly. But this was not play. This was desperate work. She moved quickly, trying not to think about the trouble she'd be in when her mom found out what she'd done. Nothing else mattered but that she finish what she'd started when she first brought the dollhouse home from the miniatures show. *Get rid of the house and the doll,* she told herself. That's what was important. It was hurting people and it was scaring her. She'd worry later about explaining its absence.

As she lit the match and held it toward the house, ready to leap away at the first flame, Zibby could see the gray cloth of the nasty doll's dress through one of the little attic windows.

She threw the match—and as the house flared up in a column of flame, she heard the bell tolling. Her hands stung as if they, too, were on fire, and over the crackle of burning wood she heard a terrible scream.

Zibby covered her ears. *Dolls do not scream,* she thought in panic. *They can't!*

But it wasn't the doll; it was Jude, right behind her, hands on hips, looking furious. "What in the world are you doing? Are you totally *crazy*, girl? Isn't this house supposed to be an heirloom—so precious you can't even sell it to Penny?"

Zibby stared at the shooting flames and did not know how to answer. Jude ran to the hose looped next to the back door and cranked on the water. "Quick, you pyromaniac! If we hurry, we may still be able to save it—"

"No!" Zibby grabbed the hose out of Jude's hands. "Let it burn!" She watched with satisfaction as the back wall crumpled. The fire popped, and the miniature brick chimney exploded. Zibby started to laugh, exhilarated. *Take that!* She thought she saw movement at the side of the garage and caught her breath, afraid that her mom had returned. But no—it was that soldier. He stood on the other side of the fence, watching the fire. When he saw her looking at him, he raised his hands and clapped them slowly together as if applauding.

Glad you approve, buddy, thought Zibby, but her laughter broke off abruptly as Jude lunged again for the hose. Zibby fended her off. "I said, leave it!" Zibby yelled. "There's something's *wrong* with it!" She lowered her voice. "It's...evil."

Jude turned off the water and looked at Zibby, wide-eyed. "Did you say *evil*?"

"Yes." Zibby's feeling of exhilaration began to ebb as the flames consumed the last of the old wooden structure and the end-of-summer breeze blew the smoke away. She glanced around for the young soldier, but he was nowhere to be seen. She felt a shiver of apprehension as she looked back at the charred wreckage. Her mom would go berserk when she saw it.

"You are the biggest drama queen I ever met," snapped Jude. "And selfish, too—burning up that house instead of giving it to Penny."

Zibby couldn't even think how to explain. Her head ached fiercely and she wished Jude would just disappear. Then Nell's car turned into the driveway and Jude started toward it. "I think you're crazy—and I'm going to tell your mom what you did to your precious *heirloom*."

Zibby tore after Jude as she trailed into the house behind Nell. Zibby flung the screen door wide and followed. Nell had started up the stairs, stooping to pick up a pile of folded laundry on the bottom step. Jude was right behind Nell, gibbering about fire and crazy, selfish girls. Zibby, panting, grabbed Jude's arm. "Don't listen to her, Mom! Everything she says is a total lie—"

Nell turned halfway up the stairs and shook her head. "Whoa, you two," she said. "You sound like a herd of buffalo, and I can't understand a word either of you is saying."

"She burned down her—"

Zibby raised her voice to drown out Jude's. "What time are we going out with Ned?"

Nell held out the pile of laundry as if to fend the girls off. "Hold everything. First of all, Zibby, would you mind introducing your friend? It's not that I mind having people race after me on the stairs, but at least I should know who they are."

Jude blinked and ducked her head. Zibby could tell she was embarrassed. Well, she should be. "This is Jude Jefferson," Zibby said hastily. "Um, and Jude—this is my mom. Jude just moved into Amy's house, Mom—"

"How nice to meet you, Jude," Nell said pleasantly. She continued up the stairs. "So, where did you live before?"

Zibby could see that Jude was desperate to tattle about the dollhouse, but good manners prevailed. "We lived in Pennsylvania," she said. "But Noddy—my grandfather, I mean—bought the lumberyard here in town, and so we moved."

Zibby spoke up quickly, hoping to keep the conversation going. "Jude lives with her grandparents because her parents are in Africa. They're both doctors, Mom, helping to start up a new hospital. Isn't that cool? So Jude is spending the year with—"

"About Zibby's heirloom dollhouse," Jude interrupted. "I hate to tell you, but she just—"

"And Jude has an aunt—that's Penny, Mom—who's *younger* than she is, can you believe it?" Zibby interrupted. "Just think how funny it would be if Aunt Linnea was, like, *my* age!"

The girls followed Nell down the hall toward Zibby's bedroom. Zibby held her breath. What would her mom say when she saw the house was gone? But Nell didn't say a word. She walked straight over to Zibby's bed and laid half the pile of laundry on it. "Here you go," she said. "And I want you to put everything away neatly—*inside* your dresser, not just on top of it." She glanced over at Jude. "Now what's this you're trying to tell me about the dollhouse?"

Zibby squeezed her eyes shut and waited for Jude to tattle, waited for her mom's explosion. But Jude was silent. Zibby opened her eyes and looked at her. Jude was standing rigid, staring at the corner by the desk. Zibby stared, too.

The dollhouse stood intact, unburnt, complete as before.

"No," whispered Jude. Zibby saw that she was trembling.

"It's nothing, Mom," said Zibby quickly. "Jude just wanted to say—well, that she really likes my dollhouse. And she wants us to build one like it for Penny. Right, Jude?" Her voice was firm, as if a reasonable tone might change the truth of what stood before their eyes.

Jude couldn't seem to answer but just kept nodding.

Nell looked at the girls curiously, then shrugged. "Okay. Whatever. You'll have fun using your new birthday tools."

"Yes, lots of fun," said Zibby brightly. "Right, Jude?"

Jude still didn't answer. Nell left the room carrying the rest of the folded laundry.

When they were alone, Zibby touched the girl's bare brown shoulder. "Are you okay?"

Jude was shaking. Her voice came out a ragged whisper. "No, I'm not okay. I saw you burn the house down. I *saw* it with my own eyes!"

Zibby reached out a finger and unhooked the latch on the dollhouse. She hated to touch it, but she had to know. The front swung open, revealing the sack of dolls inside, and, standing in the attic, the doll in the gray dress. The painted mouth looked smug.

Zibby turned her back on the dollhouse and led Jude over to sit beside her on the bed. Zibby hugged the pillow to her chest. "Listen—let me tell you about it," she began softly. "I've been wanting to tell someone, but I was sure no one would believe me. It's just too weird..."

"I'll believe," Jude whispered back, glancing warily over at the dollhouse. "But—can we talk at my house instead? I don't want to be here with...it."

"I don't, either." Zibby jumped off the bed. "That's why I was burning it. That's why—well, come on. Let's go see that clubhouse tree that Penny was telling me about. We can talk there, and maybe we won't be overheard. Maybe we'll be far enough away."

"Away?"

As Zibby headed out of the room, she cast a fearful glance back at the gray-gowned doll in the dollhouse attic. "Away from *her.*"

CHAPTER 9

The girls didn't talk much as they walked to Amy's house—*Jude and Penny's house now,* Zibby reminded herself. The sidewalk shimmered in the heat. They found Penny and Mrs. Jefferson sitting on their living-room couch looking at a magazine together. Unpacked boxes were stacked along one wall.

"Oh…hi," Penny said in a subdued voice. She threw Zibby a cautious look. Obviously her feelings had been hurt by Zibby's abrupt manner on the telephone that morning. She held up the magazine. It had a picture of an elaborate Victorian dollhouse on the front and was titled *Nutshell News.* "Want to see the kind of dollhouse you and Jude are going to build me?"

"Want to come tell us about it?" invited Jude. "And we can show Zibby the tree?"

"That's a good idea," said Mrs. Jefferson, standing up. "You girls get yourselves involved in a project—and I'll get back to unpacking more boxes so we can walk without tripping."

Penny tossed back her braids with a click of beads. "You mean you want to see the tree after all?" she asked Zibby doubtfully.

"Yes, I really do," Zibby told her. "Come on. Hurry!"

The three girls walked out to the backyard, where the fallen tree lay like a giant ark. It was the tree where Amy's tire swing had hung. "Next time you should bring your tools," said Penny, pushing through the branches that rested on the ground, "so we can build it into a real clubhouse."

Zibby, following, found herself in a leafy green clearing. It was like a little room, with a green roof overhead, and low branch benches to sit on. Sunlight filtered in and gave it a peaceful air, but Zibby was feeling anything but peaceful as she settled herself on one of the low branches.

"I don't think I need to do anything with my tools here," she told Penny. "It's a perfect little house just as it is."

"Until Noddy gets out his chain saw and cuts it into fire-wood," said Jude, poking her curly dark head through the branches. "But that won't be till the weather gets cold." She joined Zibby on the low branch and nudged her. "Okay, this meeting is officially called to order."

"Is this a meeting about my dollhouse?" asked Penny. "Here, look at this magazine—"

"It's not about your dollhouse," Jude interrupted. "It's about Zibby's dollhouse."

"Well, go on." Penny sat cross-legged on the grass and shut the magazine. She clasped her arms around her knees and looked up at the other girls expectantly. "What about it?"

Zibby sat silently.

"Did your mom say I can buy it from you after all?" asked Penny eagerly.

"No way," replied Jude vehemently. "Just *listen*."

Zibby drew in a deep breath and exhaled loudly. "Okay, here we go." But she hesitated again. "I'm not sure where to start."

"How about the beginning?" said Penny simply, and Jude added, "Once upon a time—"

Zibby nodded. "Okay. Once upon a time," she began slowly, "only two days ago, it was my birthday. And I wanted to go to Sportsmart and buy blue Zingers, but my mom dragged me to a miniatures convention instead…"

Jude shifted from the branch to the grass and listened with her knees drawn up, chin resting on them, eyes closed. Penny sprawled next to her, eyes wide and fixed on Zibby's face, fascinated. Zibby told them how she seemed to have been looking for the dollhouse even before she saw it. She told them about following the woman in the gray dress, about the bell and the stinging palms of her hands. She told them how the dollhouse would not stay put in her mom's bedroom, and how the nasty doll vanished from the trash and reappeared. She told how she thought the gray-dress doll was somehow responsible for hurting Charlotte and Nell. She told how the dollhouse rose from the ashes.

When she finished talking, Jude remained silent, but Penny jumped to her feet. "This is so cool!" she exclaimed. "It's the kind of thing that happens in books! I can't believe it's true."

"Believe it," said Jude softly. "I saw the house in flames

myself. And now it's back in Zibby's room, just the same as ever."

"But why is this happening?" moaned Zibby. "What am I supposed to do about it?"

"You mean what are *we* supposed to do," Jude corrected her. "You don't have to deal with it alone, if you don't want to. We'll help you—if you want us to help."

"This can be the reason for our club!" cried Penny. "Not just to build my new dollhouse, but to figure out what to do with your haunted one."

The *haunted* dollhouse. The word chilled Zibby even as the girls' support warmed her. "Thanks, you guys," she murmured.

"There are really two things that bug me," said Jude. "It's very weird the way the house comes back. But what's even weirder is the way things you play in the dollhouse sort of come true—but in a bad way. Your cousin cracking her head on the rim of the bathtub after you dumped the blond doll into the toy bathtub. Your mom burning her wrist after the mother doll's sleeve caught fire during the blackout." She sat silently for a second. "But what if you played *good* things? I mean, maybe the dollhouse isn't exactly evil—maybe it's *magic*. Maybe you could make anything you wanted to have happen *really* happen! Maybe you could make all your wishes come true, just by acting them out with the dolls!"

So far Zibby had been thinking only of how to get rid of the dollhouse. That she might accept whatever magic it offered and actually get it to work for her had never entered her mind. But now she bounced lightly on the branch, mulling it over. "I suppose we could try," she said slowly.

"Let's go right now!" shouted Penny, jumping up and banging her head on a limb.

"But what will we do? I mean, *how* will we try?" Zibby felt nervous about going back up to her bedroom.

"Well," said practical Jude, "think of something you want to have happen."

"I want to go to Disney World," said Penny. "Let's play that the dolls go to Disney World and see what happens."

"No," objected Jude. "The dollhouse is Zibby's and she gets to test it first."

"Thanks," said Zibby wryly. "I'm not sure that's much of an honor." She sat thinking. She thought of her dad in Italy with his new bride, Sofia. Could she play that he left Sofia and returned to Carroway, to her and Nell? But then what about Nell and Ned's upcoming wedding? She thought of Amy far away in Cleveland, starting a new life in a new house, meeting new friends. "I've been missing Amy like crazy," she told Penny and Jude. "She's really great. We could play that Amy comes back."

"Oh, right," said Jude dourly. "Great."

Zibby stared at her, baffled by the sarcastic tone.

"And are you going to play that we moved back to Pennsylvania?" asked Penny in a small voice. "Because if you do, I don't know where we're going to live. We sold our old house, you know, to move here."

And then Zibby understood. "Oh, no!" she told them. "I don't want you to move away! I'm really glad you came to Carroway." She realized it was true. "We'll just play that Amy comes back for a visit."

Jude smiled. "Okay, but how will we know she wasn't

just planning to come back for a visit anyway? I mean, how will we know if the dollhouse has the magic or not?"

"Amy and I begged and begged for her to be allowed to stay with me until school started, but her parents said absolutely not," Zibby told her. "They said Amy *might* be able to come back during the winter vacation, but absolutely not before then. They think it's important for her to immerse herself in life in Cleveland before she can come back here— that's what they said, immerse herself, like Cleveland's a pool or something."

"Okay," said Jude. "We'll play there's a visit from Amy."

"How long does it take for the dollhouse to make what you play come true?" asked Penny.

Zibby considered. "So far it's happened almost right away."

"Perfect," said Jude, standing up and brushing off her shorts. "Let's go try it now."

THE GIRLS KNELT on the floor in front of Zibby's dollhouse. Zibby ran her hands lightly over the roof, marveling at the unburnt shingles. She felt a nervous clenching in her stomach as she unlatched the front of the house. Jude opened the pillowcase and shook the dolls out onto the rug. Penny reached into the attic for the frown-faced doll.

"Not that one!" cautioned Zibby. "That one is bad news."

Penny hastily poked the doll back into the attic.

Zibby took charge. "Okay," she said, lining up the other little dolls on the floor. It had been a long time since she had played with dolls. She and Amy had much preferred bike riding, tree climbing, and ball playing. "Let's see." Zibby picked up the doll in the green dress and set it aside. "This one will be my mom. It's the doll that got burned. And then this one can be me, because we sort of have the same color hair." She selected a servant doll with reddish-gold hair and laid it next to the mother doll.

"Now you need an Amy doll," said Jude. "Which one is she?"

Zibby considered the remaining dolls. "Well, this one with dark braids could work because Amy has dark hair—but she doesn't have braids. She has short hair."

Jude picked up a short-haired doll. "How about this one, then?"

"That's a boy doll," objected Penny. Then she shrugged. "But maybe it only matters what you play with the dolls—not what they look like."

"We'll soon find out," murmured Jude.

Zibby took up the mother doll and the Zibby doll and stood them in the kitchen. "Okay, here goes." She cleared her throat, then giggled nervously. "I don't really know what to say."

"Just say what you really would say," advised Penny, and Jude agreed.

Zibby nodded. "Mo-om," she whined, tipping the girl doll back and forth as she spoke. "Mom, I miss Amy so much. I can't wait for winter vacation! I want to see her *now*!"

"Now, Zibby," she made the Nell doll answer, "don't make such a fuss. You know how busy Amy must be getting *immersed* in Cleveland. She's making new friends left and right."

Penny giggled, but Zibby pressed on with her story. "Mom, please, please can't I invite Amy to come for a visit *now?*" She made the Zibby doll fall on the floor and kick her feet in a tantrum. Then she looked up at Jude and Penny. "How am I doing so far?"

"You're going overboard," said Jude with a smile. "I think you ought to play that Amy actually comes."

"I will," said Zibby. "I'm working up to it." She picked up the mother doll and walked her over to the dollhouse kitchen window. "Stop having a tantrum this minute, Zibby! And look—what's this? A car pulling into our driveway! It must be Ned, come to take us out for pizza—but no! Zibby, look!"

"This is totally cool," cried the girl doll, running to the window. "It's Amy's dad, and he's got Amy with him!"

"How amazing," said the mother doll. "Let's go greet them."

Jude picked up the Amy doll. Penny reached for the father doll with the mustache. "This will be Amy's dad," she whispered.

Jude settled the dolls inside the box of tissue on Zibby's night table, and slid the box across the rug to the dollhouse. "*Vvrrroooom,*" she sputtered. "This is the car, driving up." She and Penny each took a doll and marched them up to the front door."

"*Ding-dong!*" cried Jude. "We're here, Zibby! It's Amy! Open the door!"

Zibby moved the girl and mother dolls into the hallway and struggled to open the little door. Jude and Penny walked the father and Amy dolls into the house. "Hooray!" Jude made the Amy doll say. "We get to visit after all! And we're going to stay—how long should it be, Zibby? A whole month?"

"Make it two weeks. That's more realistic. And she can come to the wedding."

"Okay." Jude tipped the dark-haired Amy doll as she spoke. "We get to stay for two weeks and go to the wedding, isn't that totally great?"

Penny pushed the father doll forward. "Yes, yes, just wonderful," she said in a deep voice. "I found that I had a business trip to go on down this way, so I thought I'd bring Amy along and leave her with you."

"That's super," said the Nell doll. "Zibby was just saying that she wished Amy could visit! Now, please, come in and have dinner with us before you leave for your business trip."

"No, thank you," answered the father doll. "That's very nice of you to ask, but I must be leaving right now. Good-bye, Amy. I know you'll have a great time with Zibby."

"Bye, Dad," answered the Amy doll.

Penny marched the father doll out the door and drove him away in the tissue box. Jude pushed the Amy doll inside the dollhouse with the Zibby doll and the mother doll and pulled the little front door shut. "The end," said Jude.

Zibby sat back on her heels. It had been surprisingly fun to play with dolls. "Okay," she said. "I guess that's it. Now we wait and see if anything really happens."

They heard a car pull up outside the house. Zibby raced to the window and peered out. Jude and Penny crowded close to see if Amy had arrived so soon. But the woman who got out of the car was Mrs. Simms from across the street. The three girls watched as she walked up her porch steps and went into her house. They sighed.

The telephone rang.

The girls drew in their breath and stared at each other. Zibby jumped up and tiptoed out into the hallway. Downstairs she could hear the murmur of her mom's voice, then laughter. Zibby edged down the stairs, motioning for Jude and Penny to follow her.

"That will be wonderful," Nell was saying on the phone as Zibby, Jude, and Penny darted through the dining room and hovered in the kitchen doorway. "I'm sure the kids will have fun. And it'll be good for them to be together—"

Zibby poked her elbow into Jude's side. *This is it!*

Nell hung up with a smile and turned to the girls. She smiled at Penny. "Hello! You must be Jude's aunt."

Penny nodded shyly. "I'm Penny."

"That was Dr. Cummings, wasn't it, Mom?" Zibby hugged herself. "And he's bringing Amy to visit, right?"

"Wrong." Nell looked surprised. "That was Ned—remember we're going out for dinner tonight, all of us. And then we've got to get those attic rooms ready for his kids, Zibby. They're coming to us soon. I'll need your help—" She broke off and looked at Zibby. "Why in the world did you think Dr. Cummings would be calling me?"

Zibby's shoulders slumped at the reminder that Laura-Jane would be staying with them. "Never mind." She shook her head and left the room, the two other girls trailing behind.

"Oh, well," said Jude philosophically. "It was really just a wild guess, wasn't it, that the dollhouse might make some good magic, too."

"Yeah," said Zibby. She led the way back to her bedroom and flopped across the bed, wondering whether the evil dollhouse were somehow responsible for foisting Laura-Jane on her. At least Zibby wasn't going to have to share a bedroom with Laura-Jane because there were the two little attic rooms that could be made into bedrooms for Ned's kids.

The phone rang again, but this time none of the girls bothered to get excited. It would just be Ned again, probably to say that Laura-Jane and Brady would be moving in for a whole year or something. Or it would be Aunt Linnea with an update on Charlotte. Or somebody wanting a party catered.

But a few minutes later, Nell appeared in the doorway of Zibby's room with a puzzled expression on her face. "Honey? That was Amy's dad on the phone just now. He said he has to go to a dental convention in Columbus, and can bring Amy along to visit you. He'll drop her off here tomorrow afternoon on his way. She'll be able to stay for two days, and then he'll pick her up when he's driving home again." She came in and sat on the edge of Zibby's bed. "Of course I said we'd be delighted—but, Zibby, how could you know? Had you already called Amy and arranged this with her?"

"I didn't *know*," Zibby said. "And I didn't call Amy. I just—sort of hoped."

Jude and Penny carefully refrained from looking at each other. They each stared over at the dollhouse, looking awed and a little frightened.

Nell was still frowning. "It's just very odd—"

She broke off as Zibby threw her arms around her in a hug. "Don't worry, Mom! It's just a coincidence."

Nell opened her mouth as if she were about to speak, then closed it and left the room. The three girls hugged each other in giddy excitement. Amy was coming! She would stay only two days instead of a week, but other than that, it seemed as if the dollhouse magic had worked perfectly this time—and for good rather than ill.

"This is so cool!" Penny whispered. "Can you believe it? Real magic!"

"Are you going to tell Amy about the dollhouse?" asked Jude.

"Probably, but she might not believe me. She'll just say it was her dad's dental convention thing that brought her. But we'll know different, won't we?" Zibby shook her head in amazement. "It's so weird to think we can—wow, Jude, think of this—we can do *anything*. We can play anything with the dolls and make stuff happen! One of you can have the next turn. What will you wish for?"

Jude traced her finger along the fringe of Zibby's bedspread. "We should be careful."

"What do you mean?" Zibby wanted to run and shout her excitement in the street, and she didn't like the thoughtful look on Jude's face.

"I just mean—well, Amy isn't here yet."

"Come on, Jude," said Penny. "If you don't want a turn at the dollhouse, then let me."

Jude bit her full lower lip. "No, I'll play next."

Penny lined up the dolls on the rug. "When it's my turn, I'm going to bring over my trolls and see if the magic works with them, too. That way we'll know whether it's the house that's magic, or the dolls."

"Go ahead," Zibby urged Jude. "Choose your players."

Jude hesitated, surveying the dolls. "There aren't any black dolls. How can I play something about my family?"

"I don't have any black trolls, either," said Penny. "They should make some."

"They really should," agreed Zibby.

Jude just sat staring with a frown at the dolls. Finally she selected the mother and father dolls and stood them over by Zibby's bed. "These are my mom and dad, far away in Africa, working to set up hospitals in places that don't have any." Then she picked out the brown-haired boy doll who had been Amy. "This will be me this time. And we'll say that the dollhouse is our new house here in Carroway."

"And these two dolls can be Penny's mom and dad," said Zibby, picking out two more dolls from the lineup. "I think they're really supposed to be a cook and a butler!"

"And this doll could be me, because of the braids," said Penny, selecting the brown-haired little girl doll. She tossed back her dozens of skinny braids with a clicking of beads. "Even though she has only two."

"Okay." Jude accepted the old-fashioned dolls and stood them around in the parlor. "Here we are in the living room, just hanging out and watching TV, when suddenly there's a phone call."

"Brrrrring!" squealed Penny.

"Right. And so Nana answers it." Jude walked the Nana doll over to the table. "'Hello?' she says, and then she gets all excited. 'It's Mac! He's calling all the way from Kenya!'" Jude reached over and stood the father doll up by the bed. "'Hi, Mama, it's me, Malcolm. We're just fine, but we're calling to say we're coming home earlier than we expected. We miss Jude.'"

"Hey, wait a minute," objected Penny. "Don't play that,

Jude! I don't want you to leave. You're supposed to stay all year."

Jude ran her hands through her dark curls. "A year is too long."

"Oh, come on. Please don't play that they come home and take you away!"

Jude shook her head. "I thought you'd love to get rid of me, the way you sometimes act."

Penny picked at the rug. "Don't leave," she muttered.

Zibby intervened, picking up the Nana doll in the parlor and making her talk. "'Oh, Mac,'" she cried. "'It's wonderful to hear your voice. All the way from Africa—just imagine! But we don't want you to take Jude away. We want her to stay. Penny loves having her here and so does her new friend, Zibby, who lives down the street.'"

Jude smiled a little. She tipped the Mac doll on the bed and made him speak. "'All right, Mama. How about this for a plan? We miss Jude so much, we're going to make sure we come home for Christmas after all. We just can't stand being away from her so long.'"

She picked up the mother doll, too, and pretended that she took the phone from the father doll. "'Hello? This is Sarah. Please let me speak with Jude for a minute.'"

Penny picked up the Jude doll and walked her over to the Nana doll in the dollhouse parlor. "I'll be you, Jude," she said. "'Hi, Sarah—I mean, Mom? It's me, Jude. I'm having a super time in Carroway and you don't need to come home at all.'"

"Wait a minute," objected Jude. "Let *me* do this." She reached into the house and grabbed the Jude doll. "'Hey,

Mom? Mom, I'm glad you're having a great time in Kenya and building hospitals and everything, and I really am just fine here, but I miss you. I want you to promise to come home for Christmas at least. Okay?'"

Then Jude made the mother and father dolls answer from the bed: "'Okay, angel. We promise.'" Jude laid the dolls down on Zibby's bed. "There," she said. "That ought to do it."

"Now we just wait and see!" cried Penny. "Let's go home to our house. They might be calling us even now!" She bounced happily on the bed, and the little father and mother dolls plummeted onto the rug.

Zibby gathered them up and dumped them back in the dollhouse with the other dolls. "Good idea," she said, and started for the door. "Oh, wait—" She turned back. "I forgot. I've got to go out for dinner. But call me as soon as you hear anything, okay?"

Penny agreed she would. "Hey, Jude—let's go. You saw how fast Amy's dad called; *your* dad might be phoning from Africa right now!"

But there was no answer from Jude, who was still sitting on the floor by the dollhouse, a worried expression clouding her face.

"What is it?" asked Zibby, startled by the fear in Jude's eyes.

"What's wrong?" pressed Penny.

Jude just sat looking at the spot on the rug where the mother and father dolls had fallen off the bed. Then she looked up at the other girls and shrugged. "Nothing...I hope."

CHAPTER 10

Zibby and Nell, sitting on the front porch, watched Ned's dark blue car turn into the driveway. The car door opened and Brady tumbled out, his black eyes snapping with mischief and his round face split with a huge pumpkin grin. "Hi!" he shrieked to Zibby and Nell. "Do you like pepperoni or sausage better?"

"Or some of both?" said Ned, coming up the path behind his son. "Hello there, ladies. I hope you're hungry, because we sure are!" Ned's grin was identical to Brady's, and he exuded a similar warmth and wild energy. He was very different from Zibby's dad, who was thin and fair, tall and quiet, with a shy sideways sort of smile. Nell always said that Zibby's dad didn't smile enough. He was too serious. "Life isn't so bad," she used to tell him. "Lighten up." Instead of lightening up, he'd gone off to Italy. Zibby wondered if maybe he smiled more there—or if he and Sofia sat around being serious together.

Ned was the type who was almost always laughing, the type who made her mom laugh, too. Zibby watched as Nell ran into Ned's arms and kissed him. Right in public! *Really.*

"Ew, yuck." Brady made gagging noises. And Zibby saw Laura-Jane looking out the car window in disgust.

Ned winked at Zibby and reached for Nell's burnt hand. "Poor you!" He raised her hand to his lips and kissed the bandage gently. "But, really, why are we standing around here kissing when there are three hungry children to feed?"

Brady tore back to the car. Ned and Nell followed, fingers entwined. Zibby climbed in next to Laura-Jane, who reluctantly slid over to make room. "Hi," Zibby said. But Laura-Jane shifted away and didn't speak all the way to the restaurant.

The pizza place was packed, even at this early hour. Brady kept pestering his dad for quarters to feed into the video games along the back wall. They sat at a large round table near the salad bar. Ned and Nell ordered two large pizzas, one sausage and one pepperoni, and while they were waiting for their order, Ned entertained them by trying to teach them the Italian names for things. "This is an Italian restaurant, after all," he pointed out.

"And Zibby will need to know Italian for when she visits her dad," added Nell.

Zibby made a face. "That's not happening, Mom."

"Our dad is always teaching us words in different languages at restaurants," Brady told Zibby. "Want to hear me say 'I have to go to the bathroom' in Chinese?"

"No," said Laura-Jane and Zibby at the same time.

Nell squeezed Ned's arm. "You're so good with languages," she said admiringly. "I remember you helped me pass German back in high school."

Ned nuzzled her cheek. "*Ich liebe dich!* Can you translate that?" He grinned at Zibby. "I love languages. I'm even taking Japanese lessons now, once a week. It's slow going, though."

"But aren't you Japanese?" asked Zibby, confused.

"Well, my grandparents came from Japan," Ned told her with a smile. "But my parents never learned the language as children, and I never did, either. Neither have my kids. Their mom knows some, though."

Laura-Jane flinched at the mention of her mom. She raised her head and stared at Ned with angry eyes. "It would be easier if everybody in the world just spoke English," stated Laura-Jane.

"It's a shame you feel that way," Ned replied, "though I'm afraid a lot of other Americans do, too. It's pretty ignorant."

Laura-Jane crossed her eyes and slumped down in her seat as Ned started talking about the different kinds of English spoken around the world. When he mentioned Africa, Zibby started wondering what was happening at Penny and Jude's house. Had Mac and Sarah called from Kenya to say they'd be home for Christmas?

Then the pizzas were brought to their table. Brady broke into a cheer. Laura-Jane picked at the crust of her pizza. Talk turned to the upcoming wedding. Zibby and Laura-Jane were going to be the bridesmaids, and Brady was going to be the ring bearer, though Zibby privately thought that was a dangerous choice. He would be sure to drop the ring or something. Nell told Zibby and Laura-Jane that the bridesmaid dresses, on order from the local bridal shop, would arrive just in time for the wedding.

Laura-Jane drew a breath that sounded like a sob. "I hate that word!" she hissed.

"What word?" asked Zibby.

"Wedding." Laura-Jane slid lower in her seat and turned her face away.

Fortunately it was soon time to go home again. Zibby was desperate to phone Jude and Penny, but Nell asked her to take Laura-Jane and Brady upstairs and show them the attic rooms that would be fixed up for them. Ned had been living in two places for some time; he stayed with Nell and Zibby often but still had his little apartment near the *Gazette* offices. When he had Laura-Jane and Brady with him, they all slept over there. But now that was going to change, and it was important to Ned and Nell that Laura-Jane and Brady feel at home in their dad's new house.

With a sigh, Zibby led the way upstairs. There were two small rooms up in the attic used for storage, but Nell had already started emptying things out to make space for Ned's children. Laura-Jane looked around with a scowl.

"The walls will look nicer when they're painted," Zibby said hastily, suddenly aware that the dusty dark rooms were not at all welcoming yet.

Laura-Jane turned and stomped down the stairs.

Brady careened around the crowded spaces. "I like these rooms," he said. "I don't mind sleeping up here whenever we're staying with Dad."

Zibby smiled at him and led the way down the narrow stairs to her bedroom. There they found Laura-Jane sitting on the floor in front of the dollhouse.

"Um—don't play with that!" Zibby cried. "I mean, it's not really for playing with. It's like a museum piece. Just for show."

"That's stupid," said Laura-Jane, unlatching the front. "It's got dolls and everything."

"Don't touch it!"

"Oh, shut up. You're so selfish." Laura-Jane picked up the father and mother dolls. She started humming the wedding march. "Let's play wedding, Brady," she said with a glance over her shoulder at her younger brother. "For practice, I mean." There was a sly note in Laura-Jane's voice that Zibby didn't like at all. "Here, you be the minister." Laura-Jane handed Brady the butler doll. Then she marched the mother doll along. "Here comes the bride...all dressed in white..." Laura-Jane sang off-key. "*Dum-dum-de-dum, dum-dum-de-dum.* And here's the groom waiting for her. How very sweet." She nudged Brady.

"Give me the dolls," said Zibby urgently, reaching for them. Laura-Jane shoved her away.

"Now the minister says, 'Will you take this woman to be your wife?'" explained Laura-Jane, ignoring Zibby's attempts to stop the doll play. "And the father doll answers, 'Sure, why not? So what if I already have a wife and two kids? What does it matter?' And the minister answers, 'Yeah, no problem. You can just ditch them.'" Laura-Jane twirled the mother doll. "'That's right! Who cares about them, anyway?' And then the minister asks, 'And do you take this man to be your husband?' And the bride says, 'Oh, absolutely.'" Laura-Jane made the mother doll speak in a silly, squeaky voice. "'I just love to take away other women's husbands and break up perfectly happy families. It's sort of a hobby of mine.'"

"Oh, stop it, Laura-Jane," cried Zibby. "That's not fair. You know that's not the way it is. Your mom and dad are *already* divorced. And so are my parents. And your dad isn't ditching you and Brady—you know he isn't. And at least you get to see both your parents all the time. My dad went off to live in *Italy*!"

Laura-Jane ignored Zibby. "'And now with the power invested in me as a minister of God,'" she made the butler-minister say, "'I now pronounce you man and—whoops!'" Laura-Jane pulled with a vicious tug the porcelain head off the little stuffed body of the mother doll.

"Hey!" shouted Zibby, horrified, but Brady laughed. Zibby lunged for Laura-Jane, but Laura-Jane held the butler-minister doll aloft.

"'Oh, deary me!'" Laura-Jane made the butler-minister say in a cheerful, hearty voice. "'I'm afraid the bride has fainted. No—no, I'm wrong about that. She hasn't fainted—she's dead! Massive brain hemorrhage just at the crucial second. But, oh, well, that's the way it goes. Too bad, folks—'"

"You are disgusting!" Zibby shrieked, tackling Laura-Jane and snatching up the dolls. "I hate you! How dare you!" She raised her hand to slap Laura-Jane as hard as she could, but Laura-Jane ducked. Zibby froze as Nell's sharp voice rang from the doorway.

"Zibby! What's going on? That is no way to treat a guest, and Laura-Jane is not just any guest! Laura-Jane is going to be your *sister*."

Ned stepped into the room behind Nell, looking perplexed, his usually merry face creased in a frown. "What's happening in here?"

"We were just playing wedding!" said Brady excitedly.

Zibby was so angry at Laura-Jane she was shaking. Laura-Jane sat there on the rug looking innocent, but her dark eyes challenged Zibby to tattle. Zibby bit her lip. There was no way she could explain to her mom that the terrible things Laura-Jane had played might come true, so she just held the headless doll up for them to see.

Nell reached out and took the doll. "It's all right," she said. "I can reattach the head with a piece of wire and a few stitches. It's nothing to fight about. These dolls are antiques, remember, and fragile. Accidents happen."

"I just wanted to play with the dollhouse," Laura-Jane murmured in a sorrowful baby voice. "But Zibby said I couldn't."

"I told her not to touch it! I knew something like this would happen." Zibby's voice was strained. "And she wasn't just playing wedding. She was being horrible—"

Laura-Jane interrupted by jumping up and clinging to Ned's hand. "I don't like this girl," she whispered urgently. "I don't want to play with her anymore. Let's go back to your apartment."

Zibby slammed the dollhouse shut and latched it securely. She watched her mom, Ned, Brady, and Laura-Jane walk out of the room together. As they started down the hallway, Laura-Jane turned back. She stared at Zibby, then slowly drew a finger across her throat.

ZIBBY COULDN'T SLEEP that night. She lay awake, seeing over and over how Laura-Jane had marched the mother and father dolls along. *I shouldn't have let her play anything,*

Zibby kept thinking. *I should have known she'd do something awful.* There was a ball of sick guilt in Zibby's stomach. After all, Charlotte had hit her head, and Nell had burned her hand—because something similar had happened to the dolls. But Amy was coming tomorrow, and maybe Mac and Sarah Jefferson would be coming home for Christmas—all because of the doll play. And yet when Laura-Jane started her very nasty game, Zibby hadn't been quick enough to stop her.

Now what was going to happen to Nell at the wedding?

She fell into a fitful sleep, and...*almost immediately the smell of burning filled her bedroom. She sat up in bed, gasping for air, staring with horror at the dollhouse. Flames soared from the little windows, and tongues of fire licked the shingles on the roof. The chimney fell in a torrent of sparks. From the hot, crackling wreckage, a hand slowly reached out—a hand in a black leather glove!*

Zibby moaned and tossed herself awake. This time she sat up in her bed for real, and of course there was no fire, no sparks, no groping hand. The dollhouse sat untouched, un-burnt, its chimney of little red bricks intact. But an acrid smell of smoke seemed to linger in the bedroom.

She lay down again, afraid to go back to sleep yet too groggy to keep her eyes open. Again the dream tried to sneak back into her mind, and again she jolted herself awake. Then she thought she heard noises coming from the dollhouse. She felt sure that the doll in the gray dress was prowling around. She was certain that her mom was in danger....

Finally Zibby ended up taking her pillow and creeping

into Nell's bed until morning. Would she be able to do this when Ned had moved in permanently? She stretched out and tried to clear her mind. But even with Nell safely next to her, Zibby's sleep was not restful. She dreamed of the wedding, and of her mom's head breaking off and rolling down the aisle of their church in a trail of blood.

CHAPTER 11

Zibby woke up to find morning sunlight streaming in through the bedroom windows. Nell had left a note on the pillow next to her, saying she had gone to do errands but would be back before Amy arrived.

Rubbing her eyes, Zibby picked up the bedside phone and called Jude and Penny. Their line was busy, so she dressed hurriedly and walked down the street to their house. She wasn't hungry for breakfast. It was already September, but the day was going to be hot. She felt heavy and sleep-deprived, and underneath everything else, there ran a current of anxiety about her mom's safety.

"Any news from your parents?" Zibby asked when Jude opened the front door.

Jude shook her head. "Let's go out to the tree," she said softly. "We can talk there." Then she went to ask her grandmother to be sure to call her if there were any important phone messages. From Africa, for instance. Looking perplexed, Mrs. Jefferson promised to do so.

Penny joined them under the arching branches, and Zibby related what had happened last night with Laura-Jane. "And this girl is going to be your *sister?*" asked Jude, horrified. She reached out and pinched Penny's arm gently. "Give me good old Aunt Penelope any day."

Penny pinched her back affectionately.

"Tell me about it," moaned Zibby. "But now I'm hoping we were wrong, and what we play with the house doesn't come true—that the stuff with Charlotte and my mom and Amy was all just coincidence."

Jude shook her head. "That's too much to be coincidence."

"It's awesome to think that the dollhouse can make anything happen," breathed Penny. "We could play that there's no more hunger. Or that there's world peace!"

"It's a huge responsibility," said Jude. "We have to be very careful that the dollhouse doesn't get used by the wrong people."

"Like Laura-Jane," muttered Zibby. "Does this really mean my mom is going to *die*—just because Laura-Jane played that her head came off?" She couldn't believe it. It was too horrible and impossible. But everything about that dollhouse was horrible and impossible.

"We'll have to guard your mom," said Jude. "We'll try to stay with her every minute. Zibby—maybe you can even sleep in her room with her...and go to work with her. Say you want to help out with catering or something."

"But for how long? Just till the wedding—or forever?" Zibby scrubbed her fingers through her hair as if she could erase the nightmare her life had become. "We don't know how long it takes from the time you play something till it really happens."

"Well, Amy is coming today," Jude reminded her. "So that wasn't very long."

That was true. Zibby looked at her watch. "I'll go home now and wait for her," she said tightly. "And, you know, hang out with my mom."

"Good idea." Jude squeezed Zibby's arm. "We'll help guard your mom, too, if you tell us what we can do."

"I'll let you know," Zibby said, then pushed through the leaves and started for home.

Nell was in the kitchen filling pastry puffs with salmon cream. She looked healthy and strong and not at all like someone about to die. Trays of mini-quiches and delicate cheese straws covered the countertops. Zibby helped herself to a cheese straw. "So when will Amy get here?" she asked casually. She was hoping now that Amy *wouldn't* come after all, and that the whole dollhouse phenomenon would prove to be a big fat nothing. And Nell would be safe.

"Not for a while," replied Nell. "I wouldn't expect them till after two, anyway."

And so Zibby waited, sitting at the kitchen table, reading her mystery novel, and keeping an eye on Nell. Two o'clock came and went, then three o'clock. Then the phone rang and Zibby nearly broke her ankle leaping up to answer. But it was only Jude, asking if Amy had arrived.

"No sign of her," Zibby reported. "I'm going crazy."

"We haven't had any phone calls, either," Jude said. "I'm going crazy, too." She laughed shortly. "And of course Penny's been crazy for years already, so that's nothing new with her."

Zibby hung up and helped her mom make pear *pizzettas*

topped with Brie for a reception Nell was catering the next day. Four o'clock, then five o'clock came, and finally Nell agreed that Zibby could call Amy's house to ask her mother what time Amy and Dr. Cummings had left. But there was no answer. Zibby left a message on the answering machine, feeling frustrated, then hung up and just sat there, her hand tight on the receiver.

She gave a shriek when the phone rang under her hand. Taking a deep breath, she lifted the receiver. "Hello?"

"Zibby, dear, this is Jill Cummings. Is your mom there?"

"Mrs. Cummings! I just called you and left a message! They haven't arrived yet, and I've been waiting all afternoon. We did say today, didn't we—and not tomorrow?"

"Zibby, dear, I'm afraid I have bad news."

Zibby froze. "What bad news?" she whispered. Her mother came over to her side and stood listening, a frown creasing her smooth forehead.

"There was an accident on the way, and the car was completely totaled. Both Amy and her dad were knocked unconscious and taken to the hospital by ambulance—"

"Oh no!" Zibby's stomach churned with fear.

"—but they should heal just fine. I just came in from the hospital; they both have big bumps on their heads." She laughed shakily. "They need to stay overnight for observation, and John won't be able to walk for some time—"

"'John'?" Zibby repeated stupidly. She could hardly hear what Amy's mother was saying over the bell clanging inside her head.

"Yes, I'm afraid Dr. Cummings has a badly broken leg."

"Oh, I'm so sorry." Zibby bit her lip. Nell squeezed her shoulder.

"We're all sorry, dear," Mrs. Cummings was saying, "but we're lucky no one was killed. Still, I'm afraid this means there won't be a visit for you girls anytime soon."

Zibby mumbled good-bye and handed Nell the phone. The two mothers started talking, but Zibby wandered away. She climbed the stairs to her bedroom, her legs moving slowly as if she were underwater. She rubbed her hands together, trying to lessen the stinging in her palms.

Little girls must be obedient.

The words echoed in her head. She sank onto her bed and stared over at the dollhouse. The grim doll was now up on the roof, leaning against the chimney, seeming to survey the room.

Zibby closed her eyes so she couldn't see the doll. Was it the doll's fault that Amy and her father had been in the accident? Or was it Zibby's fault, for trying to make them come to her in the first place? She put her hands over her ears, but the bell in her head kept ringing.

She jumped when she heard footsteps out in the hall, and opened her eyes. But it was just Nell, who entered the room and sat down next to Zibby. "I'm sorry about Amy and her dad," she said, hugging her. "But it's amazing their injuries weren't worse. They swerved off the road to avoid hitting someone, and hit a tree head-on."

"Wait...you mean they swerved to avoid hitting another car?" Zibby asked slowly.

"No—a person. It's very odd. Dr. Cummings says he swerved so he wouldn't hit a figure that darted suddenly across the road, directly into their path. A woman in a long, gray dress."

Zibby glanced at the doll perched on the roof, then back to her mom. "Did they hit her?"

"No. And there was no sign of her after the crash."

Zibby closed her eyes again and tried to still the panicky feeling welling inside of her. "Don't worry, honey," she heard Nell saying. "You can call Amy tomorrow. She'll be all right."

DINNER THAT NIGHT was a subdued affair, with Zibby thoughtful and sad, and with Nell simply quiet, resting her bandaged hand on the table as they ate their soup and salad. If Amy had been there, they would have ordered out for pizza and made ice-cream sundaes for dessert, to celebrate. But now there was nothing to celebrate.

Nothing…except that the doll play had not come true exactly as planned, and that meant—Zibby hoped and prayed—that what Laura-Jane had played would also not come to pass.

She shut the dollhouse tightly, with all the dolls inside, before she went to bed. She knew that latching the house would not keep the gray doll inside, but having it closed made her feel safer. She hated having the house in her bedroom, but knew there was no point trying to move it elsewhere.

She went to bed very early and tried to read. But she couldn't concentrate. She remembered she hadn't called Jude and Penny, but it was probably too late now. Tomorrow she would call them, and Amy, too. The pillow felt lumpy. She could see a full moon outside her window, glowing like an empty face. And when sleep finally came, so did the dream.

Zibby tossed and turned under her sheet. Every time she closed her eyes, her head was filled with horrible scenes: *The dollhouse on fire. The groping hand in the black glove.* And then—a new image: *A flickering woman in gray, darting across roads into darkness.* Zibby was pulled out of her dozing when she heard the telephone ringing. After another moment, Nell was calling up the stairs to her. Zibby sat up, groggy and exhausted. In another moment Nell came into her bedroom. "Oh—I'm sorry, were you sleeping, honey?"

"Not really." Her voice came out raspy. She reached for the phone and waited till Nell left the room. "Hello?"

"Oh, Zibby!" cried Jude, and after this greeting she broke into tears.

"Oh no—what is it?" But Zibby was afraid—horribly afraid—that she already knew.

"Don't play with the dollhouse anymore. Don't even touch it!" More sobs, rising hysterically, and then Penny's voice came on the line.

"Zibby? Something bad has happened. We just got news from Kenya."

"Wh—what happened?" Zibby almost didn't dare to ask. Her palms were stinging again, and the bell that had grown quiet during the night began ringing softly.

Penny's voice sounded awed. "Mac and Sarah fell off a cliff. They were hiking with friends. Sarah—that's Jude's mom—is all scraped and bruised and has a broken hand. But at least she'll be okay. But Mac—there's no sign of him. They think he's fallen into the river and been washed away. Sarah called a while ago with the bad news. Zibby, my brother might be dead!"

Zibby closed her eyes, remembering how the father and mother dolls had fallen off the bed.

"Oh, Zibby," Penny cried through the telephone. "Was it our fault?"

"I don't know," whispered Zibby.

"I've got to go. We're all out of our minds here, worrying about Mac. But we had to tell you. And to ask how things are going with Amy. And—with your mom."

"My mom seems fine, but Amy isn't coming." And, quickly, Zibby told Penny about the accident. There was silence on the other end of the line when she finished. "What do we do now?" pressed Zibby. "We have to do something."

"I don't know." Penny sighed. "Look, let's get together now, this morning, at our tree."

"I'll be over right after breakfast."

"No one feels like eating in our house." Penny's voice was sad. "Oh, Zibby, if my brother is really dead, how can we ever eat again?"

"I—I don't know," whispered Zibby. "I just don't know."

CHAPTER 12

PRIMROSE 1919

Primrose stepped into the parlor. "Papa! Mama! You've been gone forever!"

Primrose's parents rose and held out their arms to her. She rubbed her cheek against the rough wool of her papa's jacket and inhaled her mama's flowery perfume.

"We have missed our big girl," Mama said.

Primrose cuddled closer and wished she could just stay like this, here with them, and have Miss Honeywell disappear in a flash of smoke the way witches did in fairy stories. But a harsh little cough from the doorway meant that Miss Honeywell had not disappeared at all.

"Come in, Miss Honeywell, come in and join us," Papa said genially. "We'll be wanting to hear all about Primrose's progress."

"She's doing well enough, sir," said Miss Honeywell with a rare smile. "She's studying geography, literature, mathematics, science, and French every day."

"And Mr. Pope is working out all right, is he?"

Miss Honeywell's pale cheeks grew pink. "Oh, yes, very well. He is an excellent tutor."

"My big girl," murmured Mama, stroking Primrose's hair. "Learning so much!"

This is when I should tell them, thought Primrose. *Tell them about* sweet *Miss Honeywell and how horrid she is.* But she just stood still under her mama's stroking hand and remained silent. She could feel the governess's eyes on her back. *You want me to keep quiet, don't you, you old witch? So no one will know how mean you are...Well, I'm going to tell anyway!* Then she wondered whether Miss Honeywell would tell her parents about the practical jokes Primrose had played. She knew her mama, especially, would not like to hear that Primrose had done such things.

"Getting big, that's good, but not *too* big, I hope," said Papa with a smile. "Not too big for the surprises we've brought home for you!"

"Oh, Papa. I'm never going to be too big for surprises." The moment was gone. She would have to wait to tell her parents about Miss Honeywell when she was alone with them.

"Come upstairs with us, then," Papa said. "Up to your schoolroom. I've asked John and Roger to carry up the presents we have for you. They should be unpacked by now."

John was the butler and Roger was the chauffeur. Whatever Mama and Papa had brought her must be quite large and heavy! Primrose, excited by her parents' return and by the promise of gifts awaiting her, hurried out of the parlor and raced up the stairs ahead of the adults. Normally Miss Honeywell would have admonished her. But with Primrose's parents there, the governess held her tongue.

Primrose peeked around the door of the schoolroom and caught her breath. There by the windows stood a doll-house, the most beautiful dollhouse in the world. "Oh, Papa! Mama! It is perfectly perfect! It's even better than the mouse house!"

The new dollhouse was half as tall as Primrose was her-self. It had a brown-shingled roof and two brick chimneys and a front porch with little steps leading up to the front door, which had a panel of brilliant-hued stained glass. It had three stories and a tower, and the front of the house unlatched to re-veal the rooms inside. The walls were papered in tiny floral prints, and the little floorboards gleamed with polish. A miniature chandelier hung from the dining-room ceiling.

"I can't imagine anything nicer," whispered Primrose. She hugged her parents tightly.

"That's not all," laughed Papa. He pointed to a large box on the schoolroom table. "You need to open this." He pulled his silver penknife from his pocket to help her with the cord.

Primrose opened the box as fast as she could, and gasped at the sight of all the wrapped bundles of dollhouse furni-ture inside.

"Papa picked out the house itself," Mama explained. "But I'm the one who shopped all over London and Paris for the best little furnishings. Such fun! Look—there are little tables and chairs and couches and carpets—there's even a gramophone, Primrose. It's ever so dear! And wait till you see the dolls I found." Mama dug through the box and pulled out a smaller box tied with blue ribbon. "Look," she said, untying it. "Here's the family that lives in your dollhouse!"

Primrose gazed in wonder at the dolls. There were two elegantly dressed parent dolls, and six children of various sizes, both girls and boys. One of the girl dolls had brown braids just like Primrose's, and wore a pretty blue dress. There were even two tiny baby dolls wrapped in soft green blankets. "Oh, Mama, how darling! Lots of children, and even little twins."

"Yes, and here are six servant dolls," Mama said, unwrapping the last bundle. "A housekeeper and a butler, a maid and a cook, a groom for the horses—or you could have him be a chauffeur, if you prefer—and last of all"— Mama unwrapped a doll that was dressed in gray and slightly larger than the other dolls—"a governess! Just like our Miss Honeywell."

Primrose darted a glance over at her governess, who stood watching the scene with a frown. It wasn't true that the doll was just like Miss Honeywell, Primrose thought, although the doll's painted expression was just as stern. But dolls did not have hearts of stone.

"Well, Papa and Mama, thank you for this lovely gift," Primrose said suddenly. "But I doubt I shall *ever* be able to play with it. Miss Honeywell, you see, doesn't believe in playing."

Primrose heard the hiss of Miss Honeywell's indrawn breath. Papa turned his piercing gaze on the governess. "Really, Miss Honeywell? Well, I say that is nonsense! Of course our Primrose must have playtime." He held up his hand when the governess began to speak. "I want you to schedule in a proper playtime every day after Primrose's lessons are done. Is that clear?"

"Yes sir, of course," said Miss Honeywell very sweetly. "I have no problem with play at all, as long as lessons are finished first."

Papa turned away satisfied, but Mama gave Miss Honeywell a sharp look. "Be sure that her lessons do not overtire her, Miss Honeywell," Mama said. "She must be finished by three o'clock every day and have playtime until supper. And her weekends are to be free for outings."

Miss Honeywell frowned, but her voice was pleasant. "Yes, ma'am. Of course."

Outings? That was a laugh. Primrose *never* went on outings. On weekends it was Miss Honeywell who went out with her precious Mr. Pope. Primrose wondered if her tutor knew that Miss Honeywell left Primrose locked in the schoolroom with a list of assignments while they were doing whatever it was they did—probably strolling in the park or going to the moving-picture show. Primrose just smiled at her governess now. *She* would be the one to play in the park and go to the moving pictures from now on! But she would wait till she and Mama were alone before revealing the truth about *sweet* Miss Honeywell.

In the end, though, there was no time alone at all. Primrose went with her parents to the nursery to see the toddlers, and Nanny Shanks was bubbling over with news of how well Peony could talk and how Basil could turn a somersault. Then Primrose ate dinner downstairs with her parents that night, sitting around the elegant dining-room table and being waited upon by the servants. But Miss Honeywell was invited to join them as well. And after dinner Mama came along to her bedroom to kiss Primrose good night but had to hurry away because she and Papa were going out to the theater with friends.

And in the morning they were gone.

AFTER THAT, Primrose was so sad she could not concentrate on her lessons. She had her hands smacked with Miss Honeywell's ruler so many times that her palms seemed to be permanently stinging. But she could only sit at the table and read over and over again the little note her mama had left for her:

Dearest daughter,
Papa's business calls us away once more, but we will return in the spring. Enjoy your dollhouse, and please do remind Miss Honeywell that you are to have playtime every day starting at three o'clock.

—Your loving Mama

Primrose was so miserable, she couldn't even bring herself to play with the dollhouse, though Miss Honeywell was careful to stop lessons punctually at three o'clock, ringing her little bell to indicate when Primrose must close her books and leave the table. Her steps felt weighted down as she dragged herself over to sit by the dollhouse just like she dragged herself through the long winter days. She wanted her mama and her papa. It wasn't enough that they should bring her fine gifts; she needed them to stay *home*.

ONE DAY PRIMROSE sat slumped over her schoolbooks, not even bothering to try to add the numbers Mr. Pope had set in columns on the page. He himself was sitting over by the warmth of the fire with Miss Honeywell, enjoying a cup of tea. Finally he came over to check Primrose's work; he shook his head. "Nothing at all, Miss Primrose? Surely you can do better than this."

He showed Miss Honeywell the empty page, then heaved a sigh and packed his books back into his leather satchel. Miss Honeywell glowered at Primrose but did not speak until she had seen Mr. Pope out the schoolroom door and they could hear his footsteps going down the stairs.

"Primrose Parson!" Miss Honeywell snapped. "You did not complete a single sum. You are a disgrace! I don't know why you refuse to make an effort. Now, stand up, young miss, and hold out your hands." She reached for her ruler. "Little girls must learn obedience."

Primrose clenched her hands—still stinging from the last assault—into fists. "No!" she yelled at the top of her voice. "I won't! You can't make me! You're horrid and ugly, and mean, mean, mean—and I hate you! And I bet Mr. Pope hates you, too! You think he really likes you? You think you'll get him to marry you someday? What a laugh! He just likes his cup of tea!"

In an instant Miss Honeywell had grabbed Primrose and pulled her right out of her chair. She took Primrose by the shoulders and shook her so hard, Primrose thought she heard her brains rattling. Then Miss Honeywell dragged Primrose across the schoolroom to the closet—the dreaded dark supply closet.

"Oh, please, Miss Honeywell, don't lock me in," cried Primrose helplessly as the governess opened the door and shoved her inside. "I'm sure Mr. Pope really does love you—"

But the door slammed and she heard the key turning in the lock. She heard Miss Honeywell's voice outside. "You will stay in there until you can behave yourself. You must learn your manners."

Primrose crumpled onto the floor and pressed her hands to her mouth. She had learned it did no good to cry. The air was close and thick with chalk dust and something else—a kind of mustiness that made Primrose feel light-headed. She focused on the line of light shining under the crack at the bottom of the door. It was the only light in the closet except for a sort of glow along the side wall...

Primrose sucked in her breath as the glow deepened into a shape, the shape of a head. A young man's head with fair hair and dark, glittering eyes. *Oh, I know,* he seemed to be telling her sympathetically. *Poor kid. I know what it's like. Just close your eyes...try to sleep...*

A LONG TIME LATER, the key turned in the lock and Miss Honeywell opened the closet door. Primrose had been napping on the hard floorboards. She awoke groggy and disoriented. She must have dreamed that ghostly face and comforting voice.

"Out you come, you insolent baggage. Time to *play*," caroled the governess.

Primrose struggled to her feet. She wanted to run to Nanny Shanks for comfort, that's what she wanted. She didn't feel like playing anything.

"It's three o'clock. Time to play, just as your mama ordered. So go on—start playing."

"I'd rather go up to the nursery to see the twins—" Primrose began in a soft voice, but Miss Honeywell cut her off.

"It's time to play, so play you shall. You haven't even touched the nice dollhouse your mama and papa brought all the way from Europe. You should be ashamed of yourself. Such an ungrateful girl. Think of all the children in wartorn Europe who haven't ever had such playthings! Think of the soldiers who died fighting for those little children. My own baby brother who wanted nothing more than to go off to serve his country..."

Miss Honeywell is so mean she makes even playtime feel like a punishment, thought Primrose morosely as she stumbled over to the dollhouse. Her legs felt shaky from being cramped on the closet floor for so long. She knelt by the dollhouse and, feeling Miss Honeywell's hard eyes on her back, unlatched the front. The dollhouse swung open.

She began unwrapping the furnishings her mama had packed into the box. As she set them in the various rooms she soon became absorbed and forgot about Miss Honeywell. But the governess's dry little cough reminded her, and she glanced over to see what Miss Honeywell was doing. She was on the other side of the big schoolroom, settled into the armchair by the fire with her writing pad on her lap. No doubt another love letter to Mr. Pope. But that would keep her occupied for some time.

Perking up, Primrose turned back to the dollhouse. She finished arranging the furniture, then untied the blue ribbon around the box of dolls. One by one she lifted them out and settled them into their new home. "Let's see," she said to herself. "You'll be the mama and you'll be the papa, and you're away on a long, long trip—as always." She set the two parent dolls behind her on the floor. Then she picked out one of the servant dolls. "You'll be the nanny, and you'll live up in the nursery with the two little twins." She arranged the doll and the two babies up in one big bedroom. Then she arranged that room as the nursery, with cribs and high chairs, and a tiny rocking horse by the window. She put all the rest of the child dolls up into the nursery, except for one, the little one with brown braids. This one she set up in the attic. "That's the schoolroom," she murmured to herself. "The nanny and all the other children are so happy in the nursery. While their big sister is studying up in the school-room, they get to go on outings and eat delicious snacks and play with their friends. Sometimes the nanny even takes them to the circus!"

Primrose had the idea that she could draw circus animals on her art paper and cut them out with scissors and make a circus for the dolls to go to. She crossed the room to her shelf of supplies and brought the scissors and paper to the floor by the dollhouse. She spent the next hour drawing elephants and horses and acrobats, coloring them with her brightly colored pencils. This was much more fun than coloring in rivers on a geography map! For the first time since her parents' brief visit, Primrose felt her heart lifting with the joy of play. She glanced from time to time over at Miss Honeywell, but the governess was absorbed in her letter writing and was, for once, leaving Primrose in peace.

"Now the nanny is taking the children to the circus," she murmured to herself, "but the little ones say, 'Wait, wait, we want our biggest sister to come along, too.'" Primrose reached for the doll with the brown braids like her own.

"The poor big sister lives up in the schoolroom with a horrible, mean governess," she whispered, and stood the governess doll up in the room with the girl doll. "The poor girl was practically a prisoner. The governess beat her with a ruler till she was black and blue, and then locked her in the closet. When the nanny and the children came to ask the big sister to the circus, the governess said no, that she had to stay and do lessons." Primrose acted this out with the dolls.

"So the girl decided to get rid of the governess once and for all. The nanny and the other children and even the little twins all helped. They wrestled the nasty governess to the floor and dragged her over to the window."

Primrose arranged the little dolls around the larger doll and scooted them across the dollhouse attic to the windows. She found that by pressing her fingernail into the groove at the base of the little window she was able to lift the sash. "They opened the window," she murmured. "The governess cried, 'Oh, help, help!' but they didn't listen to her. They pushed her out with a mighty shove—*WHAM!*"

Primrose pushed the governess doll through the window and let her drop onto the floor below. "And that was the end of her," she said with satisfaction.

"Primrose Parson!" snapped her real governess's voice just behind her. "What in the world are you doing? If you break those dolls, your papa will be very angry. If you can't play with them properly, I shall take them away."

Primrose obediently picked up the fallen doll and set her carefully back into the dollhouse. But her cheeks were flushed, and her eyes twinkled for the first time in ages. Getting rid of Miss Honeywell was a game she knew she would play again and again.

CHAPTER 13

Just as Zibby finished a slice of banana bread and a glass of orange juice after breakfast the next day, Aunt Linnea drove up and dropped Charlotte off. "I've got some errands to do," she told Nell, "and it's sweet of you to keep Char. I don't want to leave her home alone, not with her head still aching so badly. David's at work, and Owen's lifeguarding at the town pool till three."

Nell was setting off with her trays of food to cater a reception at the Carroway Country Club, and so it would fall to Zibby to keep her cousin company. But Zibby smiled at Charlotte and cut her a slice of banana bread.

Aunt Linnea left on her errands, then Nell said goodbye as well, and told the girls to take good care of each other. "I'll be back early," she said. "And Laura-Jane and Brady's mom leaves today, so they'll be coming here this evening to stay until she's back."

"Oh, goody," Zibby exclaimed. "Laura-Jane! My favorite person!"

Her mom gave her a *look*. Charlotte snorted. Zibby finished eating, worrying that she should have arranged somehow to go with her mom. But how long was she supposed to keep watch? The other things they'd played with the dolls happened quickly, but Laura-Jane had pulled the mother doll's head off two days ago, and so far nothing had happened to Nell.

Zibby took her breakfast plate and glass to the sink, then hesitated. "I've got to go out for a while," she told her cousin, who sat slumped at the kitchen table. "But I'll be back soon. You can lie down in my bed to rest. There's air-conditioning up there, so it'll be comfortable..."

"Where are you going?" demanded Charlotte. "My mom said I'm not supposed to stay alone. You heard her."

"You always *want* to stay alone!" Zibby pointed out. "Now's your chance."

"I'm sick of lying around," snapped Charlotte. "I'm coming with you."

Zibby sighed. She just hoped her cousin wasn't going to be bossy and rude to Penny and Jude, especially now when they were so scared and worried about Jude's dad.

As they walked down the street—slowly because of Charlotte's headache—Zibby filled Charlotte in on the bad news about Amy and about Jude's dad. She didn't mention the dollhouse—or the game Laura-Jane had played. Charlotte wouldn't believe it. She was too mature for magic.

Charlotte hung back, but Zibby pushed through the leafy branches of the fallen tree in the Jeffersons' backyard and found Penny and Jude sitting inside the clearing. The air was cooler this morning and Zibby thought she smelled just a hint of autumn. The morning sunlight filtering in through the leaves made it seem a peaceful place, but the girls sitting on the low branches inside were clearly feeling anything but peaceful. Their eyes were puffy; their cheeks were stained with the tracks of tears. Zibby sat next to Jude on a branch and bumped shoulders.

"Hi," she said softly. Jude smiled wanly. "Listen, Charlotte wanted to come, too," Zibby added. "I hope that's okay."

Charlotte ducked under the leaves and came into the little room. She brushed off invisible specks of dirt from the branch before sitting down on it.

"How's your head?" asked Jude.

"Getting better, I guess," said Charlotte.

Penny asked abruptly, "Look, is it true somebody *pushed* you in the bathroom? You didn't just, like, slip in some water or something and fall?"

"Well, I *thought* I saw somebody—," Charlotte began, fingering the bandage on her forehead, but Penny turned to Zibby before Charlotte even finished her sentence.

"See? That's the first of the accidents that the dollhouse is to blame for."

Charlotte looked puzzled. "What do you mean about the dollhouse? What dollhouse?"

"Haven't you told her anything?" Jude asked Zibby.

Zibby shook her head. She wished the girls hadn't mentioned the dollhouse. She tried to change the subject. "About your dad," she said. "I'm really, really sorry."

"Well, you should be," mumbled Jude. "It was *your* evil dollhouse—"

"Jude!" cried Penny. "That's not fair and you know it!"

Jude dropped her head into her hands. "No, you're right.

Of course it's not Zibby's fault. Not really. I mean, maybe my mom and dad would have gone on that same hike whether we played with the house or not. Maybe they would have stopped to help the woman they thought was hurt anyway—"

"What woman?" asked Zibby.

"A woman my mom said they heard calling for help."

Zibby took a deep breath. "Was she wearing a gray dress?" Her mouth was dry.

Jude looked at her sharply. "How should I know? All I know is, they heard a woman calling to them for help, but when they pressed through the underbrush to search for her, they didn't find anyone. And then they fell."

"Why didn't we notice before?" moaned Penny. "What we play with the dolls doesn't come true exactly as we play it—it comes true with something gone wrong."

"We don't know that for sure," began Zibby—then she stopped, glancing over at Charlotte.

"Know what?" Charlotte asked impatiently. "What are you talking about?"

"Listen," said Penny, "there's something very wrong with Zibby's dollhouse."

"I wish it *weren't* mine," Zibby said fiercely. "You know I tried hard to get rid of it. But if I can't even burn it to ashes—then what am I supposed to do?"

"Burn it?" yelped Charlotte. "Don't be stupid, Zib! Even if you don't want the dollhouse, you could sell it or give it away. You could give it to *me*."

"That's just the point, Charlotte," Zibby sighed. "I couldn't give it to you even if I wanted to. It wouldn't stay with you."

Charlotte tossed her long hair. "You are so silly with your little games. Grow up."

"It's hardly a game when people are getting hurt," snapped Zibby.

"Then tell me what's going on," demanded Charlotte.

Zibby sighed. "All right, but you have to promise to help us figure out what to do."

Despite herself, Charlotte looked intrigued. "I promise. Scout's honor."

So Zibby reluctantly told her about the dollhouse and the dolls, and how she'd tried to get rid of the house, and about the games they'd played with the dolls. Penny and Jude chimed in with details.

"Well," said Charlotte when they'd finished, "that is *quite* a story. I'm surprised you haven't called the *Weekly World News* to report it yet."

"I knew you wouldn't believe us," Zibby said shortly. "That's why I didn't want you to come over here with me. So just shut up while we try to figure out what to do next."

Charlotte snorted and sat cross-legged on the grass. She stripped the leaves off a twig and started shredding them while the other girls talked things over.

"Whoever sold it to you had a lot of nerve," muttered Jude. "The previous owner must have known perfectly well that the dollhouse was bad news."

"It was an old woman at the miniatures show," Zibby told them. "She sold it to me for exactly the amount of money I had. To the last cent. It seemed like such a bargain at the time."

"How did she know how much money you had—to the last cent?" asked Jude.

"I don't know," replied Zibby. "That was weird. But at the time, I thought it was just good luck. *Good* luck—can you imagine?" She shook her head.

"Well, how come she was able to sell you the house at all?" wondered Penny. "I mean, why doesn't it just keep returning to *her*?"

Zibby remembered the agreement she had signed. What had it said?

I take full responsibility for the house and all its contents. It is now 100% mine and belongs to no one else on this earth.

"Wait a sec—I think she set it up that way. So I couldn't *ever* get rid of the house."

"But why should she do that to you?" demanded Jude. "I think if we knew the answer to all these questions, we'd understand a lot more about what's going on."

Penny shook back her braids with new determination. "Look, I'm going to go crazy if I just sit here waiting to hear about Mac. Let's *do* something. How about if we try to find this old woman and make her take the house back? And get back your money, Zibby."

"Where would we find her?" Charlotte asked suddenly, looking up from shredding her leaves. "The miniatures show was only for one day. It isn't a store you can just go back to."

"Still, we should try," Penny maintained. "Do you know the woman's name, Zibby?"

"No," Zibby admitted. "But maybe there's a way to track her down anyway. Charlotte, your mom knows a lot of people in the miniatures business. Maybe she knows someone who knows something about that old woman. Let's ask her as soon as she gets back."

"I suppose we can ask," Charlotte said. She scattered the bits of leaves into the grass and pressed her fingers lightly to her head. "But—can we go now, Zib? I'm feeling dizzy again."

"Do you want my mom to drive you home?" asked Penny. "I'm sure she will."

"Nobody's home at Charlotte's," Zibby said. She stood up. "She's staying at my house today. But as soon as I see Aunt Linnea, I'll ask her about the old woman. Then I'll call you guys, and we can make a plan."

As soon as the girls got back to Zibby's house, Charlotte collapsed onto the couch and closed her eyes. "Do you want something to drink?" Zibby asked her. "Or some lunch?"

"Nothing," Charlotte moaned. "I just want to lie here. Leave me alone."

Zibby went to the kitchen and made herself a peanut butter and blueberry jam sandwich, and poured a glass of milk. She grabbed a ripe plum from the bowl on the kitchen counter and carried her lunch upstairs to her bedroom. Had she sensed autumn in the air earlier? Now there was no hint of it. She switched on the air conditioner and sank onto the bed. The dollhouse lurked across the room, but she did not look in its direction. She lay back and closed her eyes, exhausted. The broken, dream-filled nights had caught up with her. She felt the weight of the humidity outside the windows pressing in on her. The thrum of the air conditioner lulled her to sleep.

She could smell smoke—and she could not ignore the dollhouse anymore because smoke was pouring out of it, choking her. She leaped from her bed to run for the door, but her legs moved in slow motion. And then that hand in a glove—that black leather glove—was reaching out from behind the doll-house. This time it seemed to be beckoning to Zibby. Flames shot straight up from the dollhouse and—and then she was awake again, this time for real, sprawled on her bed and breathing hard.

Just a dream, the same dream again. But a noise from the dollhouse made her sit up in a panic. Charlotte was kneeling in front of the open dollhouse opening the latch. "Hey!" Zibby struggled to clear her mind to focus on what was real. "Wait—don't mess with the house!"

"Oh, come on," scoffed Charlotte. "You don't really believe what you were talking about with Jude and Penny, do you? I thought you were just sort of making up a game, Zibby. You are such a baby! I can't believe we're related."

"Just leave the dollhouse alone. Weren't you listening to anything we said about it?"

"Okay, don't freak out. I'm just looking."

Zibby sat on the edge of her bed, angry at Charlotte but without the energy it would take to fight. She wished Aunt Linnea would return from her errands so Charlotte could go home. She watched Charlotte remove all the dolls from the house and then the furniture, too.

"This house could be so gorgeous," Charlotte said. "Let's decorate it, Zib. I have some extra sheets of wallpaper at home that you can have. I bet there's enough to do the front hallway. But first we have to strip off the old stuff."

Zibby watched in stony silence as Charlotte went into the bathroom for a nailbrush, a cup of hot water, and a washcloth and set to work. She only joined her cousin in front of the dollhouse when Charlotte cried out in pleasure. "Look, Zibby! The house has a name. Did you see this?"

Zibby looked where Charlotte pointed, at the small brass plaque, green with age, fastened just below the peak of the roof on the front of the house. She hadn't noticed it before because it had been hidden under the layers of grime.

"Primrose Cottage," she read. "Such a pretty name for such a nasty house."

"You're impossible." Charlotte frowned and seemed about to say something else, when both girls heard the door opening downstairs. Nell's and Aunt Linnea's voices filtered up to them.

Zibby jumped to her feet. "I'm going to ask your mom about the old woman. But don't you say anything about why I want to know. Remember your promise—scout's honor."

Charlotte rolled her eyes. "But I'm not really a scout, Zib."

"Still, you promised!"

"I'M PLEASED YOU'RE interested enough in the dollhouse to want to trace its history," Aunt Linnea said. "But the miniatures dealers who came to the miniatures show are from all around the state. The woman who sold you the house might have come from anywhere."

Zibby shrugged. She should have known it wouldn't be easy. Aunt Linnea looked thoughtful. "I know that some of the houses on display at that show were from Lilliput—the miniatures shop over in Fennel Grove. Why don't you call the shop owner and ask whether she knows the old woman you're looking for. In fact, I'm going over to Fennel Grove tomorrow for the Labor Day sales, so if Charlotte is feeling well enough, I'll take you both along and drop you off at Lilliput. You'll have fun looking around her fascinating little shop even if she can't help you with information about the woman who sold you your dollhouse. How about it?"

"Perfect!" Zibby hugged Aunt Linnea. "And may my friends Penny and Jude Jefferson come along, too? We're going to build Penny a dollhouse, and I know they'll want to see—"

"The more the merrier," said Aunt Linnea. "That's why I drive a van."

She and Charlotte drove off. Zibby phoned Amy to ask how she was feeling. Amy sounded depressed and worried about her father, who was still in the hospital. She didn't know when they'd manage a trip back to Carroway. *Probably never, the way things are going,* thought Zibby. She tried to sound optimistic while talking to her friend, but guilt churned in her stomach.

All afternoon Zibby stuck close to Nell, helping to wash the empty food trays from the morning's reception, hurrying to put the sharp knives away, offering to carry the trash outside. She listened to Nell chattering about the upcoming wedding, and worried about how to keep her mom safe.

NED ARRIVED HOME after work carrying two billowy blue sundresses with big sashes—the bridesmaid dresses—that he had picked up from the bridal shop. Brady was carrying a bagful of Chinese takeout. There was no need to cook anything, Ned explained, and that would leave more time for them all to help Nell prepare the trays of food for a Labor

Day fiftieth-anniversary reception she was catering tomorrow evening. "At least you're not doing the food for our own wedding reception," he said to Nell. "The bride has to concentrate on other things." He winked at Zibby. "Like the groom, for instance."

"I won't make so much as a cup of tea for the big day," Nell assured him with a smile. Aunt Linnea and Uncle David were hosting the wedding reception as their gift to Nell and Ned, and had booked caterers from Columbus to take care of all the food.

Nell hung the dresses on the coat rack in the front hall. She and Zibby exclaimed over how beautiful they were, and Nell urged Zibby to try hers on right away. Zibby took her dress into the bathroom to change, and came out twirling, so the full skirt billowed out like a bell. "You look like a princess, darling!" said Nell, and Ned whistled appreciatively. "It fits perfectly. I hope Laura-Jane's does, too. Where is she?"

Ned explained that Laura-Jane had gone on a bike ride earlier but had promised to arrive in time to eat with them. He checked his watch. "She should be here any minute," he predicted. He and Nell went back to the kitchen.

Brady was his usual wild self, galloping around the house, jumping on the couches. "Hey!" he called to Zibby. "I'm going to live here for a month! And, guess what? I'm going to be in the circus when I grow up! You could be, too, and wear that dress and go on the flying trapeze!"

"Great," she said, wincing at his buoyant energy. "But my mom won't want us practicing on the furniture."

"I need a trampoline," he told her, spinning dizzily in circles. "Don't you want a trampoline, Zibby?"

Zibby's life was already too full of ups and downs just now, as it was. She didn't need any more, thank you very much. She changed back into her regular clothes, hung up the lovely dress next to the identical one for Laura-Jane, and escaped from Brady—back to the kitchen where her mom was setting the table. Nell asked Zibby to pour the drinks.

The Chinese food was hot and smelled delicious, and still there was no sign of Laura-Jane. They decided, finally, to eat without her. "We can just reheat hers," Ned said, and put Laura-Jane's plate into the refrigerator.

While they ate, they talked about decorating the attic rooms. "Can you paint spaceships with aliens on my wall, Dad?" begged Brady, jumping around excitedly and brandishing a chopstick like a laser sword.

Zibby wondered how she was going to last a whole month with Brady in the house.

After they'd cleaned out all the cartons of Chinese food, Laura-Jane still had not arrived. "It isn't like her," Ned said with a worried frown. "I hope she hasn't fallen off her bike."

"Maybe Laura-Jane rode her bike back to Fennel Grove," suggested Zibby. "Back to her own house, I mean."

Ned frowned. "You might be right. Laura-Jane does have her own house key..." He picked up the phone and punched in a number. After a long pause, he hung up again. "She's not there. Or at least not answering. I wonder if she's gone to a friend's house?"

Then they all heard the slam of the front screen door, and everyone hurried into the hall. There was Laura-Jane. "Sorry I'm late," she said in her soft, sullen voice.

Nell tactfully led Zibby and Brady back to the kitchen

and shut the door, but Ned's usually cheerful voice could be heard, clearly angry.

"Where in the world have you been? Have you got any idea how worried we've been?"

"I hate you!" rasped Laura-Jane in response. "I was just riding around, that's all, and I was doing that because I didn't want to be here—with *her* and her stupid daughter. I don't want to eat with them and act like we're a family—because we're not, and we never will be! I don't want to wear any stupid bridesmaid dress, and I don't want to be in any stupid wedding. I don't want there to *be* a wedding!"

Zibby strained to hear Ned's reply but made out only a low rumbling. She glanced at her mom and saw Nell's cheeks were flushed. Nell busied herself by emptying the dishwasher. Brady, unconcerned, was leaping from kitchen chair to kitchen chair.

After another moment, Ned came into the kitchen and took Nell into his arms. "I'm sorry you heard that," he murmured. "You don't deserve it at all."

"Oh, Ned, I had no idea she was quite so angry." Nell buried her head on Ned's shoulder. "Or maybe I've tried to ignore the signs."

"Don't let her spoil things." He hugged Nell tight. "I'm going to talk to her. She'll settle down, you'll see." But when he looked for Laura-Jane, he found she'd gone out to sit in his car.

"Take her back to your apartment," Nell urged him. Ned was still in the process of moving things from his small apartment near the *Gazette* offices. "She isn't up to being here tonight."

Ned shook his head angrily, though when he spoke, his

voice was light. "Let's get those appetizers made for your big Labor Day reception tomorrow," he said. "Brady and I are excellent chefs, and we're ready to help. Right, son?"

Brady nodded. So they all set to work and spent the rest of the evening preparing little salmon puffs and cheese straws and *pizzettas* and asparagus toasts. Working as a team was fun, but Ned's determinedly cheerful banter still couldn't make Zibby forget all her troubles, which seemed to worsen every day: people lost and people hurt and people angry, and scary, impossible things happening with the dollhouse... *How much is happening because of that dollhouse?* Zibby wondered.

How much was her fault?

And what was she supposed to *do* about it?

CHAPTER 14

Early in the morning before Ned and his kids were awake, Nell and Zibby baked the last of the special offerings for the catered Labor Day reception: treacle tarts. Little melt-in-your-mouth bursts of flavor, they were among the most popular of Nell's desserts. While they were working, Zibby decided she couldn't go to the miniatures shop with Charlotte, Jude, and Penny because she didn't dare leave Nell alone in the house. But when Nell told her that Ned had the day off from the *Gazette* and planned to stay home and paint the attic rooms, Zibby figured her mom would be safe. Zibby didn't want Nell in the house alone with the dollhouse even for a minute, and Laura-Jane and Brady would offer scant protection. Or—in the case of Laura-Jane—no protection at all.

Nell went up to take a shower. Zibby left the trays of tarts cooling on the counter and ran upstairs after her mom. She closed her bedroom door, wishing it had a lock. What if Laura-Jane went in while Zibby was in Fennel

Grove and played something else with the dollhouse? She hoped Ned would make his kids help out up in the attic so they wouldn't have time to mess with her stuff. She heard Nell singing in the shower and opened the bathroom door to call out: "Don't let Laura-Jane or Brady go into my room, Mom!"

She returned to the kitchen and opened the large refrigerator to peek inside at the food they had prepared last night for Nell's big reception. Everything looked perfect. She helped herself to a warm treacle tart from the counter and waited for Aunt Linnea and Charlotte to arrive for their trip to the Fennel Grove miniatures shop.

Jude and Penny knocked at the back door just as Aunt Linnea's van pulled up in front of the house. Zibby darted up the stairs again and opened the bathroom door. "Bye, Mom! I'm leaving now!" she called over the running water, then ran downstairs, ignoring Nell's voice urging her to invite Laura-Jane along to the miniatures shop.

Downstairs Zibby introduced Penny and Jude to her aunt. Aunt Linnea shook their hands in her formal way. "Welcome to Carroway, girls."

The girls piled into Aunt Linnea's van. As they arrived in Fennel Grove and drove down Main Street, Aunt Linnea turned her head and smiled at the girls. "Who can tell me where the name of that shop comes from?" She pointed to the wooden sign in the shape of a house that hung over the front of the shop. The sign said LILLIPUT.

"Is it the name of the owner?" guessed Zibby. "Mrs. Lilliput?"

Aunt Linnea laughed. "No, the owner's name is Mrs. Howell."

"Is it some kind of flower?" asked Penny. "Like a *lily* that you *put* somewhere. Lily-put?"

Aunt Linnea was shaking her head. Charlotte looked smug.

"It's from *Gulliver's Travels.*" Jude's voice held a faint note of superiority. "You know, the book about the guy who travels all around and gets captured on some island called Lilliput by some really tiny people. Lilliputians, they're called. They tie him up with rope."

"Cool," said Penny. "Little people? You mean dolls that could move around?"

Aunt Linnea smiled at her. "In the story—written hundreds of years ago by a man named Jonathan Swift—the Lilliputians were people, not dolls. But of course, there's no such thing in real life. No little people, and no dolls that can move around, either."

The four girls exchanged a glance but didn't say a word.

Aunt Linnea told them she would be back in an hour, when she finished with her shopping. Charlotte led the way inside Lilliput. Zibby stood silently just inside the door, looking around in amazement.

The shop was full of dollhouses. It looked, Zibby thought, like a whole neighborhood built for tiny people. There were huge Victorian houses with towers, the rooms open to view, and there were houses like her own dollhouse, with fronts that opened when you wanted to play, and latched closed when you didn't. There were town houses and farmhouses, a schoolhouse and a hospital clinic. There was even a beautifully detailed gypsy caravan. There were shadow-box rooms, single rooms decorated for display: a hat shop, a bakery, a hardware store. Some of the houses and shops were in various stages of construction while others were finished down to the last perfect detail. Zibby looked with approval at the dovetailed joints on one of the unfinished houses. Somebody was a really good carpenter. She wondered whether Mrs. Howell did her own work or hired other people.

The answer came almost at once as an elderly woman ducked out from behind the purple and blue striped curtain at the back of the shop. She was wearing a carpenter's apron like Zibby's, with many pockets. The pockets bulged with small tools and nails.

"Why hello, Charlotte, dear," said the woman, beaming at them over the sales counter. She was gray-haired and tall, with a queenly bearing and smiling eyes. "You look more like your mother each time I see you. How nice you could come by and bring your friends. I'm always eager to meet the new generation of miniaturists."

"Hi, Mrs. Howell." Looking self-important, Charlotte introduced the other girls. "My mom says to tell you hello," Charlotte said. "And we're here to get some things for building a dollhouse for Penny...but mostly we need to talk to you about Zibby's dollhouse."

"Oh?" Mrs. Howell fixed her bright blue eyes on Zibby.

"Zibby bought a house at the miniatures show last week," Charlotte rushed to explain. "And, well, she wants to return it. And get her money back."

Mrs. Howell looked puzzled. "How funny, I don't recall selling you a house, dear. Was it a kit? Which house was it?"

Zibby hurriedly tried to clarify things. "I didn't buy the house from you. But Aunt Linnea said you might know the woman who did sell it to me. I need to find her."

"Even though the receipt says no returns," added Penny. "She's got to take it back!"

Mrs. Howell raised her eyebrows at Zibby. "So you've changed your mind?"

Zibby looked to Jude for help. Jude looked at Penny. Penny shrugged. Charlotte fiddled with a miniature bed on the sales counter. "Well," Zibby said finally, "it's just that I want to buy Rollerblades instead." That was the truth, at least in part. "The dollhouse is very, very old, and in pretty bad condition. And the woman who sold it to me was also very, very old, with white hair and *masses* of wrinkles." She realized this description would fit thousands of senior citizens, and that it wasn't the most tactful of descriptions, since Mrs. Howell was pretty old herself, but she couldn't remember anything more particular about the strange old woman—except for the intense relief on her face when Zibby said she wanted to buy the house. "Oh, wait..." Zibby remembered another detail. "She had very bright blue eyes."

Mrs. Howell was frowning, deep in thought. "Well, I may know *exactly* the woman you mean, if she's the one I saw at the miniatures show in Columbus, and I don't mind saying I was very surprised indeed! You see, it was more than a year ago that I had an encounter with her myself— right here in the shop. It was closing time, and I was just locking up, when a woman drove up in an old pickup truck. She was very elderly, as you say, in her nineties, I would guess. With bright blue eyes, and her face a map of wrinkles. She introduced herself as Mrs. Smythe, and said she wanted me to have her dollhouse. I told her I had dollhouses up to my ears already and didn't need to purchase any more, and she said no, no, she wasn't trying to sell the thing to me. She wanted to *give* it to me. She said she was moving into a nursing home and couldn't take the dollhouse with her. So I went out to look at the house—it was in the back of her truck—and it was lovely, or at least it could have been fixed up to be lovely. It reminded me of my own childhood dollhouse—in fact, it seemed exactly the same model. This one needed a lot of cleaning and some repairs, but I felt a sentimental attachment for a house that looked like my own from when I was a girl. So I said I'd take it. We carried it inside and put it in the back room—" Mrs. Howell gestured to the purple and blue curtain. "And then she drove away. I locked up and left, too. But then the strangest thing happened. The next morning when I came into work and wanted to inspect the new house, I found it was gone."

"Gone," repeated Zibby, nudging Jude.

Mrs. Howell nodded. "It seems it had been stolen, and yet nothing else in the shop had been disturbed. And the door had been locked—I know I'd locked up when I left, and I had used my key when I entered the shop the next morning. So I was very puzzled, and I still am...I reported it to the police, of course, but they never found any trace of it. And I wanted to call Mrs. Smythe and tell her what had happened, too, but she wasn't listed in the phone book. Then I remembered she said she was moving into a nursing home. There's only one here in Fennel Grove—it's called Fennel Hills—so I tried there. And I found her! But can you believe it? When I told her the dollhouse had been stolen, she told me not to worry about it. And then she said something very odd: she said she hadn't really expected me to be able to keep the house."

"That *is* odd," agreed Jude. "What did she mean?"

"I don't know," said Mrs. Howell, "but I must admit I was very surprised indeed when I saw her at the miniatures show in Columbus last weekend—with the same house! I was shocked, in fact. But when I confronted her and asked how she'd gotten it back, she just looked vague and started mumbling something about how bad pennies always turn up." Mrs. Howell shrugged. "I think she stole the house back herself—though why she would do that I have no clue. And how she managed it, with the door locked, I can't imagine. All I can say is that there was something very weird about the whole business, and I wanted no part of it—or her."

The doorbell jangled and a young woman walked in holding a little girl by the hand.

"Excuse me, girls," said Mrs. Howell, and she went to greet the newcomers.

"Fennel Hills," Jude whispered to Zibby. "That's where we'll find her."

"I wish Aunt Linnea would hurry up," Zibby whispered back. "We're hot on the trail!"

"I know Jenny's probably too young," the customer was saying in a pleasant voice after Mrs. Howell had greeted her. "She's only three, but I can't wait to get her set up with a dollhouse. I think every girl needs a dollhouse to play with and decorate and love."

"I couldn't agree more," said Mrs. Howell, with a smile for the child. "It's a cornerstone of childhood for girls and boys both."

"I still have the one my grandfather made," the young mother continued. "It was my mother's and then my sister's and mine, and we decorated it exquisitely. I'll pass it down to

Jenny when she's old enough. But for now, a good sturdy dollhouse for her little stuffed mice is what we need."

"Mouse house," piped up Jenny.

"Yes, sweetheart." Her mother laughed. "And we'll make a little sign for above the front door that will say 'Jenny's Mouse House.' Maybe a little engraved plaque. Would you like that?"

"Mouse House!" Jenny chortled gleefully. Zibby stood silently, staring at the little girl. She was remembering the little brass plaque Charlotte had discovered on the front of the old dollhouse.

Mrs. Howell and Jenny's mother had turned to the simple wooden dollhouse kits and were talking about which one would be best for the little girl. "What was that old woman's first name?" Zibby asked abruptly, not even bothering to excuse herself for the interruption. "Mrs. Smythe's?"

Mrs. Howell looked perplexed. "Why, I don't think she ever said, dear."

"Was it Primrose?" Zibby pressed.

"I just don't know," replied Mrs. Howell uncertainly. "I'm sure she never mentioned her first name. Why do you ask?"

Zibby explained about the plaque inscribed PRIMROSE COTTAGE on the front of the dollhouse. Jenny's Mouse House had given her the idea that Primrose might be someone's name.

Mrs. Howell looked puzzled. "That's very strange indeed. The house I had as a child was called Primrose Cottage. I guess all the models must have had the same name." Then she shrugged. "It was a lovely house, and probably a popular kit." Then she and her customer started examining the boxed kits on the shelves.

Aunt Linnea's van pulled up outside the shop, and it was time to leave. "Hey—that wasn't a whole hour!" objected Charlotte.

"I know!" agreed Penny. "I wanted to get some stuff…"

"Well, it's good, really," said Jude practically. "Because now there's time to ask her to take us over to the Fennel Hills nursing home!"

But Aunt Linnea came in and told the girls in a low voice that Nell had phoned and needed Zibby back home immediately. As the girls thanked Mrs. Howell for her time, Zibby's heart thumped hard. She remembered again the nasty scene Laura-Jane had played with the dolls; she saw again the beheaded mother doll lying on the dollhouse floor. *I never should have left Mom alone.* She felt sick with dread.

Aunt Linnea drove home to Carroway fast. When she pulled up in front of Zibby's house, Zibby jumped out first and ran up to the porch, where she was relieved to see Nell sitting with Ned and Brady on the porch swing. Then she saw that Nell's face was tear-streaked, and Ned's expression was very grim. He kept his arm tight around Nell's shoulders. "What happened?" cried Zibby. "Mom, are you hurt?" *At least she's alive!* Zibby thought wildly. She wrapped her arms around her mom.

"Oh, Zibby. I'm all right—I'm just so shaken," said Nell. She looked up at her sister and the other girls who hurried up the porch steps.

"Robbers came here!" crowed Brady. "But they got away!"

"Mom! We've been robbed?" Zibby pulled open the screen door and stepped inside.

Ned came in right behind her. "Whoever it was didn't have time to do much damage," he said. "Must have heard us. We were up in the attic rooms, painting them…"

"I was helping, too," reported Brady. "But Laura-Jane wasn't helping because she was out riding her bike again. I'm a really good painter, Zibby! You should see the alien I painted on the closet door. I was painting it, and then suddenly we heard lots of thumping and banging! Dad ran right down the stairs to see what was wrong, and I ran down, too!"

"There was nobody in the living room or dining room," Ned said. "But then we came to the kitchen—" He broke off. Zibby pushed ahead of him and ran to the kitchen— and stopped.

Every single platter of the elegantly presented food they'd worked so hard on now lay scattered on the kitchen floor. The china serving trays were shattered into a thousand pieces. And as if that weren't bad enough, the food had been stomped on, and ground into the kitchen floor. Dark, sticky smudges from the treacle tarts led a trail across the room to the back door.

Zibby sucked in her breath and tried to back out of the room, but the other girls and Aunt Linnea were right behind her in the doorway, and they pushed into the room. Aunt Linnea let out a little scream. Nell raised both hands to clutch her head as if in agony. Ned wrapped his arms around her from behind. "Who could have done this?" he demanded.

"What was stolen?" asked Aunt Linnea. "Have you made a list and called the police?"

"Nothing was stolen," Nell said brokenly. "Just completely destroyed. And what am I supposed to serve at the reception downtown that starts in"—she glanced up at the wall clock—"just a few hours?" She laughed, but it was not a happy sound. "Not that I'm in any condition to do business with my head feeling like it's going to explode…"

Zibby looked at her mom in alarm. Would Nell's head *really* explode? She felt so dizzy at the thought, she had to lean against the wall for balance.

Aunt Linnea and Ned led Nell out of the kitchen. Zibby clutched her hair with both fists to try to clear her head, then ran to the bathroom medicine chest. She grabbed a bottle of pain reliever tablets. She poured a glass of water and handed it to Brady. "Here," she said. "Take this and the bottle to my mom. That'll be a way you can help." As the little boy obediently ran off, Zibby turned to the other girls.

"Zibby," Charlotte whispered, clutching her cousin's arm, "I'm not sure it was really robbers. Look!"

The grim-faced doll in the gray dress was sitting atop the toaster. Then Zibby, turning, caught a flicker of gray outside the kitchen window, and her stomach churned. She felt she might be sick. She ran to the back door and wrenched it open—but no one was in the yard or on the patio. She took a deep breath to calm herself. No one was there at all, and at least Nell's head was still firmly attached to her body. But what if Nell hadn't been painting the walls upstairs in the attic? What if she'd been down here in the kitchen? Zibby regarded the wreckage of Nell's hard work— the knives, long and sharp, laying amid the spoiled food— and thought that her mom had had a very, very narrow escape that day.

CHAPTER 15

Zibby heard the clatter of a bike on the front porch, and in another moment Laura-Jane was banging the screen door. "What's everybody looking so gloomy about?" she asked when she saw her dad and Aunt Linnea comforting Nell, who was lying on the couch with a pounding headache. "Has the wedding been called off?" She grinned at Zibby and gave her a thumbs-up, but there was something else in Laura-Jane's face. Fear?

"Shut up," hissed Zibby. "We've had a burglary—no, an *attack*. Mom's food for the reception she's catering is completely ruined."

"Awww," said Laura-Jane. "Too bad." But her voice sounded shaky.

"It's horrible," said Jude angrily. "Go see for yourself."

Ned called to them from the living room. "Don't touch anything in the kitchen, kids! We want the police to see it just as we found it."

"The *police*!" squealed Laura-Jane. "Why call them—if no one was hurt or anything?"

"Home invasion is a crime," Ned said. "And so is destruction of property."

Zibby, Charlotte, Jude, and Penny all followed Laura-Jane into the kitchen. Zibby was glad to see that Laura-Jane looked appropriately horrified at the sight of the kitchen. "Whoa," Laura-Jane whispered after a moment of shocked silence.

"What will the people whose party Mom was catering do now?" Zibby wondered aloud. "Poor Mom—I don't see how she'll be able to make everything again in time for tonight."

"She can if we all help," said Ned firmly, coming into the room behind the girls. "She's worked too hard making her business as successful as it is to lose important customers because of some jerk's viciousness. After the police check this out, I'll go to the store and get what we need. Then we'll all start cooking!"

"It'll take *forever*," objected Laura-Jane. "And I had plans..."

Zibby had plans, too—namely to call the Fennel Hills nursing home—but Laura-Jane's reluctance angered her.

Penny spoke up in her sprightly voice. "We'll help, too, won't we, Jude?"

"Of course," said Jude. She shot Laura-Jane a look. "Gladly."

"I'll help, too," said Charlotte regally. Zibby, knowing how much Charlotte despised anything resembling housework, was impressed.

"Wonderful," Ned said approvingly.

"I'm going to help, too," cried Brady. "I'm going to be a chef when I grow up!"

"Too many cooks spoil the broth," Laura-Jane said sulkily. "I'm busy."

"Many hands make light work," retorted her dad. "That's the proverb telling the other side. Now, why not go upstairs and see the progress Nell and I have made on your new bedrooms—and then after the police leave, we'll start cooking."

Laura-Jane shook her head obstinately, dark hair swinging. "Dad—"

"Enough!" he snapped. "Nell is very upset, and we all need to help out now. When there's trouble, families pull together."

"This isn't my *family*!" yelled Laura-Jane. Then she bolted out of the kitchen. They could hear her feet pounding up the stairs. Ned started to go after her, but the arrival of the police officers at the front door stopped him. He let them in and directed them to the kitchen.

They were a man and a woman, and one took notes and the other asked questions. Then they dusted for fingerprints and looked for footprints while Zibby and the other kids watched with interest. "We'll need to take your fingerprints," the policewoman told them, "and the prints of everyone else in the house—just for purposes of elimination."

"Of course." Ned nodded.

"What does that mean, Dad?" asked Brady. He was hopping up and down in excitement. Laura-Jane edged into the room again as Ned explained that the police would check the prints of people who normally used the kitchen. Then, if they found a print that didn't match, they could investigate whose it was.

"Cool!" Brady's dark eyes shone. "Hey, guess what, Dad? Guess what, Zibby? I'm going to be a policeman when I grow up!"

Zibby watched silently as her family pressed their fingers onto an ink pad and then onto white paper. Then it was her turn. It was on the tip of her tongue to tell the officers they didn't need to waste their time. Dolls didn't leave fingerprints.

But she said nothing. When the police had spoken to Nell and checked the rest of the house, they drove away in their squad car. Everybody washed the ink off their fingertips. Brady started zooming around the house, pretending to drive a police car. Laura-Jane stomped up to the attic.

"Now let's get to work," said Ned.

Nell wrote out a list of things for Ned to buy at the market. He was adamant that if they worked fast, Nell could still be ready to cater the evening party. Never one to be down for long, Nell was entering into the spirit of the race. "The cheese straws are easy and fast," she murmured, "and so are the *pizzettas*...but the chocolate tartlets will take too long. I'll make a cake instead. See if you can get some good, ripe peaches..."

"Will do," said Ned.

Nell pushed back her hair and the half-smile she gave Ned was almost back to normal. "You're a wonder, Ned Shimizu. First giving up half a holiday to paint the attic bedrooms, then giving up the second half to shop and cook. *Now* I know why I'm marrying you!"

"You mean, not for my rugged good looks?" He grinned back at her.

When they started kissing, Zibby left the room to get the brooms and dustpans. They acted like teenagers in love, and it embarrassed her. But she knew that her own dad would have reacted to the disaster in a very different way. Of course he would have been sorry to hear that Nell's work had been ruined, but he would have left it all to her to clean up and fix things as best she could.

The hard thing about cleaning up was knowing where to start. The chaos in the kitchen looked impenetrable to Zibby, but Nell and Aunt Linnea took charge and soon made a dent in the mess. First they swept all the ruined food into one huge gloppy mass and scooped it into a cardboard box to take out to the trash bins. Then Jude and Zibby carefully swept up all the broken glass and china into a large pile by the back door, and Aunt Linnea collected it into a trash bag. Charlotte washed the silver platters and dried them. Penny loaded whatever was unbroken into the dishwasher. Aunt Linnea gave Brady a sponge to wipe up the counters and table. Then Nell washed the floor.

Just as they were finishing, Ned returned with the bags of groceries. "Where's Laura-Jane?" he asked.

"Still upstairs," said Nell. "But please don't drag her down to help. We need only willing workers right now."

Ned scowled but nodded. Zibby froze. She had forgotten about Laura-Jane. What if she was in Zibby's room playing with the dollhouse? Quietly Zibby tiptoed up the stairs and along the hall to her bedroom. From the doorway she peeked inside and saw Laura-Jane sprawled across the bed, reading Zibby's mystery novel. The doll in the gray dress lay on the bed next to Laura-Jane. But the dollhouse was closed and latched. Zibby hesitated, wanting to kick Laura-Jane out. How dare she just go in and make herself at home? But at least she wasn't messing with the dollhouse. Frowning, Zibby turned away. She went back downstairs, where the cooking and baking were beginning in earnest.

All the helpers donned the black cotton aprons printed with the large yellow daisy that was the DaisyCakes logo. They set to work under Nell's direction, and soon tiny curry pies, savory quiches, cheese straws, pasta salad, mushroom pâté, cream puffs, and a gigantic peaches-and-cream layer cake materialized, as if by magic. Zibby made a batch of cookies all by herself.

"You're all hired!" Nell exclaimed gaily as the assembled helpers put finishing touches on the platters of food. Zibby looked up with a smile.

"And I think you'll actually get to the job on time," Ned said, "if we get these things out to the car quickly." He called up the stairs for Laura-Jane to come down and help.

"You can take my van, too," said Aunt Linnea, "and I'll stay here and wash these dishes."

Ned thanked her, but then his face darkened with anger as they heard the screen door in the front hall slam. Zibby darted after him into the hall, just in time to see Laura-Jane speeding down the street on her bike. Ned looked furious, but he said nothing. He went back to the kitchen and picked up two of the platters. Zibby helped him load the van, thinking about how Laura-Jane would probably be grounded for a year.

Serves her right, thought Zibby.

Charlotte and Penny agreed to stay with Aunt Linnea,

but Zibby, Jude, and Brady rode along to help set up the food. The event was a reception held at a church hall in the town center for a Mr. and Mrs. Gminksi, who were celebrating their golden wedding anniversary. "Golden means their fiftieth," whispered Jude, after Nell had introduced the girls to the couple. "Can you imagine being married to anybody that long?"

"Fifty million years?" Brady danced along, carrying a container of whipped cream inside.

"I can't imagine being that old in the first place!" Zibby replied. "But it's nice that their marriage has lasted so long."

"I guess you've got to find the right match," said Jude. "I think my mom and dad are that kind of match." Then she grew quiet, and Zibby knew she was wondering if her dad were even alive anymore.

Zibby glanced at her mom and Ned as they opened the van and started unloading platters of food into the hall. It would be nice, she thought, if her own parents' marriage had lasted fifty years. But maybe Nell had now found the right match in Ned instead, and the two of them would grow old together. She realized that the thought didn't bother her; in fact, it made her feel happy.

But the thought of her dad and Sofia being together for fifty years was another story.

"We wondered if you were coming," Mr. Gminski said to Nell in a querulous voice. "Thought maybe you'd forgotten about us."

"Not at all, Mr. Gminski," Nell replied in her bright, professional voice. "We had a bit of trouble, but everything is fine now. Of course we couldn't forget an occasion like this!"

Zibby watched as the Gminskis' guests surged into the reception hall. Zibby felt proud when people started to exclaim over the lovely food.

Nell stayed at the reception, but Ned drove Brady and the girls back home in Aunt Linnea's van. They found Aunt Linnea sitting in a rocking chair on the front porch, reading a magazine. Penny, Charlotte, and Laura-Jane were all sitting on the porch swing. Zibby was surprised to see the girls giggling together.

But Laura-Jane stopped giggling as Ned and Nell walked up onto the porch.

"Everything all right?" Aunt Linnea asked.

"Yes, thanks," said Ned. "But no thanks to you, Laura-Jane. Come with me, young lady. We need to have a little talk."

"Uh-oh," whispered Jude as Ned ushered his daughter inside the house.

"We need to get home now, Charlotte," Aunt Linnea said, closing her magazine.

"Oh, just a few more minutes!" Zibby protested, and beckoned for her cousin, Penny, and Jude to follow her upstairs to her bedroom.

"Let's call Fennel Hills Nursing Home now, while we're all together. And before I have to hang out with Laura-Jane. That girl is bad news."

"She's not so bad, really," Penny said. "I mean, when you get to know her."

"Not so bad?" Zibby stared at her. "Well, I bet she

sneaked in here while we were at Lilliput, and played with the dollhouse dolls. She probably played that Mom's business would be ruined—and that's what happened to all the food."

"Well, I feel sorry for you, getting that girl for your step-sister," said Jude.

"She's just really upset about the wedding," Penny said. "She told me she's been hoping and hoping that her mom and dad would get back together again."

"You can't blame her for that," Charlotte added. "You were hoping that about your own parents. Remember, Zib?"

"Yeah, I know. But I still didn't play that Sofia's head would fall off!" Zibby picked up the phone book and started searching for the nursing home's number. "Anyway, if we can get Mrs. Smythe to take back the dollhouse, then maybe all this bad stuff will stop happening." She underlined the phone number with a pencil. "Here it is." Jude, Penny, and Charlotte pressed close as Zibby made the call.

"Fennel Hills," announced a warm male voice on the other end of the line.

"Um, I'd like to speak with Mrs. Smythe," Zibby said.

"Mrs. Smith?" asked the man. "We've got three—no, two—ladies with that name."

"No. Smythe." Zibby corrected him. "Um—Primrose Smythe."

There was a silence, then the sound of a throat being cleared. "Ah, yes. Mrs. Primrose Smythe. Are you a relative?"

"No—" Then Zibby wondered whether she should say she *was* a relative.

"Oh, too bad," said the man. "We've been trying to trace her relatives since she was transferred."

"Transferred?" Zibby was confused. Her dad's job transfer had taken him to Italy. Surely old Mrs. Smythe wasn't going to Italy?

"Transferred to the hospital," the man on the phone was explaining. "I'm afraid she had a heart attack a few days ago."

"Oh, no!" Zibby clenched her hand tightly around the phone. Jude and Penny and Charlotte stood by her side, looking puzzled.

"Yes, I'm sorry to say it's true. Perhaps you can reach her at the hospital."

"Which hospital?" asked Zibby, and Jude groaned.

"Highland Hospital, right here in town," he answered.

Zibby thanked him and hung up.

Jude grabbed the phone book. "Want me to make the next call?"

Zibby shook her head. "She sold the house to me, so I'd better be the one to talk to her." She pressed the buttons, and in another second was speaking to a nurse who told her that Mrs. Smythe was out of her room having tests done and could not come to the phone at present. But visiting hours went until eight at night and began again at ten the next morning. Zibby asked whether she could leave a message for Mrs. Smythe.

"Certainly," said the nurse.

"Please tell her I'm the girl she sold her dollhouse to. Tell her—tell her that I want her to take the dollhouse back."

"Take it back?" asked the nurse in surprise.

"Yes," Zibby replied firmly. "And right away. Because there's something terribly wrong with it."

"Now, now," laughed the nurse. "What could be wrong with a dollhouse?"

Zibby glanced over at the solemn faces of her cousin and friends. She saw the ache in their eyes as they worried about Mac, about Amy and her dad in the hospital, about Charlotte's stitched forehead and Nell's damaged food. "What's wrong with it?" repeated Zibby slowly. "It's nasty and horrible, and it's...*possessed,*" she said. "That's what."

CHAPTER 16

PRIMROSE 1919

"You're nasty and horrible, and you deserve to be fed to the dogs," said Primrose Parson gleefully, speaking for the little girl doll. She and the other children dolls had tied up their governess and were stuffing her into a closet. "Now we'll just sit here and wait until the dogs are hungry enough." Primrose laid the dolls on the schoolroom floor and ran to her bedroom for the stuffed dog she kept in her bed. His name was Fred, and he was worn and limp. She had slept with him since she was a baby. She carried him back to the dollhouse, checking, as she passed, that Miss Honeywell's sitting-room door was still closed.

Miss Honeywell had ended Primrose's lessons an hour earlier today because she needed to have a conference with Mr. Pope—about Primrose's progress, she said. She had sent for the kitchen maid to bring up some hot tea and slices of cake, and when Mr. Pope arrived, Miss Honeywell invited him into her private sitting room, where, she told him with a simpering smile, they would be able to talk undisturbed.

Primrose was delighted with the extra playtime; she had been having some wonderful games with the dollhouse dolls lately.

She had created stories for the whole doll family, and servants, too. The dollhouse parents traveled a lot, just like her own parents. Primrose had a hard time imagining parents who stayed home all the time. And when the parents were gone, the children were in the care of the governess, Miss Sourpuss. Primrose made Miss Sourpuss act every bit as nasty as the real Miss Honeywell, but unlike Primrose, the dollhouse children managed to find fitting punishments for their governess every time she stepped out of line. Primrose could only dream of such vengeance against Miss Honeywell, but she had fun planning the punishments and acting them out with the dolls. In fact, torturing the governess doll had become her favorite game. It wasn't as satisfying as playing practical jokes on the *real* governess, of course, but at least she didn't get her hands smacked or get herself locked in the closet nearly as often these days.

Primrose stuffed floppy Fred into the dollhouse schoolroom. "Here's Fred," she murmured. "The most ferocious creature this side of Lake Erie. His chief pleasure is eating mean people. Go ahead, Fred—enjoy yourself!" And then she acted out how Miss Sourpuss ran around trying to escape the huge, dripping fangs of Fred, and how the children laughed when she was finally chomped to little bloody bits.

But then Primrose realized that if Old Sourpuss were dead, the children wouldn't have any more fun punishing her. So she played that Old Sourpuss didn't *quite* die but lay badly injured for hours while the children went out to play with their friends. And when she recovered at last, she was more menacing than ever. She tried to beat the children and lock them into the closet, but they attacked her and overpowered her instead! The dollhouse didn't really have a closet, so Primrose stood a small box on end in one corner of the dollhouse room. It made a perfect prison, and Miss Sourpuss spent hours locked inside.

When Miss Sourpuss was let out, the children decided to hang her upside down and swing her by her heels—something the real Miss Honeywell had threatened to do to Primrose more than once, yet so far never had. Primrose carried the governess doll over to the windows and looped the cord from the window blinds around the doll's feet. "There you go, Old Sourpuss!" she murmured, and giggled as the doll swung wildly from side to side.

She could hear laughter from inside Miss Honeywell's sitting room. Laughter—from *Sweet* Miss Honeywell? It was not to be believed. Abandoning the doll, Primrose crept closer to the room and put her ear to the closed door. Yes, Miss Honeywell was *laughing* in there! It was a sound completely unfamiliar to Primrose. She could hear the high lilting voice of her governess, and the deeper tones of Mr. Pope's reply, but she couldn't quite make out the words.

And yet she must know what was making her governess laugh! Primrose pressed her ear harder against the wood. She wished she dared to turn the knob and push the door open just a crack. Well—why not?

Slowly the door crept open—just enough for Primrose to position herself so one eye could peer into the room. Enough so she could hear what was going on in there.

What she saw was Miss Honeywell and Mr. Pope sitting in two armchairs in front of the fireplace. A cozy fire burned in the grate. On the small table between the chairs lay a tray with teacups, teapot, and slices of cake.

What she heard was her tutor talking about her!

"I'm worried that young Primrose isn't really understanding the principles of electricity, Miss Honeywell," Mr. Pope was saying.

"Oh—*do* call me Calliope," urged Miss Honeywell. "And I shall call you Thaddeus, or do you prefer Tad or Ted? After all, we knew each other as children, and I think there is no need to remain so formal." She laughed gaily. "I know my father was not happy with our association because your father was a sales clerk whereas mine owned the entire department store…but we must not let such differences matter to us now, dear Tad."

"Thaddeus will do," he said. He reached up a hand to smooth back his unruly dark hair. "But as I was saying, Calliope, I do worry that I'm not reaching Primrose with my teaching methods. Perhaps I tend to be a bit old-fashioned—a bit stodgy in my approach. Perhaps the child would respond better to something new—"

"Nonsense, Thaddeus! You aren't the least bit old-fashioned. If you're not reaching Primrose, it is simply because the girl is as thick as two planks. She is unteachable, Thaddeus, and you mustn't trouble yourself about her for one second."

"Well, I do think that if the young lady had some way of applying the principles of electricity to her own interests, she would understand much better what I've been trying to teach her," Mr. Pope pressed on as Primrose listened intently. "So I'd like to propose a project that she and I could work on together. Electrifying that dollhouse of hers with real lamps!

It would make a pretty plaything, in the end—and in the meantime, our Miss Primrose would learn something. What do you say, Calliope?"

Primrose grinned. *What a good idea! Mr. Pope isn't such a dry old stick after all!*

But Miss Honeywell was shaking her head. "Oh, I don't think so, dearest Thaddeus." She leaned across the space separating their chairs and placed one hand on his arm. "Either the child is stupid—or just plain willful. And if she is willful, she needs discipline, not coddling. She must be made to mind. And she already has too many fancy playthings, in my opinion, so an electrified dollhouse is unnecessary. If she is to learn the principles of electricity, she will learn them through good old hard work. I will see to it myself, if you'd like. A taste of the belt might help her focus—"

"Well, that's another thing, Miss Honeywell—Calliope," said Mr. Pope mildly. "I think you are rather harsh with the girl. She is only a child—and a lonely one at that. And yet you work her like she's preparing for university study! I urge you to be more gentle with Primrose."

Hooray for Mr. Pope! thought Primrose.

Miss Honeywell let her hand drop from Mr. Pope's arm to his trousered knee. "Oh, Thaddeus," she said sadly. "I see the little minx has got you fooled as well. It is I who need a gentle touch, not little Miss Primrose. Thaddeus…" She dropped to her knees by his side and pressed her cheek against his thigh. He hesitantly placed one hand on top of her hair.

"My dear Miss Honeywell—" Mr. Pope sounded uncertain. "I don't believe—"

She reached her arms out and embraced him. "I want to be your bride, Thaddeus!"

Primrose couldn't help it. She burst out laughing. Snickering and snorting, she backed away from the sitting-room door, fighting for control. But—too late. Miss Honeywell had heard.

The sitting-room door flew open and Miss Honeywell leaped across the room, raining smacks down on Primrose. "You sneaking brat! I'll teach you a lesson you'll *never* forget!"

"I'll never forget the sight of you getting all swoony over Mr. Pope! Begging him to marry you—what a riot!"

With a shriek of rage, Miss Honeywell yanked Primrose's braids.

"Calliope!" shouted Mr. Pope, and he grabbed Miss Honeywell's hands in his. He pulled her to him and held her tightly. "Restrain yourself, my good woman." Then over his shoulder to Primrose he added, "Sneaking at doors is never a good thing, young lady. I'm afraid you brought this on yourself, and you owe Miss Honeywell an apology."

"I'm sorry, Miss Honeywell," said Primrose meekly, rubbing her sore head. "But, oh, Mr. Pope...I couldn't help overhearing what you said about putting lights in my dollhouse! What a wonderful idea!"

His expression softened. "Well, then, we shall try to make it happen. But you will have to do the electrical work yourself, to prove to me you understand everything."

"I will, Mr. Pope. Thank you!" said Primrose. "*You're* a really good teacher."

Miss Honeywell glared at Primrose and struggled in Mr. Pope's arms for a moment, then stopped and leaned against him. She closed her eyes. Primrose edged toward the stairs.

"Don't think I'll forget this, you little horror." Miss Honeywell's eyes were still closed, and she spoke in a soft, menacing voice. "I'm not finished with you yet."

Primrose took a deep breath and hurried out of the schoolroom. This might prove to be a very good time for a nice visit with Nanny Shanks and the twins.

CHAPTER 17

It started raining. Aunt Linnea said it was getting late and time she and Charlotte headed home. Jude and Penny announced that they'd better go home for dinner, too. Ned suggested he and Zibby, Laura-Jane and Brady all go out for Mexican food, but Zibby wished Ned would just take his kids and go away. She needed to phone the hospital and track down Mrs. Smythe.

Ned was not going away, of course, so Zibby went out with the Shimizus for tacos and burritos. She wasn't used to being with Ned without her mom there, too. She concentrated on joking with Brady the whole time they were at the restaurant, and more or less ignored Laura-Jane, which was easy to do because the other girl would never meet her eyes, anyway. Ned entertained them with stories about his travels as a reporter in Europe, and that was pretty interesting. But still, Zibby was relieved when it was time to go home again, and she was glad to see her mom's car in the driveway.

Nell was lying on the couch with a terrible headache, so Ned gave her some more pain reliever and then sent his kids off to watch a video. Zibby was relieved to get rid of them. She sat with her mom a while longer, worrying that the headache might be the work of the dollhouse evil, worrying that somehow her mom's head would...what? Heads didn't really come off. Still, she worried.

After Ned helped Nell up the stairs to bed, Zibby decided reluctantly that it was too late to phone Mrs. Smythe in the hospital. She went to her own bedroom, checked that the dollhouse was securely latched, then flopped onto her bed and picked up her mystery novel. But she couldn't concentrate. Her head was full of anxious thoughts, and sleep, when it came, was filled with dreams of danger much more troubling than the story in the novel. *Danger to her mom, danger to herself, both of them chased by a shadowy figure in gray...and then flames, flames shooting out of the dollhouse windows, and the hand in the black glove reaching out, beckoning, searching...*

She slid out of bed and approached the dollhouse slowly, though every instinct told her to run out of the room and get far away from the double danger of fire and intruder. She walked across the bedroom, noticing as she did that her rug was gone and the floor was of polished shiny wood—except where the flames had charred it. The walls of her bedroom seemed to fall away, and the space expanded until she was in some larger sort of room—a familiar place, if only she could place it. But her head was clouded with smoke. It filled her eyes and nose, and choked her throat.

The hand opened, stretching out its fingers as if sensing her nearness.

"What?" she screamed at the top of her lungs. *"What do you want from me?"*

A gust of fresh air with more than a hint of autumn blew through Zibby's window and woke her up. She struggled to sit up, relieved to be awake. That dream— *again?* Why did she keep having it? She'd never had the dream until she'd bought the dollhouse. But how were they connected? What did the dream mean?

The room was dark. Zibby reached over to turn on her bedside light—and recoiled. The doll in the gray dress was leaning against the alarm clock. The time read 2:20.

Zibby knocked the doll to the floor. *You horrible thing!* She lay there, listening to the silence. Then the silence was broken by a moan from Nell's bedroom. Zibby shot out of bed and raced across the hallway.

Nell was sitting up in bed, clutching her head in her hands. Ned stood next to her, rubbing her neck. "Sorry to wake both of you," Nell said in an agonized whisper. "This is the worst headache I've ever had. And the painkillers don't do a thing—"

She broke off with another groan.

"Call the doctor!" Zibby cried in a panic, but Nell just lay down again and burrowed into her pillow. Zibby appealed to Ned. "We have to get her to the doctor!"

"She's been like this off and on all night," said Ned worriedly, "but she doesn't want the doctor. He'll just want her to come to the emergency clinic, and she says she can't bear to go anywhere." He stood up and paced across the room. "I'll give her another half hour to see if the pain reliever kicks in—otherwise I'm taking her to the clinic whether she likes it or not."

Zibby reached out and massaged the back of her mom's neck.

"It feels like my head is exploding," whimpered Nell. "I wish I could just pull it off."

The way Laura-Jane had pulled the head off the mother doll? Zibby bit her lip so she wouldn't start crying along with her mom.

"Mmmm," Nell said after another moment. "That feels good, honey. Can you rub harder?"

Zibby applied herself to giving her mom a really good long head rub. Finally Nell fell asleep and Ned tucked her in. "I'll sit here with her for a while," he whispered to Zibby.

She crept back to her own room. The doll in the gray dress mocked her now from atop the dollhouse, leaning against the chimney. Zibby slid wearily into bed. Her last thoughts before she fell back to sleep were of her mom, lying in the next room, and of old Mrs. Smythe, lying in the hospital.

IN THE MORNING Nell needed to go to the church to meet with the musicians who would play chamber music at the wedding. Ned worried that Nell wasn't up to it, but she insisted. After he left for the *Gazette,* taking Laura-Jane and Brady with him, Zibby gave Nell a hug. "I'd better come with you," she announced.

Nell hugged her back. "No need, honey. I'm fine. What are your plans for the day?"

"Well, I wanted to go on a bike ride." Zibby had decided not to call the hospital ahead of time after all. Because what if Mrs. Smythe refused to see them? Better just to show up during morning visiting hours. "But I think I should come with you to meet the musicians at the church first." More important than visiting Mrs. Smythe was keeping Nell safe.

"I feel nearly back to normal. There's no reason you need to come. But why not invite Laura-Jane and Brady to ride with you? They're just hanging out at the *Gazette* office, playing computer games while Ned works. I'm sure they'd love to go along. I'll give you money for ice cream, too."

"Oh, Mom, I already have plans with Jude and Penny. And Charlotte!"

"Come on now, be a good stepsister."

Zibby sighed. "Mom—you have no idea how awful Laura-Jane can be."

"She's having a hard time, honey. But I'm sure she'll improve when she gets to know us better. And it would mean a lot to Ned if you'd include her in your fun with Charlotte and your two new friends."

"Another time," Zibby said firmly. "I'm not a stepsister till *after* the wedding." She got dressed quickly, then grabbed her helmet and left the house. She stopped at the Jeffersons' house first to pick up Jude and Penny. She realized she thought of the house that way now—the Jeffersons' house rather than Amy's house.

Mrs. Jefferson came to the door looking haggard and sad. Zibby knew that meant there still had been no word of her son in Kenya. Mr. Jefferson—Jude's grandfather and Penny's dad—greeted Zibby solemnly. He was glad, he said, that the girls had found a friend so soon after moving to Carroway. "Being with you helps take their minds off Mac," he added, patting Zibby on the shoulder as he moved past her into the living room. He heaved a sigh and sank onto the couch. Jude and Penny came downstairs then, and the girls said good-bye and left the house.

"Poor Dad," said Penny. "He's so distracted about Mac, he can't even go to work."

Zibby shook her head in sympathy. Jude mounted her bike in silence and set off through the park ahead of them. Zibby knew Jude was near tears with the worry about her dad. Zibby felt glad suddenly that her own dad was safe and well—even if he was far away and married to Sofia.

They picked up Charlotte and pedaled along their way. The ride on the bike path between Carroway and Fennel Grove followed the river and took about half an hour. The morning was warming up, and the end-of-summer sun beat down. Charlotte lifted her heavy blond curls off her neck, and Zibby was glad for her shorter bob. All the girls were hot and sticky, though, by the time they biked to a stop in front of the big hospital.

At last, at last, thought Zibby, leading the way through the front door and over to the reception desk in the lobby. She asked the silver-haired nurse sitting there where they would find Mrs. Primrose Smythe.

The nurse consulted a sheaf of papers. "Ah," she said slowly. "Here she is." She glanced up at Zibby and the other girls. "Are you family members? Any of you?"

The girls glanced at each other.

"Well, no," Jude said. "But we've come to see Mrs. Smythe on urgent business."

"Urgent?" The nurse looked skeptical.

"Yes." Penny smiled her brightest, most eager smile at the nurse. "It's about her childhood dollhouse."

The nurse shook her head. "I'm afraid Mrs. Smythe was moved to intensive care last night. She won't be able to see you."

"But why not?" demanded Zibby. "Is she unconscious or something?"

"It's hospital policy that only family members are allowed to visit intensive care."

The girls looked at each other, downcast. Zibby was just opening her mouth to argue when Jude spoke up suddenly.

"Okay, then," said Jude cheerfully, "we *are* Mrs. Smythe's grandchildren. And so we'd like to see her right away."

"But you *aren't* her grandchildren," objected the nurse. She peered at them over her wire-rimmed glasses. "You quite clearly said you weren't."

"We...got confused," said Jude firmly. "But we are definitely her grandchildren, and we know Grandma would like to see us. Just for a very short visit."

"I don't believe you can be her grandchildren!" protested the nurse. "You look nothing like her. Next thing you know, you'll be trying to convince me you're all *sisters*!"

"Well, we *are* sisters." Charlotte spoke up pleasantly. "All of us. And you can't prove we're not!"

Penny smiled angelically. "We're quadruplets. Just not identical."

"Look," Zibby said hastily, as she could see they had seriously annoyed the nurse, "please just phone Mrs. Smythe's ward and ask somebody to see whether she would like to visit with her four grandchildren who have come to talk about her old dollhouse. *Please!*"

"If she says no, we'll go away," promised Jude. "But if she says yes..."

"We promise not to upset her or make any noise," Charlotte added in her prim way.

The nurse glowered at them, then sighed. She picked up the phone on her desk. "All right. I'll check with the head nurse."

The girls waited impatiently while the nurse talked on the phone. "Some children here to see Mrs. Smythe…about a dollhouse. They say they are her grandchildren. Her *quadruplet* grandchildren, no less. Is she awake? Will you ask her—?" The nurse listened. "Yes, I'll wait."

The girls held their breath.

Then the nurse raised her eyebrows. "Really? Hmmm. Really. All right, thank you." She hung up the phone and leaned toward the girls. "Well, it's hard for me to believe, but Mrs. Smythe says she is very eager to see her grandchildren. So you may go up. Eighth floor, turn right past the elevators." She shook her head disapprovingly. "It's highly irregular. Be sure to check in at the nurses' station first."

The girls thanked her and rushed to the elevators. "Quadruplets!" giggled Penny as the elevator doors slid open. The girls, snorting with laughter, sobered up as doctors and nurses got on and off at the different floors. People wearing green surgical scrubs pushed important-looking carts of instruments covered with plastic down the hallways. The girls followed signs to the intensive care ward, then hesitated at a circular counter in the middle of the hallway.

"Is this the nurses' station?" Zibby asked tentatively.

"Yes, it is," answered the nurse on duty. "And you must be the determined young quadruplets who have come to see Mrs. Smythe. Come right this way." She set off down the hallway, then stopped in front of a closed door. As she opened it, she looked back at them over her shoulder. "Mrs. Smythe wants to see you, but she is very weak. Her heart has been giving her some problems lately."

"What's the point in living," came a querulous voice from the single hospital bed inside, "if you can't see people or do things? It's boring just lying here helpless all the time."

"I believe I'd feel the same way, Mrs. Smythe," said the nurse in a soothing voice, leading the girls over to the bed. "I'll leave you now to your visitors—but only for a few minutes."

And there lay the old woman from the miniatures convention, at last. Her white hair frizzed out from her head like dandelion fluff. Her blue eyes were very bright. "Ah, yes," she said, peering at Zibby. "You're the little girl who bought the dollhouse. I've been wondering how long it would take you to come looking for me."

CHAPTER 18

PRIMROSE 1919

On a cold wintry afternoon, Primrose knelt before the doll-house. Recently she'd had a lot more playtime with the doll-house than she usually did, because Miss Honeywell was ill. Her hoarse voice had grown raspier than ever, and she had developed a nasty cough. Soon the doctor had to be called in, and he diagnosed a bronchial inflammation. Poor Miss Honeywell was put to bed for two weeks in a bedroom on the second floor, where the maids could tend to her more easily. When Mr. Pope came to teach Primrose, he brought a bouquet of flowers for Miss Honeywell, and Miss Honeywell was cheered for a short time. But she slept badly, tossing with fever, and called out all sorts of garbled nonsense. One afternoon Primrose had been walking past the sickroom on her way to visit Nanny Shanks and the twins in the nursery, and she heard Miss Honeywell shouting. Was the governess calling *her*? Primrose stopped and listened outside the bedroom door.

"No, no. I forbid it!" gasped Miss Honeywell. "You're all I have left, and you must obey me in this matter. Our parents left me in charge, Lester, and you must obey…I insist—" She broke off with a moan and a terrible fit of coughing. Primrose crept away down the hall.

It was a wonderful two weeks. Out from under the governess's watchful, repressive eye, Primrose was able to play with Peony and Basil whenever she wanted. And Nanny Shanks arranged sleigh rides to visit the big house on the other side of the park, where her sister was nanny to a nice boy named Oscar Smythe. Mr. Pope was Oscar's tutor, too, and while Miss Honeywell was indisposed, he taught Primrose and Oscar together in Oscar's schoolroom. "You work better together with another pupil," Mr. Pope commented to Primrose. "When Miss Honeywell is well, I shall urge her to continue this arrangement."

It *was* a delightful arrangement, and Primrose liked Oscar very much. But she knew Miss Honeywell would never agree to it. Anything that took Primrose out of Miss Honeywell's direct control would be forbidden.

When lessons with Mr. Pope were over, Oscar and Primrose played checkers and pick-up-sticks while the two nannies drank tea and the twins rode around in Oscar's metal pedal car. Some afternoons, Nanny Shanks would leave the twins in the care of the cook, and she and Primrose would go to the ice rink at the lagoon. At first Primrose tottered on her ice skates, but after a few days she could circle around the rink without falling. At the end of the first week, she could skate arm in arm with Nanny Shanks. One day Oscar joined them at the ice rink, and he taught Primrose how to bend low and race, and how to skate backward. Primrose was happier than she had ever been.

And then in the evenings, after the twins were asleep, Primrose would sit with Nanny Shanks. Primrose tried to tell Nanny how horrible Miss Honeywell was, but Nanny Shanks recollected that Primrose had always been an imaginative girl and reminded her that exaggerations were not kind.

"But everything I'm telling you is *true,*" insisted Primrose.

"Then I shall speak with your father when he returns," replied Nanny Shanks, and Primrose had to be content with that.

She and Nanny enjoyed reading aloud together. They read *Little Women,* Primrose's favorite. Primrose was so busy and so happy during the days Miss Honeywell lay sick in bed, there wasn't any time left over to play with the dollhouse.

But then Miss Honeywell recovered. She ordered Primrose back to the schoolroom and heaped work upon her "to make up for lost time," as she said. She refused to consider Mr. Pope's proposal that Primrose and Oscar be taught science and mathematics together, saying that it would not be suitable or proper. She seemed to find it entirely proper, however, to flirt with Mr. Pope whenever he came to teach Primrose. She urged him to leave Primrose in the schoolroom with piles of work so that she and he might sit together by the fire. She giggled like a young girl. Once Primrose even saw Miss Honeywell perch herself on the arm of Mr. Pope's chair and reach out with her fingertips to neaten his unruly dark hair. He did not encourage her, as far as Primrose could tell, but he did not push her away, either, or laugh in her face as Primrose wished he would.

While Nanny Shanks and the twins were out in the fresh air making snowmen, Primrose sat at her table, memorizing lists of spelling words. While Nanny Shanks sang and played, Miss Honeywell scolded and shouted. While Nanny Shanks cuddled, Miss Honeywell smacked, declaring Primrose to be the most unmannerly and ill-behaved child she had ever met.

Primrose turned to her dollhouse again with a sense of desperation. *There,* at least, the governess was put in her place. *There* the governess was punished for her viciousness. Primrose played that the doll children pushed the governess doll out the window, stuffed her down the chimney, hanged her by the neck from a hook in the ceiling. She felt some measure of relief from this play, but the real Miss Honeywell still loomed large and fearsome. Primrose always felt choked around her governess, never knowing when Miss Honeywell's anger and disapproval would be roused, never knowing when she would be pinched or paddled or put into the closet.

One afternoon in December, after lessons had ended—and Primrose had been smacked twice for not being able to locate China on the world map fast enough to please her governess, who accused her of laziness and indifference—Primrose opened the dollhouse for solace. Miss Honeywell left the schoolroom on some errand of her own, and it seemed the air grew immediately clearer and easier to breathe.

Primrose took the mother and father dolls, who had been traveling over by the wardrobe in her bedroom, and set them on the back of her stuffed dog, Fred. "Here come the

parents, galloping home on their horse," she murmured.
"They want to be home in time for Christmas. They've
brought so many presents for the children, even Santa Claus
would have a hard time bringing anything more." Her own
mama and papa had written to say they would be home for
Christmas, too. It was the one bright star keeping her spirits
up now that Miss Honeywell was recovered. "And just as the
parents arrive home from their trip, Old Sourpuss is upstairs
taking a tonic for her sore throat. It has been bothering her
for a long time, and the children hate the sound of her *hack,
hack, hack.* It keeps them awake at night, even worse than
her snoring." Primrose picked up the two littlest dolls and
made them speak.

"James the gardener made the rats in the walls be quiet
by giving them some of this special powder in their rat hole,"
the tiny girl doll said. "Maybe it would help to quiet Old
Sourpuss's cough, what do you think?" And the boy doll answered: "What a fine idea! Let's ask Big Sister to help."

Primrose marched the girl doll into the dollhouse schoolroom. "Why, what a wonderful idea. You are such smart
children!" The doll children tipped the whole box of rodent
killer into Old Sourpuss's medicine bottle. Then Primrose
moved the governess doll into the room. *"Hack, hack, hack,"*
she coughed for the governess doll. "I shall need another dose
of tonic. And after that I will punish the children again since
they didn't know where China was on the map today."

Then the governess doll swallowed a large spoonful of
tonic. Then another. "My, oh my, this tastes even more delicious than usual—" Primrose made the doll stagger around
the dollhouse attic. "But, oh dear, I feel so dizzy and short of
breath. Oh—just the way I feel when the tutor is near me.

He wants to marry me, you know, I can tell, and he just takes my breath away! But no, wait, this is bad! I feel the most dreadful, painful cramps! *Hack, hack, hack!* Help! I can't breathe at all!" The governess doll tumbled to the floor. Primrose grinned as she moved the doll children over to her.

"I'm afraid she's dead," said the boy doll.

"Oh, well," said the girl. "Nothing to be afraid of. Not anymore."

Primrose smiled with satisfaction. Then she got the dolls ready for the funeral. The parents arrived home just in time. "Hooray, Mama and Papa are home!" she made the doll children cry. "Just in time for the funeral—hooray!"

She turned from the house to get the parent dolls riding home on Fred the dog and drew in her breath sharply.

There stood Miss Honeywell, right behind her. She had entered the schoolroom and walked across to the dollhouse without making a sound. And Primrose, so engrossed in her play, had not noticed. Miss Honeywell had been watching. She had been listening. She had seen and heard everything.

The skin on Miss Honeywell's pale face looked tight, and her eyes glittered with a dangerous light. "Killing off the governess, eh?" she said in a low, hard voice. "Killing me off, were you?"

"N—no! Miss Honeywell, it wasn't you—of course not!"

The yank on Primrose's braids tumbled her sideways. She stumbled into the dollhouse, then quickly regained her balance and turned to run away. But Miss Honeywell had her now, her grip like a trap around Primrose's arm. "Into the closet with you, my girl. Into the closet now—and out you'll come tomorrow morning and not one moment sooner."

All night in the closet? "No!" cried Primrose.

She kicked and screamed for Nanny Shanks, but Miss Honeywell dragged her to the closet and slammed the door. Primrose heard the key grate in the lock. "Please, please let me out, Miss Honeywell," begged Primrose. "Please!"

"That's *Sweet* Miss Honeywell to you," came the reply, and then the *tap-tap* of Miss Honeywell's firm footsteps moving swiftly away.

Primrose sank down into the darkness of the closet and pressed her fist to her mouth. All night! How could she bear it here in the dark for hours and hours and hours? It was cold, and the floor was hard, and she was all alone. She huddled on the floor and pressed herself into the corner.

She cried until she could cry no more and her breath came in ragged gasps. The crack of light under the door faded to a deep gold, and Primrose knew the sun was setting. Her stomach felt hollow, but there would be no dinner. She told herself to be strong, to be a brick. She wouldn't let *Sweet* Miss Honeywell win.

She must have dozed, because when she next opened her eyes, the crack of light under the door was gone. She heard footsteps on the wooden floor and Miss Honeywell's harsh voice: "Primrose? I hope you are thinking about your behavior. Such a sinful game. Your parents, when they hear, will be deeply shocked. I hope you are properly repentant."

Primrose did not answer.

"Are you, young miss? Are you repentant and ashamed?"

Primrose pressed her lips together and did not say a single word. Let Miss Honeywell open the door to see if she were properly ashamed—and then she'd dart past her so fast that Miss Honeywell would be caught off balance and crash to the floor, breaking her neck! And Primrose would run and run and run…

But Miss Honeywell did not open the door to check on Primrose. She stood outside the closet and ranted about how ungovernable Primrose had become. There was *never* a more willful and spoiled child, and so on and so forth. Primrose felt tears coursing down her cheeks again, because she knew her escape was only a fantasy. The door was thick. It was locked. It was going to stay locked because Miss Honeywell was not going to open it, and because Primrose didn't have the key.

She put her hands to her ears to block out the governess's hateful rasping voice. Her fingers touched something hard. Her hairpins!

Primrose's long brown hair was braided into two plaits and then pinned up into loops behind each ear. Miss Honeywell had yanked out one loop, but the other was intact. Primrose pulled at the pins eagerly now and held them in her hands tightly. Hard, thin, long enough to fit into the lock; maybe she could escape from the closet after all?

Finally Miss Honeywell finished berating Primrose. "I'll be back for you in the morning, young miss." She rattled the doorknob for emphasis. "And not a moment before."

Primrose waited until she heard the *tap-tap* of Miss Honeywell's footsteps across the floor and was sure that the governess had gone downstairs for dinner. Then Primrose set to work. She poked the end of the hairpin into the lock and moved it up and down. She tried the door handle—but no, the door was still locked. She tried the other hairpin, jiggling it back and forth. But again, the door remained locked. Primrose did not give up hope. She had tools, she had time, and she had patience. She would stay here at the door all night if she must, trying to pick the lock. Thieves did it all the time; this she knew from tales Nanny Shanks had told her. And if nothing else, trying to pick the lock gave Primrose something to do, for the hours in the dark closet passed very slowly indeed.

As she worked on the lock, one wall of the closet started to glow. Primrose stared. Was she imagining this? Or was the same head forming there—out of thin air—as before? A young man's head. And a young man's voice, whispering to her: *Poor kid. I know what it's like. Poor kid...* The face faded away and the glowing wall darkened. Primrose rubbed her eyes, uncertain, then applied herself to the locked door with renewed energy.

After a long while, Primrose had the idea of using both hair pins at once. She twisted them together and pressed them into the lock. At first nothing happened, but she felt a stronger resistance—something more to push against. She pushed the pins up and down, then rotated them slowly in the lock. And then she half heard, half felt the tiny *tock* as the lock opened. Holding her breath, Primrose cracked the closet door and stepped out cautiously into the schoolroom. She exhaled slowly and looked around.

The schoolroom was dark. The doors to her bedroom and Miss Honeywell's bedroom stood open. So did the door to Miss Honeywell's sitting room. That meant Miss Honeywell was still downstairs. That meant there was still time, if she acted quickly, for a really good practical joke. This was one that Miss Honeywell would not forget in a hurry!

Primrose sidled into Miss Honeywell's bedroom and went

straight over to the dresser. On top of the dresser stood the large china bowl and pitcher full of water for washing. The third floor didn't have a bathroom, so both she and the governess had to wash and brush their teeth from the water in their pitchers, changed daily by the maids. For bathing they used the big bathroom downstairs. Next to the china bowl and pitcher was Miss Honeywell's ring of keys. Primrose picked it up and slid the closet key off the ring. She put it in her pocket.

Then Primrose lifted Miss Honeywell's pitcher. It was nearly full. *Perfect!* She ran back to the schoolroom for one of the chairs and carried it into Miss Honeywell's bedroom. But when she stood on it, she still couldn't reach...so she jumped down and looked around for what could be used to lift her even higher. *Aha! Miss Honeywell's night table!*

As fast as she could, Primrose cleared the lamp and the book and bottle of cough medicine from the night table and dragged the table over to the chair she had positioned behind Miss Honeywell's bedroom door. She stopped and listened but heard no sounds from downstairs. Nonetheless, she must be quick or Miss Honeywell would return before she could get everything ready. And then it would be the closet again—probably for the rest of her life—with only the glowing head from her imagination for company.

Primrose smiled grimly to herself as she heaved the little table up onto the wider base of the chair. The table wasn't very heavy but it wasn't very stable, either. She would have to be extremely careful, or she'd fall and ruin everything, and the trick would be on her.

Once the table was stacked on top of the chair, Primrose clambered up, cautiously hanging on to the door for support. Yes, now she could reach the top of the door. But—*oh, no, silly me*—she had left the pitcher back down on the dresser. So she had to go down and get it. Climbing back up again while holding the heavy pitcher was not easy. In fact, several times Primrose nearly dropped the pitcher. Water sloshed out everywhere—all over her clothes and onto the floor. But at last she had the pitcher where she wanted it: balanced right on top of the door.

The slightest movement would dislodge it, pouring water all over whoever touched the door. That was the plan. *Whoosh!* Miss Honeywell would get the surprise of her life when she came up to go to bed.

But first Primrose had to get down from her tower without detonating her surprise. She held her breath as she considered how to climb off the night table and chair without jostling the door. Finally she decided just to jump, and so she leaped from her makeshift ladder right onto the middle of the governess's bed. The night table wobbled up on the chair, but it didn't touch the door, and the pitcher of water remained upright on its precarious perch.

Success! thought Primrose, grinning with gleeful relief. She quickly went about smoothing out the bedcovers, returning the night table to its place by the bed, and placing the lamp, book, and medicine bottle carefully where she had found them. Then she carried the chair back into the schoolroom.

She had just pushed the chair neatly into place at the table when she heard the telltale tapping of Miss Honeywell's shoes on the stairs. She darted toward her bedroom to hide, then froze. No—not there. The safest place to wait and watch her practical joke would be in the closet. She would lock the door again from the inside for extra protection. Miss Honeywell would get her ring of keys and not find the one for the closet, but she wouldn't be able to prove that Primrose had taken it.

Primrose raised herself on tiptoe and tucked the key high on the closet shelf, inside one of the books. She grinned in the dark at the thought of a dripping-wet Miss Honeywell yelling at her through the door, clearly wanting to blame her for the soaking. "But Sweet Miss Honeywell," Primrose planned to say, "here I was, locked up in the closet all the time. How could I have done anything? Maybe it was your darling, devoted Mr. Pope instead!" She stifled a giggle. And then she would beg to be let out, but Miss Honeywell wouldn't be able to find the key. She'd have to call one of the menservants to take the door off. And then everyone would know how cruel she was to poor Primrose, and word would even get to Primrose's parents. And Miss Honeywell would be fired and sent away.

Miss Honeywell's shoes *tap-tapped* into the schoolroom. Primrose waited, forcing herself to breathe deeply and evenly. But Miss Honeywell did not come near the closet. The footsteps headed straight for her bedroom. Primrose jumped up and pressed her ear to the door, listening. Then she reached up and retrieved the key from its hiding place. This she had to see. She unlocked the closet door soundlessly and opened it just a crack. She didn't want to miss out on Old Sourpuss's good soaking.

Miss Honeywell put out a hand to push open her bedroom door. She took a single step into the room, and at the same time, the heavy pitcher of water—the entire china pitcher, not just the water—fell straight down onto her head with a solid thunk, raining water all around. Primrose watched from the closet with round, wide eyes as the governess crumpled onto the floor atop the shattered china.

It had worked even better than Primrose could have hoped. *Old Sourpuss will be plenty wet and bruised now,* thought Primrose with satisfaction. She waited for her governess to jump up and start screeching. "What's wrong, Sweet Miss Honeywell?" she would call in her most innocent voice. "Why do I hear water dripping out there?" She laughed under her breath at the wonderful satisfaction of this joke, her best practical joke ever.

But Miss Honeywell did not jump up. She didn't move at all.

After a moment Primrose opened the closet door a little wider. "Miss Honeywell?" No answer. Could the governess have been knocked unconscious?

Primrose edged out of the closet, her heart beginning to pound. Miss Honeywell was lying just inside the doorway of her bedroom, with her legs twisted oddly. One look at Miss Honeywell's open glassy eyes and ashen skin confirmed a most horrible truth.

No, thought Primrose. *No, it can't be. I didn't mean...I never meant—*

Primrose started to whimper, then the whimpers became screams. And as she screamed for Nanny Shanks at the top of her lungs, Primrose heard, quite distinctly, Miss Honeywell's voice inside her head.

"You did this to me, you vicious little practical joker. But I'll get you back for it, mark my words. Even if it takes until the end of time, I shall have my revenge!"

CHAPTER 19

Zibby edged closer to Mrs. Smythe's hospital bed. "I'm Zibby Thorne," Zibby introduced herself. "Isabel Thorne—that's my real name, remember? And this is my cousin, Charlotte Wheeler. And our friends, Jude and Penny Jefferson."

"But we're not sisters," Penny piped up. "I'm her *aunt*."

Jude elbowed Penny. Charlotte stepped forward with adult poise. She held out her hand. "How do you do, Mrs. Smythe. It's really good of you to see us."

"That's the only girl I want to see." Mrs. Smythe pointed a gnarled finger at Zibby. She opened her mouth to speak again, but the words turned into a cough. The nurse hurried back into the room and over to her side, and when Mrs. Smythe finished coughing, the nurse helped her lie back on her pillows again. The old woman was pale.

"Are you sure you're up to having visitors?" pressed the nurse.

"Yes, yes, I'm fine," muttered Mrs. Smythe. "Now, you leave me to my company."

"Well—" The nurse hesitated. "All right." She showed the girls a button at the side of Mrs. Smythe's pillow. "Buzz me if you need me." She left the room, and this time closed the door.

The four girls pulled up chairs and sat in a row across from Mrs. Smythe's bed. Mrs. Smythe fingered the folds of her white hospital sheet. Her voice was breathless and light, and the words came out fast, as if she couldn't hold them back. "All right, girls. What do you want to say to me? It's about the dollhouse, of course. I know that. But what has been happening? You must tell me. Oh, I was clever, wasn't I? My brilliant inspiration—after all these years! And it worked—at last! Hasn't it?" She frowned at Zibby. "You do still have the dollhouse, don't you?"

"Oh yes," said Zibby. "I can't seem to get rid of it." She watched Mrs. Smythe carefully to see if that would sound surprising to her.

But it didn't. Mrs. Smythe just smiled. "Yes, yes! Ha-ha-ha! Free at last."

Zibby stared at her in astonishment, then felt the pressure of Jude's hand on her arm. "Well, Mrs. Smythe," Zibby continued, "that's why I'm here. I don't want the house anymore. I want you to take it back."

The old woman smirked, her wrinkled face creasing with what looked to Zibby like mischief. "No refunds, no returns. You signed a contract, my dear."

"I'm not even asking for my money back! I just don't want the dollhouse. It's doing horrible things. We think it's evil—and I bet you knew that when you sold it to me!"

Mrs. Smythe was shaking her head wearily. "Ah, no, my dear. The dollhouse isn't evil. It's a lovely plaything. If anyone's evil, it's Sweet Miss Honeywell."

"Sweet—who?" asked Penny.

"Miss Honeywell?" asked Charlotte.

Zibby and Jude glanced at each other. "Is Miss Honeywell the doll?" Zibby ventured. "The nasty doll in the gray dress?"

"Well, not exactly," answered Mrs. Smythe, and again her voice held that breathy, weary note. "No, Miss Honeywell is only *using* the doll. It became her body, you see, after she didn't have one anymore."

The back of Zibby's neck prickled. "No body?" she asked. "What do you mean?"

Mrs. Smythe just sat there, fingers plucking at her sheet, a rather unpleasant little smile playing at the corners of her mouth. "You have a ghost in your dollhouse, my dear."

Jude spoke up impatiently. "Really, Mrs. Smythe, I think you owe us an explanation! The dollhouse is scaring us, and it's causing all sorts of trouble."

Mrs. Smythe looked surprised. She leaned forward intently. "What kind of trouble?"

Charlotte fingered the edges of the bandage covering her stitches. "Well, people getting hurt, for instance."

"Car accidents," said Penny.

"And falls off cliffs!" cried Jude. "My father might be dead because of the dollhouse!"

Mrs. Smythe looked impressed. "My goodness. Sweet Miss Honeywell must be feeling very powerful indeed. I was sure her malice was directed only at me. I never thought she would reach out to torment others…"

"I don't understand any of this!" said Zibby. "What are you talking about?"

"All right." Mrs. Smythe drew a deep, raspy breath. "I

will tell you everything. But first let me make one thing perfectly clear: I will never take that dollhouse back. Do you understand me?" She peered at Zibby, blue eyes hard. "Never. It is yours. You bought it. I've rid myself of Miss Honeywell—outfoxed her at last!—and I'm not taking her back."

Zibby shivered. Mrs. Smythe looked harmless enough, lying there in her hospital bed, but her breathless voice masked a cold strength. Zibby decided she didn't like Mrs. Smythe much, even if she *was* old and sick. "All right," she agreed. "You don't have to take the house back. But will you at least tell us what's wrong with it—and help us to get rid of it in some way?"

"Shall we burn it?" laughed Mrs. Smythe, breaking off in a coughing fit. She lay back on her pillows and tried to catch her breath. She struggled to sit up again, then peered at Zibby with knowing eyes. "Shall we chop it up with an ax? Drop it into the ocean off a boat? Oh yes, don't look surprised. I've tried all those ways and more—but nothing works, as I think you know."

"But *why?*" demanded Penny. "Why does the house always come back?"

"Miss Honeywell makes it return." And suddenly the spark was gone from Mrs. Smythe's voice and she was just an old, sick woman again. She slumped back against the pillows. "Miss Honeywell is haunting it. It is her revenge. She's been haunting it for decades—since I was a girl. She was my governess, you see. My parents were gone a lot of my childhood, traveling, visiting friends, who knows why? They never took us children along—we hardly knew them. We always stayed home with the servants. I was left in the care of Miss Calliope Honeywell."

"But why should your governess haunt your dollhouse?" asked Charlotte.

Mrs. Smythe gazed up at the ceiling. "A pleasant sounding name—Calliope Honeywell," she said as if she had not heard Charlotte's question. "Ca. Lie. Oh. Pee. A pretty, musical sort of name, don't you think?"

"My real name is Penelope," Penny interjected. "Pen. Ell. Oh. Pee. I hate it."

"Miss Calliope Honeywell came to us when I turned eleven years old," continued Mrs. Smythe, still gazing up at the ceiling as if the story she were about to tell them was written up there in the plaster. "She arrived, she stayed, and in a very short time she made my life a sort of hell."

Zibby settled back in her chair and listened. Jude's shoulder touched Zibby's, and Zibby felt comforted by the touch. Penny and Charlotte leaned forward to hear better.

The breathy voice was low and soft but perfectly clear. "I hated her, you see," Mrs. Smythe said. "I hated her very much indeed. And so I was always thinking up ways to get even with her for the meanness she inflicted on me. I was a great one for practical jokes, anyway, and so I started trying to teach her a few lessons. Maybe everything would have turned out differently if I hadn't felt the need to take revenge on her. It all began simply enough, though, before I'd even been given the dollhouse as a gift. The first practical joke was a simple one. I just clipped a clothespin onto her beaky old nose to stop the terrible snoring…"

The four girls listened, rapt and horrified, as Mrs. Smythe told her story.

CHAPTER 20

PRIMROSE 1919

The days leading up to Miss Honeywell's funeral passed in a blur. Primrose was not able to stop shivering. Immediately after she'd heard Miss Honeywell's voice in her head, Primrose had stopped screaming and started shivering instead. She had run back to the closet, locked herself in, and hidden the key. When Nanny Shanks, having heard the screams, came running into the schoolroom, she found Miss Honeywell—dead—and Primrose crying inside the closet.

Primrose sobbed to Nanny Shanks through the closet door that she'd been locked up for hours, and that she'd heard a terrible crash, and she was frightened, and could she *please* come out now.

Nanny Shanks called for help. She found Miss Honeywell's key ring, but the closet key was not on it. So the menservants had to take the door off at the hinges to get Primrose out. Then Nanny Shanks called the doctor, though anyone could see there was nothing to be done for Miss Honeywell.

Primrose was moved down to the nursery to be near

Nanny Shanks and the twins. She lay in bed that first night after Miss Honeywell died, shivering so hard that Nanny Shanks built up the fire in the bedroom grate and piled on extra blankets. She brought up Primrose's dinner on a tray. But it was impossible for Primrose to eat.

Primrose stayed in bed for two days, until Mama and Papa returned from their trip. They had come home to celebrate Christmas, which was just a week away, arriving to find the house in turmoil and a funeral being planned. Primrose had never been to a funeral, and she certainly did not want to go to this one, but Mama and Nanny Shanks got her out of bed and dressed her in a black dress and shawl, and they all went to the church to say their farewells to Miss Calliope Honeywell.

The only people at the funeral were Primrose's own family, the servants, and Mr. Pope. The minister described how Miss Honeywell had tripped while carrying her water pitcher, striking her head fatally. He spoke about the sadness of accidental death, of a useful life cut short. The service was over after a few prayers and one song, and the minister's assertion that the Lord alone knew when each of us would be called back to the fold.

Only Primrose knew that it wasn't the Lord who had called Miss Honeywell home to heaven. Only she knew about that last practical joke.

It was a lonely feeling, but Primrose wasn't sorry at all that Miss Honeywell was gone forever. She did feel sad for Mr. Pope, hunched over in his black overcoat. He might have been the only person in the whole world who actually had liked Miss Honeywell. She steeled herself to speak to him after the service. "It—it must be terrible," she said, "losing the person you loved and were planning to marry…so suddenly this way…"

Her voice trailed off as he looked at her in surprise. "Well, yes, Primrose," he said soberly. "It *is* terrible that Miss Honeywell should lose her life so suddenly—especially after the other losses she had to bear. Her parents both died of influenza when she was quite young, you know, and then after she raised her younger brother, to whom she was entirely devoted, he went off against her advice and was killed in the war. But you must have misunderstood, child; I had not asked Miss Honeywell to marry me."

"Oh! But she said—well, you did spend a lot of time with her…"

"Young girls have romantic imaginations," said Mr. Pope mildly. "Miss Honeywell and I enjoyed discussing matters of pedagogy—in other words, we talked about teaching, Primrose."

Well, that might be what Mr. Pope wished were true, but Primrose had seen her governess swooning over the tutor and knew she longed to be his bride. That such a marriage would never be possible now was something else Miss Honeywell would consider Primrose's fault.

Later that same day, after the funeral, the shivering finally stopped. Primrose felt warm and comfortable as she played in the nursery with the little twins. She lay in bed that night, snug beneath her quilt, and felt that it was almost too wonderful to be true—that at long last she was really and truly free. Miss Honeywell would never be able to shout at her or lock her in the closet or smack her hands again. Primrose pressed her toes against the hot-water bottle warming her bed and felt a little thrill of pleasure.

But suddenly Primrose heard a bell ringing. And there in the darkness, Primrose's hands began to hurt—the palms stinging just as if they were being struck by Miss Honeywell's ruler. Primrose clenched her hands into fists and pressed down on her mattress. "You can't do anything to me now," she whispered.

Don't be so sure about that, you ungovernable child.

Primrose held her breath. She peered around the small bedroom. The twins and Nanny Shanks slept in rooms nearby; but no one was in this bedroom now but her. And yet...she knew that voice. "Horrid old Honeywell!" Her voice hissed through the darkness. "Get out of here!"

That's Sweet *Miss Honeywell to you, young miss!*

Primrose moaned and ducked beneath the covers.

She heard a noise outside her door—and footsteps coming toward her room—and hardly dared to look. She was afraid to see Miss Honeywell's ghost. But no—it was only Nanny Shanks coming to check on her. "Please stay with me, Nanny, please!" begged Primrose. And Nanny Shanks obligingly settled herself in the chair by Primrose's bed.

"Poor child." Nanny's voice was comforting. "It's been a long, hard day. You go to sleep now. I'll be here."

Primrose closed her eyes and rubbed her hands against the soft blanket until they didn't hurt anymore. She told herself that Miss Honeywell was dead and buried, and there were no such things as ghosts. Miss Honeywell had no power over Primrose anymore. She couldn't do anything to Primrose now. Nothing at all.

But that didn't turn out to be quite true. Primrose learned very soon after Miss Honeywell's death that, indeed, even from beyond the grave, the cruel governess still had some amount of power. She had the power to haunt.

Primrose discovered this terrible truth when her father carried the dollhouse downstairs to the nursery after Christmas. Her parents had given Primrose a dear little grandfather clock for the dollhouse. Primrose opened the latch and swung the front of the house wide and set the new clock in the parlor. Then she gathered all the doll children. "Oh, children," she made the mother doll say in a sorrowful voice, "I'm sorry to tell you your governess has died. It is a shame—but now we must have the funeral."

Primrose moved the dolls into the parlor and laid Old Sourpuss, in her gray dress, on the floor by the piano. "May she rest in peace," intoned the father doll. Primrose tipped the other dolls forward to show that they were bowing their heads in prayer. Then she made the girl doll with the brown braids sit at the piano and play a hymn. All the dolls sang along.

"And now for the burial," said the father doll. And Primrose wrapped Old Sourpuss in the map of Europe, stuffed the bundle into a brown paper bag, and then put on her overcoat. On her way downstairs she met up with Nanny Shanks and the twins, who were planning to ride in the sled and play in the park.

"Come with us, dear Primrose," invited Nanny Shanks. "We were just coming to find you! It's a lovely day. I wouldn't be surprised to find that nice young Oscar Smythe in the park as well."

"Oh, goody," said Primrose, and she skipped down the stairs with them. They left the house and went to fetch the sleds from the back porch. As they passed the trash bins overflowing with Christmas wrappings and ribbons, Primrose plunged the brown paper bag deep down inside and pressed closed the lid. The garbage collectors would come by later in the afternoon, and that would be the end of Old Sourpuss.

But it wasn't. When they returned from the park, Primrose watched with satisfaction from the nursery windows as the garbage collectors trundled the bins to their wagon and tipped the garbage into it. Relieved, Primrose went over to her dollhouse to play. But she had to press her hands against her mouth to hold in her scream—for there in the dollhouse attic sat Old Sourpuss in her gray dress. Primrose reached out her hand, disbelieving her eyes.

How could this doll be here? Had someone somehow found the doll and brought it back?

Then inside her head she heard the bell ringing softly. It sounded like Miss Honeywell's school bell, rung from a great distance. As she picked up the doll, her palms started stinging, and she heard Miss Honeywell's deceptively soft voice in her head again: *You've robbed me of my life, my job, and my one true love! And you will pay for it, young miss. Oh, yes, you will pay.*

"Mr. Pope never planned to marry you—and who would? And you *can't* hurt me," Primrose gasped, dropping the doll and clasping her smarting hands together behind her back. "You're dead and gone!"

Dead—yes, thanks to you. But gone? Oh, no, my dear. Two can play at practical jokes, and I shall teach you to mind if it takes me forever and ever…until the end of your days.

CHAPTER 21

"Till the end of my days!" chortled Mrs. Smythe. "That's what she said! But *I'm* the one having the last laugh, aren't I? Finally *I've* won!" She beamed at Zibby. "I tried all my life to get rid of that old dollhouse and the doll, but they always returned. What luck that the other week I had a sudden inspiration to take the house to the miniatures convention in Columbus. Just out of the blue I decided to go— shortly before I became so ill. And there you were—just ready to buy the house!"

"Out of the blue?" murmured Zibby. "That's how it was with me, too. Out of the blue I ended up buying a dollhouse I hadn't been planning to buy at all." Something was tickling the back of her mind, some understanding she couldn't quite pin down. She tried to concentrate, but it slipped away.

"You paid for the house and signed the contract, and that's why Miss Honeywell can't come back to me." Mrs. Smythe smiled. "You've got her now, and I say good riddance!" She turned her head feebly on the pillow. "What a relief, after all these years! She has been nothing but bad news. She ruined my childhood as best she could when she was alive, and even after death continued to plague me. It was because of her that I was deprived of playing with my beautiful dollhouse. I'll never forgive her for that—or for anything else!"

"Why couldn't you play with the house after she'd died?" asked Jude.

"It was too dangerous," the old woman replied. "Sweet Miss Honeywell's ghost made it impossible. Whatever I played came out wrong. If I played that the doll children went sledding in the park—then my real baby brother and sister were hurt when their sled tipped over. If I played that the doll parents came home from a trip with lots of gifts, my own real parents came home to find that all their luggage— with the gifts they were bringing to us inside—had been stolen. Once I played that the nanny doll baked cookies for a lovely dollhouse tea party, but then my real Nanny Shanks caught her apron on fire and ended up in the hospital. Old Sourpuss was using that dollhouse to keep control of me, to show me her power. So I never played with the house again."

"It's exactly the same sorts of things that have been happening to us," said Jude.

"Well, I am sorry about that," admitted Mrs. Smythe. "But Miss Honeywell likes to be in charge. You should lock up the house so she can't bother you."

Penny was frowning. "So you mean that Zibby has paid all her money for a dollhouse she can't even play with? I think it was really *mean* of you to sell her the house, knowing all along that the ghost was in there!"

"Now, my dear, I had no reason to think Miss Honeywell would bother anyone else. It's *me* she has a grudge against, after all. I thought that if the house found a new owner, she'd just go away—to wherever people like her go when they die. It isn't likely to be heaven, though, is it?"

"Well, she hasn't gone anywhere," said Zibby fiercely. "She's inside the doll, and she's making trouble for us just as much as she ever did for you."

Charlotte nodded in agreement. "And we never even did anything to her. *You* did."

Mrs. Smythe shook her head weakly on her pillow, smiling a sly sort of smile. "No, no, I didn't do a thing to her! Not a thing. That was just a prank gone wrong, that's all. She was always a horrid woman. And she certainly did take her revenge on me, so don't you think that makes us even? Wherever I went, all my life, that dollhouse has come, too. I daresay you'll soon see for yourself."

"What do you mean?" asked Zibby fiercely.

"On New Year's Eve after Miss Honeywell died, I covered my tracks." Mrs. Smythe winked at Zibby. "I dropped that closet key into the river when Nanny Shanks took us for a walk. And that same night, I dragged the dollhouse down to the backyard and smashed it to pieces with a sledgehammer. I took that governess doll and smashed its porcelain head. I ground the china to dust under my boot. Then I shredded the body to pieces with scissors, and I burned all the scraps in the grate in my bedroom. It felt wonderful—liberating!—to destroy everything. And yet, what do you know? When I woke up on New Year's Day, that dollhouse was right back in my bedroom. Without a scratch on it, and the doll was sitting on the roof smirking at me, believe it or not."

"Oh, I believe it," said Zibby wryly.

"When I was twelve I went away to boarding school," whispered Mrs. Smythe. She lifted her head off the pillow briefly, then let it fall back. "I was happy to go. I thought that at last I'd be rid of the dollhouse. But no. Even there, she found me. The house appeared in my room at school, and I had a devil of a time explaining to the headmistress where it had come from. We weren't allowed to have toys in our rooms, but the dollhouse wouldn't stay away. My roommates thought it was a wonderful joke I was playing on the headmistress, but of course it wasn't. Finally I hid the house in the closet, behind my dresses."

She winked at the girls, a slow flicker. "And even when I married, the dollhouse came along on my honeymoon trip to Europe. Poor, dear Oscar—dear Mr. Smythe—he always humored me, though I never told him the story." A weak smile flickered on the woman's dry lips. "The dollhouse has been an unpleasant reminder of my last practical joke all these years. Though I couldn't destroy it, I tried several times to *give* it away—but nothing worked. Then at last, as I told you, I had an inspiration to *sell* it at the miniatures show. All of a sudden."

"And that's where I came in," said Zibby slowly. "But I wonder why Miss Honeywell would want to stay with me?"

"Oh, I don't think she wanted to stay with you," Mrs. Smythe corrected her calmly. "She *had* to, I believe, because I made you sign the contract. That's what did the trick." Her cool blue gaze was steady. "You were just in the right place at the right time to suit my purposes."

Zibby sat silently, trying to figure it all out.

"One thing's been bothering me," Jude said suddenly. "Why did you choose to sell the dollhouse for such a low price, when it's worth so much more? I mean, why that odd amount—what was it, Zibby?"

"Exactly one hundred eighty-six dollars and seventy-three cents," said Zibby. "Exactly what I had, down to the last penny."

Mrs. Smythe shrugged. "I don't know. It just seemed a good price, all of a sudden."

All of a sudden. Zibby frowned. A lot of things seemed to have happened all of a sudden. "But that's the point," she said slowly. "How could you know *to the last penny* the amount I had in my pocket that day? I didn't even know myself that I had the extra change."

Mrs. Smythe shook her head. "Of course I didn't know. It was just a lucky coincidence."

Jude gazed at Zibby. "I don't think coincidences happen like that," she said. "*Someone* must have known."

Again, the niggling sense of something just beyond her understanding tickled Zibby's mind. A puzzle piece not yet in place.

Penny chimed in, breathless. "Someone?"

And then Zibby knew. "Miss Honeywell!"

Mrs. Smythe laughed gaily. "Nonsense! Why would Miss Honeywell *choose* to allow the dollhouse to change owners after all this time? No, no, *I* was the clever one that day. I've had the last laugh in the end."

In the end. Distantly Zibby heard a bell ringing. It was Miss Honeywell's school bell, ringing again inside her head. With the ringing of the bell came a new clarity, as if the governess's unseen hand had dropped the last piece of the puzzle into place.

The last laugh? Zibby stared at Mrs. Smythe, lying so weakly there in her hospital bed, and then the terrible truth dawned. Zibby shook her head. "I don't think so," she murmured. "I'm afraid you haven't had the last laugh after all."

"No?"

"No. I don't think it was chance at all that you suddenly decided to sell the house at the miniatures convention. I think Miss Honeywell *made* you go. I think she *wanted* you to sell the house this time because she knew it was, well, time for a new owner. I think she chose me herself. A woman wearing a gray dress led me toward the dollhouse! A ghost could know exactly how much money I had—*you* couldn't, but *she* could. It wasn't anything to do with your sales contract, Mrs. Smythe. Miss Honeywell is haunting me now because she wants power."

"Now, why would she want a change after all these years?" queried Mrs. Smythe. "She vowed to be with me always—till the end of my days, she said, and—"

Mrs. Smythe broke off, staring at Zibby in shocked realization. Then she started coughing, gasping for breath between each cough. Her pale face turned alarmingly red. Jude pressed the call button, and the nurse came rushing in from the hallway. She helped Mrs. Smythe lean forward, tapping her gently between the shoulder blades. At last the coughing subsided. The nurse lowered Mrs. Smythe back onto her pillows.

Zibby watched as Mrs. Smythe slumped sideways on the bed. A little fleck of foam at the corner of her open mouth slid slowly down her chin. The nurse wiped her face with a cloth.

Mrs. Smythe's voice came out as a moan. "You mean—you mean you think Miss Honeywell knows I don't have long—is that it?"

Zibby glanced at the nurse, then nodded soberly. "That would explain why I found myself wanting to buy the dollhouse—all of a sudden—when I'd been planning to buy Rollerblades. It would explain why I felt I was looking for something, and why I started following that woman in the long gray dress, and why a dollhouse that should cost about a thousand dollars cost just exactly the amount of money I had that day. Miss Honeywell was manipulating both of us. She made you go to the miniatures convention, out of the blue. She made you price the house at exactly the amount I had in my pocket. She made me long to buy it—out of the blue."

"She wanted you." Mrs. Smythe's voice was only a whisper now. "Because she knew she wouldn't have me much longer. She always needed to be in charge of someone, you see. First she had her brother, Lester, to raise. Then, after he died, she came to be my governess. Oh, she talked about him all the time—said Lester wouldn't have died in the war if he'd only learned to mind her. She was determined to teach *me* to obey her, and then even when she was dead, she couldn't let go of me. Now she's turned to you." The nurse hovered over her, impatient for the girls to leave. "I suspect she thought *you* were in need of governing. She would look for a child who was weak."

"Weak?" Jude was bristling. "Zibby's healthy and strong."

"I mean emotionally weak, my dear. In turmoil, perhaps. Sad about something, maybe. Sweet Miss Honeywell could always find a person's weak spots and use them to her advantage. And how was your behavior that day? She was always on the lookout for unmannerly behavior."

Charlotte cleared her throat. "You were sort of having a tantrum, Zib," she said quietly. "You were kicking the wall…"

And Zibby recalled how she had been feeling on her birthday. Sad and bereft because Amy had just moved. Angry because Nell wanted to look at dollhouses instead of taking her to Sportsmart as promised. Anxious about the upcoming wedding and the prospect of having Laura-Jane for a stepsister. Maybe she had been a little weak that day, Zibby admitted to herself. And a little unmannerly. *Weak and unmannerly enough, anyway, for Miss Honeywell to choose me for her new little girl.*

The nurse motioned for the girls to leave. Zibby reached out impulsively and squeezed Mrs. Smythe's gnarled hand where it lay atop the sheet. There didn't seem to be anything left to say. But Mrs. Smythe spoke faintly: "I guess the joke's on me."

CHAPTER 22

Zibby lay in bed that night thinking about the girl who had killed her governess so many years ago. She thought about the angry and determined Miss Calliope Honeywell, whose need to wield power and exact revenge had reached out to Primrose Parson Smythe from beyond the grave.

It was hard to believe that things like this could really happen. Zibby's parents had always scoffed at the notion of ghosts. But Zibby had been seeing Miss Honeywell's power in action ever since her birthday. Ever since she'd bought the dollhouse.

Ever since she had been *forced* to buy the dollhouse.

Miss Honeywell, knowing that Primrose Parson was old and sick, couldn't bear the thought of giving up her power. So she had chosen a new child to govern: Zibby herself. How *dare* she? Zibby was angry now as well as scared.

She figured that all the dollhouse play resulted in trouble because Miss Honeywell wanted to show Zibby her strength. Miss Honeywell didn't care who she hurt. And so Charlotte and Amy and Dr. Cummings and Jude's parents all suffered after somebody played with the dollhouse. And also Nell. Especially Nell.

Zibby's strongest fear was for her mom. School would be starting in two more days and Zibby would be gone for hours—hours in which Nell would be unprotected. And then there was the upcoming wedding. What would happen to Nell at the wedding?

But if Miss Honeywell thought she could haunt Zibby the way she had been haunting Primrose Parson all those years, she could just think again. "I believe you're powerful," Zibby said aloud in the darkness of her bedroom. "You don't have to prove it to me anymore!"

How could Zibby bear to live the way Primrose had— always being followed by Miss Honeywell? She couldn't and wouldn't—that was the easy answer. But how to stop this governess who was so bent on wielding power from beyond the grave?

Finally Zibby slept, and of course she had the dream. It didn't even frighten her quite as much because she'd fully expected it. Even in sleep she was aware that this nightmare had to be tied to Miss Honeywell. *I won't let you have power over me,* she thought, challenging the governess even while still dreaming. *I won't let you win.*

In the morning Zibby jumped out of bed and hurried to find her mom. Ned had left early for work and he'd taken his two kids with him, thank goodness, but Zibby didn't want Nell left alone for long. Nell sat at the breakfast table with her red-gold hair pulled carelessly back in a shining ponytail. She wore a loose, light blue T-shirt and jeans. The newspaper was open on the table and Nell held a mug of coffee, but she was not reading the paper and her coffee went untouched as she stared off into space with a dreamy smile on her lips.

"Mom, I hate to say it, but you look like somebody in love!" Zibby greeted her. *Nothing must happen to hurt Mom,* she thought desperately. She would be extra-vigilant now that she knew about Miss Honeywell.

"Oh, I am." Nell grinned and put down her mug. "Believe me, I am. My headache is gone and the sun is shining, and I feel I've been waiting to marry Ned all my life. I've been in love with Ned since we were teenagers."

Zibby poured herself a glass of orange juice. "But didn't you ever love Dad?" she asked hesitantly. "I mean, you say you always loved Ned—so why didn't you marry him in the first place? Why did you marry Dad instead?"

"Oh, honey," said Nell, "I did love your dad. I wouldn't have married him if I hadn't. And I still think he is a very fine man with many wonderful qualities. I wish you would open your eyes to them." Zibby scowled at her, and Nell sighed. "Well, anyway, I'd known Ned forever—he was my boyfriend all through high school, as you know. But we'd never really dated anyone else—either of us. So when I went off to college and met your dad, he was exciting and different. He was older, and I felt more grown-up when I was with him than I did with Ned. Your dad is a good man, Zibby. He's very reliable and organized and methodical and always very busy, and always very...practical."

"You make Dad sound boring," Zibby pointed out.

"No—not exactly boring. Just very earnest." Nell smiled. "Ned's not so serious. He and I can laugh together. He makes me feel that life is full of wonder. He doesn't have half the energy for work that your dad does, Zibby; he's not *driven* that way. Yet I know we'll be happy, and I'm lucky that we found each other again when we were both free to come together." She reached out and touched Zibby's hand. "You know, I'm glad your dad found his Sofia. Maybe they're as perfect for each other as Ned and I are. I really think you should go visit Italy soon to check it out. Check *them* out."

Zibby felt strangely happy and sad mixed together, but she shook her head. Her dad was a traitor. "Maybe in about fifty years," she said. She drained her orange juice at the same time Nell drained the last of her coffee, and they both set the mug and glass down on the table at the same moment. Zibby laughed, then reached out to grab her mom's wrist. "Hey, look! Your burn's all healed! That's *incredibly* fast. Yesterday it was still all red and sore looking."

Nell looked at her wrist in surprise. "Strange. But lucky—I'll look good in my wedding pictures. And speaking of which, Linnea will be here in a minute. We're going to the photographer's studio to discuss things. I'd better get ready!" She dashed out of the room, leaving Zibby to wash up the breakfast dishes.

As Zibby was wiping the counters, the telephone rang. It was Jude, and her excited jabbering was unintelligible at first. "Calm down, calm down," said Zibby. "I can't understand a word you're saying."

"Oh, Zibby, he's okay, my dad's okay! We just had a call from my mom, in Kenya—right when Penny and I were eating breakfast. My mom says that Dad was found lying trapped in the bottom of a gorge. He was sure that he'd broken both legs, because he was pinned under a huge boulder, but when the rescue party got him out, he could walk! Can you believe it?" Jude's voice trembled. "Oh, Zibby, it's amazing—he didn't even have any water or food left. Another day or two and he would have died. He's dehydrated now, and very weak, and he has a gigantic bump on the head, but he's going to be just fine!"

"Wow!" cried Zibby, gladness flooding her. "This is *super.*"

"My grandparents say it's a miracle, and Penny is dancing around the house for joy. Mom says that since Dad's going to be okay, they're going to stay on and get back to their work with the new hospital, but they'll come home for Christmas for sure. I'm just so excited, I don't even care that Christmas is still months away. Just as long as my dad's safe. That's all that matters."

Zibby agreed. She talked to Penny, too, then asked both girls to come over after breakfast. She hung up and sat at the table with a smile on her face, happy and relieved.

A tapping on the kitchen door made her jump. She ran to the door, and there was Charlotte with Aunt Linnea. Charlotte looked different, but it took a second before Zibby realized that the bandage on her forehead was gone.

"Your head," Zibby said, opening the screen door for her cousin and aunt.

"I know," said Charlotte, touching her head in wonderment. "Isn't it amazing?" She twirled around the kitchen. "As soon as I woke up, the bandage just sort of suddenly dropped off. And the gash is so much better, my mom couldn't believe it."

"I can't!" said Aunt Linnea with a smile. "It's amazing how fast she healed. As soon as the stitches are out, the scar will hardly show." Charlotte pirouetted around the kitchen.

"That *is* amazing," said Zibby slowly. "In fact, this seems to be the day for good news." Zibby told them about Mac Jefferson's rescue in Kenya.

Nell came downstairs then, and she and Aunt Linnea left to organize some further details about the wedding. After they'd driven off in Aunt Linnea's van, Zibby sank down into a chair at the kitchen table. "All this good luck— so suddenly... it's a little bit strange, don't you think?" She looked at Charlotte. "I mean, even the fact that your head is nearly healed, and my mom's burn is gone..."

Charlotte considered this. "Too good to be true, you mean?"

The phone rang again before Zibby could answer, and it was, astonishingly, more good news. Amy was calling to say that her dad was out of the hospital early. He was walking a little already, and his leg was nearly as good as new, she reported. He still had his cast on but didn't need to lie in traction anymore. "The doctors say he can come home!" She laughed. "And he's promised we'll drive down for a visit just after Thanksgiving. Will that be all right?"

Zibby assured her it would be wonderful. She hung up and turned to Charlotte. "Remember what Jude said to Mrs. Smythe about coincidences not just happening? Well, this is definitely not coincidence, either, I bet." She told her cousin about Amy's dad. "Isn't it just too weird that everything is turning out okay—all at once?"

Charlotte nodded. "It's got to be something to do with

Miss Honeywell, don't you think? Maybe she's sorry about all the trouble she's been causing."

"Somehow I doubt it." Zibby frowned. Miss Honeywell did not seem the type to start feeling sorry, all of a sudden, or ever, about anything.

Zibby reached for the phone. "I'm going to call Mrs. Smythe at the hospital," she told Charlotte. "I think she'd like to know that all the trouble Miss Honeywell caused is getting fixed."

When the receptionist answered, Zibby asked to speak to the head nurse in intensive care. She was connected promptly. But when she asked for Mrs. Smythe, there was a silence.

"Are you one of the children who visited her yesterday?"

"Yes," said Zibby. "I just wanted to talk to her for a minute."

"Well, I'm afraid that won't be possible," the nurse said slowly.

"You mean she's feeling worse?"

There was a silence, and then the nurse's voice came over the line, gentle and solemn. "I'm afraid that Mrs. Smythe passed away very early this morning."

"Passed away?" yelped Zibby, and Charlotte gasped. "You mean she *died*?"

"Yes, dear. I'm sorry, but her heart was very weak."

"Did we—I mean, did our visit somehow—" Zibby could barely ask the question.

The nurse's voice was firm and reassuring. "Absolutely not. Mrs. Smythe was very old, and her heart was just plain worn out. The doctors knew she didn't have long to live. She knew this herself. It was only a matter of time. I'm sure your visit made her last hours more pleasant; she didn't have any family left, you know—except for her quadruplet granddaughters!"

Zibby tried to laugh but couldn't. "Well, I just hope you're right."

"It's hard when a friend dies," said the nurse kindly. And Zibby agreed, although Primrose Parson Smythe had not been a friend, not exactly.

She set down the phone and sat staring silently at Charlotte for a long minute. "Well," she said, "so much for good news." She explained what the nurse had told her.

"Dead," said Charlotte. "That's sad, isn't it? So—is it over now, you think? Everything with the dollhouse?"

"Well, it must be," replied Zibby. "That must be why all these good things are happening so fast. Miss Honeywell has got her final revenge, and Primrose is dead, and now it's all over. End of story." Zibby felt relieved that she would not have to figure out how to outwit the nasty governess after all. If Miss Honeywell's revenge ended with Primrose's death, she would not need a new girl to govern after all. So—good news again.

"I think we should phone Jude and Penny and tell them what's happened," Charlotte said.

"They'll be over here in just a few minutes," Zibby told her, and sure enough, the Jefferson girls arrived at the back door a moment later. They all went up to Zibby's bedroom and sank down in front of the dollhouse.

How frightened Zibby had been last night—frightened and angry. But now that Mrs. Smythe was dead, there would be no more haunting. She reached out to unlatch the house. It swung open and Zibby smiled. Things that had been stuck, broken, ruined, whatever, were now going to go smoothly. Primrose Parson Smythe was dead, and Miss Honeywell could rest in peace, and Nell would be safe now, too. Zibby felt giddy with relief.

"Why is this little doll with the brown braids sitting on the roof?" asked Jude, reaching over to pick it up. She set the doll on the little couch in the parlor.

"I don't know," said Zibby. "I left the house locked up, with all the dolls inside—including the governess." Zibby pointed to the gray-dressed figure lying facedown in the attic room. "Old Sourpuss herself."

A little sound from the dollhouse made them all stiffen. It was a small rustling sound, the sort of sound Zibby had heard before and attributed to mice. She didn't believe in mice now. She believed in ghosts. Did the other girls feel the sudden weirdness—the *tension*—in the air? Her relief of a moment before evaporated.

Penny pressed against Zibby's shoulder. The beads at the ends of her many braids clicked comfortingly.

"I heard something," she whispered. "Did you?"

"Yes," Zibby whispered back.

"I heard it, too," moaned Charlotte. She inched backward, away from the dollhouse.

Jude's lips were pressed tight.

Zibby reached out and flicked the gray-gowned doll with her finger. "Miss Honeywell?"

A giggle. A rustle of petticoats. All in Zibby's head? Could the others hear it, too? "Did you hear that?" she asked Jude.

Jude shook her head. "No, but there's a sort of chill..."

"I feel it," whispered Zibby. Then she heard it, what she had been fearing—and almost waiting for at the same time. A voice in her head.

I'm here now. I want to stay with you.

A voice, high and light. Different from the other voice Zibby had heard in her head. The rustling sound came again and Zibby saw the girl doll shiver. Holding her breath, Zibby slowly reached out for the little doll. It seemed to shift under her fingers. She nearly dropped it.

Silly girl! Don't you recognize me?

"Listen," Zibby said in a shaky voice. "Miss Honeywell, you don't need to haunt us now. Primrose is gone. She's dead—just like you. You've had your revenge on her. And I don't need a governess, so go away!"

"What are you talking about, Zibby?" shrieked Penny.

"You mean you didn't hear that?" cried Zibby. "Did you hear what she said?"

"What who said?" demanded Penny.

"We didn't hear anything but what *you* said," Jude murmured. "Zib, what's going on?"

"She asked if I recognized her."

"*Who* asked?" demanded Charlotte. "We didn't hear anything!"

"Who are you?" breathed Zibby, bending over the little doll. "Who?"

Silky laughter filled Zibby's head. *Come on, take a guess. Isn't this a good joke?*

"Mrs. Smythe?" Zibby asked wildly. "Primrose Parson? But—you can't be. I mean, we just saw you in the hospital. I mean, you're dead now!"

That's right, but I don't want to be dead. I want to be a girl again.

"Oh no. No way! Not in *my* dollhouse," said Zibby.

"Who are you talking to? What are you saying those things for, Zibby?" shouted Charlotte. "You are totally freaking us out!"

"*Sshh!*" hissed Jude. "I think she's hearing something. Someone." Jude reached out for Zibby's hand and held it.

"Well, I don't hear anything," cried Charlotte. She jumped off the bed. "I'm going home."

"Me, too," whimpered Penny. She stared at Zibby, who was hunched over the little girl doll, and at Jude, who was holding Zibby's hand tight. "Right now!"

"No, wait," said Jude, still holding on to Zibby. "Primrose?" She addressed the little doll.

That's my name, don't wear it out.

"I can hear her, Zibby!" shouted Jude. "Listen, you guys, hold hands with Zibby. She's in Zibby's head, but if you're touching Zibby, you can hear her, too!"

Charlotte grabbed Zibby's shoulder. Penny took hold of Jude's hand, then linked arms with Charlotte. The four girls sat in a cluster in front of the dollhouse with the little girl doll on Zibby's lap.

Zibby couldn't believe any of this was happening. She had come back to her dollhouse ready to celebrate that Miss Honeywell was gone, and instead found another ghost in residence. She could feel Charlotte's fingers jabbing into her shoulder. She could feel Jude's hand sweating in her own. She could see Penny's trembling. Zibby took a deep breath and spoke to the ghost of Primrose Parson. "I'll lock up the house just as you did, and I'll never open it again," she threatened. "I don't want *any* ghosts around here—not Miss Honeywell, and not you."

But that's not fair, whined the voice of Primrose Parson. *Miss Honeywell is the one who played all the mean tricks. I'm the one who made everything all right again. I've been trying all morning to undo her mischief. You girls should be thanking me!*

Penny trembled harder. "I can hear her right in my head!"

Zibby squeezed Jude's hand. Then she addressed the small doll on her lap. "What do you mean you've been making things all right again, Primrose?" She couldn't imagine calling the doll Mrs. Smythe. Mrs. Smythe was the old woman in the hospital. This—the voice, anyway—was clearly a girl about their own age.

Peals of girlish laughter. She *burned your mother's arm; I healed it! Same with this girl here—Charlotte. Her head is all better now, isn't it? That's thanks to me. And your friend and her father are coming to visit, right? And the man in Africa— well, that was my biggest accomplishment!* She *left him for dead—but now he's going to be fine. I saved him!*

"Thank you so much," said Jude fervently.

It's hard, summoning power without a body, the little voice mused. *I don't know how Miss Honeywell has managed for so many years. I find it to be very draining. But then, of course, I'm just learning. I daresay with practice I'll be as powerful as Miss Honeywell herself—no, even more powerful! Soon I'll be able to move objects, too—and then who knows what else I'll be able to do? Once I learn how to siphon her power, I shall get rid of Old Sourpuss once and for all.*

That will be Sweet *Miss Honeywell to you, young miss.*

Now there seemed to be two voices in Zibby's head and a cold prickle under her shoulder blades. The other girls gasped. Zibby drew a deep breath. "Primrose?"

You won't get rid of me so easily. I'm not finished with any of you yet.

It was Miss Honeywell's voice. Not high-pitched and girlish, but hard. If Miss Honeywell was still around, then what did that mean for Nell? Fear made Zibby bold. "Look, you're both dead now," she shouted, "so it's got to be finished! Go away!"

You think things are over? asked the lower, menacing voice. *You have no idea. There's quite a bit of unfinished business, don't you think, Miss Primrose Parson? You've sapped my strength, you think—well, so you have, for now! But I'll be back, stronger than before.*

You think that scares me? mocked Primrose's reedy, high-pitched voice.

Perhaps not. But it should. And then the cold prickle left Zibby, and she knew Miss Honeywell had gone. For now.

"I'm scared," said Penny in a small voice. "They both scare me. Let's get out of here."

"We're going home," agreed Jude. "You can come, too, Zibby and Charlotte."

Zibby put the little doll with brown braids back in the house. Her mind was whirling with what had just happened. Voices in her head? Battling ghosts?

Wait! Primrose's reedy voice spoke again in Zibby's head. Jude tightened her grip on Zibby; she heard it, too. Penny and Charlotte linked arms with Zibby and Jude so they could also hear.

Miss Honeywell is gone for now, said Primrose in Zibby's head. *But it's strange—there's a feeling of someone else in the dollhouse.*

"What do you mean?" Zibby began cautiously.

I can sense that I'm not alone here. There are other...presences.

Zibby shivered. She swung the house closed. Primrose Parson's voice skittered around in Zibby's head. *Wait—come back! I want company! I'm new at this ghostly stuff.*

"Then don't be a ghost," said Jude. "Go on—to wherever people go when they die. Go to heaven and leave us alone."

But I never had much of a chance to play with my dollhouse, you know. Listen, we can have fun. Primrose's voice became wheedling. It seemed as long as Zibby was touching the dollhouse or the doll she could hear the ghost. *We'll be friends. You'll like having me here! But I want you to fix up the house...fix it up the way it should have been all these years, with all the nice furniture and some new wallpaper. And get rid of the bad smell.*

"What bad smell?" asked Penny. "I don't smell anything."

The smell of smoke, Primrose told them. *Smoke—and fire.*

"That's like my dollhouse dream," Penny said. "Smoke and fire..."

Charlotte pulled away from the group. "Ugh. I don't want to hear any more. It was bad enough when there was Miss Honeywell to worry about. I don't like this—this Primrose. Having a voice in my head is creepy." She looked pale. "Let's go."

Zibby stepped away from the dollhouse. She was looking at Penny soberly. "What was that you just said, Penny? What did you say about your dream?"

Penny dropped hands and moved back from the other girls. "It's just a dream I've had twice now. A nightmare, really. About a dollhouse on fire. And an awful hand reaching out of the flames—a hand wearing a black glove."

CHAPTER 23

"But—you can't have dreamed about that. That's my dream!" Zibby stared at Penny with round, frightened eyes. Vengeful governesses, haunted dollhouses, dangerous attacks on her family and friends, voices inside her head— all this was enough to drive anyone over the edge; still, Zibby had felt she was handling it bravely enough. But this shared dream made her aware there was something else going on.

It was another thing that *just didn't happen*—and yet was happening anyway.

"What are you talking about?" Jude asked. "Tell us about these dreams."

Quickly Zibby told them. Then she leaned toward Penny. "Do you remember when you first had the dream?" she asked.

Penny nodded. "It was that first day I met you. And then again last night."

Charlotte looked nervous. "But people just don't have the same dreams."

"People don't have ghosts talking to them in their heads, either," said Zibby. "But *we* do.

"I think Zibby and Penny must have had a *similar* sort of dream," said practical Jude.

"Brought on by all this stuff with the dollhouse."

"But what could the dream have to do with the dollhouse?" asked Charlotte, frowning.

"Maybe it's like a prophecy," said Penny brightly. "Maybe it means the dollhouse is going to burn down, and then we'll be rid of it—and rid of Primrose and Miss Honeywell, too."

If only it could be that easy, thought Zibby. But she didn't believe it for a moment.

THE JEFFERSON GIRLS went home at dinnertime. Aunt Linnea came to pick up Charlotte. Then Ned arrived with his kids. Both Laura-Jane and Brady hurried straight up to their new attic rooms, but Zibby settled into a kitchen chair and listened to her mom and Ned chat about the wedding photographer, the deadlines at the *Gazette,* and their honeymoon plans. "Short but sweet," Nell said about the honeymoon, but Zibby fretted silently. Would her mom be safe on a trip—even a short trip? Would Miss Honeywell strike then—or at the wedding itself?

When Ned left the room, Zibby stayed with Nell and started chopping vegetables for soup. She wondered if she could explain to her mom all that was going on. How was it possible they could be in the same room and Nell didn't notice how much was wrong?

"Mom?"

"Hmm?" Nell's voice was dreamy. "Here, add a few sprigs of rosemary to the pot."

There was no easy way to start. Just plunge in. "You know my dollhouse?"

"What about it?"

"There are ghosts in it." Zibby braced herself, ready to start telling her story from the very beginning. But Nell just laughed.

"The Haunted Dollhouse—that's a good game," she said approvingly. "Original. When Linnea and I were kids, our dollhouse dolls just had very ordinary, normal lives— though sometimes we threw in a kidnapping or a mystery to solve." She handed Zibby a pile of place mats. "And you're lucky, having Jude and Penny and Charlotte interested in the dollhouse, too. You girls can really get some good games going together. And speaking of the girls, Zib—how about asking Laura-Jane to play with you, too? I don't want her feeling lonely while she's living here with us."

Zibby sighed. It was no use. She took the place mats and set the dinner table. She made a big salad, and her mom baked homemade croutons. Normally she would enjoy spending this time with Nell, chatting, but now everything seemed unimportant with Miss Honeywell still at large.

"And now there's Primrose, too," she muttered to herself. "Can't forget Primrose."

Nell looked at her curiously, then asked her to call the other kids down for the meal. Reluctantly Zibby left the kitchen and climbed the stairs in the hallway. "Brady!" she shouted. "Laura-Jane!" She glanced quickly into her own bedroom on the way down just to be certain Brady and

Laura-Jane weren't messing with the dollhouse. But her room was empty, and the dollhouse appeared to be as she'd left it. Closed up. Latched.

She yelled up the narrow stairs to the attic. "Come to dinner!"

Brady clattered down right away. Laura-Jane followed more slowly, her face strangely pale. "Do you feel all right, honey?" asked Ned when he saw her.

"I don't like it here," she told him angrily. "I don't see why I can't stay at one of my friends' houses till Mom gets back from her trip."

That sounded like a fine idea to Zibby. "I think she should be allowed to," Zibby said.

Laura-Jane glanced at her in surprise.

"Look, girls," Ned said wearily, sitting down and picking up his soup spoon, "I wish you would try to make an effort with each other."

"It's not about Zibby," muttered Laura-Jane. "Or even Nell. It's this house. Things are weird here."

"*You're* the weird thing here," Brady said, then shrieked as his sister kicked him under the table.

"Kids!" Ned admonished them. The doorbell rang and Brady raced to answer it.

"It's some guy wanting our money!" he called back from the front hall. "He says he knows Zibby!"

Zibby went to the front door. The boy wanting money was Scott Guerrero, a kid in her class at school, who was also their newspaper delivery boy. He handed her the bill. "Your money or your life," he told her. "It's twelve dollars and fifty cents."

"I guess my life's worth twelve-fifty," she said. She'd

known Scott since kindergarten and liked him most of the time. "Hold on while I go see if my mom agrees."

Nell told Zibby to take the cash from her wallet. "My purse is on the table in the hall." Zibby found the purse and rummaged around. But there was no wallet inside. She walked back to the kitchen to report this. Nell looked perplexed and went upstairs to check in her desk. Still no wallet. So Ned opened his own wallet and paid for the newspaper.

"Hey—maybe you guys will get the *Gazette* for free now that Ned Shimizu is your stepfather," Scott Guerrero told Zibby.

"I don't think it works that way," she replied. "And he's not really my stepfather—yet. The wedding is next week. But, anyway, see you at school."

"Only two more days!" he said, and made a gagging sound. "Can you believe how fast vacation went?" As he bounded down the porch steps, Zibby returned to the dinner table. Nell was looking puzzled.

"I'm sure I had my wallet today," she was saying slowly. "I paid the photographer's first installment, so I had to have it then. And I went to the grocery store—I know I had it then, too. Maybe it fell out in the car. I'll look after we eat."

Laura-Jane squirmed in her chair. "May I please be excused?"

"You haven't eaten much," Ned pointed out.

"I'm not hungry." She pushed back her chair and left the room.

"I'll help you search in the car," Brady offered, and after everyone had finished eating, he and Nell and Ned went outside while Zibby stacked the soup bowls in the dishwasher.

Laura-Jane should be helping with chores if she's going to live here, Zibby thought resentfully. *But she'd probably drop the dishes on purpose, just to be mean.*

Nell, Ned, and Brady came inside again, all looking glum. "No sign of it," said Nell.

"I bet robbers stole it!" said Brady. "The same ones who came in here and wrecked the food and stuff."

"Was there a lot of money in your wallet, Mom?" asked Zibby sympathetically.

"Oh—only about twenty dollars in cash, I think, and some change," Nell answered. "But of course there's my driver's license and credit cards—and the wallet itself. It was the one you gave me, honey, and I treasure it."

"Don't worry, Mom. I'll find you a new one," Zibby replied staunchly. But she was sorry that particular wallet was lost. She had saved her money and chosen it carefully. It was supple black leather with top stitching in a golden thread. The stitching formed a pattern of daisies, the flower symbol of DaisyCakes. Zibby had been so excited when she'd seen it by chance at a department store in Columbus that she'd asked the clerk to hold it for her until she could return with her money. It was the perfect gift for Nell, and now it was gone.

After the dinner dishes were washed and put away, Ned and Nell brought out a jigsaw puzzle and sat at the dining-room table together. Doing puzzles was something Zibby used to do with her mom and dad, and it felt strange to see Ned there in the place where her own dad used to sit, searching for the corner pieces.

"Come on, Zib—help us out," Nell invited her.

Zibby hesitated.

"But would you first go up and ask Laura-Jane and Brady if they'll join us?" Ned asked. "Brady is especially good at puzzles."

Laura-Jane was not going to want to do a puzzle with anybody, Zibby could almost guarantee it. But she shrugged. "Sure, I'll ask."

Zibby headed up the stairs. She couldn't help glancing at her closed bedroom door. Should she check what was happening in the dollhouse? Drawing in a resolute breath, she continued up the attic stairs. "Brady!" she called. "Laura-Jane!" Brady's door was open. He was sitting on the colorful rag rug, surrounded by Legos. "Hey," he said cheerfully. "Your mom said I could play with this stuff. It used to be yours—she found a whole basket of it down in the basement. Is that okay? Do you mind? Wanna help me make a spaceship?"

"It's fine—I don't mind at all," Zibby assured the little boy. But the sight of all the Legos gave her a twinge. She and her dad had loved to build intricate Lego structures together when she was little, and even when she wasn't so little anymore. Once he moved out, she packed all the Lego blocks away. "I'll build a spaceship with you later—promise. But your dad wants you. He says you're great at puzzles."

Brady stood up, brushing tiny Lego bricks from his jeans. He clattered down the stairs as Zibby crossed the landing to tap on the closed door of Laura-Jane's room.

There was no answer. Zibby opened the door and saw that the room was empty. Was she down in Zibby's room, behind the closed door, messing with the dollhouse? But then Zibby heard the toilet flushing on the floor below and knew that Laura-Jane was down in the bathroom.

Zibby looked around the room appreciatively. It was amazing how Ned and Nell had transformed the attic room for that ungrateful girl. It looked cozy and inviting now in the glow of the bedside lamp. She sat down in Laura-Jane's armchair to wait, and reached back to adjust the cross-stitched pillow (Grammy's contribution) behind her.

Her fingers touched something hard. Something smooth and firm. Zibby shifted in the chair and moved the pillow, drew out the object, its golden thread gleaming in the lamplight. She sucked her breath sharply.

Nell's black leather wallet.

CHAPTER 24

Through the pounding in her head, Zibby heard Laura-Jane's footsteps on the stairs. She shoved the wallet back under the pillow just as Laura-Jane came into the room.

"What are you doing in here?" Laura-Jane demanded.

"Your dad wants you to come down and work on a puzzle." Zibby was surprised that her voice came out sounding so normal while her mind raced like a wild thing.

"Like I really want to spend my time with your stupid mother." Laura-Jane snorted and turned away. "Like I want anything to do with her."

With a surge of anger, Zibby withdrew the wallet from behind the pillow and threw it onto the bed. "But you want her money," Zibby said flatly. "How dare you?"

Laura-Jane sank onto her bed. Her face grew very pale and her almond-shaped eyes closed. "I didn't," she whispered.

"Oh, yes, you did, and here's the proof."

"No." Laura-Jane opened her eyes. They blazed hotly at Zibby. "I *thought* about taking it—when I came home earlier and saw your mom's purse in the hallway. I even lifted it out—and looked at it. But I put it back. I *swear* I did..." Her voice faltered.

Zibby reached out and scooped up the wallet. "Swear all you like, but this pretty much speaks for itself." She walked to the door. "My mom will be glad to get this back. Or did you spend all the money already?"

"I *didn't*—oh, Zibby, listen to me!" Laura-Jane's voice was choked, and Zibby turned back in surprise. The black eyes were pleading. "Something really weird is going on," Laura-Jane whispered. "I'm—I'm scared." She reached out for Zibby's arm.

But Zibby shook her off. Anger burned in her like a torch. It made her skin feel tingly, as if an electric current blazed inside her. She laughed coldly.

"It was sort of like what happened last time," cried Laura-Jane. "In the kitchen! I only meant to tip *one* tray of food into the sink—"

"What are you talking about?" Zibby moved closer.

"The way things are happening." Laura-Jane started sobbing. "It isn't me!"

Zibby wanted to drag Laura-Jane downstairs and toss the wallet right onto the table where Ned and Nell and Brady were working on their puzzle. But something about the other girl's reaction struck her: Laura-Jane wasn't acting guilty. She was acting...frightened.

"Tell me what happened in the kitchen," ordered Zibby.

Laura-Jane wrapped one of her long ponytails around and around her fingers in agitation. "I was mad—okay, I know it's mean of me, but I *was* mad. And there were all those trays of food. So I tipped the one tray into the sink.

That's all I did. One tray. Then…" She stopped. "I don't know exactly. There was this bell ringing in my head, and my hands started hurting, and then there was this force—forcing me to dump a second tray. And then suddenly all the other trays and the dishes and glasses started flying around the kitchen—I had to duck so I wouldn't get hit—and everything was crashing and breaking. I ran outside and jumped on my bike. I had to get away, *far* away, as fast as I could!"

Laura-Jane was breathing hard. Zibby watched her stonily, not wanting to believe a word of her story. But she kept hearing Laura-Jane's words: *I heard a bell ringing in my head and my hands started hurting…* Unmannerly, tantrum-prone Laura-Jane. Could it be that Miss Honeywell was trying to govern Laura-Jane, too?

"What about the wallet?" Zibby asked. "Did you hear a bell ringing before you stole it?"

"But I'm telling you I didn't steal it! I only *thought* about stealing it, but I swear I never took it. I just found the wallet on my desk when I came into the room. I hid it in the chair while I was thinking how to put it back—without anyone seeing me. Because, face it, no one's going to believe I didn't take it." She scowled at Zibby. "But I *didn't*!"

Laura-Jane's story had the ring of truth—because how could she know about the bell and the stinging hands when she'd never heard Primrose Parson's story? But then Zibby glanced over at Laura-Jane's dresser and her voice hardened. "First a wallet, then a doll. What else are you going to take that doesn't belong to you?"

"What doll?" cried Laura-Jane.

Zibby pointed to the dresser, where she had just spied

the little girl doll with the brown braids propped against Laura-Jane's freshly painted wall.

"I never touched that doll! I don't know how she got there!"

Zibby stood up and crossed the room. She snatched up the doll. With wallet and doll in hand, she stamped over to the door. She would go straight down and show her mom and Ned what she'd found here in Laura-Jane's room and let them decide what it meant. But she was stopped by a little voice inside her head.

That was fun, said Primrose Parson.

"What was fun?" demanded Zibby. "What do you know about this?" Zibby saw Laura-Jane's startled look and realized that the other girl could not hear the ghost's voice.

I'm getting the hang of it, Zibby. Now I can move objects around! I moved the doll—as you see! The ghost's high-pitched voice was gleeful. And I moved the wallet. It's wonderful having power! I can see now how Miss Honeywell did it—moved the dollhouse around. But it's hard. I'm not nearly that strong—yet. But it was I who took your mother's wallet, Zibby. I meant it as a joke, that's all! Just a little practical joke. You mustn't be so quick to jump to conclusions, my dear girl. You'll hurt people's feelings.

Zibby blinked. She took a deep breath, then reached out and linked arms with Laura-Jane. Laura-Jane tried to pull away, but Zibby held tight. "Wait a sec, I want you to hear something."

"Let go of me," yelled Laura-Jane. "Are you crazy—or what?"

I have seen no sign that Zibby is crazy, said Primrose calmly. *She seems to be a bit wild, but so many young girls are like that nowadays, aren't they? You yourself are no gem, and you can be quite sure Miss Honeywell would agree with me.*

Laura-Jane screamed.

"What is going on up there, girls?" Ned's voice sounded both angry and wary at the same time. "Laura-Jane? Zibby?"

The girls stared at each other.

Shall I go to him? asked Primrose. *I'm still just learning how to do this, but I bet if I concentrate my energy very hard I might be able to make the doll float all the way downstairs. Wouldn't that be funny?*

"No!" said Zibby, and she tossed the little doll onto the bed.

"It's okay, Daddy," called Laura-Jane in a shaky voice. "We'll be down in a minute." She looked desperately at Zibby. "Whose voice is that? What's happening with that doll?"

Zibby regarded her mistrustfully. "Do me a favor, and I'll do you a favor. Stop being horrible to my mom."

Laura-Jane glanced nervously at the little doll on the bed. "I'm telling you—I didn't steal your mom's wallet, and I meant to tip only *one* of those trays of food!"

"Well, you thought about taking the wallet, and that was enough to give Primrose the idea for her stupid joke. And it must have been Miss Honeywell who helped you with destroying the kitchen, if you really didn't do it all yourself."

"I swear I didn't! Now tell me, who is Primrose? Who is Miss Honeywell?"

"Promise to stop being nasty to my mom."

"I just don't want them to get married." Laura-Jane's voice was choked. "It ruins everything! How can my mom and dad get back together when he's married to someone else?"

"Laura-Jane, he's never going to get back together with your mom." Zibby wanted to shake her. "Listen, I felt the same way when my parents got divorced. I wanted my dad back so much—and I wanted my parents to get married again. But my dad married someone else. Someone in Italy! I've never even met her, and I haven't seen my dad in two years. At least you see your dad *and* your mom all the time. I wish my dad had never gone to Italy, but at least I don't try to take it out on his stupid wife."

Laura-Jane stared at her, then down at the doll on the bed. She was silent for a long moment. Then she whispered, "Did that doll really talk?"

"Yes—and I'm going to tell you about it. But first we have to return my mom's wallet," Zibby said firmly. She took the wallet and headed out of the bedroom. Laura-Jane followed.

Zibby went downstairs to her mom's bedroom—soon to be her mom and Ned's bedroom, she remembered— and dropped the wallet onto the floor by the desk. "I'll just put it there," she told Laura-Jane, who hovered at her side. "So she'll find it later. I'd like to tell her the whole story—but it's getting so complicated..."

"Tell *me* the whole story," begged Laura-Jane. "I'm getting really scared."

Brady's voice, yelling up the stairs, interrupted her. "Aren't you guys going to help us with this puzzle?"

Zibby's laugh held a note of hysteria. "He thinks *they've* got a puzzle?" She started down the stairs. "We'll talk later, at bedtime."

It was the first time they'd spent all together that was even halfway congenial. Nell, Ned, Zibby, Laura-Jane, and Brady all crowded around the big square coffee table in the living room and tried to fit together the pieces that would make up the whole picture. They were working on Zibby's birthday puzzle: the scenic photograph of Venice's Grand Canal. Zibby and Laura-Jane worked on it in silence, and slowly the canal took shape. Ornate gondolas crowded the waterway, each poled along by a gondolier in a striped blue and white shirt. Zibby wished herself into the picture, away from these people and all the tensions. "You can almost hear the gondoliers singing," said Ned, and then he started bellowing something in Italian in his deep voice. Nell joined in, harmonizing perfectly, and Zibby saw Laura-Jane's mouth tighten. But they all worked on the puzzle until Ned said it was time for Brady to be in bed.

"I'll take him up," said Laura-Jane quickly, earning her a surprised look from her father. "Come on, Brady."

"I'll help," said Zibby, getting to her feet—and got even more baffled looks from both Ned *and* Nell. Brady, who normally would have put up a fuss about being sent to bed, scrambled up the stairs, delighted to have both girls at his service.

Once he'd brushed his teeth and was tucked into bed, he demanded that each girl read him a story. Finally they said good night and crossed the landing to Laura-Jane's little room. "He's cute," Zibby said. "You're lucky to have a little brother."

"Forget him. Tell me about the doll," ordered Laura-Jane. "Tell me about that voice." She looked over to her bed, but the doll was not lying where Zibby had left it. "That

Brady!" cried Laura-Jane. "Now you'll see what a pain it is to have a little brother. He's always into my stuff."

"Wait," whispered Zibby. "I don't think Brady took it. He was downstairs or with us the whole time. Come down to my room for a minute."

Sure enough, the little girl doll was sitting on Zibby's pillow. Zibby picked her up. Then she reached for Laura-Jane's hand. "Laura-Jane, meet Primrose Parson."

Hello again, said Primrose's voice in their heads. *I've been lonely just waiting around.*

Laura-Jane dropped Zibby's hand as if it had sent a shock through her.

"Sorry," said Zibby. "It's still pretty much a shock to me, too." She sat looking at the doll for a long minute, then tossed her down on the bed again. She moved over to sit in front of the dollhouse. "Come here, Laura-Jane, and tell me something. Do you believe in ghosts?"

CHAPTER 25

PRIMROSE 1920

Nanny Shanks tied the green satin ribbon on Primrose's dress. Primrose twirled in front of the long mirror, pleased at her reflection. The whole family, Nanny Shanks included, was invited to Mr. Pope's wedding. Primrose hugged herself with excitement. She had never been to a wedding before. The invitation was delivered some weeks ago, and Primrose's mother had opened it at the breakfast table (Primrose was now old enough to join her parents downstairs for breakfast in the dining room) and had read it aloud:

MR. AND MRS. THOMAS E. MAYBERRY REQUEST
THE HONOR OF YOUR PRESENCE
AT THE WEDDING OF THEIR DAUGHTER
EVELINA LYDIA
TO
MR. THADDEUS POPE
SATURDAY, DECEMBER 10, 1920

"You mean *my* Mr. Pope?" Primrose had asked in surprise. "Mr. Pope is getting married after all? He never said anything to me about getting married!"

Indeed, Mr. Pope was always too focused on lessons to talk about anything other than science and mathematics with Primrose. He had continued to tutor her after Miss Honeywell's death, but now Primrose's parents had enrolled her in a boarding school in Cleveland, and she was to begin after the Christmas holidays.

"It would seem the man has a private life outside of his tutoring sessions, dear girl," said her father with a chuckle.

Primrose reached for the invitation and studied it with a frown. "Who is this Evelina person? I never heard of her."

"Her father is a professor at the university where Mr. Pope studied," said Papa.

Primrose wondered whether Mr. Pope had already been courting Miss Mayberry while Miss Honeywell was still alive. But she kept her wondering to herself. Primrose never mentioned Miss Honeywell if she could avoid doing so. Just hearing the governess's name made her stomach churn, and there were other, more complicated feelings, too—quickly pushed away. No one knew that the vengeful spirit of the governess haunted Primrose. Her parents were careful not to talk about the governess, not wanting to upset their daughter. Mr. Pope himself had been careful to stick to the academic subjects he taught, and rarely discussed anything else with Primrose or with Nanny Shanks, who often sat in on the lessons now that Miss Honeywell was gone.

Resolutely Primrose had pushed the governess out of her thoughts. Talk turned to the wedding and what new dresses must be purchased. Primrose, flushed with delight, was allowed to accompany her mama to the dressmaker's later that same afternoon. This would be her first grown-up event!

And now, the day was at hand. Shortly, they would motor to the church where the wedding would take place. Primrose sucked in her breath to make her waist appear smaller as Nanny Shanks finished tying the beautiful green bow. The sash and her hair ribbons were both pale green satin; the dress was a creamy white. Primrose's brown hair, usually tied back in two braids, had been carefully curled and now hung in long sausages over her shoulders.

"You look quite the young princess," said Nanny with satisfaction, reaching out to smooth back one of Primrose's curls. She draped a green velvet cloak around Primrose's shoulders. "And now, milady—your carriage awaits!"

Primrose looked out of the nursery window, down at the curving drive where the chauffeur waited with the automobile. She loved getting out of the house. Since Miss Honeywell's death, there had been many more chances to spend time in town, to visit other children, to play. But Primrose just couldn't seem to enjoy herself the way she knew she should. She often had a feeling that she was being watched. She didn't play with her dollhouse anymore, though she regretted not being able to fix it up the way she'd planned. Her parents asked her about the house from time to time, wondering at her lack of interest in the very toy she had wanted for so long. But she told them she'd grown too old for doll play.

The chauffeur drove Primrose's family to the church. He parked the long black automobile at the curb and got out first to open the doors for his passengers. Primrose jumped out and skipped up the steps ahead of her parents.

Inside the big stone church, she glanced around with interest. It was festively decorated in holiday greenery. There was an air of hushed expectancy as the minister walked in, followed by Mr. Pope, who looked unexpectedly handsome in a black tailcoat. Then the organ surged, and everyone stood up to watch as three bridesmaids walked down the aisle, followed by the radiant bride, on her father's arm. Primrose grinned at the expression of awe and love shining on Mr. Pope's face as he watched his bride approach. Surely now—for once—even this single-minded tutor was not thinking about electricity and mathematical formulations!

When the bride and groom turned to face the minister, Primrose and her parents sat down again. But Primrose jumped straight up again because she had sat on something hard. She tugged it out from under her and gave a little shriek: in her hand was the governess doll from her dollhouse, stern-faced and garbed in gray.

"Really, dear," murmured Primrose's mama. "I think you might have left your playthings at home today."

"I didn't bring it!" Primrose's voice came out as a high-pitched squeak. She dropped the doll onto the pew cushion. Panic rose in her throat. The people sitting behind her frowned.

"*Tsk, tsk.*" Nanny Shanks, sitting on Primrose's other side, gave her a reproving glance. "Sit yourself down and be quiet, Miss Primrose!" She stowed the doll in her handbag.

Primrose sat down again, heart pounding. She tried to listen to the minister, talking about eternal love, in sickness and health, for richer and poorer.

The bride and the groom exchanged rings. Mr. Pope kissed his bride gently. Triumphantly the two of them started down the aisle arm in arm, now man and wife. They beamed at their guests as they passed. But then the bride tripped and stumbled. If Mr. Pope had not been holding her arm, she would have fallen. He reached down to pick up whatever she had stumbled over—and found himself holding the gray-gowned governess doll.

Primrose started shaking. He looked down at the doll in surprise, then handed it to Primrose as he and his bride passed on.

"Really, Primrose!" exclaimed Mama. "You are too old to bring toys out in public!"

"I didn't—"

"That's strange," said Nanny Shanks, as she and Mama and Papa stood to leave the church. "I'm quite sure I just put that doll in my handbag…"

Mama swept out of the church with Papa at her side. Nanny Shanks and Primrose followed. Primrose took a handful of rice out of the pretty lace bag one of the bridesmaids held out at the door, then walked into the frosty air. But before she tossed the rice at the departing bride and groom, she hurled the governess doll into the bushes at the side of the building.

The groom's automobile had been decorated with tin cans and streamers and a banner that said JUST MARRIED. The car waited in front of the church as Mr. Pope and his bride shook everyone's hands and thanked them for coming to the wedding. The two of them were motoring off for a week at Niagara Falls.

"I hope you will enjoy boarding school," Mr. Pope said to Primrose as he shook her gloved hand, "and do well in science and mathematics."

They all watched as Mr. Pope settled his bride carefully in the front seat of the automobile, while the best man hurried to start the auto by turning the crank at the front. Mr. Pope walked to the driver's side. He put his head inside, then withdrew in surprise. He walked back over to Primrose.

"Your doll again, I believe?" He held it out to her—the doll in the gray dress.

Primrose recoiled. "No! Keep it away from me! That's not a doll—that's Miss Honeywell!"

His face paled. "Calliope Honeywell?"

I want to be with you, Thaddeus. I am the one meant to be your bride!

"She wants you!" Primrose backed away. "Can't you hear her?"

"I'm sorry, Mr. Pope," said Primrose's papa. "I don't know what has gotten into Primrose today, bringing a plaything to your wedding!" He took the doll and tried to return it to Primrose, but she thrust her hands into her pockets and wouldn't take it.

"Mr. Pope has to keep it," she whispered.

"I think not," said Mr. Pope, trying to smile now. "My wife and I have no need of a governess to chaperone us!"

Papa handed the doll to Nanny Shanks, who tucked it firmly into the pocket of Primrose's green cloak. Primrose stiffened, but knew she had made enough of a scene already and so forced herself to join her parents and the other guests in shaking hands and saying cheerful celebratory things. The best man cranked up the automobile again, and finally the newlyweds drove off, with the wedding guests waving. Then Primrose sat alone on the cold stone steps of the church, shivery in every bone.

She slid her hand into her cloak pocket. It was empty.

Mr. Pope thought he'd left the doll behind, but Primrose was willing to bet that since the doll wanted to be with him, nothing would stop it from joining him—on his honeymoon, or wherever. Forever.

She had a dreadful feeling that none of them had seen the last of Miss Honeywell.

CHAPTER 26

In the morning Jude phoned to invite Zibby to a slumber party. "Tonight," she said. "It'll be our first party in our new house. A sort of end-of-summer, back-to-school party. I'm inviting Charlotte, too, so we can talk about everything—figure out what we're supposed to *do* about the dollhouse and the ghosts and everything."

"Sounds good," Zibby said. "But—um—Jude? Can Laura-Jane be invited, too?"

"Laura-Jane?" asked Jude. "Are you feverish...or out of your mind?"

"Definitely out of my mind," agreed Zibby. "But things have sort of changed. We'll tell you when we see you."

"We?" Zibby imagined Jude shaking her head in astonishment. "Sure. Whatever."

Mr. and Mrs. Jefferson welcomed all the girls with big smiles. Mr. Jefferson carried on about how nice it was that Penny and Jude had made new friends before school started.

"It's much easier to start a new school when you know some of the other kids," he said. "So you'll all be at Carroway Middle School?"

"All of us except Laura-Jane," Zibby told him. "She lives in Fennel Grove with her mom most of the time."

Mrs. Jefferson served spaghetti for their dinner, made a big fruit salad, set out one pitcher of apple juice and another of milk. She left the girls in the dining room, gathered around the big table. It should have been a pleasant meal, the start of a fun slumber party, but the atmosphere was guarded because the other girls weren't sure why Laura-Jane was with them or what to say to her. But Zibby couldn't talk about the ghosts with Mr. and Mrs. Jefferson walking in and out of the room.

Laura-Jane wasn't making things easier by just sitting silently, nibbling a strand of pasta. Zibby tried to liven things up by telling Penny and Jude about the different teachers they were soon to meet at Carroway Middle School and which ones were her favorites. She recommended Ms. Durkee. "Get her for science if you can." Charlotte offered advice about which school clubs to join and where the cutest boys hung out, and then she started in with makeover advice: Penny would look great with blush on her cheekbones, Jude could definitely use mascara to highlight her curly lashes, and Zibby really needed to pluck her eyebrows and do something about her hair. It was so *limp*. Maybe a perm...

She didn't offer any suggestions for Laura-Jane.

"Let's go up to my room now," said Jude hastily as Mrs. Jefferson breezed into the dining room again to clear the dishes. Mr. Jefferson came in with a big bowl of popcorn for the girls to take upstairs.

Zibby unrolled her sleeping bag next to Jude's bed and sat down on it. She reached for a handful of popcorn, waiting for the other girls to set up their sleeping bags. She looked around the room and thought how different it looked from when it was Amy's bedroom. Amy's room had been all pink and purple and ruffly, with lots of stuffed animals displayed on shelves. Now the walls were creamy yellow, with simple white curtains at the window. Three pots of healthy green spider plants sat on the window ledge, sending down green baby shoots. A tall pine bookcase held Jude's books, and Zibby was pleased to see some of her own favorites among them.

It was a peaceful room, and Zibby breathed in deeply, hoping that the atmosphere would keep all the girls calm as Laura-Jane confessed her part in the attack in the kitchen— how she had tipped the first tray into the sink out of nastiness but then watched in terror as the other trays were hurled by unseen hands. "Plates and glasses and pots, too!" Laura-Jane told them, holding her hands to her cheeks as if still feeling the shock. "I raced out of there like...like..."

"Like a ghost was chasing you," said Penny, wide-eyed. "And it sounds like one really was." She turned to the others. "Poor Laura-Jane!"

"Poor Laura-Jane?" Jude's tone was dry. "She tossed one tray all on her own, remember? She's not totally innocent."

"I know," agreed Charlotte, "and that was really mean."

"Primrose said *she* was the one who took the wallet— but she couldn't have been the one who wrecked the kitchen," Zibby spoke up. "She wasn't a ghost yet."

Laura-Jane looked ashamed of herself. But then she shook back her long black braids and spoke determinedly. "I don't care if you don't believe me, but it wasn't me who wrecked the kitchen. It felt like someone else was taking over my body and making me throw the trays around. It was…like being imprisoned. I couldn't move the way I wanted to! Someone else was *making* me move!"

"*Sweet* Miss Honeywell," murmured Penny. She shivered.

Jude noticed the shiver. "It's what you do at slumber parties, isn't it—tell ghost stories?"

"Yes—but they're not usually true!" Laura-Jane exclaimed. "I *hate* ghosts. I don't even *believe* in them. But Zibby's house is full of them, and I hate living there! It's creepy," she added in a small voice. "But I am sorry about… Nell. Zibby, I really am sorry for…being unfriendly to your mom."

Zibby studied her for a long moment. The other girls were watching carefully. "Well," Zibby said finally, "if you're *really* sorry, you have to prove it by helping us figure out what's going on. I don't like ghosts, either, and I didn't believe in them, either, until I got stuck with the dollhouse. But they're real—and they're really there. In my creepy house."

Laura-Jane slipped deeper into her sleeping bag. "I'll help if I can," she said. "But creepy stuff gives me bad dreams."

"Welcome to the club," Jude said ominously. "The bad-dream club."

"Only Zibby and I are in *that* club!" said Penny with a nervous giggle.

"Have you told Laura-Jane about the dream yet?" Charlotte asked Zibby.

"I don't want to hear about it," moaned Laura-Jane. "Can't we please stop talking about weird things? I'm on weirdness overload."

Weirdness overload, thought Zibby. That was a perfect description of what she herself was feeling these days.

So they tried to put ghosts out of their heads. They ate the popcorn and played Monopoly, and Laura-Jane proved to be a hilarious companion, making many outrageous business deals. Mr. Jefferson called them down to the kitchen and taught them an amazing trick: Charlotte sat in a kitchen chair and the others stood around her, pressing their hands firmly down onto her head while breathing rhythmically in and out, in and out, in and out for one hundred breaths, and then simultaneously placing two fingers each under her arms and knees and lifting her up over the back of the chair and down to the floor again. When Zibby first heard the plan, she laughed and said it would be impossible for four girls to lift a fifth up high—just using two fingers each. "Try it," Mr. Jefferson said, and they had, and it really worked. "It's to do with concentrating your energy," he told the girls. "Joining forces." Then they went back upstairs and listened to music and talked about the upcoming school year that was starting the day after tomorrow. It was nice to do something *normal,* Zibby thought, looking around at the other girls. Something *ordinary* for a change. Laughing companionably, the girls chattered until sleep finally overtook them.

But in the stillness of sleep, the dream came creeping. It seeped into Zibby's head and filled her mind with smoke.

She was home in her own bedroom, and the dollhouse was on fire. Zibby told herself not to panic. It was just a dream, and she'd had this dream before. And yet the heat of the fire was so intense, it must be real. She had to hurry, had to escape from the bedroom—

But then she realized suddenly that she wasn't in her bedroom, after all, but in some large, echoing space. A familiar place—but where? The smoke covered everything. She could not see anything beyond the fire.

She stared at the burning dollhouse as the hand wearing the black glove—scant protection from the darting flames—reached around the porch. Zibby could see the glove clearly despite the billowing smoke. She could see the cracked black leather with a jagged tear at the base of the thumb. She could see the zigzag stitching along the wrist.

The gloved hand hit out desperately at the fire, then groped along the charred wooden floor, scrabbling as if trying to fasten onto something just out of reach. Then the hand jerked upright, index finger raised. Zibby stared at the hand.

It beckoned to her, finger crooked invitingly. "Come to me, my lamb, come to me!" She heard the deep voice all around her reverberating off the walls of the vast smoke-filled room.

Then screams filled the bedroom, but they were not Zibby's screams. She struggled awake, sat up in her sleeping bag, shaking the dream out of her head.

The panicked screams were coming from the sleeping bags beside her, from Laura-Jane, from Charlotte, and from the bed—from Jude. Zibby reached out a hand to shake Laura-Jane awake just as the bedside light flicked on. Jude sat up groggily. Charlotte struggled to sit up in her sleeping bag and peered at them through a mass of tangled yellow hair, gasping. Penny threw open her sleeping bag. "It's the dream!" she burst out. "I was having the dream again!"

"We all were, I think," sobbed Laura-Jane. "It's awful!"

In seconds Mr. Jefferson burst into the room with his

wife right behind him. "What's happening in here? Nasty dreams, you say? All of you?" Mr. Jefferson looked dubious.

Laura-Jane looked around the room and her eyes flickered with remembered horror. She gazed into the far corner by the windows. "I dreamed about Zibby's dollhouse. It was over there—in the corner," she whispered. "It was on fire."

"There were huge flames shooting out—and smoke! It was a fire, it was in our gym at school...and then there was a—a hand!" Charlotte's voice rose in panic. "A hand in a glove reaching out of the flames!"

Yes, thought Zibby. That large, familiar room—it was the gymnasium.

"I dreamed the same thing," said Jude from her bed. "I could see every detail. A horrible hand in a horrible black leather glove with a tear in the thumb—reaching for me!" She buried her face against Mr. Jefferson's shoulder.

Zibby and Penny stared at each other wordlessly. Now they had all had the dream. But how was it possible—and why was it happening?

"It sounds dreadful," Mr. Jefferson said in a soothing voice, and Mrs. Jefferson brought all the girls cups of water.

"This is what comes of too much popcorn and too much party," she said gently. She waited until all the girls lay back down in their sleeping bags, then turned off the light. She and Mr. Jefferson returned to their own bed, leaving Jude's door open and the hall light on.

"Are you guys all okay now?" asked Zibby.

"I don't know." Laura-Jane's voice was still shaky. "I don't think I'll ever get the image of that thing—that *hand*—out of my head."

"You get used to it," Zibby told her quietly. It seemed she and Laura-Jane were finding more and more things in common, she thought ruefully.

Penny propped herself up on one arm and looked over at Zibby. "Did you hear the voice, Zibby?" She looked around at the other girls. "Did you all hear the voice? I never heard that voice in the dream before."

"That was a new part of the dream for me, too," said Zibby. "*'Come to me, my lamb, come to me!'*" Zibby gulped out the words and then lay down again. "It was a man's voice," she added softly. "And you know something else?"

"What?" asked Jude.

Zibby took a deep breath. " I think—I think I've heard that voice somewhere before. I just wish I could remember *where*."

CHAPTER 27

The next day, Nell put aside her wedding plans and her DaisyCakes commitments and took Zibby, Laura-Jane, and Brady to the mall for some last-minute school shopping. They bought notebooks, binders, pencils, markers for their new backpacks, and clothes, too. The whole day was taken up with errands, and this was a relief to Zibby. She didn't open the dollhouse. She ignored the governess doll sitting on the roof, leaning against the chimney. And she ignored the little girl doll when it appeared on the kitchen table.

They all went to bed late. There were lunches to pack: tuna sandwiches, a crisp apple each, and little chocolate puffs from a tray meant for one of Nell's catered parties. Zibby took a long shower and washed her hair, then laid out her new clothes for the next day. Then Nell made Zibby's traditional night-before-school hot chocolate for all the kids, and they sat on the porch steps to drink it. It was nice sitting outside. The air was crisp with the promise of autumn.

When Zibby finally went up to bed, she made herself stay on guard against the dream. Each time she smelled that first puff of smoke, she forced herself to wake up. And so when morning finally came, she was nearly as tired as if she had not slept at all.

ZIBBY STUMBLED OFF the school bus, hoping she wouldn't fall asleep in her classes. But despite her fatigue, it was fun showing Jude and Penny around, and introducing the girls to the other kids.

By the last period, science, Zibby was yawning. She slid into a seat at the back of the room and closed her eyes briefly while kids filed noisily into the room. A deep, raspy voice called for quiet, and Zibby's eyes flew open, her heart thumping.

The voice from the dream.

She stared with surprise at the teacher. The shaggy-haired man she had seen around town stood at the front of the classroom, his hair as unruly as ever, wearing the same vest patterned in brightly colored diamond shapes. "Mrs. Durkee is staying home with her new baby this semester," he told them in a gravelly voice, "and so I will be your substitute teacher. My name is Mr. Potts."

Now Zibby remembered where she'd heard his voice before. He had leaned over the backyard fence the afternoon she'd burned the dollhouse, asking whether she had seen his lamb.

"It's *Ms.* Durkee!" shouted Scott Guerrero from his desk at the back of the classroom.

Mr. Potts frowned. "I don't believe in such ridiculous forms of address."

The other kids sighed or laughed, but Zibby's head was in a whirl. How could this man's voice be the one she heard in her dream? *Come to me, my lamb, come to me!* It didn't make any sense.

"I see from Mrs. Durkee's syllabus that she likes to start the school year talking about the genetic modification of plants." Mr. Potts glanced down at the sheaf of papers in his hand and shook his shaggy head. "But I am not particularly interested in genetic modification of any sort. Are you?"

The class laughed and assured him they were not the least bit interested.

"However," continued Mr. Potts in the soft, deep voice that compelled the kids to lean forward to hear him, "I am something of an old hand on other topics of scientific investigation. So we shall start with"—he smoothed his hair and raised his raspy voice—"electrical power."

The class cheered. But Zibby felt uneasy.

"Silence!" ordered Mr. Potts. "Now let's begin. Open your notebooks and prepare to jot down some facts about this fascinating but potentially very dangerous form of energy."

Zibby sat back and let his words wash over her as he began to lecture about electrical power. She took a few notes and ended up doodling in the margin of her notepad. When she saw what she had drawn, she gasped.

Hands. She'd been drawing hands wearing gloves.

She crumpled the paper and tried to concentrate on Mr. Potts's lesson. He was writing on the board about volts and currents. He was explaining that the class would be making batteries using an ordinary lemon. "It may sound impossible," he said, frowning sternly out at the class, "but the key to scientific experimentation is seeing for yourselves. You need proof. And you shall see the proof."

Zibby tried to listen, but her hands were hurting—stinging as if they were being smacked by Miss Honeywell's ruler just as Primrose Parson's had been. She rubbed her palms gently in her lap. She placed them flat on the cool surface of the desk, trying for some relief. How could Miss Honeywell be here at school? *Why* would she be here?

Finally the bell rang and Mr. Potts, after assigning the students to bring lemons to school, dismissed them. Zibby struggled from her desk, ready to flee. But Scott Guerrero stormed up the aisle first and bumped into her. Her backpack fell, dumping everything out onto the floor. "Sorry!" he shouted, without stopping.

Zibby knelt to gather up her books and papers and pencil case, her hands still aching. The classroom was nearly empty by the time Zibby retrieved the last pen from beneath a desk two rows away. Only Mr. Potts remained, waiting for her to leave so he could lock up the classroom. He waited impassively as she shouldered her backpack, then he reached for his heavy overcoat on the back of his chair and shrugged into it. From the pocket of his coat a scarf and gloves fell to the floor. Zibby, passing on her way out the door, bent down and picked them up for him.

"Here," she said, holding them out—then froze.

The scarf in her hands was an old one, knitted of gray wool. It was completely unremarkable—except for the fact that it seemed inappropriate for such a nice autumn day. The gloves were inappropriate, too. They looked hot and thick, of peeling black leather with a zigzag pattern stitched along the wrist in gray thread. And there was a jagged tear near the base of the right glove's thumb.

Zibby couldn't move. For a moment she couldn't even breathe.

This time when Mr. Potts spoke, his voice was even softer than before. "Thank you kindly," he said, taking his belongings from her trembling hands.

Zibby edged out the door with a glassy smile fixed on her face. Then, in the hallway, she turned and ran, gulping in great gusts of breath. She ran until she was outside the school and hurtling down the sidewalk toward home. She ran until it hurt to breathe.

As she ran she tried to convince herself that she had been mistaken somehow—that Mr. Potts did not have a glove with zigzag stitching and a tear by the thumb, that she had not really recognized his voice as the voice from the dream.

Ripples of terror coursed through her body each time she thought of it. She ran all the way home on the strength of that terror. She ran until she was sitting on her own front porch steps, breathing hard, trembling, hearing the voice over and over. Somehow the impossible was still possible, and the nightmare had turned real.

What could Mr. Potts have to do with Miss Honeywell and Primrose? What? What? Her mind asked the question over and over. There had to be a connection, but what?

She took out her key, opened the front door, and ran up the stairs to her bedroom. She knelt in front of the doll-house. Taking a deep breath, she unlatched the house. "Primrose!" she cried. "Where are you?"

I'm here—just thinking about a chandelier, said the little voice in her head when Zibby lifted the little girl doll from the couch in the parlor. *The parlor could be made very elegant. I think it needs a chandelier. And what about a new couch? The one I was sitting on looks fancy, but it's hard as a board.*

"I need to talk to you, Primrose," said Zibby, clutching the doll. "Do you know a man named Mr. Potts?"

Not that I recall, replied the ghost promptly. *What do you think about getting some framed artwork up on the parlor walls?*

Zibby shook the doll impatiently. "Listen, Primrose, some very strange things are happening and I think they're to do with Miss Honeywell."

She's trying to get stronger, but I'm in the way, the little voice said gloatingly. *I can feel her trying to suck my energy, but I won't let her! There's no room for her anymore. The dollhouse is mine, all mine—and I want you to help me make it fabulous. Starting with—*

"Forget fixing up the dollhouse for now," said Zibby. "Listen to me. There's this dream I keep having. And not just me, but all of us. Ever since I brought the dollhouse home." She stopped and took a deep breath.

All right, all right. Calm down and tell me the dream, Primrose said. So Zibby told her about the fire and the glove, and the voice of Mr. Potts.

That's a very strange dream, and it reminds me of something… began Primrose.

"I knew you could help!"

But I can't really help, because…I can't quite remember, replied the ghost. *Everything is going all foggy in my mind.*

Primrose's voice was fading like a wisp of fog itself. It was sounding weaker every time she spoke, as if Primrose were losing power. Was it Miss Honeywell, as she'd said, sucking energy?

"Are you there, Primrose? Can you hear me?"

There came no answer. Frustrated, Zibby put the doll in the pocket of her jeans and headed downstairs to the kitchen. She peeled a banana and popped a piece of bread in the toaster.

She saw the day's mail lying on the kitchen table with her weekly postcard from Italy on top. The postcard showed people on boats in a narrow street of water—just like in the birthday puzzle they hadn't gotten around to finishing. Zibby studied the picture while she ate her banana, then turned the card over.

Dear Zib,

What about Christmas in Venice? We can sail into the New Year in a gondola! Please think about it. How would you like to start learning some Italian? I know you're probably busy with French in school, but if you have time to fit it in, I'll happily make the arrangements with your mom for private lessons. Just let me know. Sofia is taking a course to brush up on her English in hopes of meeting you soon. I miss you very much.

Love, Dad

Another cheerful card. He never berated her for refusing to write back or for not coming to the phone when he called. He just kept writing, week after week. She stared at the words until they blurred.

Oh, Dad! she thought. Missing him was an ache in her chest. He was so sensible and ordinary, and he did not believe in ghosts. He had always made her feel safe. She tried to push him out of her mind, but he was lodged there, part of her. *There are different kinds of ghosts,* Zibby thought shakily. *Different kinds of hauntings.*

She jumped up, needing to get out of the house. Carrying the postcard and her toast, she left by the back door. Red and gold leaves, hints that summer was almost over, drifted down onto the patio in the cool breeze.

The stamp on your postcard would look very nice in a frame on the parlor wall, piped Primrose's faint voice in Zibby's head, and Zibby jumped. She'd forgotten the doll in her pocket. Zibby ignored the voice and walked to the Jeffersons' house. Just as Zibby reached their driveway, she heard a tap on a horn, and Ned's car pulled up to the curb. Zibby was surprised to see Charlotte, Jude, and Penny all squashed into the backseat. Laura-Jane sat in the front.

The girls tumbled out, and Ned smiled at Zibby out the window. "Brady has soccer at the middle school field, so we dropped him off on the way over from Fennel Grove—and we found the other girls just starting for home."

"Yeah," said Charlotte. "We waited for you after last period, Zibby! How come you left without us?"

Zibby smiled what she hoped looked like a natural, normal smile. "Oh—I just forgot." She waved good-bye to Ned, and then turned to the girls. "I forgot," Zibby told them succinctly, "because I was totally terrified."

"What happened?" Penny asked quickly.

I'm thinking a beaded glass chandelier, came Primrose's faint, dogged voice. *There's a miniatures shop in Fennel Grove that would be a good place to shop for such a thing—*

"Oh, will you be quiet already?" snapped Zibby.

Penny looked at her in hurt astonishment. Zibby grabbed her arm. "Sorry—I wasn't talking to you, Penny! It's Primrose." She withdrew the doll from her pocket. "She's a nag."

"Let's go to the tree," said Jude. She pushed her way through the branches to sit inside the little clearing. The other girls followed.

"*Brr,*" said Laura-Jane, sitting down next to Penny on a low branch. "Now that it's September, it feels like summer is over for good." She pulled up the hood of her sweatshirt.

"Tell us what scared you," Jude ordered.

Zibby leaned back against a sturdy branch and took a deep breath. "My new science teacher," she began, "well, his voice. It's the one from the dream. And there's more…" She shivered. "He has the same glove."

"You mean Mr. Potts?" whispered Charlotte. "He's my new homeroom teacher, filling in for Ms. Durkee. But we were only in homeroom for ten minutes. I didn't see any gloves."

"Well, he had them," replied Zibby darkly.

"Who *is* Mr. Potts?" asked Laura-Jane.

"Mr. Potts is a new substitute teacher at our school," Zibby explained. "In science."

"But how can he have anything to do with the dream?" asked Laura-Jane. "How can he have anything to do with anything?"

"That's what we want to know," said Jude. "None of this makes sense."

"Our problems keep multiplying," said Zibby slowly, trying to think it through. "First there was Miss Honeywell, and then just when we thought we'd solved that problem, along comes Primrose. And now there's Mr. Potts and the dream—"

"But we were having the dream before we met Mr. Potts," Jude pointed out.

"I'd seen him around a few times," Zibby said slowly. "Starting the day I got the dollhouse."

They all considered this in silence.

"It's all to do with the ghosts," said Penny. "It's got to be!"

"He has the glove," Zibby murmured, trying to make the connection, "and the voice from the dream. He even asked me if I'd seen his 'lamb' when I saw him looking over the fence last week! And I never had the dream until I'd bought that stupid dollhouse!" She was shivering now, and she knew it wasn't only the brisk wind that caused the chill. "And my hands were stinging in his class today as if Miss Honeywell were there, too, smacking me the way she smacked Primrose."

"Did you see that governess doll at school?" asked Penny.

Zibby shook her head. "No, thank goodness."

"But you felt her vibes," said Jude. "Bad vibes."

Something is wrong. Primrose Parson's reedy voice sounded suddenly inside Zibby's head. Zibby jumped. *Someone is stuck.*

CHAPTER 28

"What do you mean—'stuck'?" demanded Zibby. She hurriedly told the other girls what Primrose had just said. They all linked hands so they could hear the ghost's reply.

"Is whatever's wrong to do with Mr. Potts?" Penny prompted.

When the little voice came again it was weaker than before. *I—I can't seem to…Everything is so very fuzzy…ohhhh!* The little voice was a distant whisper. *Miss Honeywell, is that you?*

"Is she sucking your energy, Primrose?" cried Zibby. "Is that it?"

No answer. Zibby dropped the other girls' hands. "This is impossible."

"I think Primrose sounded scared," ventured Penny. "Didn't you? What did she mean about Miss Honeywell?"

Jude frowned. "And what did she mean by 'stuck'?"

Charlotte tossed back her long hair. "Maybe Primrose just sounded so far away because she's going to disappear forever. Maybe she's just going on to wherever ghosts go when they're finished haunting people. To heaven. That would be good, wouldn't it? *I* think it would."

"Well, I don't want her to disappear until she's told me what she knows about Mr. Potts," said Zibby. "She knows *something*."

"Maybe bribery would work," suggested Jude drily. "Fix up the dollhouse the way she wants. Buy her a chandelier or something."

"Well, I guess we could start by framing stamps from my postcards," said Zibby resignedly. "Primrose wants some fine art on the walls."

Just then Mrs. Jefferson came outside and told the girls she had errands to run in Fennel Grove and she would be back in about an hour. Penny jumped up and called after her.

"Wait, Mom! Are you going near Lilliput—the miniatures shop? Could you take us there?" She turned back to the others. "Maybe we really can buy Primrose a chandelier!"

"I don't have any money," Zibby reminded them sourly. "Remember? Sweet Miss Honeywell saw to that." But she followed Penny, ducking beneath branches.

"We don't have to buy anything today," Jude said. "We'll just see how much it costs."

Mrs. Jefferson peered at the girls emerging from the fallen tree. "All of you? Well, I guess we'll fit in the van. But first you girls need to phone for permission." She reached into her purse and fished out her cell phone. Zibby took it but handed it to Laura-Jane.

"Can you call your dad at the *Gazette*? If he says you can go, my mom will let me, too."

"Oh, he'll say yes," Laura-Jane predicted, pressing the little buttons. "Anything we want to do together will get a big thumbs-up." And sure enough, Laura-Jane quickly secured permission for them both.

Then Charlotte phoned home, too, and they were set to go. Before they left, however, Zibby tucked the little girl doll into a nook in the tree. "I won't forget you," she promised, "but I don't need you in my head in public." She felt a surge of relief at leaving Primrose behind.

Mrs. Jefferson waited till everyone was buckled into the van, then drove off. She let them out in front of Lilliput with instructions to be ready to go again in twenty minutes. The girls opened the doors and hopped out. They waved as Mrs. Jefferson drove down the street.

Mrs. Howell greeted the girls from behind the counter. "First day back to school, girls?"

"Yes," said Charlotte politely. "We've just come to browse around for a while."

"Take your time," Mrs. Howell told them cheerfully. "Once the homework starts piling up, you may not have so much time to think about dollhouses!"

That would be just fine with me, thought Zibby.

The girls looked at the lighting kits. There were little chandeliers and lamps of all sorts. Some were wired to light up, and others were merely for show. All seemed expensive to Zibby. "I'll never be able to keep Primrose happy," Zibby complained. "I'll be broke."

"Oh, look over here at these little families," Penny said, leaning over a glass case full of tiny dolls. "They're so perfectly detailed! And they come in different colors, just like real people."

"But the sets are all the same," objected Laura-Jane. "Mother, father, brother, sister, baby, dog. What if I wanted a family with more kids? Or with grandparents? Or with parents from different races, like my dad and Zibby's mom? Or a cat instead of a dog?"

Mrs. Howell, overhearing her, laughed. "The good miniaturist thinks of everything," she said, and pointed to a higher shelf where boxes of single dolls were displayed. "You can mix and match all you like, and build as big a family as you want! Add teenagers. Add old folks! I even have parakeets in cages for doll families who don't want dogs *or* cats."

Laura-Jane giggled. She reached up and removed one of the single dolls that had been displayed separately on the shelf inside a glass dome. "Oh, look, this one is sweet, and it looks like an antique."

It was a little girl with fair skin, black curly hair, and bright blue painted eyes. The head was made of china instead of plastic, and the pink dress was faded. It was about the size of the little girl doll with the brown braids—the one that Primrose had taken over.

"That one isn't for sale," Mrs. Howell said. "I just keep old Sally on the shelf with the others so she won't be lonely." She took the doll from Laura-Jane and smoothed the little dress. "It was a doll I loved as a child," she said. "My special baby. She first belonged to my mother."

"I like the old dolls even better than the modern ones, I think," said Laura-Jane. "They have more character. Zibby has a whole bagful of old dolls for her dollhouse."

Zibby shot her a warning look. She did not want anyone to mention the ghosts.

"Yes, Zibby, I've been meaning to ask you whether you ever found that Mrs. Smythe person who sold you the dollhouse," said Mrs. Howell. "The one you were asking about."

"Oh, um," faltered Zibby. She cast a desperate look over at Jude. "Well, yes, I did. But she was in the hospital and had something wrong with her heart. And then she died."

"Oh dear," said Mrs. Howell, lifting the glass dome to replace her special baby inside. "Oh my!" she exclaimed in a startled voice. "How did this get inside? Look at this lovely little doll, girls. She's an antique, too, if I'm not mistaken—"

"That's Zibby's doll," said Penny hastily. "Here, Zib, don't leave your doll behind."

Zibby stuffed the doll roughly in her pocket. She had left Primrose Parson in the tree, but that hadn't stopped her from accompanying them to the shop. Could *anything* stop these ghosts?

"We came to look at chandeliers," Jude said quickly.

Mrs. Howell smiled. "Lamplight adds a cozy feeling to any home, large or small."

"Zibby's dollhouse isn't wired for electricity," stated Charlotte. "But maybe we can just sort of hook something up."

A shadow of worry crossed Mrs. Howell's face. "Oh, don't do anything electrical without having a professional install the wires, dear."

"Is wiring a dollhouse hard?"

"Not really difficult. But it's very important to have it done correctly—and safely."

"*My* dollhouse already has lights," Charlotte said proudly, tossing back her blond mane.

The other girls made elaborate motions of tossing their hair back, too. Jude's hair was too short, but she shook her head in as disdainful a manner as she could.

"Well, if you do electrify your house," Mrs. Howell said to Zibby, suppressing a smile at all their tossing, "then I'd advise you to have it done professionally. Wiring is tricky. And it can be dangerous." Her expression grew serious and her forehead creased in a frown. "Things can go wrong— badly wrong."

AT BEDTIME ZIBBY lay very still, listening. There was a rustling sound. Maybe it was just wind from the window left open a crack, blowing papers on Zibby's desk. But Zibby slipped out of bed and walked to the dollhouse.

The little girl doll was sitting on the front porch. Zibby picked her up. "I left you in my pocket."

I want to get inside the dollhouse, replied Primrose in a whisper. *She won't let me.*

"You mean Miss Honeywell?" whispered Zibby.

She's in there, I'm sure of it. I can feel her.

Zibby sat on her bed. "Can't you make her leave?"

She's getting stronger. Much stronger. I think she's trying for a body.

"A *what?*" demanded Zibby. She hoped she hadn't heard what she thought she'd heard.

I think she wants a body—instead of staying in the doll. But that would take a huge amount of energy. I'm still very new at this ghost stuff, you know, but I'm learning that it all takes power. Moving objects around. Inhabiting the dolls. Speaking in people's heads. But she's had years of practice gaining power. And now she wants more.

Zibby glanced uneasily at her closed bedroom door. She'd left Nell downstairs with Ned, both of them reading in the living room, cups of tea at their sides. Was she still down there with him? Was she safe?

Put me inside the dollhouse, Zibby. Open the latch and put me in the parlor! Then I can try to show her who's boss—

"No way!" hissed Zibby. No way could she bring herself to open the dollhouse where Miss Honeywell was lying in wait, hoping for a body. She crawled back under her covers and pulled them to her chin. She set the doll on the bedside table. "Try to sleep," she said. "That's what I'm going to do."

Ghosts don't sleep.

Zibby did, somehow. Uneasy sleep. Sleep full of dreams.

CHAPTER 29

At school the next day, Zibby was careful to avoid Mr. Potts. She wished she were brave enough to cut her science class, but she knew cutting would only land her in the principal's office. At lunch she saw Mr. Potts in the cafeteria. Her heart started thudding, and she looked away. Then she snatched another quick glance at him. He sat alone, reading the newspaper, not eating a thing. Later he strode off down the hallway briskly—as if he knew right where he was going. Usually substitute teachers got lost in the large middle school and had to ask directions.

When Zibby came out of her math class, Mr. Potts was coming straight toward her down the hall. She dodged around the corner and leaned against a wall of lockers, taking deep breaths. *Safe.* Then the thought came unbidden: *Poor Mr. Potts.* It wasn't his fault if she and her friends were dreaming about him. Was it?

Or did he know fully well that he was a nightmare come to life?

The last period of the day arrived, and it was once again time for science. Zibby hesitated outside the door to the classroom, trying to think of an excuse not to go inside. She hesitated so long that the late bell rang.

Sucking in her breath and praying for courage, Zibby slipped into the science room and closed the door. Mr. Potts stopped speaking until she found her seat at the back of the class. "One tardy is excused," he announced. "A second tardy earns you an after-school detention. Are we all clear about this?"

The class murmured that they were. Zibby sat at her desk, hardly daring to breathe. Mr. Potts stood up at the front of the classroom, wearing the same suit and diamond-patterned vest he had been wearing every time she'd seen him. His black coat lay on the table next to his desk.

He lectured in a loud, stern voice about electrical currents. He drew diagrams on the board. Then he stuck wires into a lemon to make a lightbulb light up. Students raised their hands to ask eager questions, but Zibby watched the darkening sky outside the classroom windows. It was starting to drizzle. She wondered what her mom was doing. She hoped fervently that Nell was out catering a party for Daisy-Cakes or buying flowers for the wedding this weekend, not sitting in the house at the mercy of Miss Honeywell.

"A scientist must be a careful technician," barked Mr. Potts, making Zibby jump. She forced herself to pay attention. "Knowing about how electrical power works is not enough. It is utterly important that each connection be correctly fixed. Loose screws or crossed wires in a terminal mean the electricity starts arcing—"

"What's that mean?" Scott Guerrero called out.

Mr. Potts paused. He singled the boy out with a fierce frown. "Listen carefully, young man. *Arcing* means that sparks start jumping on the loose terminal. Then the wires get hot, and the insulation starts to melt and burn, and anything combustible lying around will ignite. That means *fire!* Do you hear me, children? Horrible fire—all because a screw was loose—"

"He's got a screw loose, if you ask me," someone muttered, and some of the kids giggled. They stopped when Mr. Potts raised his voice in a shout.

"Never play with electricity! Get rid of all your electric toys!" He stopped, then continued in a softer voice. "My daughter had a dollhouse once, with tiny lights—" He broke off.

"What happened?" asked Liz, the girl sitting in front of Zibby.

Mr. Potts was shaking his shaggy head back and forth, his expression anguished. "Faulty wiring," he said. "A loose screw. Arcing. Fire…" His voice trailed off. The class waited.

A dollhouse on fire, Zibby thought. *Just like in the dream.* Her hands were aching. She saw Scott Guerrero rub his own hands back and forth across the surface of his desk. Were other kids feeling Miss Honeywell's ruler smacking their palms, or was she the only one?

After a moment Mr. Potts collected his thoughts and continued. "Parents have no business giving children electrical toys," he said. "It's criminal."

"What happened to the dollhouse?" asked a boy whose name Zibby didn't know. "Did you buy your daughter another one?"

"No," he replied curtly. "No…I couldn't do that." Then

he pressed his lips together and turned his back on the class. He picked up the eraser and wiped the diagram off the board.

The bell rang and Zibby gathered up her books and rushed from the classroom. The pain in her palms faded away. She met Charlotte, Jude, and Penny at the lockers, and the four of them left school together.

Zibby told them what Mr. Potts had just said in class about his daughter's dollhouse catching fire. "So something *did* happen with a fire and a dollhouse—just like in the dream."

"This is too creepy," said Jude, glancing over her shoulder. "Let's go to my house—"

"No, come to my house," pleaded Zibby. "I don't want to be alone with the dollhouse, and I promised Primrose I'd start fixing it up. We can frame some art for her walls."

"I can't come," Charlotte told them, and Zibby thought her cousin sounded relieved. "I have piano."

No one was home yet at Zibby's house. Nell had left a note on the table saying she would be home before six and would Zibby please put the casserole in the oven at five thirty. Ned had left a phone message saying that he had Laura-Jane and Brady at the *Gazette* office with him, and they'd be home in time for dinner. Zibby was surprised how lonely the house felt without Laura-Jane and Brady. *Laura-Jane's starting to fit in,* Zibby thought. And Brady never had been any trouble at all, really.

The Jefferson girls and Zibby popped popcorn in the microwave and took it up to Zibby's room. The little girl doll was no longer on the bedside table where Zibby had left her the night before. The dollhouse was latched, but Zibby couldn't bring herself to open it and look for Primrose. What if the governess doll were there instead—waiting for a body?

Zibby unearthed all her dad's postcards from the bottom desk drawer and found a big box of matches. The girls cut out the prettiest stamps and clipped the heads off the matchsticks, trimmed the sticks to size, then glued them together. When the tiny wooden frames were dry, they colored them brightly with Zibby's felt-tipped markers and glued them around the stamps.

Leaving the stamps to dry on Zibby's desk, the girls went down to the kitchen so Zibby could put the casserole into the oven. Then Ned came home with Laura-Jane and Brady. Nell arrived at the same time, bearing a load of empty serving trays that needed washing. She set her trays on the counter and turned to Ned for a long hug. Then a kiss. Laura-Jane looked away. Brady whistled. Jude and Penny retreated into the hallway.

"Mom! Ned! Come up for air," Zibby demanded. "You're acting like high school lovebirds. It's embarrassing."

Ned peered at Zibby over her mom's shoulder. "But I haven't seen my bride all day!"

Nell laughingly extricated herself from Ned's arms. "Speaking of high school, Zib, why don't you and Laura-Jane get busy with that project Grammy suggested? It would be really nice to have some old photos from our school days displayed at the reception. You can check out my old yearbooks—look at the ones from junior high, too. They're in the dining room cupboard, bottom shelf."

"Mmm, I remember junior high," said Ned, pulling

Nell back into his arms. "That's when I first saw this skinny redheaded girl in my math class. She wore two long pony-tails, just right for pulling."

Nell giggled girlishly, and Laura-Jane snorted.

"Oh, get over it," said Jude to Laura-Jane.

"I think Zibby's mom and Laura-Jane's dad are very sweet together," said Penny. "So, come on, let's see these old yearbooks. I'll help you make the display."

"We'll both help," said Jude, as Zibby led the way into the dining room.

Zibby pulled out the first yearbook in the stack. She leafed through the pages. Her mom and Ned were seniors in high school. The kids in the photographs looked funny to Zibby, though Ned was immediately recognizable despite his long hair and sideburns, and so was Nell, with her long hair parted in the middle and hanging straight down over her shoulders. It was strange to think they'd known each other way back then, even before Nell had gone to college and met Zibby's dad. She flipped through the pages and had to smile at the fresh-faced pictures of Aunt Linnea and Uncle David. Aunt Linnea looked just like Charlotte, and Uncle David looked just like Owen.

"But these are high school yearbooks," said Jude. "Your mom said to start with the earliest ones. The ones from middle school."

"Junior high," said Zibby. "That's what they called it then."

Laura-Jane reached into the cupboard and pulled out two thin yearbooks. "Here they are." She flipped through the pages. "Zibby, look—it's your mom in seventh grade.

With ponytails." She stared down at the photograph for a long moment, then turned the pages until she found the photo of her dad. "I guess they really have known each other a long time," she said thoughtfully.

Zibby took the book back into the kitchen to show Nell and Ned. Ned reached for the yearbook, laughing, then flipped to the faculty-and-staff section. "Recognize this lady?" he asked Zibby, and she exclaimed in surprise.

"That's Ms. Wilson, our school librarian—but look at that afro and those beads! Very cool. Now she wears her hair back in a sort of elegant twist, and it's gone gray."

"Well, time changes everyone," said Nell.

Ned added, teasingly, "And she *is* the head of the media center now, with a dignified image to maintain. Back then she was a fiery new English teacher."

Zibby reclaimed the yearbook and checked to see whether any of her other teachers were at the school so many years ago. Then she froze, her eye caught by the photo of a familiar round-faced man with a shock of wild hair, wearing a dark coat and diamond-patterned vest. The caption beneath the photo said T. POTTER, ASST. CUSTODIAN.

Time changes everyone, Zibby thought, her mind spinning dizzily.

"What is it, honey?" asked Nell at Zibby's sharp intake of breath.

"That's him," said Zibby faintly. "That's my science teacher."

"Mr. Potter, the janitor?" Ned sounded surprised. "I remember him. Well, he must have gone to college and gotten his teaching credential."

Zibby took the book and walked slowly out of the

kitchen, back to the girls in the dining room. Without a word she handed the book to Jude, pointing with a trembling finger at the picture of T. Potter. Jude's mouth dropped in surprise. Penny and Laura-Jane leaned over to look as well.

Penny's eyes grew round. "What's wrong?" demanded Laura-Jane, looking at their shocked faces. Zibby led the way into the living room and collapsed onto the couch. The other girls sat down and looked at her expectantly.

"What is it?" persisted Laura-Jane.

"It's Mr. Potts," whispered Jude, and showed her the picture. "But it's from twenty-five years ago, and the name says Potter instead."

"Okay," said Laura-Jane. "I see it. But so what? Maybe he changed his name. Maybe he used to be the janitor, and now he's a science teacher. Why are you guys so freaked out?"

"Because...of this." Zibby retrieved the yearbook from Jude and flipped frantically through the pages. "Look here," she said. "And here, and here." There was Nell in twin ponytails and a shy smile. There was Ned, with his wide grin identical to Brady's. Ms. Wilson's calm smile in the photo was the same as now, but her face was unlined and her hairstyle outrageous. *Everybody* looked different than they did today. And so they should. After all, more than twenty-five years had passed.

"Why hasn't anything about Mr. Potts changed in twenty-five years—anything but his name?" whispered Zibby fiercely. "Why does he look exactly the same in this picture as he did in class today?"

"He's even wearing the same clothes," observed Jude.

"You mean this Mr. Potter looks *exactly* like Mr. Potts?" asked Laura-Jane.

"Exactly," said Jude.

Maybe it isn't Mr. Potts after all, Zibby thought in desperation. *Maybe it's his father or uncle!* "I think this whole thing is probably just another one of those weird coincidences," she said to the other girls as firmly as she could. "Don't you think?"

"I think I'd stop going to that school, if I were you, and transfer to mine right away," whispered Laura-Jane. "That's what I think, if you really want to know the truth."

CHAPTER 30

The girls had phoned Charlotte to tell her what they'd discovered, but no one was home. So their news had to wait till morning, when they met up at the lockers. "I *know* it sounds impossible," Zibby shouted over Charlotte's screeching. "But so is everything else."

"I've got to see this for myself," cried Charlotte. "Let me see the yearbook!"

"I didn't bring it to school," Zibby said, "but why don't we talk to Ms. Wilson?" The school librarian, after all, should know about Mr. Potts—Mr. Potter, whatever his name was. "She's been at the school such a long time, she might remember the guy."

The other girls agreed, and they arranged to meet at the school library after their last class. But first there was the entire school day to get through. Zibby dreaded that final period when she would have to sit in Mr. Potts's classroom. When the time came, she walked so slowly down the hallway that the tardy bell rang before she got there. She took a deep breath to calm her pounding heartbeat and slipped inside.

There was Mr. Potts, looking just as he had in the old yearbook photo, wearing his suit and diamond vest. He frowned at her. "Second tardy equals one detention after school," he reminded her sternly. "Today, this classroom, at three thirty."

Zibby lowered her eyes and slunk to her seat at the back of the room. School ended at three fifteen, so she would have just a few minutes to meet Charlotte, Jude, and Penny in the library, to talk to Ms. Wilson. The thought of having to sit for an hour in the room with Mr. Potts made her skin crawl. Maybe other kids had detention, too, and she wouldn't be alone with him. She fervently hoped so. When the bell rang for class to end, she dashed from the room and hurried to the library.

The library was a large room built onto the side of the middle school, with windows along two sides, letting in sunlight and a view of the orchard. Zibby waited outside the door until Jude, Penny, and Charlotte came down the crowded hallway. "I don't have much time," Zibby told them. She explained about her detention, and Jude squeezed her arm in sympathy.

Ms. Wilson was standing behind the checkout desk, helping a boy sign out some computer software. As soon as the boy had gone, the four girls went straight to the desk and asked if they might see the old yearbooks.

"Which year?" asked Ms. Wilson, leading them to a low shelf of books along the back wall. "Here they are—every yearbook from 1910 up until last year. The new yearbook for this year won't be out until spring, of course."

"Nineteen ten!" exclaimed Penny. "The school seems too modern to be that old."

"Well, dear, don't forget about the fire of 1934," said Ms. Wilson.

"Fire!" the girls exclaimed in one breath. But Zibby was calculating quickly. Nineteen thirty-four was too long ago. Mr. Potts couldn't have been here then.

"Yes, the school burned to the ground in 1934," explained the librarian. "And it was rebuilt in a more modern style. A lot of people complained that the new building wasn't as nice as the old one had been, but people always do complain about change. And then the new school was remodeled again in the early nineties—that's when we got the computer center and the new auditorium."

Zibby reached for the yearbook she'd looked at the night before and flipped to the faculty pages. "Look," she said, smiling at Ms. Wilson. "Here's somebody you might remember."

Ms. Wilson laughed at the photograph. "Love that hair," she said. "But you kids will laugh at your own yearbook pictures someday, too." She left them then to answer a phone call, and the girls clustered together to peer down at the book. Zibby turned the page to show Charlotte the picture of the janitor. There it was: T. POTTER, ASST. CUSTODIAN.

"That's him," breathed Charlotte. "It really is."

"Look at that vest." Penny moaned. "It's just like in my dream."

"I told you," whispered Zibby. "He's exactly the same."

Jude silently reached for another book on the shelf. She opened it to the back, scanning the index. Then she closed the book and reached for another one.

"What?" asked Zibby. "What are you doing?"

Jude flipped through the next book, put it back, then reached for another. And another.

The bell rang. It was time for Zibby to report to detention.

Then Jude gasped, stabbing her finger down onto an open page of the yearbook she held. Zibby leaned closer to see. This yearbook was from 1957. The black-and-white photographs were clear and crisp. And there on the last page, among the faculty, was a picture of Mr. Potts—their Mr. Potts—looking just as old as he did now, sporting the same diamond-patterned vest and the same unruly dark hair.

But this time the name under the photo read: T. PORTER, MATH TUTOR.

This time, thought Zibby, her mind spinning.

How could Mr. Potts be pictured in two different yearbooks, decades apart, still looking just the same as he had today in class? Was his name really Mr. Potts, at all—or was he T. Potter? Or T. Porter? Zibby reached out and pulled other yearbooks off the shelf, and so did the other girls—all turning the pages hastily, checking the indexes. Zibby didn't even feel surprised when they discovered pictures of Mr. Potts in some of the other yearbooks. It was almost as if she had been expecting to find him.

Practical Jude opened her backpack and took out a notebook. "Okay," she said, writing down all the dates of the yearbooks in which Mr. Potts appeared. "Let's get to the bottom of this. Look at how many times he's pictured. The first time is in 1932. There he is—as Mr. T. Pope, the principal of Carroway Junior High. And look—he's not wearing the vest. Then there's Mr. T. Pope again, still the principal, in 1933—still no vest, and he's wearing glasses! Then in 1934 he's got on that funny bow tie."

"After 1934 he shows up only once per decade," murmured Charlotte, leafing through the yearbooks. "With a different name each time, but always the same clothes and hairstyle."

"I hate that stupid diamond vest," announced Penny.

Jude was writing furiously, trying to get everything down in her notebook. "T. Pope, principal from 1932 until 1934. And then he's back in 1944 as T. Popper, cafeteria staff. That was sort of a step down in his career, I'd say."

"In 1954 he's T. Porter, math tutor," read Penny aloud. "And in 1964 he's T. Pape, gardener."

Zibby frowned down at the books. "In 1979—that's when our parents were here, Char—he's T. Potter, assistant custodian. But that's not just a decade later—it's fifteen years since he last showed up."

"And then he skips the 1980s completely and comes back in 1997 as T. Post, reading tutor," said Jude. "That's even more than fifteen years. I wonder why?"

"But now he's back," said Charlotte in a whisper. "And it's been only a few years."

"I don't understand the pattern, but I think it's important somehow." Jude threw down her pen and rubbed her fingers through her short curls in frustration.

"All of these pictures with the diamond vest—do you think it's somehow the *same* photo just printed again and again in all the books?" asked Penny.

"No, look closely," said Charlotte. "You can see the pose is slightly different in each one even though the clothes are the same. Like here, in the 1944 picture, he's sort of smiling, and in the 1964 picture his eyes are nearly closed. And in 1997 his head is turned a little to the side."

"But the clothes don't change at all," mused Jude. "And the hairstyle. It's him, all right, in every single photo!" She closed her notebook. She shut all the yearbooks, too, and slid them neatly back onto the shelf. Then she looked at the other girls expectantly. "So, now what?"

"So...now I'm late for detention." Zibby groaned.

"Forget it," said Charlotte. "No way are you going anywhere near that man—whatever his name is!"

Zibby had to smile a little at her cousin's protectiveness. Charlotte was a lot nicer these days, she reflected, since they'd been battling ghosts together.

Penny spoke up comfortingly. "Don't worry. We'll go with you." She looked at the other girls eagerly. "Right? We'll ask Mr. Potts about the pictures. It's the obvious thing to do."

"Aunt Penelope's a brave woman, you have to say that for her," said Jude, with a little, nervous laugh.

Charlotte moaned. Zibby felt the fine hairs on the back of her neck prickle. Nonetheless, they all said good-bye to Ms. Wilson and followed Penny down the hall to Mr. Potts's classroom.

"Hello, Mr. Potts," Penny said as they filed inside.

He sat at his desk, eyes closed. When he opened his eyes and saw the girls, he pointed a finger straight at Zibby. "You," he said gruffly. "*Double* detention for being late. But not now, not today. I must leave. We shall schedule it for another time."

"I—I'm sorry—" Zibby's voice quavered. Her heart

began to thud painfully. "But before you leave—um—we wanted to talk to you."

He waited. "About science? About electricity?"

Zibby turned to the other girls.

"Not exactly," Jude spoke up. "About photography."

"I know very little about that subject," Mr. Potts said. "Now, I really must go." He stood up on shaky legs and gripped the edge of his desk for balance. "Perhaps when Mrs. Durkee—that is, *Ms.* Durkee—returns, she will teach you about photography." He picked up his scarf. Zibby watched in fascinated horror as he wound the fabric around his neck, then reached for his overcoat on the back of the desk chair.

"We think you *can* help us," Charlotte said bravely.

"Oh?" Mr. Potts's voice sounded edgy. He slid his arms into his coat and started doing up the buttons. He drew from his trouser pocket an old-fashioned pocket watch on a chain. "I'm afraid my time is up, young ladies."

"We were looking in the old yearbooks," Jude continued. "In the library."

"I—I really must be off!" Mr. Potts gazed past them to the door.

"We found your picture in some of them," Penny pressed on. She walked nearer to him, her dozens of braids dancing on her shoulders. "It really amazed us how you manage to stay looking so young—after so many years." She looked up at him with her most dazzling smile. "We wondered if you would tell us how you do it?"

Mr. Potts's eyes widened. He started to back away from the girls, his expression frantic. He no longer seemed stern and gruff. He was *afraid* of them.

His obvious fear gave Zibby confidence. She spoke up clearly. "We also wondered why you changed your name so many times, Mr. Potts. We're wondering what's going on."

Mr. Potts shook his head, reaching into his pockets for his gloves. Zibby sucked in her breath as he slid them on to his hands. There they were—two black leather gloves with zigzag stitching around the wrists. The right thumb had a tear. Zibby couldn't look away.

"I'm sorry," Mr. Potts whispered. "I simply cannot stay. It is impossible..." He backed up against the chalkboard.

"Why are *you* so afraid?" demanded Zibby. The more he trembled, the bolder she felt. "*We're* the ones who should be afraid!"

She took a step in his direction, and he held up his hands as if to ward her off. She could see that the palm of the left glove was worse than cracked—it looked burned. It looked as if it had been charred in a fire.

A fire in a dollhouse?

"Tell us who you are!" she cried, taking another step toward him. "Tell us about the dollhouse and the fire!"

Mr. Potts let out a cry, and then—something was happening to him. He had backed against the blackboard, but it didn't seem to be supporting him. Somehow he was falling, no—he was melting. No—it was as if Mr. Potts were *dissolving* right before their eyes.

And then he was gone.

The girls stood in shocked silence. Then Zibby started to cry. She felt filled with a desperate, inexplicable sense of loss.

"I should have known," she wept. "After everything that's been happening, I should have seen it right away." She drew a deep shuddering breath and wiped her eyes. "I can't believe we didn't see it right away, you guys," she said to the others in a calmer voice. "We should have guessed."

"Guessed what?" Jude was edging to the classroom door, carefully avoiding the spot where Mr. Potts had stood.

"He's a ghost," Zibby said gently. "Mr. Potts is another ghost."

CHAPTER 31

PRIMROSE 1923

Nanny Shanks telephoned Primrose at her boarding school in Cleveland every Sunday afternoon. That was the time when the girls sat in the common room, reading by the fire or playing board games at the round tables by the windows. They were allowed to receive phone calls in the headmistress's office on Sunday afternoons. And this is where Primrose would be called each Sunday around four o'clock to speak to faithful Nanny Shanks.

Not that there was ever much news—just updates on the twins, or reports of Primrose's parents' latest travels. And Primrose never had much to report to Nanny Shanks, either—just about her progress in learning to swim, or about her A on a French test. She didn't want to tell Nanny Shanks about the hateful girls who teased her for having a dollhouse in her room, and she certainly couldn't tell her how often she'd tried to get rid of the dollhouse only to have it return, intact, every time.

But this Sunday Nanny Shanks had interesting news.

"We've had a letter from Mr. Pope," she told Primrose on the telephone. "He and his wife are living quite near you up in Cleveland now, where he has been teaching science at a private academy since leaving us. And now I've had a lovely announcement come in the mail yesterday to say they have had a baby girl! Isn't that lovely news? I thought you might like to send them a special gift for the baby."

An idea lit up Primrose's face, though of course Nanny Shanks could not see it through the phone lines. "Nanny, I would like to give my old dollhouse to Mr. Pope's baby."

"Oh, you dear girl! That is very sweet of you. I know how you love that dollhouse—why, you've taken it off to school, haven't you? And even brought it home for the summer holidays! Are you quite sure you can part with it?"

"Absolutely," said Primrose firmly. She knew it was only a slim chance that she could get rid of the house this way. After all, she had tried many times to give it to other girls at school, to break it to pieces with a sledgehammer, and to burn it—all with no success. But...Mr. Pope's baby daughter might be different. The gray doll, after all, had disappeared from Primrose's cloak pocket at the wedding and not returned. Mr. Pope had been Miss Honeywell's great love. So maybe the house would also like staying with the Popes.

And so it was arranged that when the Parsons' chauffeur came to collect Primrose at the Easter break, he would take Primrose to deliver the dollhouse to the Popes herself.

THE POPES LIVED in a small house in a respectable neighborhood very close to the school in Cleveland where Mr. Pope taught. The chauffeur stopped the car at the curb and opened the door for Primrose and Nanny Shanks, who had

driven up from Columbus with him. As they walked to the
front door, Nanny Shanks murmured she had heard that
Mrs. Pope's health had not been well since the baby's birth.

"What a lovely baby, Mrs. Pope," Primrose said in her
nicest voice when she and Nanny Shanks had been welcomed by Mr. Pope and led into the master bedroom to
meet the baby for the first time. "You must be very proud."

The baby was dark-haired and pink-cheeked, the very
picture of health. But her mother lay in bed, pale and gaunt.
Primrose was shocked. Mrs. Pope looked nothing like the
radiant bride she had met at Mr. Pope's wedding three years
before.

Mr. Pope lifted the baby from his wife's thin arms and let
Nanny Shanks hold her, sitting in the rocking chair beside
the big bed. Nanny Shanks and Primrose made baby talk
while Mr. Pope and the chauffeur together wrestled the
large dollhouse into the room and set it by the windows.

Mrs. Pope gasped with pleasure when the dollhouse was
unveiled. "This is a fabulous gift, Miss Parson. I am very
touched that you would give away such a piece of your
childhood. It's too generous of you."

"I'm happy to do it," Primrose replied truthfully. She
pointed out the several cardboard boxes stacked by the chair.
"And there are the furnishings and little dolls for it as well. I
hope the baby enjoys it when she is older."

"You are so sweet to give us this gift," replied Mrs. Pope.
"Isn't she, Thaddeus?"

"Indeed she is," agreed Mr. Pope. He smiled at Primrose
and didn't seem at all the long-faced tutor she'd once
known. Married life seemed to have lightened his spirit,

though Primrose could see in his eyes the worry when he looked at his wife. "This is the same dollhouse we once planned to fit with electric lights, is it not?"

"Yes, the same one," said Primrose.

"But Miss Honeywell put a stop to that." He rubbed his hands together. "Well!"

Primrose, who always felt a little prickle at the back of her neck at any mention of her governess's name, remained silent.

"Indeed!" Mr. Pope said awkwardly into the silence. "Perhaps I will electrify it myself for our little girl someday. Thank you again, so very much."

"You're most welcome," Primrose said. Then she and Nanny Shanks were offered tea and little cakes, which they accepted, and Primrose got to hold the baby on her lap. She touched the soft cheek gently with one finger, then said good-bye, and left with Nanny Shanks.

Primrose held her breath as the chauffeur stopped the car back at the Parsons' house. She tiptoed up to her bedroom and peered inside, fully expecting to see the dollhouse in the corner. But it wasn't there, or in the playroom, or in the twins' bedroom. And when she returned to school at the end of the one-week break, the house was not there, either.

Primrose was joyful. At last she could sleep well at night, untroubled by ghostly noises and morbid thoughts. She had finally found the only other place for the dollhouse: the home of the only other person Miss Honeywell would want to haunt!

Primrose breathed free and easy for exactly ten days. During those days she aced her French exam and learned to dive beautifully into the school swimming pool. She was even invited to share a secret midnight feast with some of the other girls on her hall.

But her pleasure was short-lived. On the tenth day of freedom, the telephone rang in the headmistress's study. It was, as expected, Nanny Shanks. Nanny sounded very upset.

"Oh, Primrose, dear girl, I've had the most terrible news. Poor Mrs. Pope has died! Mr. Pope is beside himself with grief, as you can imagine. That poor, poor man. And that little baby without a mother! Oh, it is too tragic for words."

"What happened? How did she die?" Primrose was sorry to hear this news. Mr. Pope had been so happy with his bride.

"Complications from the birth, I heard. She was very weak, as you saw. Now the funeral service will be on Friday, and of course we must go."

Primrose agreed that they must. She said good-bye to Nanny Shanks and, feeling very unsettled, wandered out of the headmistress's study and back to her room. Something was going to happen. She could just feel it.

What do I mean by that? Primrose asked herself, but didn't know. Nonetheless, she wasn't the least bit surprised when just after dinner, when the biggest girls were organizing a game of charades, she was called into the headmistress's study to take another phone call. It was Nanny Shanks with further news.

"Dear girl, now there's something else. Something very strange. I've just had another call from Mr. Pope. He had more bad news to tell me. On top of the tragedy of his wife's death, he must cope with thieves! It seems that the lovely dollhouse you gave the baby has been stolen! Imagine that—furnishings, dolls, and all. It was there in the morning but now it's gone."

"Oh no—" Primrose took a deep breath.

"He called in the police, of course, but there is no trace of it. Nothing else seems to have been stolen. Now he is saying he would like to speak to you, Primrose. And he asked permission to come to your school—tonight! I have spoken to the headmistress, and she says it will be permitted, though it is highly irregular. He is on his way now, and I just wanted to alert you. He is terribly agitated."

"But what does he want to see *me* about?" cried Primrose. She was sweating.

"Perhaps just to tell you himself about the dollhouse," Nanny Shanks replied.

Primrose said good-bye and hung up in a daze. *Nothing that happened is my fault!* Primrose went to sit on the window seat. She looked out at the darkening evening. Almost immediately she saw a sweep of headlights come up the drive.

The headmistress showed Mr. Pope into the study where Primrose waited, and ordered them both cups of tea. Mr. Pope thanked her, then asked to speak to Primrose privately. The headmistress nodded and left the room, leaving the door ajar. In a flash, Mr. Pope crossed the room and sat on the window seat, next to Primrose.

"I am very sorry to hear of your wife's death," she began politely—but he interrupted her.

"I have been visited by a ghost," he said hoarsely. "And I believe you have, too."

Primrose hesitated. "But why would your wife appear to me?" she asked carefully.

"No! Not Evelina!" He rubbed his hands across his face. "It was Miss Honeywell."

The back of Primrose's neck prickled.

"I'm sure it was Calliope," he continued. "When my wife and I were first married, strange things kept happening. The doll in the gray dress—the one you brought to our wedding—kept turning up during our honeymoon. It was frightening the way it would suddenly appear on our breakfast table or be sitting on the sink in our bathroom. It even showed up one night at the theater, waiting in our reserved seats." He took a deep breath. "And then it disappeared again. Until you brought us the dollhouse. Then the doll was back. It appeared on the bed next to my wife! It lay on the pillow next to her head, and no matter how many times I returned it to the dollhouse, it moved somehow to the pillow! It caused me great distress, though I always made a little joke about the doll, and I believe Evelina thought I was playing some sort of game."

"First of all, let's get one thing straight," said Primrose staunchly. "I did *not* bring that doll to your wedding. I've already told you that."

"Yes, well, I did not believe you then," Mr. Pope said, "but I do now. I believe the doll is able somehow to move… by itself."

Primrose pressed her lips together and did not comment.

Mr. Pope took a deep, shuddering breath. "The day she died, Evelina had spent about an hour arranging the furniture in the dollhouse. She seemed so happy—chattering away like a girl as she set up the dolls. But by late morning she was feeling faint and took to her bed. She fell into a deep sleep and she died that same evening—only three days ago."

His voice broke. Primrose waited, holding her breath, until he had composed himself.

"When I walked into the room and found her—I also found the doll. On the pillow next to her head! I put the doll into the dollhouse and latched the house closed. Several hours later my housekeeper made me a light supper and urged me into the dining room. I tell you, I had no appetite. But I sat at the table—and found that the doll was lying next to my plate as if waiting for me. The housekeeper denies all knowledge of how she came to be there—yet there was no one else in the house, except for the baby, of course. So who put it there, Primrose?"

Primrose remained silent.

Mr. Pope's voice grew even more agitated as he continued his story. "Then this morning the doll was on my desk, leaning against the lamp. And I heard a voice in my head— it was Calliope Honeywell's voice! I recognized it! It was frightful, Primrose. She said she was *waiting* for me. She said that our love would never die."

Primrose stared at him. "W—what did you do?" she whispered finally.

"I shouted that 'our love' had existed only in her imagination. I told her my one true love was Evelina!

"That was the wrong answer, because," Mr. Pope explained, "suddenly the desk in my study started vibrating. Then I noticed that the dollhouse was there in the corner of the room," he continued, "and *it* was vibrating! Little pieces of doll furniture started flying about the room—they narrowly missed hitting me, I tell you! I ran from the room, bolting the door from the outside." Mr. Pope's eyes were wild. "And when I went back a few hours later and dared to check, I found that the dollhouse was gone—though the room was still locked!"

He stared at Primrose. Two splotches of red marked his cheekbones. "Like a crazy man, I started checking the house, though I knew I would not find the dollhouse. Still, I searched the study, the kitchen, even the bathroom. Nothing. It was gone. It must have been stolen…," he concluded shakily. "Yes, stolen. At least that is what I must believe. Because to think otherwise is to admit that Calliope—" He broke off, shuddering.

"Stolen," agreed Primrose in a strained voice. "I'm so sorry."

"Good riddance to it," Mr. Pope said softly. "But I wanted to come tell you in person, because you were so kind to give us the dollhouse. And I wanted to ask you whether you have heard from Calliope—ah—Miss Honeywell yourself."

They sat in silence a long moment and Primrose could hear the clock ticking on the mantel. She could not speak about Miss Honeywell. She rubbed the back of her neck and shook her head. "No," she whispered the lie, "I have heard nothing."

Then the headmistress poked her head back into the room and said it was bedtime for Primrose. Mr. Pope hastily stood up and shook Primrose's hand in farewell.

Primrose slowly climbed the stairs, lost in thought. She stood outside in the hallway, not wanting to open the door, knowing fully well what sight would greet her eyes when she finally did. And she was right.

There it was, front and center: the large, imposing dollhouse standing importantly in the middle of the room again, as if it had never been gone. And Primrose heard distant laughter borne on currents of air, vicious and triumphant.

CHAPTER 32

"So you mean we're dealing with *three* ghosts now?" Penny's voice rose to a shriek. "I can't stand it!"

But, strangely, Zibby herself felt much calmer now that she realized Mr. Potts was a ghost. Her terror of the science teacher seemed to fade away as Mr. Potts himself had done.

"At least three," she said. "And they all have to be connected to the dollhouse."

"But Primrose wasn't a ghost yet when you bought the dollhouse," objected Charlotte.

"I know, but everything that's happened is because of her. They're all connected, somehow—Primrose and Miss Honeywell and Mr. Potts. They're connected as ghosts—so they were probably connected in life, too. We still need to find out where Mr. Potts fits in. I saw him for the first time the same day I bought the dollhouse. He was in the park. And later I saw him walking along our street, and another time he was looking over the fence into my backyard when I burned up the dollhouse. He asked if I had seen his lamb, and I thought he was talking about a *sheep*. Now I'm not so sure."

"I think he was looking for a person," said Penny thoughtfully. "A person he likes. He said, 'Come to me, my lamb,' as if it meant 'my sweetie pie,' or something."

"Hmmm," said Jude, musingly. "What's weird is how nervous he is. Really shaky and weak. For a ghost, that seems strange. I mean, Miss Honeywell is so strong."

"Primrose isn't always strong," Zibby pointed out. "When Miss Honeywell is there, it's as if she pulls the energy right out of Primrose."

Jude's dark eyes widened. "Maybe Miss Honeywell is somehow sucking the energy out of Mr. Potts, too. He always looks like he's about to fall apart. And just now he seemed as scared of us as we were of him."

"As we *are* of him," corrected Charlotte. "*I'm* still scared of him. Remember that dream?"

"Yeah—even if he's a sad sort of ghost, there's still that awful dream," Penny agreed.

"I'm not forgetting about the dream. But I'm not sure he even knows we're having it." Zibby shoved her hands deep into her jacket pockets. Newly fallen autumn leaves swirled around their feet as they walked. "I think we need to figure out the dream. How it's connected to him and to Miss Honeywell and to Primrose—and why we're having it."

"So—first of all we'll ask Primrose if she knew Mr. Potts when they were alive," Jude said decisively, kicking leaves along the sidewalk. "And then we'll try to interpret the dream. Maybe she can help us with that, too."

"Let's go tell her what we've found out," agreed Zibby.

"Right now. If she knows Mr. Potts is a ghost, she should be able to tell us what his trouble is."

"His trouble, plain and simple, is that he's *dead*," said Charlotte sternly. "That's the trouble with all these ghosts. They've caused nothing but trouble so far."

"You're right," Zibby allowed, "but there's got to be a reason all this is happening. Everything is connected somehow to that dollhouse, and Miss Honeywell's at the heart of it. I never saw a ghost in my life until I got that dollhouse. I didn't even *believe* in ghosts." She jumped up the steps to her front porch and turned back to Charlotte. "But now my life is nothing but ghosts. I don't want to go on being haunted forever. In ghost stories, the ghosts haunt people for a *reason*."

"Like they want people to find their bones and give them a decent burial," said Penny. "I saw a movie where there was this ghost who needed help because its bones were all scattered—"

"You mean we have to find Mr. Potts's *bones*?" shrieked Charlotte.

Zibby frowned at her cousin impatiently. "I don't think it's like that, exactly," she said, trying to keep her voice mild. "But I do get the feeling we're supposed to *do* something."

"Mr. Potts gave you a detention," Charlotte pointed out. "Double detention, even. Are you just trying to be noble?"

"Grow up, Char," said Zibby wearily, though it pleased her to be able to say those particular words to her oh-so-mature cousin. "I just have the feeling that he's a sad, tortured ghost, and he's only a part of what's been happening, and I am desperate to figure out what it is—and how to stop it."

"Me, too!" said Penny.

"Me three," said Jude. "And I bet Laura-Jane will make it four. Aren't *you* with us, Char?"

Charlotte shrugged, but she followed the girls into the house. With a finger pressed to her lips to signal that they should stop talking about the ghosts, Zibby headed for the kitchen. The girls found Nell in there, in the midst of preparations for another catered party. Trays of delicacies covered the table and every countertop.

"We're hungry," Zibby announced, watching her mom deftly cut thin pasta strips and hang them on a wooden rack to dry. She was pleased to see that Nell had been so busy. That must mean her head wasn't aching.

Nell paused with a noodle hanging from her fingertips. "Apples?"

Zibby eyed the three-tiered chocolate cake. *"Apples?"* Sometimes it seemed that all the best food was reserved for DaisyCakes.

"Well, there's some caramel dip to go with the apples," said Nell with a smile. Then she added, "Laura-Jane got home half an hour ago. She's up in her room. Where have you been?"

Zibby started slicing apples and arranging them around a little bowl of the dip. "I got a detention in science for getting to class late."

"Walk faster, then," Nell said. "But I do remember how crowded those hallways get."

"Yeah," said Zibby noncommittally. She still wasn't used to keeping secrets from her mom.

The girls took their snack to Zibby's room and called up the attic stairs for Laura-Jane to join them. Sitting all to-

gether on the floor in front of the dollhouse, they filled
Laura-Jane in on what they had learned about Mr. Potts
that day. "Why am I not surprised?" Laura-Jane asked,
with a shiver. "Every single day in this house *something*
bizarre is happening."

Zibby looked at her sharply, then realized that Laura-
Jane had not intended to be insulting. She was simply stating
the truth. Things *were* bizarre here. Zibby opened the dollhouse and reached inside for the little doll in the blue dress.
"Primrose?"

At your service, came the peevish little voice in her head.
*And it's about time you returned to me. I've been having quite a
battle. But this is my dollhouse and I won't leave!*

"Is Miss Honeywell here?" Zibby asked urgently. "Is she
in there with you? What's going on with the two of you?"
She reached out for Jude, and the other girls linked arms so
that they, too, could hear Primrose's fretful voice.

Oh, yes, she's here. And she's trying to kill me!

"But you're already...dead," Zibby reminded her.

*She's trying to suck all my energy. She's a parasite—siphon-
ing off every drop of energy so that she can grow stronger. But
she mustn't win. I shall stay here as long as I want!* The little
voice in Zibby's head rose to a shout. *Do you hear me, Old
Sourpuss?*

That will be Sweet *Miss Honeywell to you, my girl.* The
whispered reply seeped coldly into the girls' heads.

Zibby realized with dread that Miss Honeywell's power
was so strong that she didn't need to speak through a doll at
all. She could reach inside the girls' heads any time she liked.

"Listen, Primrose," Zibby said in a low voice. "We
wanted to talk to you about Mr. Potts." She glanced uneasily

around the room, picked up Primrose, then beckoned silently to the other girls. They trooped out into the hall and back down the stairs and outside to the front porch. Jude had the presence of mind to bring along the plate of apple slices and caramel dip.

Logically she knew it didn't make any difference at all, but Zibby felt safer out of sight of the dollhouse. They sat on the stairs, touching arms or legs so they could all hear Primrose's voice. Zibby held the little girl doll on her lap. "Primrose, we need you to help us with Mr. Potts."

I told you already, I don't know anybody called Potts.

Zibby met Jude's eyes. There must be something connecting all three ghosts—but what? "Listen, the point is, we've found out that Mr. Potts is a ghost, Primrose. Just like you. And he keeps coming back to our school. We need you to help us find out what he wants."

The little girl doll vibrated in Zibby's hands. *Your teacher is a ghost? You're quite certain of this?*

"That's right," said Zibby firmly. She helped herself to a slice of apple.

The man must be very powerful. Primrose sounded awed. *Tell me more!*

The girls told her how Mr. Potts wore the same gloves as appeared in the dream, and how all the girls were having the same dream, and how it seemed Mr. Potts kept coming to the school every decade. "He's looking for something," said Zibby. "I think it's a lamb. Or—a person he calls 'my lamb.'"

They told Primrose how Mr. Potts had vanished when they confronted him. They told her about the terrible sadness emanating from him.

Hmmm, Primrose said from time to time. *Hmmm.*

Then the little ghost fell silent. Zibby huddled with the other girls together on the steps. Wasn't Primrose going to help them?

"Come on, Primrose!" prompted Zibby.

Then at last Primrose began to speak. *Ghosts have different strengths, I'm learning.* Primrose's voice came to them faintly, as if she were far away. *They—we—have to practice. I can haunt the dollhouse—and speak to you. But it's much harder for me to move things—like the doll. Or the wallet. Miss Honeywell spent her whole life trying to force people to obey her—first her brother, Lester, then me; and the whole time she's been dead, she's been learning how to gather power. She's had lots of practice.*

"Like making me throw all those dishes and glasses in the kitchen," murmured Laura-Jane. "That took a lot of power. I could feel her power in the air all around me, like evil vibrations."

Exactly. She's very strong. And when she gathers her power, I feel myself growing weaker, losing power...There's not enough room in that house for both of us. And remember I told you I felt some other *energy in the house?*

"Yes," Zibby said.

I'm wondering if that might be your Mr. Potts. If it is, and if he's the very strong ghost you say he is, then Miss Honeywell is probably trying to gather energy from him, too.

"I'm not sure he's really so powerful," Zibby objected. "He always looks worn out."

Primrose's voice rose in their heads. *Manifesting himself in a real body—that takes up the most energy of all! The man probably saves up his energy little by little over time, storing it*

up until he grows strong enough—amassing that much energy
could take a decade, which would explain why he shows up at
school only every ten or fifteen years. And even then he would
only be able to stay visible a short time. He must have a very
compelling reason to work so hard. You say Mr. Potts can actu-
ally walk around the school and touch things? And speak aloud
so people can really hear him?

"Yes," said Zibby. "He walks and talks and writes on the
board like any normal teacher."

"He puts on his own horrible gloves," added Penny.

He has complete control over matter. Primrose sounded
mightily impressed. *And you say he has even been photo-*
graphed?

"Many times," sighed Jude. "As far as we can tell from
the yearbooks."

What yearbooks? gasped Primrose.

Zibby told her.

Show me—right away! Now the ghostly voice was urgent.

"They're in the school library—well, wait, I do have one
here at home." Zibby dashed inside, returning to the porch
with Nell's yearbook. "Look—this was my mom's." She
flipped through the pages until she found the photo of
T. Potter, Assistant Custodian. "See?"

Aaaaiiiieeeee! The screech jabbed through the girls'
heads like a jolt of electricity.

"Ow!" moaned Charlotte, clutching her forehead.

"What is it? What's wrong?" cried Laura-Jane and Penny.

That's him! Oh, dear me, that's him!

"Who?" shouted Zibby.

"So—you recognize him?" asked Jude.

The ghost's voice was agitated. *Oh, yes indeed, I recognize*

him. But that is not Mr. Potts, and that's nobody called T. Pot-
ter. That is Mr. Thaddeus Pope, my former tutor!

"T. Pope," said Jude with satisfaction. "That's what Mr.
Potts was calling himself when he was the principal back in
the 1930s, remember?"

"You mean you knew Mr. Pope?" Zibby's voice rose excitedly. "For real? Before you were ghosts, I mean?"

I told you about him. He was my tutor. He was quite a nice
man...And Miss Honeywell was in love with him. Primrose's
voice came to them very faintly. Her power seemed to be fading. *She thought she'd end up marrying him someday!* The
weakest little giggle hovered in their heads.

Zibby held the little doll up in front of her face. "Primrose—tell us!" she begged. "What happened to Mr. Pope?"

But there came no answer, even though the girls sat with
arms linked for a full five minutes, waiting.

"Do you think Miss Honeywell stopped her?" whispered Penny.

"Do you think Miss Honeywell is listening to us now?"
Charlotte glanced uneasily around the porch.

"I don't know," said Zibby. She held up the little doll.
"Primrose?" she asked pleadingly. "Can you hear me?
Please tell us what happened to Mr. Pope!"

They waited again, finishing off all the apple slices and
caramel dip, but still there came no reply. Primrose had
gone. *Or she was overpowered,* thought Zibby. All the girls
sat quietly. They didn't seem to have a lot of energy themselves anymore.

Distantly Zibby could hear the sounds of activity inside
the house: Nell's voice singing down in the kitchen. A bell
ringing—was it the phone? Or Miss Honeywell? Zibby was

ready to head inside to check on her mom, but Nell came to the front door and opened the screen.

"There you are, girls," said Nell. "Mr. Jefferson just phoned to say Jude and Penny need to come home for dinner now. And Charlotte—what about you, honey? I can drive you home, or you're welcome to stay for dinner with us. Ned is picking Brady up from soccer, and I'm afraid they're bringing pizza, too. We'll have to stop eating so much fast food after the wedding!"

"I'd love to stay, Aunt Nell, but—um—I'm really tired, and I'd better go," Charlotte replied, her voice sounding perfectly normal despite her pale face and trembling hands. "I've got tons of homework."

"Zibby and Laura-Jane, would you please set the table in the dining room so we can eat as soon as I get back from Charlotte's? And make a salad so I don't have to feel like a bad mother."

"Sure, Mom," said Zibby. Her voice sounded normal, too, but tired. It was exhausting, dealing with ghosts and worrying about her mom. She felt so very, very tired, as if all the energy were being... *Oh no.* The thought slammed into Zibby hard.

Was Miss Honeywell drawing power from other sources besides Primrose? Besides Mr. Potts? Could ghosts get energy only from other ghosts, or could they tap into live people, too? Zibby dragged her fingers through her hair.

The girls stood up. Zibby and Laura-Jane said good-bye to Penny, Jude, and Charlotte. Nell gave Jude and Penny a wedding invitation to take home to Mr. and Mrs. Jefferson, and the girls thanked her excitedly. Nell and Charlotte climbed into Nell's DaisyCakes van and drove off.

Then Zibby opened the screen door and went slowly inside. On the stairs, up at the level of the landing, a flicker of gray caught Zibby's eye. Resolutely, Zibby climbed the stairs.

There atop the bookcase on the stairway landing stood the governess doll. Her steely eyes stared boldly at Zibby. *We have some business to attend to, young miss,* said the governess's voice in Zibby's head.

"Oh no we don't," whispered Zibby. She grabbed the doll and ran back downstairs. Outside, in front, Ned and Brady were just arriving home and Laura-Jane was greeting them. Zibby knew she should go help carry in the pizza, but she hurried into the kitchen instead and opened the back door. She threw the gray-gowned doll outside across the patio with as much force as she could muster.

It was probably a pointless gesture, but getting the doll out of the house even for a short time made her feel better. She slammed the door and sank into a chair at the kitchen table.

The table was crowded with covered trays of desserts for another DaisyCakes catered event that night—which explained why Nell wanted to eat in the dining room instead of the kitchen. A luscious chocolate cake stood on a glass pedestal. Normally Zibby might have been tempted to stick out one finger and steal just the tiniest taste of frosting. But not tonight. She felt shaken. She wanted her mom. She wanted to tell her everything.

You will not speak to anyone about this, young miss.

Zibby jumped up from the table and looked wildly around the kitchen. There was the doll, returned from the patio, standing by the toaster. Zibby could hear Ned and Laura-Jane talking in the front hall. She edged past the counter and inched toward the kitchen door—toward their voices, and, she hoped, toward safety. But the door slammed shut—right in her face.

You must learn to mind me.

"Shut up! You have no power over me! You aren't my governess!"

You must be taught to obey.

Zibby pulled on the door handle, but the door was stuck. She raised her hands to pound the door with her fists but felt an inexorable pressure pushing her arms down to her sides again. She opened her mouth to scream for Ned, but no sound came out. Her jaw was forced closed. She found herself marching against her will right back to the table where she'd been sitting. An unseen force pushed her back into her chair.

Now sit there quietly. Like a lady.

Zibby struggled to break free from the unseen hands that held her in place. She was frantic to scream, to shout— but her mouth simply would not open. As if from very far away, she heard Brady laughing. Where were Ned and Laura-Jane?

You must learn to mind.

Why hadn't Nell come back from taking Charlotte home? Zibby tried desperately to stomp her feet, to make enough noise that Ned would hurry to the kitchen to investigate—but her feet felt bolted to the floor.

Now lift your right hand, young miss. Lift it up and put it on the table.

Against her will, Zibby saw her right arm move, saw the hand lift off her lap and hover in space for a moment before settling onto the tabletop next to one of the trays of food. It was as if it were someone else's hand. She watched, mesmerized.

Little puffs of sugar. Pretty morsels of chocolate. You would like to eat them, wouldn't you, greedy girl! And without her volition, Zibby's hand rose in the air and peeled back the foil from the tray. Her fingers reached for one of the chocolate puffs and lifted it. Her hand waved it around in front of her face, then moved it toward her mouth.

But little girls must not spoil their dinners with sweets. The cold voice sifted through Zibby's mind like a freezing wind. An unseen hand slapped the puff out of her fingers.

Now pick up the whole tray!

"No!" The word burst out of Zibby's mouth even as she saw her hands moving toward the tray. She stared hard at her hands, willing them to stop. She would *not* pick up the tray.

Do it this minute, you disobedient child. Pick. Up. The. Tray.

"No!" gasped Zibby—but her hands grasped the sides of the large tray and tightened around the metal rim anyway.

Now you will stand up and hold the tray as high as you can. Over your head, my girl. Yes, yes, very good. That's the way.

Again Zibby struggled to pull away from this mind control. She fixed her eye on the governess doll even as her arms hefted the tray high. "You will not win," she hissed at the doll.

Now dump the tray onto the floor.

"No!" whispered Zibby. She stared hard at the doll, pictured it toppling backward into the sink. Willed it to topple.

You must learn to mind. The voice was implacable. *Dump. It. On. To. The. Floor.*

Zibby thought of all Nell's hard work on this food. She visualized the doll falling into the sink and down the garbage disposal. Imagined flipping the switch to start the blades chopping inside the drain. "No way." Zibby's voice was implacable, too.

The pressure in Zibby's brain was immense. She felt that her head was going to explode.

Dump it, ordered Miss Honeywell. The cold menace of her voice was like a vise around Zibby's brain, squeezing tight.

But Zibby resisted the pressure with all her might. She gasped for air. "NO!" she shouted at the top of her lungs, and immediately the kitchen door burst open and Laura-Jane stood there, openmouthed at the sight of Zibby holding the large tray over her head.

"Zibby!"

"H—help me," whispered Zibby. "I can't—" The pressure in her head was so great she knew she was going to drop the tray anyway. She was going to fail. "I *can't...*"

But Laura-Jane could. She leaped forward to whisk the tray out of Zibby's arms just as Zibby collapsed onto the kitchen floor.

CHAPTER 33

Laura-Jane set the tray back on the table. She pulled Zibby to her feet. "It's Miss Honeywell, right?" she asked urgently. "Just like before. Just like when she forced me to break all the china and stuff. Are you okay?"

Zibby ached all over. She sank shakily into the kitchen chair again. Rubbing her sore knees, she took deep breaths to calm herself. "Okay?" The pressure in her head receded and she looked up at Laura-Jane gratefully. "I'll never be okay as long as that ghost is around. But, oh, Laura-Jane, thank you, thank you, thank you for coming in when you did. I don't know what she would have tried next."

"I can still feel her." Laura-Jane scanned the kitchen. "But where?"

The governess doll was no longer by the toaster. "Check the sink," whispered Zibby.

And that's where they found the doll, headfirst down the disposal.

"Quick—let's turn it on!" cried Zibby, and was reaching for the switch just as the back door opened and Nell stepped inside.

"Ready to eat, girls?" Nell asked cheerfully, then stopped, looking down at the floor. "What's going on?"

Zibby drew back from the switch regretfully. She stepped away from the sink and looked where her mother pointed. There on the table was the tray with the foil folded back. There on the floor was the chocolate puff Miss Honeywell had slapped out of her hand.

"Sorry, Mom," she murmured. "I—I was just going to try one. Just a little taste. I guess I...dropped it."

Nell bent down to wipe up the mess. Swiftly, Laura-Jane tugged the governess doll out of the sink and with a single underhand motion tossed it into the adjacent laundry room, where it landed in a basket of folded clothes.

"You know I don't like you to help yourself, Zib," chided Nell. "All this food has been paid for by my clients. It's all meant for the banquet tonight."

"I know, Mom. I guess I...just couldn't help myself."

"Well," Nell said, standing up again, "get a better grip on yourself. Now, let's eat quickly, because I've got to get this food over to the reception. Where are those pizzas?"

"Dad put them on the dining-room table," Laura-Jane told her. "Everything's ready. I'll get the drinks."

Nell smiled at this helpful version of Laura-Jane, and they all went in to eat.

THAT NIGHT ZIBBY sat slumped at one end of the living-room couch, with Ned at the other end, reading. Laura-Jane and Brady had gone to bed. She was trying to read her history assignment, but her eyes kept closing. Finally Ned reached over and shut her textbook.

"Bedtime," he said firmly.

"I'm waiting for Mom."

"She could be another hour."

"I need to talk to her," Zibby said, her voice trembling with stress and fatigue.

"Can't it wait till morning? Or is it something I can help you with?"

Zibby rubbed her eyes. "I don't think so." She looked up at him. "Well, maybe." Her own dad would listen gravely to whatever she told him, but he would never, ever believe in ghosts. He didn't believe in anything unseen. Not even God, probably.

What did Ned believe in? Zibby had no idea. She took a deep breath. "Ned, what do you think about ghosts? Not the white-sheet, Halloweeny kind, but real ghosts? Spirits that can't rest? That hang around after the person has died?"

He stared down at her, then sat next to her on the couch. "You're asking this for a reason. Do you think you've seen a ghost?"

"Well…yes."

"Here? In the house?"

"Sort of. And at school. And…I've heard voices. Ghosts' voices."

Ned leaned back and looked at her, brow furrowed in consternation. "Go on."

Zibby felt a rush of gratitude toward her soon-to-be stepfather. He wasn't laughing his head off or telling her there were no such things as ghosts. He was going to listen. She opened her mouth to tell the whole tale, beginning with the purchase of the dollhouse, when her mouth was forced closed so hard that she bit her tongue.

"Ow!" she cried, tasting blood.

Hold your tongue, my girl.

"What's wrong?" asked Ned, looking confused.

"I bit my tongue."

Zibby found herself standing up. That was it: She just stood up suddenly as if pulled upward from the couch by invisible wires. Her math textbook tumbled to the floor.

Ned picked it up and sat there, holding it and looking at her. "About these voices you hear, Zib? Go on. Tell me about them."

Zibby's mouth opened and an odd little chuckle came out. "Oh, it was nothing," she heard herself saying. "I was just teasing you, sir. You know, I was thinking maybe I'll dress up as a ghost for Halloween this year." There came that little chuckle again.

"What's with you, Zib?" Now Ned sounded annoyed. "I think you'd better get to bed."

"You are quite right," Zibby said politely. "I'm sorry to be such a silly, disobedient girl. Good night, sir." Then she turned—was made to turn—and marched out of the room and up the stairs to her room. She was made to enter her bedroom and close the door behind her. She was made to walk over to the closet. She opened the door, and then a mighty force shoved her from behind and she tripped over her laundry basket and slammed to her knees. There came a sharp slap across her cheek. Zibby tried to cry out, but the force settled onto her body and kept her pinned to the floor, immobilized. She could barely breathe. She could barely think.

The closet door slammed.

The force held Zibby down so she could not move. But in the darkness of the closet she could see the side wall start to glow, and a face shaped itself out of the blackness. She closed her eyes in terror, but could not move to cover her ears, and so she heard quite clearly a voice whispering mournfully: "Poor kid...I know what it's like..."

MAYBE IT WAS an hour later, maybe more. But when the force holding her down drifted away, Zibby could finally sit up and breathe deeply again. There was no glowing head, no ghostly voice. She crept weakly out of the closet and sat on the edge of her bed. She knew she should go find Nell and Ned and try to tell them what was happening, but fear kept her sitting quietly. She knew she should at least go into the bathroom and brush her teeth and wash her face, but she felt as limp as a wet rag. She wanted to talk to Primrose, but she didn't dare go near the dollhouse in case Miss Honeywell was lurking there. Fear made her slip silently under the covers and huddle down into the pillows.

CHAPTER 34

Zibby's sleep was deep and dreamless, for a change, and she even slept through her alarm. But when she finally woke up, the first thing she saw was the governess doll standing triumphantly on the dollhouse roof.

Good morning, young miss. I hope you have learned your lesson.

Zibby threw her pillow as hard as she could and knocked the governess doll off the roof.

Bull's-eye.

But it was hard to get out of bed. Zibby felt sluggish, as if her brain and body were weighted down or as if she were moving underwater.

Ned had already left to take Laura-Jane and Brady to school, and Nell was just leaving to cater a brunch, when Zibby shuffled into the kitchen. "You're very late this morning, and you've missed Jude and Penny," Nell said, handing her a glass of orange juice and a bagel with cream cheese. "Get in the car and I'll drop you off at school, but don't make this snail's pace a habit. Ned told me you were up late waiting for me. Is everything all right?"

"Oh, sure," said Zibby vaguely. There seemed no point in trying to talk about it now.

At school the heavy fog around Zibby lifted. Away from Miss Honeywell, Zibby's exhaustion dropped away and she hurried through her day, eager for lunchtime and a chance to talk to Jude, Penny, and Charlotte about what had happened. She found them waiting for her by the library doors. She had forgotten their plan to talk to Ms. Wilson about Mr. Potts.

"I've got to talk to you guys," Zibby began. "Desperately!"

But the librarian beckoned them inside with a smile, her dark eyes welcoming. "I see it's the school-history committee," she joked.

"Well, actually we did want to ask you some questions about school history," Jude began. "Because you've been here such a long time."

Ms. Wilson laughed. "Yes, sometimes it does seem like forever. But fortunately for me, it's a job I love. Not everyone can say as much, I'm afraid. I hope each of you girls will end up working because the job is something you enjoy, and not just something you do to earn a living."

Zibby hoped so, too, but right now her mind was not on her choice of future career.

"We wanted to ask you about one of the principals," Jude said. "Mr. Thaddeus Pope."

"He was here from 1932 till 1934," added Charlotte helpfully.

"*Way* before my time," said Ms. Wilson, smiling. "But as it turns out, I do know something about him. It's a matter of historical record. He was a very well-respected principal, by all accounts. He was the principal here when the school burned down in 1934."

"Can you tell us about it?" Penny urged Ms. Wilson.

Ms. Wilson checked her wristwatch. "I don't have time to tell you the whole sad story before the bell rings for lunch to end," she said. "Why not come back after school? I'll have time then to talk to you—and in the meantime I can look for some newspaper articles about the fire. They'll probably tell you more than I can about poor Mr. Pope."

Good, thought Zibby. She needed to talk to the girls, tell them what had happened with Miss Honeywell. She couldn't concentrate properly on Mr. Potts—or Mr. Pope, or whoever he was—with her brain still swamped in the effects of Miss Honeywell's battle for control.

"Why do you call him 'poor' Mr. Pope?" asked Jude. "I mean, if he was so well respected and everything?"

Ms. Wilson's reply blew the last wisps of fog out of Zibby's brain.

"Well, because as I understand it, the fire was his fault, through his own carelessness," Ms. Wilson said. She put a hand to her neatly styled hair and shook her head. "And because he died in the fire that night."

OUT IN THE HALLWAY the girls clutched at each other. "That's it!" said Jude. "That's why Mr. Potts is haunting the school. Because he died here—in the fire."

"He comes back every decade because that's how long it takes for him to save up enough energy to become visible," reasoned Penny, her voice rising with excitement. "Changing his name each time so people won't know who he is."

"Now it's up to us to find out why," Jude continued, "so that he can rest in peace."

"Then all this haunting will be *over,*" Charlotte said. "And maybe things can finally be normal again!"

"Nothing will be normal as long as Miss Honeywell is in the picture," said Zibby flatly. And she told them how she had battled with the governess in the kitchen the night before and been saved by Laura-Jane.

"I'm telling you guys, Miss Honeywell was taking over my mind," Zibby continued. "Talk about nasty scenes. It was horrible. I felt like my brain was being pulled out of my head. After last night, I forgive Laura-Jane totally. She couldn't help it anymore than I could. And thank goodness she heard me trying to cry out and came into the kitchen just in time. Because otherwise Miss Honeywell would have made me destroy all of Mom's trays of food—and who knows what else she would have done to me? Everything with her is about being in control of somebody. Being in charge." Then she told them what had happened when she tried to talk to Ned. About the slap. And the closet. And the glowing head and ghostly voice.

"That's what happened to Primrose," Jude looked perplexed. "The same sort of thing. But how does Mr. Potts fit into the story?"

"I don't know," Zibby admitted. "But if he was Primrose's tutor, Mr. Pope, as she says, then he's connected to her and Miss Honeywell both."

"In homeroom today Mr. Potts was totally quiet," reported Charlotte. "He didn't say two words."

"Let's hope he doesn't say two words in science, either," muttered Zibby. "I don't think I can stand anymore." And then the bell rang to send them off to their afternoon classes. Zibby couldn't concentrate in any of them. Her mind was a whirl of disjointed facts like pieces to a puzzle scattered across a table. But what picture would emerge once all the pieces were in place, she could not imagine.

As her last-period class approached, Zibby steeled herself for another encounter with Mr. Potts. She consoled herself thinking that it couldn't be worse than the fearful scenes last night with Miss Honeywell. Mr. Potts, at least, did not seem to be out to hurt anybody, even if he did star in their nightmares.

Mr. Potts sat slumped at his desk. When the bell rang, he looked up at the class wearily. "Today you will read chapters three and four in your textbook," he said in a weak, raspy voice. "I am not well today. I would appreciate your cooperation." He glared at them from beneath his shaggy brows, and something in his look made even the most boisterous students sit quietly. There was a tension in the room, and Zibby wondered whether all the other students could feel it as she could. The air seemed to vibrate. When she looked up at Mr. Potts again, she saw him staring into space, thin tears sliding down his cheeks. The sight made her want to comfort him, at the same time she longed to grab her backpack and run from the room. The other students shifted uneasily, and at last Zibby couldn't help it. She cleared her throat and spoke to him.

"Mr. Potts? Can we help you somehow?" Her voice rang out more loudly than she meant it to in the quiet classroom. All the other kids turned to look at her with relief.

But Mr. Potts seemed to have difficulty focusing on the

source of the question. He peered around the room in confusion, then finally shook his shaggy head. "No one can help me," he whispered. "No one. Please just continue with your work."

When the dismissal bell finally rang, the other kids bolted out of the classroom, but Zibby lingered. "Mr. Potts—," she began.

He lifted his head and peered at her. "You again," he muttered. "Go on home. No detention. Just go home."

"Thank you," said Zibby. "But I wanted to ask...are you, I mean, were you really Mr. Pope? Mr. Thaddeus Pope—the principal of this school? And before that—the private tutor of a girl named Primrose Parson?"

He dropped his shaggy head and covered his face with his hands. He mumbled something. Zibby had to edge closer to hear the words. It was just one word over and over again: "Liddie-liddie-liddie-liddie." She stood next to the desk, not sure what to do, and then Mr. Potts started changing. He was...fading away. He was there, yet not there, getting fuzzy and transparent right before her eyes. Zibby sucked in her breath and ran.

Jude, Penny, and Charlotte were waiting for her outside the door to the library. Frantically Zibby told them what she had seen. She dragged them to look into the science classroom—but the room was empty.

"Don't say anything to Ms. Wilson yet," hissed Jude. "Let's wait and see what she can tell us." They walked down the hall to the library.

"Ah, here you are," Ms. Wilson said when she saw the

girls. She sat at a table with a thin book open before her. "This book is called *A Concise History of Carroway, Ohio*. It was published in November 1934 by the local historical society."

Penny reached for the book. "Does it mention the fire here at school?"

"Yes, dear," said Ms. Wilson. "Although in the introduction it does say that the manuscript was ready to go to the printer when the school burned down, so they added a chapter quickly. There may be other details that came to light later. But here—let me tell you some of the background."

The girls settled back in their chairs and looked at her expectantly.

"In 1932 old Miss Chippenham retired," began Ms. Wilson. "Miss Chippenham had been the principal of the school for more than thirty years. The school board appointed Mr. Thaddeus Pope as the new principal." Ms. Wilson tapped the *Concise History* with her finger. "It's all in here. Mr. Pope had been a science teacher at other schools in Columbus and Cleveland, and had also been a private tutor. When he came to Carroway, he was a widower with a daughter just about your age.

"He was a successful principal, but he missed being a science teacher. So in his very first year here, he started a science fair. He encouraged all the students to take part. There were prizes for the best science experiments, and lots of local publicity, and a special family night here at school when all the exhibits would be on display for the public. He and his daughter were well liked and had settled in happily to life in Carroway—until tragedy struck."

"The fire!" said Penny.

"Exactly." Ms. Wilson nodded. "The science fair was being held again, and everyone was getting ready for the family-night exhibition. The children brought in all of their experiments that demonstrated different scientific principles: botany experiments with plants, chemistry experiments with cooking, biology experiments with pet rats and guinea pigs, physics experiments with burglar alarms...well, you can read all about it in these articles.

"Mr. Pope decided to electrify his daughter's dollhouse as a special exhibit. He and his daughter were here quite late the night before the show, setting up the dollhouse display and getting everything ready. Mr. Pope wanted everything to be perfect."

"Uh-oh," murmured Zibby. She could sense what was coming.

Ms. Wilson ran her hand over the book on the table. "Uh-oh is right. Mr. Pope and his daughter worked for hours, late at night—and something went wrong. There was a fault with the wiring or maybe a surge of electricity—*something* that gave Mr. Pope a hefty shock and knocked him out for a minute; no one knows exactly. While he lay unconscious, the sparks of electricity must have set the dollhouse and little furnishings on fire, and it spread to some cans of paint and then leaped to the other display items—paper kites, games, wooden constructions...all sorts of experiments using who knows what in terms of chemicals. I imagine it all went up in flames quickly, with the entire gymnasium full of smoke, and there would have been explosions...It must have been total chaos. By the time the firemen arrived, the school was in ruins. Mr. Pope's body was discovered among the ashes of what had been the dollhouse." The librarian shook her head. "A terrible tragedy."

The girls sat in silence. Then Zibby spoke up. "What about Mr. Pope's daughter?"

Ms. Wilson paged through the book. "Well, it says that the girl was presumed dead."

"You mean they couldn't find her body? You mean she was burned up completely, bones and all?" asked Penny, her voice tinged with horror.

"I suppose it was possible." Ms. Wilson nodded. "The flames reached incredible temperatures. It would have been like an incinerator in our school." She handed some papers stapled together to Jude. "Here you go. I've photocopied for you the chapter about the fire. And there may be more coverage in the public library or *Gazette* archives." She checked her watch. "Oh, dear, I must run to a meeting!"

The girls stood up and thanked her for helping them. As they were leaving the library, Zibby turned back. "Is there a picture of Mr. Pope's daughter in the yearbooks?"

Ms. Wilson looked distracted. "Go check the 1934 book—quickly! The book says she was in the seventh grade."

Zibby ran to the back shelf and pulled down the 1934 yearbook. She flipped past the faculty pages, noting the photo of Mr. Pope, Principal. And then, there among the group of seventh graders, she found the black-and-white picture of his daughter. The girl had dark hair like her father, waved around her face in soft, full curls. Her face was pale, but her bright eyes looking out of the old photo held a spark of mischief. Zibby felt a sudden stab of pity. It was horrible to think of this pretty, cheerful-looking girl—who had been just about Zibby's own age—dying so painfully, charred beyond recognition.

Above the picture was the list of the girl's extracurricular activities at school: drama club, school newspaper, volleyball team, science club. Then Zibby read the name beneath the photograph, and nodded to herself. *Lydia Pope.*

It was all beginning to make sense.

CHAPTER 35

PRIMROSE 1934

Mrs. Primrose Smythe heard the clatter of the metal flap in her front door. She untied her apron and walked down the hallway of her trim little house, thinking with resignation that she was almost but not quite used to wearing an apron now, and to doing her own cooking. She was getting good at it, but she still looked forward to the day she could have servants to help out again. Nanny Shanks had come to live with Primrose when she married, and Nanny was the one who showed Primrose how to cook and clean the house on her own after the troubles of 1929 meant the Smythes could no longer employ her. That was when the stock market crashed and Primrose's father and her husband, Oscar, both lost most of their savings and investments. Nanny Shanks had left the Smythes to live with her widowed nephew, who needed help caring for his children, and Primrose was on her own. She hated doing her own housework, but there was nothing she could do about it.

Still, Primrose reflected as she knelt to pick up the envelopes that lay scattered on the floor inside the front door, money troubles were nothing compared to the trouble she'd lived with for most of her life. Ghost trouble.

It was the only thing she could not tell dear Oscar about. Of course he noticed that her childhood dollhouse was always with them—it had even come along on their honeymoon aboard the S.S. *Olympia* as they sailed to England and back—and, though he might think her attachment to it just a bit strange, he was a true gentleman and never let on.

When they'd had to sell their big house and move into this small one on the other side of Columbus, Oscar suggested they pack the dollhouse into the attic to leave more room in their bedroom—but Primrose had to insist the dollhouse be allowed to stay. She knew, though she couldn't tell Oscar, of course, that the dollhouse would unpack itself from wherever they stashed it and return as it always did.

Oh! A letter from Nanny Shanks! Primrose took the mail to the small kitchen table and sat down with her letter and a cup of tea. She always enjoyed hearing from Nanny.

Dear Primrose,

A piece of interesting news has come my way via my friend, Eleanor, who lives in Carroway—that little town on the river just south of Columbus. It seems our Mr. Pope and his daughter moved from Cleveland to Carroway a year or two ago, where Mr. Pope has taken a job as principal of the junior high school. Eleanor's children go to the school and say he is a kind principal—firm but fair. Sounds like he's still the same as we remember him. Perhaps you will want to pay them a visit now that you are nearly neighbors once again.

Primrose read the rest of the letter, which was full of news about Nanny's nephew's children, and what was blooming in Nanny's garden. She sat sipping her tea, thinking about Mr. Pope living in nearby Carroway! She had not seen her former tutor since he had visited her at school more than ten years ago. He had taken his baby daughter to live with his parents, in New York, and she had heard no further news of them. Primrose hoped little Lydia Pope was having a happy childhood, despite being motherless. Or perhaps Mr. Pope had married again. The baby would now be... what? Eleven or twelve?

The same age Primrose herself had been when Miss Honeywell died.

Primrose had a glimmer of an idea. Perhaps the ghost— who seemed so determined to stick by Primrose—might prefer a *new* little child now...especially one who was the daughter of the man Miss Honeywell had loved. It had nearly worked before; the dollhouse had stayed with the Popes for ten days when Primrose gave it to the baby. It was only Mrs. Pope's death that seemed to upset things, somehow causing the dollhouse to return to Primrose. Giving it back to Lydia Pope now was certainly worth a try. Why should Primrose be the one to suffer so long? It was time for a change.

THE NEXT DAY Primrose asked Oscar to help her carry the dollhouse down the stairs and out to their automobile. He agreed to take the train to work that day so Primrose could drive the auto to Carroway to call on Mr. Pope and his daughter. She had telephoned ahead of time to ask if she might come, and Mr. Pope had seemed pleased to hear from her. She did not mention the dollhouse but simply arranged to be there in time for coffee after school. He was not to cook, she said; she would bring a cake. "Nonsense," he had replied. "Lydia will bake something. She's a very good cook and a wonderful little housekeeper."

The Popes lived in a small house several blocks from the school. Primrose parked her automobile at the curb and made her way up the brick path. A tall girl with dark hair worn in a fashionable bob opened the front door at her knock. "Hello," she said politely. "You must be Mrs. Smythe. My father said you were coming to see us today."

"And you must be Lydia." Primrose smiled at the girl.

"Yes. Please come in." Lydia stood aside so Primrose could enter, but Primrose pointed to the automobile where the dollhouse was wedged in the rumble seat. It had been difficult packing the house into the auto, but Oscar had managed it. He was delighted that Primrose wanted to give the dollhouse away.

"I've brought you a gift, my dear. Would you like to see it?" Obviously the child would not recall that Primrose had given her this same gift once before.

Lydia's face lit up as she saw the dollhouse. "Oh— really? For me?" Her thin, serious face lit in a smile very like her father's. "Baba!" she called. "Come out here and see what Mrs. Smythe has brought me!"

"What is this?" Mr. Pope stepped out of the house. He shook Primrose's hand. "Hello, Primrose. You are looking very well. And so grown-up! I'm afraid I'll always think of you as a girl of Lydia's age."

"Look what Mrs. Smythe has brought," repeated Lydia, grabbing onto his arm. "Help us get it into the house, Baba, please! I can't wait to see inside it."

Mr. Pope noticed the house wedged into the automobile for the first time and his face darkened. "The dollhouse!" He stared at it, then turned to Primrose. "It *is* the same one!"

"Yes," she said. "It should be Lydia's."

Mr. Pope frowned. "But it was stolen years ago. How did you come to get it back?"

Primrose hesitated. In her eagerness to be rid of the dollhouse she had not thought through her story. How to explain that the dollhouse had returned to her? How it would never leave her?

Before she could think of what to say, Mr. Pope crossed his arms and shook his head. "Lydia, dear girl," he said, "please go into the house so I may speak to Mrs. Smythe in private."

The girl opened her mouth as if to object, then caught her father's warning glance and closed it again. "Yes, Baba," she said obediently, and looked back only once over her shoulder as she walked up the path to the house and closed the door.

"Primrose, this is very strange indeed," said Mr. Pope in his stern tutor's voice. It made Primrose feel like a child again—an uncomfortable feeling. "Was it Calliope?" he whispered urgently. "Tell me, Primrose! Did she have something to do with the dollhouse's disappearance?"

"It came back on its own," she replied evasively. "It always does. I can't explain why. But I really do want Lydia to have it—and that is why I gave it to her the first time."

"You're asking me to believe the dollhouse just *appeared*?"

"It did." Primrose stared longingly at her automobile. She wanted to jump in and drive away from here. But *not* with the dollhouse.

Mr. Pope was silent for a long moment. "It appeared rather in the same way that doll in the gray dress keeps appearing?"

Primrose hesitated. She had realized that sometimes the governess doll was missing, but she had not known where it went. "More or less."

Mr. Pope pressed his lips together. "Listen to me, Primrose. I heard Calliope's disembodied voice in my head that once, and it is something I will never forget. And I saw—at least I believe I saw—the dollhouse furniture flying around the room the night my wife died. Something else I will never forget. I asked you years ago if you had ever heard from Calliope after her death—and you said you had not. I am asking you again. Have you seen her ghost?"

"Miss Honeywell has been dead for fifteen years," said Primrose, attempting to sound lightly scornful though her heartbeat was loud in her ears. "You're a man of science. I am sure you cannot believe in ghosts."

"No, of course not," he said, but without conviction. "But I don't want this dollhouse all the same."

"Baba!" Lydia called from the door. "The coffee is ready now! Shall I help you bring the dollhouse inside first?"

"We're not keeping the thing, Liddie."

"Why ever not! It's gorgeous!" The girl came out and put her hand on Mr. Pope's arm. "Baba, I was just inside thinking about how the dollhouse could be the very best display at the science fair!" She turned to Primrose, cheeks rosy with excitement. "My father has been teaching me all about electricity, Mrs. Smythe," she explained eagerly. "And I've just had the most wonderful idea that we could electrify the whole dollhouse so that there are real lamps lit in every

single room! It would be so lovely, Baba! We could do it together, so I can show you what I've learned. And then we'll
put the house on display, with signs explaining the electrical
process. Oh, please, may we?"

Mr. Pope looked uncomfortable.

"It sounds like a fabulous idea for a project," Primrose
said heartily.

Mr. Pope cleared his throat. "It's what I had once suggested as a project for you, Primrose," he said. "Do you remember? To apply your lessons about electricity!"

"I do recall," said Primrose. "It's a very good idea. And
of course the dollhouse would be at the school—rather than
here at your house." She looked hard at Mr. Pope.

"Yes, that's true, it *would* have to remain at school," he
said. *"Hmmm."*

"Please, Baba?" begged Lydia.

Primrose saw his expression soften as he looked at his
daughter. "All right, my lamb. We will electrify the dollhouse for the science fair, and then keep the dollhouse at
school on display. But we will *not* keep it here at home. Do
you understand?"

"Thank you!" cried Lydia.

"Then, shall we take the house indoors?" asked Primrose quickly before he could change his mind. "We'll all
need to help. It is quite heavy."

"Perhaps in the garage?" suggested Mr. Pope.

"No, Baba! Please!" protested Lydia.

Reluctantly, Mr. Pope helped Primrose bring the big
dollhouse into the house. They set it in the dining room,
where it loomed on the table like a mansion atop a cliff.
Lydia hurried to open the latch and brought out the bags

full of furniture and dolls. Exclaiming with pleasure, she immediately set to arranging the rooms.

Mr. Pope ushered Primrose into the parlor and offered her coffee. Primrose felt she could not refuse, though she wanted nothing more than to get away from the dollhouse as fast as her auto could drive her, before Mr. Pope changed his mind. No one knew how she had been suffering all these years! It wasn't fair that she should have to be burdened with the dollhouse all her life, and if there were any chance at all the dollhouse would stay with the Popes, she wanted to give it the chance. "Just a quick cup," Primrose acquiesced. "I'm afraid I really must be going."

"Oh, Mrs. Smythe! Before you leave, I want to show you something." Lydia handed Primrose a little dark-haired porcelain doll about four inches tall. "Isn't she the dearest thing? She belonged to my mother. I think she'll like living in such a fine dollhouse, don't you?"

"Yes, I think she will," said Primrose.

Mr. Pope asked Lydia to bring in the cake, and the girl darted off to the kitchen, returning with plates of the chocolate cake she had baked. Primrose listened for a while as father and daughter discussed how they would illuminate every room of the dollhouse. Then she picked up her handbag, praised the cake, and said she must be going. As she chugged off down the street, she felt years of stress rolling away. She cranked open the side window and took what she felt to be the first deep cleansing breath she'd had in ages.

Now if only that dollhouse will stay put! she thought.

A WEEK PASSED and Primrose enjoyed every day with a glad heart. Her step was light, she smiled frequently, she sang as she went about her errands. Even housework seemed more pleasant now that she was free of the dollhouse.

Then a few days later, Primrose woke up after a sound night's sleep. She reached for her dressing gown and came downstairs as usual to start breakfast.

The sky outside the kitchen windows was growing brighter as she heard Oscar's footsteps on the stairs. And then he was in the kitchen, giving her a quick good-morning kiss as she flipped his omelet onto a plate. He went to the front door to bring in the newspaper, then returned to the kitchen, reading the front page. His face was somber.

"Bad news," he said. "Big fire over in Carroway last night."

Primrose reached for the paper. The bright morning darkened as she read the headline:

Carroway Junior High School Burns to Ground

And in smaller print: **Principal and Pupil Perish**

Primrose staggered, and Oscar steadied her. "Take a deep breath," he said. He led her to the table and tried to get her to sit down in a kitchen chair. But she pushed him away and ran upstairs. She had not noticed anything amiss when she'd first awakened and gone downstairs. But there it was, back in the far corner of their master bedroom:

The dollhouse.

She'd given it away once, and Mrs. Pope had died. She'd given it away a second time—and now look what had happened. Primrose sank into a chair with a shudder. She clutched the newspaper to her breast and thought she heard the crackle of flames, thought she smelled the smoke as Mr. Pope and Lydia met their fates.

You have quite a knack, whispered a voice in her head. *Quite a knack for killing people—don't you, young miss?*

"It's not *my* fault!" screamed Primrose. "You know it's not!"

"Of course it's not, dearest," agreed Oscar, patting her shoulder comfortingly. "How in the world could it have anything to do with you?"

CHAPTER 36

"Mr. Pope's daughter's name was Lydia." Zibby clutched Jude's arm as the four girls left the school building and started walking home. "And when Mr. Potts was starting to disappear, I heard him whispering, '*Liddie-liddie-liddie-liddie.*'"

"You mean you think he was calling for his daughter?" Jude's voice was thoughtful.

"But why is he calling for her *now*?" demanded Charlotte. "They've both been dead for ages. You'd think he'd know that."

"Primrose might be able to tell us, I bet," said Penny. "If she *can*."

"I bet Miss Honeywell could tell us, too," Zibby said grimly. "But I won't be asking her, that's for sure—not after what happened last night. I was no match for her. She was able to control my body completely."

"Let's go see what Primrose has to say." Practical Jude was ready for action.

"I can't go," Charlotte said, and there was a measure of relief in her voice. "I have ballet."

"We'll fill you in later," said Jude. "All the gory details."

Aunt Linnea pulled up in front of the school and took Charlotte away, and the rest of the girls set off for Zibby's house. Zibby was glad to have her friends with her. She hated the feeling of not being safe in her own house. When they arrived, they found Ned dropping Laura-Jane off in the driveway. Zibby hadn't seen him since the night before, when he'd seen her acting so strangely and calling him "sir." She steeled herself to smile naturally at him, though she felt embarrassed.

"Hey, girls," he greeted them through the open window of his car. He raised an eyebrow at Zibby. "Hello, Zib. How are you?"

"Fine, thanks."

"Glad to hear it." Then he hugged Laura-Jane. "I've got to run back to work for another hour, but I'll pick up Brady at soccer practice on my way home. Will you please tell Nell?"

"Okay, Dad," said Laura-Jane. "See you later."

"Wait—Ned?" Zibby called to him. "Do you think we could come with you to work and look at old newspapers?"

Penny caught on right away. "Like—from 1934?"

Laura-Jane looked intrigued.

Ned shook his head. "I've got a deadline for an article, and I need to finish it now. But tomorrow... yeah, tomorrow will work. Is it for a school project?"

"Um, yes," said Zibby, and Penny said at the same time, "Well, not really."

Ned raised his thick black brows. "Whatever. Anyway, come tomorrow straight after school and I'll find you what you need." He waved, then drove off.

The girls walked inside together. Nell wasn't home yet, but the kitchen smelled wonderful. A note on the table explained that she was delivering food for a fancy tea party to the Ladies' Guild in Fennel Grove.

"It's funny," said Laura-Jane softly, sniffing appreciatively, "how coming here sort of feels like home now. A couple of weeks ago I would never have believed it could happen."

Zibby glanced at Laura-Jane, then reached out and gave her a brief, impulsive hug. "Well, now there's been more happening that you won't believe," Zibby told Laura-Jane in a dark voice.

The four girls went upstairs and settled in Zibby's room on the floor in front of the dollhouse. Zibby looked around to see where the governess doll was this time. No sign of her. The coast was clear.

Zibby told Laura-Jane about what had happened last night after she and Brady went to bed. "I was going to tell your dad about everything—but Miss Honeywell stopped me. Then she locked me in the closet!"

"I think I'll take back what I just said," murmured Laura-Jane. "About how this house feels like home?" She touched Zibby's arm. "Maybe you should come and live part-time with me and Brady at our mom's house."

Zibby gave her a brief smile. "Thanks. But I have a feeling the dollhouse and the ghosts would just follow me. I have a feeling there's no running away from this. We have to *solve* it. We have to *stop* it." She steeled herself before reaching out to open the latch on the dollhouse. Who would be inside this time?

The little girl doll lay on the parlor couch. Zibby reached for her. "Primrose? We have a news update."

I have been waiting for you, said Primrose. *I have a news update, too.* Her voice, Zibby was glad to hear, was loud and strong again. She had obviously regained her power. Zibby was relieved, and she hoped that a powerful Primrose resulted in a very weak Miss Honeywell.

"You go first," said Zibby.

No, you, said Primrose.

So Zibby leaned back against her bed and laid the doll on her knee. She held out her hands to Penny on her left and Jude on her right, and then Laura-Jane linked arms with Jude so they all could hear when Primrose spoke. Connected this way, Zibby told Laura-Jane and Primrose all they had learned from Ms. Wilson. She told about the fire in 1934 and the principal's heroic but doomed attempts to put out the fire and save his daughter, Lydia. She told how she had seen Mr. Potts start to fade away. How she had heard him crying in anguish: "Liddie-liddie-liddie-liddie!"

Laura-Jane listened, twisting her long black ponytails.

"We think he's calling for his daughter, Lydia," clarified Jude. "That was the name of Mr. Pope's daughter—he was the principal, you know, when the fire broke out."

I told you that was my tutor, Mr. Pope. Primrose's reedy voice filtered through their heads. *And what I've learned about him is that he's been trying to find his daughter ever since he died. He is terribly, horribly stuck.*

"What do you mean, 'stuck'?" asked Zibby. "You said that once before."

Someone is stuck—and I've been feeling it, but I didn't know then who it was. Now I know. It is Mr. Thaddeus Pope, your Mr. Potts. Stuck means "stuck." Unable to move on—

"Wait a sec," interrupted Jude. "Translation, please. 'Move on'?"

A brisk wind rattled the window. From downstairs came the slam of the front door as Brady and Ned returned home. Zibby hoped Brady wouldn't come upstairs.

Primrose's reply was like a sigh through their heads. *Moving on,* she said, *is like finishing up. Graduating. Being ready for the next thing. Mr. Pope's wife, Evelina, for instance, moved on long ago. I've learned that he would like to go with her, but he can't. He won't rest until he finds Lydia. And if Miss Honeywell's sucking his energy, too, he might never find her.*

"I think it's a really sad story," Penny murmured.

"I do, too," said Laura-Jane.

"It's worse than sad," objected Zibby, "because Miss Honeywell hasn't moved on, and she's a danger to everyone! But I do feel sorry for Mr. Potts and Liddie both." She lifted the little doll and peered at its small painted face. "And anybody else who is stuck, Primrose."

The little voice was tinged with outrage. *I am not the least bit stuck!*

"Well, why aren't *you* resting in peace?"

I am perfectly able to move on whenever I want! I have chosen to haunt this dollhouse! I—I like it here! The little doll trembled. *I never got a chance to enjoy my dollhouse! Miss Honeywell was always spoiling things. I just want to fix it up. I want a chandelier. I want some new wallpaper.*

"Okay," said Zibby hastily. "Keep your hair on." She patted the doll with one finger. "We'll fix up the house soon. But now it's more important to help Mr. Potts—Mr. Pope, I mean. Isn't it?"

"Poor Mr. Potts," said Laura-Jane. "He doesn't seem like a nightmare now."

He most likely doesn't even know about the nightmares, offered Primrose, sounding slightly mollified. *His energy stirs things up—maybe sends off all sorts of vibrations, memories of the fire...*

"What I've been wondering," said Penny, "is how come a man who was the principal of the whole school when he was alive would choose to come back as a janitor. It would be a big cut in pay."

"I think it makes perfect sense, because becoming visible takes huge amounts of energy," Jude pointed out. "He would hardly have enough strength to take on a full-time job. He just needs a job that lets him look around the school for a few weeks, searching for Lydia. I doubt he ever stays around long enough to get paid. He keeps on searching until his energy runs out. Isn't that right, Primrose?"

Energy is very hard to hold on to. Especially when someone is trying to suck it away.

Zibby smoothed the doll's little blue dress. "What if Miss Honeywell is able to suck away all his power as well as yours, Primrose? What happens to you then?"

The doll shuddered in Zibby's lap. *It's not just about*

what would happen to me, she told them. *It's about what she'd be able to do.*

"You mean, like, to my mom?" Now Zibby was the one who shuddered.

"If we could help Mr. Potts to rest in peace, somehow," ventured Jude hastily, "then he could move on. Right? And if he were gone, then Miss Honeywell wouldn't be able to steal his energy to make herself more powerful. And if she isn't able to gather more power, maybe she won't have enough to be able to hurt anyone else…"

"I bet it was Miss Honeywell who burned your school down," Laura-Jane said. "I bet she started the fire that killed Mr. Pope and Lydia."

"And—wait a second—how did *Mrs.* Pope die, Primrose?" Jude queried. "Did Miss Honeywell kill Lydia's mother, too—out of jealousy? Did she kill *all* the Popes?"

Laura-Jane clutched Zibby's arm. "This is giving me the creeps," she whispered.

Zibby knew all about the creeps. She was having them badly just now, in fact, even though there was no sign of Miss Honeywell. She had the feeling that the governess was lurking nearby, listening to everything that was said, biding her time before exerting her power again.

I was away at boarding school when Mrs. Pope died, replied Primrose. *But…I had given the new baby my dollhouse. And I know the dollhouse was in the room the night Mrs. Pope died. And after that…it returned to me. So probably Miss Honeywell was around.*

"You gave your haunted dollhouse to a new baby, knowing full well it had Miss Honeywell's ghost in it?" Jude's voice rang with disgust.

I meant it as a gift, whined the ghost. *And I was desperate to be rid of the thing. I didn't know anyone would die!*

"Could any other dollhouse in the whole world have such a terrible history?" wondered Laura-Jane.

The air in the room seemed to deepen, grow heavy. Zibby felt heavy, too.

Miss Honeywell is around here somewhere. I can feel her evil energy!

"Where?" Laura-Jane glanced around the room nervously.

Zibby thought she saw the curtains moving at the window. Just the breeze? Or was the governess doll hiding behind them?

"What about Lydia, then?" asked Penny, clearly still thinking about the Pope family. "Is Lydia stuck now, too? Can you feel her energy?"

Liddie is nowhere.

"But that's not possible, is it?" said Zibby. "Probably she's 'moved on' to be with her mother. That's why Mr. Potts can't find her." Wind rattled the windowpanes and the curtains billowed. Zibby could see that no one was hiding there.

Primrose was adamant that Lydia Pope had not moved on, because ghosts know who has moved on and who is stuck. But there was no trace of Lydia's energy among those who were stuck. She was nowhere at all.

Zibby frowned. How could that be possible? Was Lydia hiding somewhere—like Miss Honeywell? She stared at the billowing window curtains, at the place where no one was hiding, and the answer came to her with a start.

Not hiding. Not *stuck*. "Wait—I know!" she whispered. "What if Lydia Pope didn't die that night in the fire after all? What if she's still alive?"

CHAPTER 37

When Zibby hesitantly slid into her seat in science the next day, Mr. Potts wasn't up at the front of the classroom. Instead, a young woman with frizzy red curls sat behind the teacher's desk. She had written her name on the blackboard: Ms. Glover.

"Please open your books to page eighty-seven," she was saying when Zibby sat down at her place.

"Hey!" bellowed Scott Guerrero. "It's Friday the thirteenth! That's my lucky day!"

Ms. Glover ignored him. "Page eighty-seven," she repeated. "Any questions?"

Zibby raised her hand. "What happened to Mr. Potts?"

"And who would that be?" asked Ms. Glover.

"Our other substitute teacher," Zibby told her.

"He was cool!" called out Scott Guerrero. "Even though he never changed his clothes!"

"I don't know a thing about him," said Ms. Glover. "Now, open to page eighty-seven."

"He was really into electricity," added Scott. "It really, you know, turned him on. Get it? Electricity turned him on!"

The class laughed, but Ms. Glover did not.

"Get it?" Scott was never one to leave the limelight once it was shining upon him. "In fact, it really shocked us—how much Mr. Potts loved electricity. Get it? *Shocked* us?" He grinned and the class tittered.

"I assure you I don't know a thing about Mr. Potts," snapped Ms. Glover. "But I suspect he left because he just got tired of trying to get you to open your books to page eighty-seven."

The class roared with laughter—all but Zibby.

Zibby slouched in her seat. Her curiosity was aroused. She would go see the principal after school, she decided. Someone must know where Mr. Potts had gone.

She found Charlotte, Penny, and Jude at the lockers after school. "Want to come with me to see Ms. Hooper?" Zibby asked. "I want to ask about Mr. Potts."

"Maybe he ran out of energy," Jude suggested.

"Or," said Penny slowly, "he just got tired of looking for Lydia."

But Zibby remembered the anguish in Mr. Potts's face and knew he would never stop looking. She opened the office door. "Are you all coming in with me?"

Ms. Hooper, an elegant white-haired woman, was talking agitatedly into the telephone. She motioned the girls to sit down on the bench inside the door to wait. Soon she put down the phone and ran her hands across her hair, tucking stray hairs into the neat bun. She seemed to be making an effort to calm herself. "What can I do for you girls?"

Jude, Penny, and Charlotte looked at Zibby. Zibby cleared her throat. "Um, we were wondering about Mr. Potts, our science teacher. When he'd be back, I mean…" Her voice trailed off as the principal's friendly expression darkened.

"That man!" Ms. Hooper frowned. "He's caused no end of trouble."

"Well, we were just wondering. Because he didn't say good-bye. To the class, I mean."

Ms. Hooper looked out the window. "It was strange, really." She spoke softly. "Early on the first day of school, Mr. Potts appeared at my office. He said he had come to be the substitute teacher, and of course I assumed the board of education had sent him as a replacement for Ms. Durkee—so I took him to the classroom…He seemed to know the way already. He strode down the hall in front of me."

"So, why isn't Mr. Potts here now?" asked Zibby.

The principal's eyes sharpened. "I was talking to the superintendent yesterday and he apologized for not having found a substitute yet to be Ms. Durkee's replacement. I was baffled and told him we had Mr. Potts…but he said the board had not sent Mr. Potts. I was amazed! People can't just walk in off the street and pose as substitutes. So, of course, I called Mr. Potts to my office immediately…But he never came in to see me. He just—disappeared."

"We saw him do that, too—," began Penny, but Jude stopped her with a sharp elbow.

The principal frowned at the girls. "I shouldn't be speaking to you girls about this matter. The whole thing is highly irregular."

The girls said good-bye and left the office.

"Highly irregular!" Penny giggled.

"And she doesn't know the half of it," said Zibby.

ALL FOUR GIRLS biked over to the *Gazette* office at the end of the day. Ned had picked up Laura-Jane and Brady after school, and they were waiting for them.

The *Gazette* had been Carroway's local newspaper for nearly one hundred and fifty years. The offices were a busy place, with phones ringing and people bustling in and out. It reminded Zibby of a beehive, with all the background droning and buzzing and flying around. Brady sat in an empty office across the hall from Ned's, playing a computer game.

Laura-Jane led the way down to the archives in the basement. "I was here last year to do a report on the Civil War," she told them with a proprietary air. "Dad found me loads of old articles of the *Gazette* from 1865 that told about Abraham Lincoln's assassination. And there were lists of all the names of the soldiers who had fought and died. It was really cool—but sad."

"You can research other wars, too," Ned said. "Here— look. We have databases with information on all the battles and even lists of the casualties and prisoners of war." He typed in the name "Shimizu" and "World War Two," and pressed RETURN. Immediately a listing of names of soldiers called Shimizu appeared on the screen. "This is a list of the American casualties," Ned said solemnly, and highlighted one name: Albert Shimizu. "My uncle," he said. "My father's older brother."

Zibby could imagine what a terrible loss it would be to have a father or uncle or brother die in battle. Luckily for her, her own dad was safe and happy over in Venice. A little tickle of memory reminded her that Miss Honeywell had had a brother die in the First World War. Primrose had told the girls how much the governess talked about that brother, Lester.

"Hey, Ned, can I look up somebody who died in the *First* World War?"

"Sure, Zibby," he said. "Turn on that computer there and type in whatever name you're searching for."

Zibby pushed the button to turn on the computer, then shrieked as a puff of smoke and a flash of light burst forth. The other girls shrieked, too. "What did I do?" Zibby cried. "I didn't mean to break it!"

"It's Friday the thirteenth," said Laura-Jane. "These things happen."

Ned sighed. "It's not Zibby's fault. It's just a circuit overload or a power surge. This old building has been rewired—but evidently not down here in the archives." He examined the computer. "Look at these wires—all plugged into one extension cord. Ridiculous. It'll blow every time. But—never mind, Zibby. Here, use this other computer. It's on a separate circuit. What name did you want?"

"Um...Lester Honeywell."

"Who is he?" asked Ned, typing in the name.

"Oh—somebody from school mentioned an old uncle with that name who died in World War One," lied Zibby. Charlotte looked at her curiously.

"No listing for Honeywell." Ned squinted at the screen. "Sure you've got the right war?"

"Maybe not," said Zibby, although she was sure. She didn't know why she'd wanted to check, anyway. She felt flushed, as if she'd been running, though the basement was cool.

"So, what *are* you sure about?" asked Ned. "When was that school fire?"

"Nineteen thirty-four," Zibby replied promptly. She wiped her sweaty hands on her jeans. She felt they were on the brink of some discovery that was going to lead some-where...somewhere she was not sure she wanted to go. Jude pressed a shoulder against hers reassuringly.

In a very short time Ned found the microfilm of the fire articles, and Laura-Jane competently showed the girls how to use the machine to view them. Once he saw that the girls knew what they were doing, he unplugged the broken com-puter and carried it away, upstairs.

The very first headline made Zibby's heart pound harder. They were getting closer. But—closer to what?

CARROWAY JUNIOR HIGH SCHOOL BURNS TO GROUND

PRINCIPAL AND PUPIL PERISH

1 OCTOBER 1934

Flames consumed Carroway's junior high school last night in an unexplained blaze that Fire Chief Davis LeZak says started in the gymnasium sometime after 10 P.M. The gymnasium was to be the site of the Family Science Fair, which was scheduled to open today. Sci-ence teacher Mr. James Logston says he left the school shortly after 9 last night, leaving Principal Thaddeus Pope and his daughter, Lydia, age 12, working on their display for the fair. "They were planning to electrify Lydia's dollhouse," Mr. Logston told police.

Investigators believe that sparks from the experiment may have ignited other displays and started the conflagration.

The community mourns the loss of Mr. Pope, principal for two years, whose body was found in the wreckage. It is believed that Lydia Pope, a popular seventh-grade student at the school, also perished in the tragic blaze.

An article two months later was accompanied by the same photograph of the dark-haired girl they had seen in the yearbook. Zibby read the accompanying article aloud.

DOLLHOUSE DOLL HOLDS CLUE TO MISSING GIRL

10 DECEMBER 1934

Albert Fielding of Carroway, a repairman for the Carroway Coach Company, was installing new seats on a bus yesterday when he discovered a small, smoke-blackened doll wedged beneath one of the old seats. He took the doll home for his daughters, Eleanor and Sarah. Eleanor, a seventh grader at the junior high school, identified the doll as one belonging to a schoolmate, Lydia Pope, presumed dead in the fire that destroyed the junior high school last September. Her body, however, was not found in the ruins.

"Liddie and I once played with this doll in her doll-house," reported Eleanor Fielding, "so I am quite sure it is hers."

Mr. Fielding took the doll to the police, who now believe it may provide evidence that the Pope girl survived the fire and possibly made her way by bus to Columbus. Police in Columbus have been contacted and are joining the search for the missing child. Anyone with information should contact the Carroway police.

"Now we're getting somewhere," Jude said with satisfaction. "Scroll down to the next article, Zibby! There's got to be more!"

And there was, a full six months later.

"Here it is!" Zibby's voice rose in excitement. "Look, everybody, here it is!"

AMNESIA VICTIM REMEMBERS

15 JUNE 1935

It was a happy day for Lydia Pope, age 12, missing since the Carroway school fire and believed dead. The missing child was traced through a small doll she had left behind on a bus the night she fled the fire. Police now know she had been struck on the head as the school building crumbled and burned around her, and she wandered through town in a daze while emergency services were busy at the scene of the fire. No one noticed the child board a bus for Columbus, where she ended up with a band of street urchins, living rough. She claims to have no memory of the fire, of her own name or circumstances, and recalls only that she had lost her doll.

She was known as Dolly among the street children. This week when Children's Social Services rescued the street children and sent them to the local orphanage and foster homes, "Dolly" was also placed in care. With her closely cropped hair, shorn by the children themselves in an attempt to keep lice at bay, and wearing tattered clothing, the child looked nothing at all like the photograph in police files of the missing daughter of Carroway Junior High School's principal Thaddeus Pope, who perished in the September fire. But by happy circumstance, the matron of Fennel Grove Orphanage took photographs of all the street children and passed these on to the local police, hoping to find many of their families. In at least this one case, the chief was able to make a positive identification. Final proof was had today when Eleanor Fielding, age 12, and a friend of Lydia Pope's in happier days, hearing that her friend was alive, brought the child the doll that had been found on one of the city buses after the fire. When Lydia Pope was reunited with her little doll, she remembered everything and her memory was restored. (continued, p. 18a)

Zibby's fingers trembled as she scrolled along to page 18a. The article concluded with information about long-term memory loss, and a photograph.

Doctors at Westview Hospital in Columbus agree that although Lydia Pope has been traumatized by her experiences and by the news of her father's death (Lydia's mother passed away when the child was an infant), she should make a full recovery. "Youth and fortitude are on her side," confirmed Dr. Patrick Morton, who treated Lydia. "And time, of course, is a wonderful healer."

The child will go to live with relatives in Michigan.

Zibby's eyes flew across the lines of words, but what caught and riveted her attention was the photograph of Lydia, holding her little doll. The girl looked very different from her yearbook picture. Her face was thin and pale; her hair was as short as a boy's. Her eyes were half closed as if she were exhausted. Zibby didn't blame people for not recognizing her as the missing child. But the doll was easy to recognize.

"Look," breathed Zibby, hardly able to believe what she was seeing.

Jude leaned forward to see, and sucked in her breath sharply.

And Penny's voice rose shrilly. "It is! It really is!"

Charlotte tossed her hair. "I can't believe it."

"What?" cried Laura-Jane. "What is it?"

Tears sprang to Zibby's eyes. "I already suspected that Liddie didn't die. And now here's proof. She *is* still alive— and we know just where we can find her!"

For there it was, in grainy black and white: Lydia's little doll was the one they had seen so recently in the miniatures shop in Fennel Grove, the doll that wasn't for sale. The one Mrs. Howell had called her special baby.

CHAPTER 38

Zibby led the way up to Ned's office. He was on the telephone. The girls waited, simmering with excitement. When he hung up, Zibby nudged Laura-Jane forward.

"Dad?" began Laura-Jane. "We need a huge favor!"

The telephone rang. "Hold it, honey," Ned told her. "I've got to get this one." He answered, then sat down at his desk and, with the phone wedged between his ear and his shoulder, he started typing furiously. He answered the next call as well while the girls hovered anxiously. Finally Laura-Jane was able to ask her question: Would he drive them to Fennel Grove, to Lilliput—right away, this minute?

Ned shook his head, distracted by the sight of three of his colleagues rushing toward him waving sheaves of paper. "No, sorry, girls, I can't today. Usually I would—you know I would! But I'm up against a deadline, and I'm swamped. You can use the phone in the office across the hall, where

Brady's playing, to see if some other parent can drive you. But I won't be finished here for at least another hour."

Laura-Jane led the way across the hall into the office where her brother was busy zapping space aliens. He looked up briefly and grinned at them, then turned back to his intergalactic war. Zibby closed the office door firmly, then moved to the far corner by the windows. "There's not enough time to bike over to Fennel Grove," she said in a low voice. "And Laura-Jane doesn't have her bike here, anyway. Our parents are going to be busy, you know they are—and there isn't time to get anyone else to drive us." She took a deep breath. "So why don't we just call her?"

Charlotte cleared her throat. "She might have a heart attack or something."

"Poor thing," said tenderhearted Penny. "It'll be such a shock."

"What makes you think she'll believe us?" asked Charlotte, tossing her hair. "I sure wouldn't."

"Maybe we shouldn't even be telling her," mused Laura-Jane. "I mean, isn't it Mr. Potts who needs to know? He's the one who is so sad and desperate, not her."

Zibby frowned. *Should* they try to tell Mr. Potts first? But—where was he? At least they knew where to find Liddie. She turned to Jude. "Will you call? You make the most sense."

Jude smiled a little at that and walked over to the desk. "Sorry, Brady," she said, "but we need the phone. And can you turn that volume down on your game?" She picked up the receiver.

Brady continued his game with the sound turned low.

While Zibby looked up the phone number, Laura-Jane pulled up a chair so Jude could sit comfortably. Zibby and Laura-Jane hovered on either side of Jude. Penny perched on the edge of the desk. Charlotte walked across the room to look out the window.

"It's ringing," whispered Jude. She took a deep breath. "Hello, Mrs. Howell? This is Jude Jefferson. I was in your shop the other day with my friends—yes, that's right. Oh, we haven't started building it, but we will. Anyway, that's not what I'm calling about…"

Zibby, Laura-Jane, and Penny looked at one another with expectation. Charlotte turned from the window and came back to the desk.

"Well, I need to ask you a question," Jude continued. "And, um, this is kind of hard. But, first of all, just to be sure, I need to ask if your first name is Liddie. I mean, is it Lydia? And was your father named Thaddeus Pope?"

Jude picked up a pen with her thin brown fingers and twirled it nervously. "Yes! Yes, that's what we thought. That's right! I know—we've heard a lot about the fire recently. Well—" She paused, listening. "I know, I know. And normally it wouldn't be any of our business, of course, but, well, a lot of things have been happening. Things you probably should know about."

Zibby found herself clenching her hands into fists. How was Mrs. Howell going to take this? And where was it all heading? She felt they were hurtling headlong into the unknown. But that was not a new feeling, not really. She'd felt this way ever since she'd first brought the dollhouse home.

Again Jude listened, shifting uncomfortably in the chair.

She dropped the pen and ran her fingers through her short dark curls. She raised her brows expressively at Zibby.

"The sooner the better, I think," she said into the receiver. "Because...well, because we have a, um, message for you." Again she paused, then added carefully, "From your father."

Jude held the phone away from her ear, and the other girls could hear the squawk but not the actual words of Mrs. Howell's agitated reply. Zibby was not surprised that Mrs. Howell wanted to see the girls at her shop right away. She wanted to hear their whole story and would close early and come pick them up herself. She would drive them home again, too.

Jude hung up slowly and leaned back with a huge sigh. "That was *hard*. I hope I don't have to make any more bizarre calls like that—ever!"

"What did she say when you told her the message was from her father?" asked Laura-Jane.

"It was strange," Jude answered slowly. "First she said, you know, that can't be, that's ridiculous, my father died years ago!—and everything. But then she sort of sighed and said maybe that explains the voices..."

"Voices!" shrieked Penny. She looked at Brady and lowered her voice to a whisper. "Don't tell me she's got a ghost in *her* head, too."

"I don't like any of this," muttered Laura-Jane. "And if I have that dream one more time, I'll go crazy, I know I will."

"That's why we need to see Mrs. Howell," said Zibby, cutting off the younger girls' rising hysteria. "Now let's go tell Ned that we've got a ride to Fennel Grove."

"I bet she'll be here any second," predicted Jude. "I know *I'd* be driving like a rocket if I heard that *my* dad was trying to contact me."

"Yeah," murmured Penny. "And *he's* only in *Kenya!*"

Mrs. Howell picked them up in her old station wagon. The seats were strewn with wood shavings, shreds of cardboard, and rolls of plastic bubble wrap. "Just push all the debris out of your way," Mrs. Howell said as the girls climbed in. "I always mean to clean out the car after I've gone to a miniatures convention, but somehow I never get around to it."

During the drive to Fennel Grove, Mrs. Howell chattered brightly about the most recent miniatures show she'd been to—up in Cleveland. She'd sold three of her handmade dollhouses as well as lots of furniture. And there was another show next month in Philadelphia. She planned to be at that one, too.

Zibby, sitting next to her in the front seat, listened politely. She suspected that the chatter was a cover for Mrs. Howell's nervousness. *Who wouldn't be nervous about getting a message from a long-dead father?* she thought ruefully. Look how upset she got with each postcard from her own dad, who was still very much alive.

At Lilliput, Mrs. Howell unlocked the door and led them straight through the shop back to her workroom. She sat down on one of the battered wooden chairs around the large table and motioned the girls to sit as well. The table was covered with balsa wood and various tools.

Mrs. Howell rubbed a hand across her face and sighed.

"All right, let's hear what you've got to say. My father has been dead for seventy years. How can you possibly have a message from him?"

"Well, we've met him," Zibby said softly. "In our dreams." She decided to talk only about Mr. Potts for now. She would not mention Miss Honeywell if she didn't have to.

"And then at school," added Jude.

Mrs. Howell closed her eyes briefly. "I don't understand."

"We don't really understand, either," Zibby said. She tried to think of a starting place. Had the story begun when she'd bought the dollhouse on her birthday? Or long before, on the night of the fire in 1934? Or with a girl named Primrose Parson, whose practical joke had misfired into the first tragedy?

Seeing Zibby's hesitation, Penny spoke up first. "Back in the summer, just after Jude and I moved here, we started having bad dreams. The *same* bad dream. We had it the day after we met Zibby, and that was the day after she had bought the dollhouse at the miniatures show. Zibby and Charlotte and Laura-Jane all had it, too, the very same dream. About a dollhouse on fire..."

Now that Penny had broken the ice, all the girls clamored to add to the story. Zibby described the terrible dream in detail. Jude told how they found the old yearbook photos and learned the story of the school fire from Ms. Wilson. Charlotte related how they'd identified the new science substitute as the same man in the unchanging photos—and as the same man they had seen around town after Zibby had bought the dollhouse. Laura-Jane added that they'd read the old articles about the fire in the *Gazette* archives just that very afternoon.

"And that's when we saw the picture and finally figured

out who Liddie was," Zibby told Mrs. Howell. "I knew I'd seen the doll before. And you had told us it was your own, from when you were little. You called it your special baby— and now I can see why! It was the thing that jogged your memory when you had amnesia, and it was the thing that made me realize you had to be Lydia Pope—the lost 'lamb' that Mr. Potts has been looking for."

Through all their explanations, Mrs. Howell sat gazing at them without a word. But now she covered her face with her wrinkled old hands. "It's unbelievable," she whispered. "But you must be telling me the truth. No one in the world could know that my father always called me his lamb." A sob caught in her throat, and she had to stop and press the back of one wrinkled hand to her mouth. "You see, when I was a toddler, I never said 'Papa' properly. It always came out like 'Baba'—and my father said I sounded like a little sheep. I always called him Baba, even when I was much older. And he called me his lamb."

The girls looked at one another uncertainly, then Zibby touched Mrs. Howell's shaking shoulder and Penny gave her a comforting hug. The ghostly words that once sounded so menacing now seemed unbearably poignant—a father's lament for the much-loved child he had lost.

"And, impossible as what you're telling me seems," the woman continued shakily, "it makes sense of the strange feeling I've had sometimes—maybe only once every ten years—of someone calling to me. Calling my name."

Zibby took a deep breath. "Your father has been haunting the school," she told Mrs. Howell, "looking for you. When he saves up energy to materialize, he comes—but he is able to stay just a few weeks, searching the school—and around town, too. He knew you hadn't died with him, but he couldn't seem to find you alive, either. I'm sure it is his voice that you've heard."

"I've been wondering if it was the amnesia that confused him," mused Jude. "You know, you often read about how a newly dead spirit will contact the loved ones they've left behind. Well, maybe Mr. Potts—I mean, Mr. Pope—tried to contact you, but then couldn't because your mind was sort of, you know, disconnected after the fire. He couldn't make contact, and he got confused."

"And then," added Penny, eagerly taking up the theorizing, "and then he got stuck. So even when you got your memory back and moved to Michigan, he was still haunting the school, looking for you *here*. And now he's come back again—still looking—but there is another ghost who is trying to take his power. He can't let her because he needs all his energy to keep searching for you. They're fighting for energy, for power, and the vibrations are giving people nightmares...Dreams of fire."

Mrs. Howell was staring at her, shaking her head. "'*Another* ghost,' you say? 'Energy'? 'Nightmares'?" She dabbed at her eyes. "I can't bear to think of Baba so unhappy and confused all these years, calling for me," she whispered. "He was such a kind man and a good father. He raised me alone, did you know that? My mother died when I was only a few months old." She looked thoughtful. "I was sent to my cousins up in Michigan, and they were good to me. I grew up busy with friends and school, and, later, work. I never let myself think much about what happened to me as a child. Too painful, perhaps. But I wonder—if I had come back to Carroway, might I have seen my father?"

"When did you come back to this area, then?" asked Charlotte.

"My husband and I moved to Ohio—near Cleveland—about ten years ago, when he retired. But even then, I had no interest in coming back to Carroway. Then, two years ago, my dear Hugh died, and I heard that this little shop was for sale here in Fennel Grove. So I decided to move back to this area to work. I keep meaning to retire, but I enjoy the shop too much. Still, I don't go to Carroway very often."

"We want you to come to our school," said Jude, "to see if your dad can find you now."

Mrs. Howell looked intrigued. "You think I might be able to see him? Really see him?"

"It might work," said Zibby. "There can't be an end to this haunting unless Mr. Potts—I mean, Mr. Pope—knows that Liddie is alive. So we have to get you two together somehow. And we need to do it before my mom's wedding on Sunday—" She broke off. It was too complicated to explain.

"Come tomorrow," Penny begged. "Please, can you come to school tomorrow?"

"But it's Saturday tomorrow," Jude reminded them. "And besides, Mr. Potts has disappeared."

"There's a girls' volleyball tournament at eleven o'clock," Charlotte told them. "So the school will be open. We'll be able to go inside. Let's go earlier. Let's go at ten."

"Mrs. Howell's presence might give Mr. Potts new energy—enough to return," theorized Zibby. "At least it's worth a try."

"I'll come," said Mrs. Howell resolutely. "Ten o'clock sharp." A shadow flitted across her face. "And this time if I hear a voice calling to me, I shall answer."

CHAPTER 39

Mrs. Howell drove the girls home. Zibby and Laura-Jane slipped into the house just as Nell was putting dinner on the table. With an effort, Zibby dragged her mind off Mr. Potts and Mrs. Howell. Brady chattered on about soccer; Ned and Nell talked about going out to see a film that evening; Laura-Jane kept her head down and picked at her food, glancing up at Zibby from time to time with knowledge of their shared secrets in her eyes.

After dinner Ned and Nell left for their film. Zibby and Laura-Jane parked Brady in front of a video and went up to Zibby's bedroom together. Zibby looked carefully around her bedroom for the governess or little girl doll, but she couldn't see either one. The girls knelt in front of the dollhouse. Zibby held her breath as she opened the latch. She found the little girl doll sitting at the tiny kitchen table. Zibby plucked her out of the dollhouse. "We need your help, Primrose. A favor."

Laura-Jane put her hand on Zibby's shoulder so that she, too, could hear the ghostly voice.

"It's about Liddie—we found her," Zibby said. "Lydia Pope! She didn't die in the fire, after all." Quickly Zibby recounted the afternoon's developments.

You're saying Lydia Pope isn't dead? Primrose's eager voice soared in their heads. *That's what you're telling me? That she's alive?* The ghost seemed to forget about her chandelier. She sounded happy. She sounded…relieved.

"Yes, she is totally alive, and always has been." Zibby's voice rose excitedly. "She's Mrs. Howell! And we've made a plan to try to get her together with her father—tomorrow. We want you to help us by contacting Mr. Pope *now* to tell him that Liddie will be at school tomorrow at ten o'clock. We can't tell him ourselves because he's disappeared, and we think he's run out of energy. But even if he can't be visible, we're thinking maybe he can show up some other way. We'll take along one of the dolls, and maybe he'll inhabit it the way you do."

"We'll take the father doll," said Laura-Jane. "That will be the best one."

"Right," agreed Zibby. "We'll bring the father doll to school—and if you can get him to show up even for just a few minutes, it might be long enough for him to see that Liddie isn't dead. That she just had amnesia for a while. He's been confused for so long."

Amnesia, you said? Primrose sighed. *That explains a lot.*

"It explains everything, doesn't it?" said Zibby. "Amnesia is like a great big nothingness. Mr. Pope couldn't make contact with Lydia after the fire because her amnesia acted as a block."

"Poor Liddie," murmured Laura-Jane. "And poor Mr. Pope."

She reached out and touched the doll's blue dress. "Will you help us, Primrose?"

I do want to help— The ghost's voice was very faint now. *But Miss Honeywell...*

Zibby glanced around uneasily. "Where is she?"

In the distance a bell started ringing. Primrose's school bell. And then, like a slow burn, an ache spread through Zibby's palms. It was painfully clear where Miss Honeywell was.

Right here.

Laura-Jane cried out and held her own hands, outstretched, toward Zibby. "My hands—"

"I know." Zibby's words came out as a harsh whisper. "Miss Honeywell is back."

That's Sweet *Miss Honeywell to you, my impertinent girl.*

The air in the bedroom seemed heavy. Zibby felt a slow paralysis weakening her limbs. She pivoted slowly and spied the governess doll, propped against her bed pillow.

"Let's go up to my room," said Laura-Jane. "I feel so... limp. I can't stand being in here with...her."

Zibby set the little girl doll back on the dollhouse parlor couch. She shut and latched the dollhouse and followed Laura-Jane out of the room, with relief.

The girls climbed the attic stairs to Laura-Jane's room, where the air seemed lighter and less oppressive. They sat on Laura-Jane's bed and looked at each other. "How many hours till morning?" asked Zibby shakily. She just wanted to be back at school, with Mrs. Howell and all the girls, laying Mr. Potts to rest. It *had* to work. It had to happen the way they wanted it to. This was the first step toward getting rid of the dream—and maybe getting rid of Miss Honey-well herself.

"I know what we can do while we're waiting till morning." Laura-Jane went to her dresser and opened her jewelry box. She held up a pair of dangly beaded earrings. "I was saving these for when I get pierced ears. But they could make a good chandelier instead. You know, for Primrose."

The earrings were made of clear beads that looked a little bit like diamonds. "It might help her get her energy back—if she's feeling happy," Zibby agreed.

"My idea is that we'll bend them together, sort of," said Laura-Jane, "and then add little wires and more beads and stuff. We can make other things for her, too. Have a craft night."

Why not? thought Zibby. It might keep their minds off their troubles. They set to work. When Brady's video finished, they let him help. They made the chandelier, framed six more stamps, and made some pretty houseplants by sticking snips of dried flowers from the bouquet on the dining-room table into little balls of clay stuffed into toothpaste cap pots.

When Nell and Ned came home, Zibby could see they were surprised to find the girls together. "Homework piling up already?" Nell asked, looking curiously at the diagrams Zibby had sketched for the chandelier.

"Yes, loads," she replied. And it was true enough; Zibby had quite a lot of homework assignments going undone because she had not been able to concentrate on anything but ghosts since school began.

Ned put Brady into bed and told the girls they should

go to bed, too—but he looked so delighted that they were getting along, Zibby thought he would probably let them stay up all night, if they asked. Nonetheless, they promised they would turn the light off soon. He and Nell went back downstairs.

"Voilà." Zibby held up their finished products. The two earrings, painstakingly reshaped, with additions of other beads, glittered in the lamplight. The framed stamps looked like real paintings. The potted plants would look lovely on top of the table in the dollhouse parlor.

"I think everything looks great," approved Laura-Jane. "Let's hope Primrose likes it."

But that meant they had to go back down to Zibby's room to put the things they'd made inside the dollhouse. Neither girl wanted to do that.

"If we don't take the stuff down until tomorrow, that might not be enough time for Primrose to gather her strength and find Mr. Potts to tell him to be at the school." Zibby was worried. "I'd better do it now."

Laura-Jane handed Zibby a roll of tape. "Be careful," whispered Laura-Jane as Zibby started down the attic stairs. Laura-Jane watched from the top step.

Zibby peered into her bedroom from the hallway. She could see her bed; she could see that the governess doll had vanished from the pillows.

Zibby tiptoed over to the dollhouse. Nothing stopped her. "Primrose?" she called softly. "I have some presents for you." She unlatched the front of the house and swung it open—and gasped because there lay the little girl doll on the parlor floor with the governess doll standing over her, arm raised. The malevolence emanating from the dollhouse was palpable.

My parents taught me how to mind, and I taught my brother—though he had to learn the hard way—and I shall teach you...

The voice in Zibby's head was Miss Honeywell, but was she talking to Zibby or to Primrose? Zibby couldn't be sure, but fury welled up in her. She snatched the gray-gowned doll out of the dollhouse, ran to her window, threw up the sash, and hurled the doll out into the night. She slammed the window and returned to the dollhouse. "Don't worry, Primrose," she said, picking up the little girl doll.

She'll never be gone! She craves power—complete power! She'll never rest, never, never—not until she has a body again. And if she can't manifest one on her own, she will take over someone else's...

"Whose body, Primrose?" cried Zibby frantically. "Whose body will she take?"

Miss Honeywell never had a chance to be a bride, whispered Primrose in Zibby's head.

Terror thumped in Zibby's heart. Pieces of the puzzle were clicking into place in her head. Calliope Honeywell, twisted and angry, and never a bride. Bent on revenge. Reveling in her power. Longing for more. Making all the doll play come true with nasty twists...but nothing yet had happened since Laura-Jane had pulled the head off the mother doll. When would Miss Honeywell strike again? "The wedding," whispered Zibby. Miss Honeywell would come for Nell in two more days, at the wedding. Unless they could stop her.

She took a deep breath. "Look, Primrose. Laura-Jane and I have made you a nice chandelier. Something to brighten up the house, even though it won't really light up, of course. But we hope you like it." Hurriedly, because she knew Miss Honeywell could reappear at any moment, Zibby tore strips of tape from the dispenser and used them to secure the chandelier to the parlor ceiling. It dangled prettily, though whether it would help Primrose regain power, Zibby had no idea. Hurriedly she rolled little pieces of tape into pellets, stuck them on the backs of the stamp paintings, and adorned the parlor walls. She set the toothpaste-cap planters on the table. "Enjoy these things," she whispered to the little girl doll, and sat her on the parlor couch. "I'll be back for you in the morning." Then she hesitated. "Or should I take you upstairs to Laura-Jane's room with me? Are you afraid to stay here, in case Miss Honeywell comes back?" The irony of a ghost's being afraid of another ghost was not lost on Zibby, but she didn't blame Primrose for being terrified.

It's no use. She will find me wherever I go. And this is my *dollhouse! Not hers.*

Zibby was pleased to see Primrose regaining some of her spunk. "So you'll stay and try to gather up all the power you can?"

I shall stay.

Zibby slept in her sleeping bag on the floor of Laura-Jane's room. Neither girl slept well, but at least neither had the dream, for a change. Both were up early and dressed before Brady had even awakened. Zibby sidled into her bedroom, scanning the room for danger. She heard a noise from

the dollhouse—a sort of scuffling sound. Slowly she unlatched the house and swung the front of it open.

Miss Honeywell was back, none the worse for her flight
out the window to the bushes below. The governess doll sat
in the velvet armchair in the parlor; Primrose sat on the
couch, across from the armchair, where Zibby had left her
the night before. The beaded chandelier twinkled in a shaft
of morning sunlight.

Zibby extracted the little girl doll and the father doll
from the dollhouse and latched the front securely. Then she
stowed the dolls deep in the bottom of her school backpack
and hurried down to breakfast. Ned was making coffee.
Nell was buttering slices of toast. She looked wan and pale.

"I've got an incredible headache," she murmured. "I'm
glad I don't have to cook today."

"Isn't it time to pamper yourself?" Ned inquired gently.
"After all, tomorrow is the wedding, and you're the radiant
bride."

The *bride.* Zibby's heart fluttered.

Nell smiled up at him weakly. "I'm feeling far from radiant just now, but I will be tomorrow. If only I didn't have
this raging head—"

"We're not supposed to be meeting our parents for lunch
till 11:30, so let me put you back to bed and take care of
things here," Ned said. "My sweet bride. You just get another few hours of sleep and you'll feel much better."

Thank you, Ned, thought Zibby fervently. "Should I
come to the lunch?" she asked. "I could come—to help out,
or something."

"No, honey," replied Nell. "This is just for the bride and

groom and our two sets of parents. Ned's are driving up from Columbus, and we're all going over to pick up Grammy and Gramps."

"Well, okay." Zibby was glad that her mom would be surrounded by people today. She kissed Nell good-bye. *I'm trying hard to keep you safe,* she thought. *Sweet bride.*

THE JEFFERSON GIRLS, Laura-Jane, and Zibby all rode their bikes to school while an autumn storm brewed. Charlotte met them on the front steps of the brick building. Their greetings were interrupted by a loud clap of thunder overhead and a flash of lightning. They dashed inside and the lights in the hallway flickered briefly.

Electricity in the air, Zibby thought. She hoped the extra charge might help Mr. Potts gain strength so that he would be visible when Mrs. Howell came to school.

The girls waited in the lobby for Mrs. Howell. Rain started pattering on the front steps. Penny waved frantically from the door as they saw the old station wagon pull up in front of the school. Zibby's heart started beating hard as Mrs. Howell stepped slowly out of the car, opening her umbrella and cautiously walking through the downpour. Jude and Charlotte hurried forward to take her arms and help her up the wide stone steps. Mrs. Howell took off her plastic rain hat and looked around the big entrance lobby with interest. "Hello, girls. It certainly looks different in here from the way I remember it."

The girls walked her down the hallway to the library. "It's open on a Saturday because the yearbook committee is having their first meeting in here today," Jude whispered.

"That's good, because we want to show you the yearbook photos first."

"Yes," agreed Mrs. Howell. "Seeing is believing."

"But please don't faint or anything," said Laura-Jane worriedly.

Jude led the way past half a dozen kids sitting around a table and chattering about the yearbook layout. She showed Mrs. Howell the shelf of yearbooks. Mrs. Howell started with the yearbook from 1934. "There we both are," she whispered, looking at the photo of her father, then flipping the pages to stare down at the one of her girlhood self. "Before the fire. Before the end."

"But it wasn't the end for you," Penny reminded her. "And, really, it wasn't the end for your father, either, because—look!" Quickly, the girls pulled the other yearbooks from the shelves and opened them to show her all the pictures of Liddie's father.

Mrs. Howell peered down in disbelief. Her face grew pale. Her hands holding the yearbooks shook a little. "Every ten years. Isn't it strange that my father would allow himself to be photographed? It seems like a lot of extra energy used for nothing."

"Not for nothing," said Zibby thoughtfully. "I bet he was hoping you might see the photos someday and know he was looking for you. And here you are."

Mrs. Howell reached out with a steadier hand and replaced the yearbooks on the shelf. "And poor Baba is going to keep on returning until he finds me..." She shook her head. "We must find a way to let him know I'm here, and I'm fine."

The girls escorted Mrs. Howell down the hallway to the science classroom. It was locked, but they peered through the glass window in the door. Mrs. Howell looked in eagerly as if expecting to see her father standing by the blackboard, but no one was there. Zibby fished the little brown-haired doll out of her backpack. "Is he here, Primrose?" she whispered.

The other girls linked arms in order to hear Primrose's response. Mrs. Howell looked frightened, but Penny took her hand.

He's not here, said Primrose's voice in their heads, and Mrs. Howell yelped in surprise. *Try the gymnasium.*

"Whose voice is that?" the woman asked breathlessly as they hurried down another hallway to the gym.

"It's just Primrose Parson, one of the ghosts in my doll-house," Zibby replied in a low voice. "She's going to help us contact your father." Mrs. Howell stared at her incredulously, but Zibby didn't elaborate. There were too many girls in PE uniforms suddenly running past, and their coach calling for quiet and no running. It was going to be hard enough finding some privacy now to summon Mr. Pope. "I'll tell you all about Primrose later," she promised Mrs. Howell.

Mrs. Howell nodded. She stood in the doorway of the gymnasium and looked around at the gleaming wooden floor, the tumbling mats stacked against the walls, the basketball hoops and volleyball nets. "Strange to think," she murmured, "that this gymnasium was built on the exact site of the one that burned. If my father haunts anyplace, it ought to be here—where he died."

Zibby held up the little doll again. "Is he here, Primrose? Is this the place?"

Silence from Primrose. Mrs. Howell looked relieved.

"How do we contact him?" asked Jude. "Here, get out the father doll."

"There isn't much time," Charlotte said, consulting a notice board hanging on the wall. "The volleyball game is scheduled to start in half an hour."

"Let me just tell him I'm here," said Mrs. Howell simply. "And see what happens." She removed her hard-soled shoes and left them just inside the door. Then she took the father doll from Zibby and walked across the polished wooden floor in her stockinged feet, stopping in the far corner by the windows. The girls removed their shoes and trailed after her. "This is the place," Mrs. Howell whispered. "This is where we were when the fire started."

Zibby pulled the little girl doll out of her pocket and closed her fingers around it. The sound of rain slashed against the high windows of the gymnasium. Muted laughter out in the hallway filtered into the vast room. Mrs. Howell held out her hands. "Help me, girls."

Wordlessly they all joined hands and stood in a circle. Zibby and Jude had Primrose clasped between their hands. Laura-Jane and Mrs. Howell had the father doll clasped between theirs. Charlotte glanced self-consciously over her shoulder toward the door. The other girls' eyes were closed. Zibby shut her own eyes and tried to visualize Mr. Potts as he had looked in her science class. She tried to recall the sound of his voice, how loud and stern it was when he lectured, how low and soft when he called out for Liddie.

"Baba?" Mrs. Howell whispered. "Here I am. It's me, Liddie. Please show yourself to me if you can." Her hand tightened on Zibby's.

Almost immediately Zibby felt a little tingle in her arm as if a mild electric current were running through her. In her head she heard Primrose's reedy voice: *Yes, yes, he's here,* she trilled. *Mr. Pope, can you hear me? Mr. Pope—come to us. We've found Lydia!*

The tingling intensified. Zibby opened her eyes and stared at the center of their circle, where it seemed to her a swirl of smoke was taking shape. She took a deep breath of anticipation—and awe.

The smoke formed itself into a figure—the figure of a young man. But this was not Mr. Potts—nor Mr. Pope— nor a shaggy-haired, middle-aged man at all. This was a teenaged boy with close-cropped fair hair and a long thin face. Two dark eyes glittered out of that face, like coals in the ashes. He was wearing a uniform—like a soldier—with knee-length breeches and sturdy black boots. He was carrying a helmet in one hand.

"That's not Baba," whispered Mrs. Howell. "Heavens—it's a World War One soldier!"

It was the young man Zibby had seen in the park and in the backyard. His mouth opened and closed as if he were speaking, but at first Zibby couldn't hear anything. Then she did, faintly: *I tried to get away. I tried to go to war!*

Another ghost, thought Zibby. She was not even surprised. In the flurry of discovery about Mr. Potts, she had almost forgotten the other stranger who had appeared several times, trying to tell her something. Almost forgotten, but not quite.

Poor kid, he said now to Zibby. His voice was very soft and sorrowful. *I know what it's like.*

She remembered he had said this to her before—when she was shut in the closet, and when she was trying to burn the dollhouse. "Are you Lester?" she asked him. "Lester Honeywell?" He had to be.

Again his mouth moved as he tried to speak, but no sound came out.

"What do you want?" she asked him insistently. "Do you know Mr. Pope? Do you know Primrose?"

The young man's wavering face looked so mournful, Zibby longed to comfort him.

A commotion at the door to the gymnasium broke the spell. It was the girls' volleyball team arriving for practice before their game. They burst into the quiet space with laughter. Their feet pounded across the wooden floor. The boy vanished.

As loud voices echoed through the room and balls started bounding everywhere, the five girls led a shaken Mrs. Howell out into the hallway. Carrying their shoes, they all walked back to the lobby, failure hanging over them like a rain cloud.

"There was only that flicker from Baba—but I felt he was trying to come," said Mrs. Howell desperately. "Did you feel it, girls? Before the soldier boy?"

"I did," Jude confirmed. "But I don't think he has enough energy to materialize, and that army guy did."

"I think he was Lester Honeywell," said Zibby. "Miss Honeywell lost her brother in World War One, remember."

"But what could that have to do with anything?" asked Charlotte.

"Everything has something to do with Miss Honey-well," said Jude. "So why not this?"

"Primrose, do *you* know who he was? Was it Lester?" asked Zibby. "The soldier?"

Her voice was fainter than before. *I don't think so—well, maybe—*

"Don't fade out on us now!" begged Zibby. "Hold on to your energy!"

"We need to help Mrs. Howell's father get more energy, somehow," said Penny.

"But how?" demanded Charlotte. "Do we wait till the volleyball game is over and try again—using the father doll?"

A boom of thunder outside the building reminded Zibby of the flickering lights in the hallway. *Power,* she thought—or was it Primrose's voice in her head?

"I don't think we should wait here at school," Zibby said slowly, "because the storm might be over before the volleyball game is. But I do think the lightning is giving him power, and since this whole thing started with the dollhouse…"

"You think that Baba's power might be stronger near the dollhouse?" asked Mrs. Howell, her smile breaking like sunshine through the rain clouds.

"I think we should try to contact your father again before the storm passes," affirmed Zibby. "Let's go to my house right now."

CHAPTER 40

Mrs. Howell parked her station wagon in Zibby's driveway. Zibby was relieved to see that Ned's car wasn't there. Nell must be feeling well enough to go out to lunch with Grammy and Gramps and Ned's parents as planned. And where was Brady? He was supposed to have soccer practice, but with all this rain it had probably been cancelled. She didn't want him barging in and getting scared to death—or scaring away Mr. Potts.

The five girls helped Mrs. Howell hurry through the rain to the front porch. Zibby slipped into the kitchen while the others took off their coats. Nell had left a scribbled note on the table saying that Brady's soccer practice had been cancelled but the coach had taken Brady to play with his kids for the day. He would bring Brady home in the late afternoon.

Perfect, thought Zibby. She held tightly to the little girl doll as she led the way upstairs to her bedroom. The governess doll was not in sight, but Zibby knew she could be anywhere. Mrs. Howell had eyes only for the dollhouse. Letting out a little moan, she approached it like a sleep-walker—arms outstretched.

"Zibby," she cried, "I believe this *is* the very same doll-house old Mrs. Smythe brought to me. You've cleaned it up so beautifully, I hardly recognize it." She ran her hands over the roof shingles, then moved down to unlatch the front. "Yes, it is the same house. And—" She frowned, perplexed. "It's also very much like the house I had as a child. The one that burned."

Jude nudged Zibby, and Charlotte cleared her throat. Laura-Jane and Penny raised their brows at each other be-hind Mrs. Howell's back. *Doesn't she know?* thought Zibby, confused. *Can't she tell it's the exact same house?*

"Mrs. Howell," said Zibby. "There's something about this house you need to know. And the person to explain it to you is right here." She held up the little doll with the brown braids.

"Your ghost girl?" Mrs. Howell turned from the doll-house with a nervous laugh.

"You've met her before," said Zibby gently. "It's Prim-rose Parson, who was your father's student when he was a tutor—way back long ago before he'd even married your mother. And Primrose Parson grew up to marry Mr. Smythe. And Mrs. Smythe is the old woman who contacted you and tried to give you the dollhouse."

Mrs. Howell sank onto Zibby's bed. Her face was creased in confusion. "Wait...Mrs. Smythe—I think I re-member that was the name of the woman who gave us the

dollhouse in the first place—the dollhouse that burned. I—
I don't understand."

"Tell her, Primrose," ordered Zibby, clutching the doll
tightly. And she sat next to Mrs. Howell on the bed and took
the old woman's hand in her free one. The other girls moved
toward them. Jude put a hand lightly on Zibby's shoulder.
The other girls linked hands so they, too, could hear what
Primrose had to say for herself. "Go on, Primrose," urged
Zibby. "Tell the whole story. Tell about Miss Honeywell."

For a long moment there was no sound at all in the bedroom except for the patter of rain on the windows. Then
Primrose's voice sounded faintly.

Mr. Pope wanted to electrify my dollhouse, you know,
Primrose said. *But Miss Honeywell put a stop to that.*

"Please tell Mrs. Howell about Miss Honeywell," urged
Zibby. "Tell her everything you know about her father and
Miss Honeywell—and the dollhouse."

And Zibby felt a little jolt—like a surge of electricity—
run through the doll as Primrose summoned all her power.
Then Primrose's voice began to speak in their heads. She
told about how her parents had given her the dollhouse,
how Miss Honeywell had been determined to marry Mr.
Pope, but then she had died....

Primrose related how Miss Honeywell had haunted her
all her life since then, and continued even now to plague her
from beyond the grave. Primrose was speaking very quickly,
Zibby noticed, and she sounded agitated. Zibby noticed,
too, that Primrose was not telling Mrs. Howell *why* Miss
Honeywell was haunting her. She'd left out the detail that it
had been her practical joke that killed the governess.

Miss Honeywell had haunted Mr. Pope, sometimes, too, Primrose told Mrs. Howell. Miss Honeywell had been so jealous that Mr. Pope had married Evelina, Mrs. Howell's mother.

I gave you the dollhouse when you were born, Liddie, Primrose continued. *But it returned to me. I gave it to you again when you were twelve, and your father said you could keep it to use for the science fair. It returned to me both times. Nothing has ever managed to destroy it.*

"So it really is the very same dollhouse?" Mrs. Howell shook her head. "Unbelievable. But then so is a ghost's voice talking inside my head." She released Zibby's hand, looking dazed.

She stood up and walked back to the dollhouse. "Not a burn mark on it." Then she looked back at the girls, all hovering uncertainly behind her. She cleared her throat in a businesslike manner. "Well, girls, are we ready to try again?"

Zibby squeezed the little doll. "All right, Primrose. You try to get Mr. Potts—Mr. Pope—to come to us now." She set the little girl doll in the parlor, then brought the father doll out of her backpack and handed it to Mrs. Howell.

"Let's hold hands again," said Mrs. Howell, slipping the father doll into the pocket of her cardigan. She seemed to be taking control, and Zibby was happy to let her.

They stood around the dollhouse, hands linked. Lightning flashed outside the bedroom window. "Baba?" whispered Mrs. Howell, and then called it out again in a firmer voice, "Baba!"

Zibby felt a shiver of current along her spine, and she sucked in her breath sharply as eddies of smoke started swirling around the dollhouse. There was no fire, only black smoke filling the bedroom. The girls coughed, but no one broke the circle of hands. Then they all saw something else, something just visible through the black smoke—and Mrs. Howell, who had never had the dream, tipped back her head and let out a cry.

The hand in the black glove was back.

Zibby gripped Mrs. Howell's hand tightly so she would not pull away and break the circle. They watched the hand grope feebly toward them from the smoke, and then a deep, rasping voice swelled from nowhere, crying out in anguish: *Liddieliddieliddieliddie!*

The swirling smoke took form. A figure of a man was visible—not the soldier this time, but Mr. Potts, in his diamond-patterned vest. Mrs. Howell wrenched free of the circle and threw herself at the man, clutching his gloved hand. "Baba!"

"Who is this old woman?" roared Mr. Potts, glaring through the smoke at the girls. "What has she done with my Liddie?"

"Baba, it's me!"

The swirling smoke began to settle, and the girls could see Mr. Potts and Mrs. Howell facing each other in front of the dollhouse, hands clasped. Mrs. Howell was hanging on tightly while the man struggled to pull away. Zibby was surprised to see how young he looked next to his elderly daughter. But of course he had been only forty-five or fifty when he'd died.

"Hello, Mr. Potts," Zibby said calmly, as if ghosts in her bedroom were nothing unusual—and indeed they weren't, these days. "Or, really, we should say Mr. Pope now. Please just listen to us for a minute. Look—it's Liddie. We've found Liddie for you!"

"This old woman?" He succeeded in pulling away from Mrs. Howell so that she was left holding only the singed black leather gloves. He shook his head disbelievingly. "I thank you for your concern, girls, but I must not waste time while this storm is giving me extra energy. I must use it wisely and continue searching for my daughter."

"But wait!" cried Jude.

"This *is* your Liddie!" shouted Penny.

"I *am*—," cried Mrs. Howell.

"And we can prove it!" yelled Charlotte.

Laura-Jane spoke up, too: "Yeah!"

Mr. Pope shook his shaggy head. "Scientific proof?" His booming voice dwindled. "I must keep looking for the child…"

His confusion was too profound, too complete. It had reigned for too many years. He could not, Zibby realized, shake the idea that his daughter was still twelve years old. Just as he himself had not changed in nearly seventy years, he could not imagine that she had, either.

What was there to connect young Liddie Pope with the adult Lydia Howell? What would break through Mr. Pope's confusion and convince him?

Zibby saw Mr. Pope flicker, and she realized they were going to lose him—not because he had run out of energy this time, but because he had no wish to stay. Frantically she turned to Mrs. Howell. "Your special baby!" she cried. "Did you bring it?"

Mrs. Howell picked up her handbag. She fumbled inside it, keeping her eyes on her father as if fearing that by looking away for an instant she might lose him. "Look here, Baba," she said, holding out the little doll to him. "Don't you remember Sally?"

The doll that once had the power to cut through the void of Liddie Pope's amnesia now cut through the decades of Mr. Pope's confusion. "It's Liddie's doll," he whispered. "Yet it can't be. That doll burned up. They both burned up..."

"The doll didn't burn!" Zibby said, gladness welling deep inside her as she saw his stern expression soften. He was starting to understand. "And Liddie didn't burn up, either. She was just somewhere else, all this time. Oh, Mr. Pope, you have to believe us."

Mrs. Howell moved closer to her father's ghost, murmuring to him, speaking fast. Zibby knew she must be worrying that the energy wouldn't last long enough for the whole story to be told.

But she told it all—beginning when she found herself lying out in the orchard with the school blazing behind her. "I didn't know what to do but get away," she said. "I made my way to the bus station and crawled inside an empty bus... and next thing I knew, I was in Columbus. I didn't know my name or where I came from or what had happened to me." She was still holding the black leather gloves as she spoke, pressing them to her heart.

Her voice filled Zibby's bedroom with her story, and to Zibby the events seemed so real and immediate, it didn't seem possible that they had happened long ago, before she was born, before her parents had been born. The other girls listened raptly, never taking their eyes from the ghost and his daughter.

Mr. Pope listened, too. "It's really you?" He raised his hand and brushed the fingers across his daughter's wrinkled cheek. "And have you grown up happy, Liddie?" he asked.

"Oh, yes. And happier than ever now that we've found each other."

"Then, at last I can be happy, too," Mr. Pope murmured, and it seemed to Zibby that he wasn't quite as much *there* as he had been at first. As if he were somehow becoming only an echo of himself. *He's losing power,* she thought. *But it's okay now.*

"Will I see you again, Baba?" asked Mrs. Howell, clasping his hand in hers.

"Not here, not anymore," sighed Mr. Pope, his voice growing fainter. "I have finally done what I needed to do. I have found you—and now I shall be moving on. But your mother and I—we will be waiting..."

"Oh, but Baba, I hate to lose you again so soon!" Mrs. Howell lifted her hand—the hand that had held his—and found it empty. The black gloves, too, had vanished. Her father's ghost was disappearing right before their eyes, flickering occasionally like a lightbulb about to expire.

"You will never lose me." His voice came to them as if from a vast distance. Faint though it was, Zibby felt the power in it, the power of his love for the child he had never forgotten. "But there's no rush to join me, my dear little Liddie. Take your time getting here. Live to a ripe old age. An even *riper* old age!" He flickered again. "I must go now, my lamb."

Then there came a flash of lightning, and a quiet voice spoke from a corner of the bedroom: "Oh, no you don't, my dearest Thaddeus. Not yet."

Zibby turned around slowly, and there, seated at the desk, was a woman in a long gray dress—the long-faced woman from the miniatures convention. A woman, solid and real, with dark, glittering eyes.

Miss Calliope Honeywell.

CHAPTER 41

Zibby broke out in a sweat. It was one thing to hear this woman's disembodied voice in her head, or to feel this woman's strength weighing her down, yet quite another thing for her to be sitting here, seemingly as solid and real as Zibby herself.

The woman in gray spoke in a hard cold voice. "You shall not move on, Thaddeus!"

"I must go to Evelina," Mr. Pope said, but Miss Honeywell stood up suddenly and glided toward him.

"You're not going anywhere," she hissed. "I forbid it. Not when I have finally stored up enough energy to have a body—like you, dearest Thaddeus. Oh, you were a clever fellow—waiting so many years and hoarding your power before appearing in a real body! I was never able to wait that long. Patience, as you know, was not one of my virtues." She laughed gaily.

Do you have any virtues at all? Zibby wondered through her terror. She doubted it.

"Besides, my dear," Miss Honeywell continued, "I had Miss Primrose Parson to attend to, among other things. But now I have discovered another way to store up energy—one that involves no waiting at all! I have summoned all possible power in order to be with you now, in my body, as you see. We are meant to be together, and I know a way we can be—permanently. Rather than struggling to manifest in the bodies we once had, we can get new ones. Other bodies, Thaddeus. Just think of it. Healthy, *live* bodies."

Zibby sucked in her breath and kept backing away until she was pressed up against her dresser. Jude was next to her, clutching her arm in an agonizing grip. They couldn't see through the smoke pall to the other girls. Miss Honeywell's malevolence blanketed the room.

"I don't need a body anymore, Calliope," said Mr. Pope. "Nor do you."

"You will not deny me, Thaddeus. Not after all I have done to bring us together. Not after I caused the fire that ended your life so that in death we would be together, as was denied us in life!" The woman's voice swirled around them, black as the smoke. "Our love must not be denied."

Zibby felt the heavy lethargy press down on her. She could not move her legs or arms. But she took a deep breath and managed to speak. "You?" she cried out to Miss Honeywell. "Talking about *love?*"

The figure flared as if lit from within, and a thin column of smoke swirled around her skirt as the ghost moved toward Zibby.

Zibby could not move, though every instinct in her was to flee. "I don't believe you know what love is," she declared recklessly.

The ghost glided closer to Zibby, eyes blazing. "There's a wedding tomorrow, with a bride and a groom. We shall take their places, Thaddeus and I. We are powerful enough to have their bodies for our own and be married as we were meant to be. And then we will deal with disobedient little girls as they are meant to be dealt with. Once and for all."

"I think that was a death threat," Jude mumbled into Zibby's ear.

Zibby squeezed her friend's hand, though she barely had the strength to move.

"Calliope." Mr. Pope sounded very far away, though his ghost was still visible. "Leave the girl alone. This isn't about her, is it? Nor about any of them. You think it's about you and me, but it isn't—and never has been. In life we were not meant for each other, and after death I have yearned only to find my Liddie, to know she was safe, before moving on to my beloved wife. All your determination cannot keep me here. I'm ready to move on now because I have found my Liddie at last." He flickered, called out, "Good-bye!" and vanished with the next flash of lightning. In the following volley of thunder, his voice bounced back to them: "Evelina? My darling!"

The room quivered with Miss Honeywell's rage.

Mrs. Howell was weeping. "He has moved on," she whispered, smiling through her tears. "He is with my mother again."

Through the swirling smoke, Zibby caught glimpses of Jude, Penny, Charlotte, and Laura-Jane. They all appeared to be frozen—or dead. They were held in place by Miss Honeywell's power, sapped of their strength as she sucked their energy to fuel this manifestation of her body.

Zibby felt herself being drained of energy, too. It was a slow sucking sensation in her stomach and it grew stronger with every flash of lightning. She fought against it, but she knew what was happening. Miss Honeywell was using the storm to drain whatever strength she could from the people present in the room.

And then Zibby was aware of another presence forming at her side—another ghost drawing power from the living people and from the electricity of the storm. It was a girl about Zibby's own age, with long brown braids. It was Primrose Parson.

"Miss Honeywell!" Primrose's voice sounded just as reedy as when it was inside Zibby's head. "I am here."

"That's *Sweet* Miss Honeywell to you, my girl. You must learn your manners."

Both ghosts flared in the rolling thunder. Zibby, still leaning against the dresser, reached again for Jude's limp hand and hung on tightly. Across the room she could see Mrs. Howell gripping the dollhouse for support.

The smoke grew more dense. The girls coughed, and Zibby was relieved to know they were still alive. Miss Honeywell's voice dripped with scorn. "Are you ready to get down on your knees before me, begging my forgiveness?"

"Beg forgiveness?" Primrose laughed weakly. She turned and appealed to Zibby. "She smacked me with her ruler! She locked me in the closet! She made my childhood into a hell, and she's haunted me all my life! She haunted the Popes, and she's been haunting you. *She's* the one who needs to ask for forgiveness, wouldn't you say?"

The force draining Zibby was nearly crushing her now. It was a struggle to draw breath. "That's true, Primrose,"

Zibby gasped out. "But don't forget—you're the one who killed her. Who knows what she might have become if she'd lived? What things she might have done—maybe even turned out to be nice, if she'd found a good husband and had a family. Or changed jobs so she wasn't a governess anymore. Who knows, Primrose? But she never had the chance because you *killed* her."

"I only meant to get her wet," said Primrose in a small voice. "I've been sorry all of my life."

"Then tell her that now."

The two ghosts stood like statues in the roiling smoke. For a suspended moment, no one moved or spoke.

Then Primrose Parson slowly sank to her knees in front of Miss Honeywell and bent her head. "I hated you," she whispered. "But I never planned to kill you. And that's the truth. I—" She hesitated. "I'm very sorry." Her thin voice caught in a sob. "I *do* beg your forgiveness, Miss Honeywell." The room was heavy with silence.

Into the silence, Miss Honeywell laughed sharply. "A nasty piece of baggage is little Miss Primrose Parson, and I knew it from the moment I met her."

The ghost of Primrose Parson flickered. Zibby held her breath. The whole room seemed to hold its breath. Outside the window the flashes of lightning and the rolling thunder were farther away.

Miss Honeywell looked around at the girls, at Mrs. Howell, then down again at Primrose. She laughed. "I always despised you, Primrose Parson," Miss Honeywell said slowly. "A girl who had everything she wanted—but who was spoiled to the core."

Primrose raised her bowed head. "I didn't have *every-thing* I wanted, Miss Honeywell. I didn't have parents to take care of me." Tears shone on her ghostly face. "I had *you.*"

Miss Honeywell's black eyes glittered. "Be that as it may, I shall never forgive you," she said. "Your practical joke is what kept me from marrying my true love."

Primrose rolled her eyes. "Believe that if you want," she said. Her shoulders drooped. She got slowly to her feet.

Miss Honeywell tilted back her head and opened her mouth, and out came a stream of laughter—laughter that chilled Zibby inside and out. Zibby saw Mrs. Howell trying to rise from the floor behind the dollhouse but sink back from lack of strength. She saw Penny and Laura-Jane and Charlotte all struggling to get off the bed, but Miss Honey-well's power forced them to lie there like butterflies pinned to a board. Jude was at Zibby's side but had no more power to help than if she'd been a sleeping baby.

Then Zibby saw a plume of smoke curling up in the corner by her desk, taking shape even as she realized with certainty who it was.

"Lester?" Zibby called out weakly. "Lester Honeywell?"

The effect of this name on Miss Honeywell was enormous. She flung herself away from Zibby and fell back across the room to the windows. Her power lessened immediately, and Zibby felt able to breathe again.

The plume of smoke took shape now as the young soldier boy, holding his helmet in one hand and pointing at Miss Honeywell with the other. *"Calliope."*

Zibby wasn't sure he really spoke or the words were in her head. But when she looked over at Jude, she saw Jude was listening with an open mouth. Jude could hear him, too. Lester was truly there.

"Where will it stop, Calliope?" he thundered. "Who will stop you?" Then he turned to the girls and spoke in a gentle voice. "Someone must stop her—but I've never been able to do it. Our parents tried to make her mind, when they were alive, but she was always headstrong and willful. She was furious with our father when he would not let her keep company with the boy she adored—our neighbor, Thaddeus Pope. Said the Popes were not of our class. Then our parents died of influenza, and Mr. Pope went off to college, and she was even more furious. She stayed at home to raise me, and I felt every ounce of that fury, believe me."

A bark of sharp laughter from Miss Honeywell made Zibby start. Then she turned back to Lester with dawning understanding. "You never really went off to war," Zibby said slowly. "She just told people you did."

"I wanted to go off to war—anything to get away from home, from her rules, from her harsh discipline. I was not eager to fight in the war, but I was desperate to be away from home, away from her control. She forbade my going, but I signed up anyway. Never made it to my regiment, though. It took just one mighty shove and a swift kick to the back of my knees on the morning of my planned departure—and she was quick with those swift kicks." The ghost chuckled, but it was not a merry sound. "I had experienced them before, many times after our parents died and left her to raise me. But never before at the top of a steep staircase."

"She killed you," murmured Zibby.

"Yes." Lester's ghost wavered, but the voice was strong.

"And I have watched her all these years, watched as her fury grew and grew and the people who came into contact with her suffered. Even after death, her power continued to increase. Where will it end?"

Miss Honeywell glided across the room to face him. "You always were a sinful liar, Lester, though I tried to beat it out of you," she snapped.

Lester ignored his sister. "She told the police I had tripped, and what a terrible tragedy it was. She may have come to believe it herself—certainly she never once accepted what she had done. Or perhaps she told herself it had been necessary—because children must be made to mind."

"That's right," Miss Honeywell cried. "They must be forced to mind!"

"You can't force people, Calliope—haven't you learned that? You can't force them to obey you, or to love you." Lester's ghost flickered. "And now what are you left with? Nothing and nobody. You've hurt countless people, and you've stopped yourself from moving on—"

"Who cares about moving on?" screamed the ghost of Miss Honeywell. "I shall never move on! I will regain a body and no one will stop me." The lights in the bedroom flashed on and off, on and off, and Zibby felt herself grow limp. Lester faded away until he simply was not there. Primrose let out a high-pitched squeal and also disappeared. "I will suck you all dry," Miss Honeywell intoned, raising her arms high. "I will triumph over all of you, all the living and the dead."

And then, like a light going out, she vanished.

"Is she gone?" asked Penny shakily. "Really gone?"

"They're all gone," said Jude. "All the ghosts are gone."

"Well, Miss Honeywell will be back, I'm sure of it," said Zibby, taking a deep breath and moving her arms and legs, testing them for damage. "After all, tomorrow is the wedding."

"Your poor mom," whispered Laura-Jane. "Oh, Zibby, I am so sorry."

Zibby just shrugged helplessly.

"You couldn't know it would lead to this," said Jude.

"I have never been so frightened in my life," said Mrs. Howell, coming out from behind the dollhouse and holding on to it for support. "But it has all been worth it for me to see my father again and to know he has moved on. No more saving up energy to come searching for me, no more dreams of fire…They're happy now, he and my mother, together."

"It's Zibby's mother we have to worry about now," said Laura-Jane.

Thunder rumbled again, but it sounded much farther away now. The flashes of lightning, when they came, were faint. The storm was moving on, taking its energy with it.

"Dreams of fire," murmured Zibby. She was sick of feeling scared and helpless. She was thinking hard.

"I want to go home," Charlotte whispered weakly from the bed.

"Wait—don't go yet," said Zibby slowly. "Not just yet because—because I'm getting an idea. You know that saying about fighting fire with fire? Well, I'm thinking about a way to get rid of Miss Honeywell for good."

The others looked at her expectantly.

"I think I've got a plan," said Zibby with a small, hopeful smile. "Or—we can call it a practical joke, if you want."

And then she told them.

CHAPTER 42

The day of the wedding dawned sunny and clear. Zibby lay in bed, staring up at the ceiling, listening to the birds singing outside her window and Ned singing in the shower. Across the room, the dollhouse was latched securely. There was no sign of the governess doll. All these things were good omens, Zibby told herself.

She lay thinking about her plan. If it worked, the dollhouse would be free of ghosts for the first time in its long, haunted life since Primrose Parson first played with it as a girl. And Nell would be safe. But if it didn't work...

Zibby sat up and pushed back the blanket. She would just have to hope and pray that it would work and the wedding would take place without a hitch and her mom and Ned would have a peaceful, happy honeymoon—and a long life together.

But first there was the wedding to get through.

Zibby rolled out of bed and went into her mom's bedroom. Grammy was already there, helping Nell fix her hair.

Brady and Gramps, Grammy told her, were downstairs making breakfast. Grammy coiled Nell's long red-gold braid into a low bun and pinned it at the nape of her neck. "Pretty," said Nell, gazing into the mirror, "but can you stop for a minute and give me a massage? I've got one of those terrible headaches starting up again."

Zibby's throat constricted. *So it begins,* she thought.

Grammy began kneading the back of Nell's neck. "Maybe you'd better go down now and eat something," she suggested. "You're probably just hungry and nervous."

"I'd better eat before I get dressed, anyway," Nell agreed.

Her wedding dress hung on the back of the door. Zibby glanced at it appreciatively. It wasn't long and white—white was reserved for first-time brides, Grammy had explained—but was short and airy, in a beautiful cream color with swirls of shimmery silver thread.

Laura-Jane appeared in the doorway. "Good morning," she said uncertainly. Her eyes sought Zibby's. *Is your mom okay?*

"Mom has a headache," Zibby said pointedly. "Let's get breakfast." The girls followed Grammy and Nell downstairs. They ate bagels and cream cheese and fruit salad. Then Gramps, Ned, and Brady got dressed for the wedding and left early in Gramps's pickup truck, which was full of flowers from his garden, ready to be displayed in the church.

Then it was time for Zibby and Laura-Jane to dress in their blue bridesmaid dresses. They twirled in front of the long mirror in Nell's room, and Zibby felt like a princess. Grammy brushed Zibby's hair till it formed a shining cap. Then Gram set to work on Laura-Jane's long black hair, twisting it up into a French braid with loose tendrils to frame her face. If only Nell were not sitting slumped on the edge of her bed massaging her temples, Zibby would have enjoyed the hustle and bustle of the wedding preparations.

They drove to the church, and Aunt Linnea and Uncle David were already there, with Charlotte and Owen in their best clothes. Ned's parents were waiting, too, and his brother, James, and James's family. There were friends of Ned's and Nell's from their school days, people Zibby didn't know at all from the newspaper office, and people she did know who had hired Nell to do their catering. There were neighbors from across the street, and then the Jeffersons arrived with Jude and Penny looking resplendent and unfamiliar in fancy dresses. Ned and Brady and Gramps all looked very impressive in their suits. Gramps was tucking flowers into their buttonholes.

Zibby saw Mrs. Howell arriving. She was not an official wedding guest because neither Nell nor Ned had met her yet. But Zibby had invited her because she was part of the plan.

Nell and Ned were waiting in the minister's study while the church filled with wedding guests. Brady, Ned's parents, and Grammy and Gramps all stood out on the steps, welcoming people as they arrived. Zibby and Laura-Jane hovered anxiously as Nell clutched her head. "Ooh," she moaned. "This is killing me."

Ned took Nell's hands. "What can I do? Is it time for another painkiller?"

She staggered against him. He held her tightly. "I feel like my whole head is about to burst," she whispered. "I feel—I feel like someone is pulling my brain out!"

"Here, sit down over here," he directed.

Zibby walked over to the minister's desk and sank into his big leather chair. She looked at the desk. There was a phone on it, and a computer, and a mug full of pens and things. The mug had writing on it: ALL WILL BE WELL. Zibby hoped that the slogan was an omen.

Then her hand suddenly reached out and plucked something from the mug. She looked down at it in surprise. It was a sharp knife—no, it was a letter opener. But sharp— like a dagger. She reached out to put it back again....

And couldn't. Her hand wouldn't obey her brain's command. Her hand, instead, moved slowly down to her side and held the letter opener, point down, hidden among the folds of the blue dress. *No one will see it there. You'll pull it out when it's time and—surprise!*

Miss Honeywell. Zibby felt her stomach drop. She opened her mouth to call for Laura-Jane, but her mouth would not open.

Across the room, Laura-Jane and Brady were talking to Nell. "It's almost time," Laura-Jane said.

"Come on," urged Brady. "We'll help you."

"Or would you rather lie down for a few minutes?" Ned asked his bride. "I'll get you something cold to drink and we can start a bit late."

Ned's mother stepped into the study. "The organist is ready. Everything looks beautiful. Shall we start?" Then she saw Nell's contorted face. "Goodness! What's wrong, dear?"

"She's not having second thoughts," said Ned with an attempt at humor. "It's just a bad headache. She's been having them a lot lately. It's nerves, I think."

"Hmm," said his mother. "I think my new daughter-in-

law should make a trip to the doctor for a checkup after this trip down the aisle."

Nell managed a small smile. "I'll be fine," she murmured, taking a deep breath and smoothing her hair. "Weddings are stressful—especially on the bride."

Zibby could hear the organ music beginning and knew that the people who had come to the wedding would expect it to start soon. She watched Ned give Nell a hug and observed how Nell winced.

"Ready, honey?"

Nell stood up slowly. "I hope I can get through this without fainting."

Again Zibby tried to replace the letter opener in the mug. Her hand would not budge. It was as if she had turned to stone.

Grammy hurried into the room. "What's holding everybody up?" Then she saw Nell's pale face. "You poor angel," Grammy said soothingly. "But I bet your head will be better as soon as you're out there saying your vows." She bustled around Nell, straightening the straps of the shimmery wedding dress. "Now, take a deep breath, and everything will be fine. You look beautiful." Her smile included Zibby and Laura-Jane. "Both of you girls look exquisite, too."

Laura-Jane picked up her bouquet. "Ready, Zib?"

And Zibby found she could stand up now, no problem. She walked over to the others, holding the weapon tightly against her side. *You can make me carry it,* she thought mutinously, *but I'm not going to* do *anything with it.*

We shall see about that, young miss.

Ned's parents and Nell's parents walked down the aisle

first and sat in the front row together. Next came Brady, looking very sweet, with no sign of his usual boisterousness, carrying the rings on a little satin pillow. He stood up next to the minister. Zibby tried to forget she had a dagger in her hand as she and Laura-Jane walked slowly, side by side, their dresses floating out around them with every step. Laura-Jane was smiling and showed no trace of the anger and resentment that she'd felt about the wedding only a week ago. Zibby nodded as she passed Jude and Penny, sitting with their family, and Charlotte, sitting with hers. Owen gave Zibby the thumbs-up sign as she and Laura-Jane glided past. When they reached the altar, Brady greeted them with a big smile. "I didn't drop it!" he exulted in a stage whisper.

They all watched as the bride and groom approached. Nell held tightly to Ned's arm. Zibby could see Jude, Penny, and Charlotte all anxiously watching as Nell approached. But Mrs. Howell was not looking at the bride at all; instead she was scanning the church, alert for the danger only she and the girls knew was lurking. She did not look at Zibby. She did not know, Zibby realized, that the danger was so close.

Nell and Ned made a storybook couple, though Nell's smile had a strange fixed quality that Zibby knew meant she was fighting back a terrible pain. Ned was so dark with his black hair and suit, and Nell was so fair with her red-gold hair and creamy dress; they seemed a perfect match. They strolled along, with Ned nodding to friends and relatives. Zibby tried again to open her hand and release the letter opener, but her fingers clenched it as tightly as if they had been welded to it.

When Ned and Nell reached the altar, they faced the

minister and the service began. "Dearly beloved," intoned the minister, "we are gathered here on this lovely morning to witness the marriage of—"

He broke off as the lights flickered and went out. Zibby peered out fearfully into the dim church. The day was sunny enough that the lighting was not necessary, but she knew that this must be some sort of sign from Miss Honeywell. She was getting ready to strike.

The minister cleared his throat and began again. "Dearly beloved—" Then the lights came back on, and he broke off again. Then they went off, then on, then off, then on. People turned in their seats with frowns on their faces, looking for ill-behaved children. But there was no one in sight who was messing around with the lights.

Laura-Jane sagged against Zibby. "Help," she whispered. "I'm getting so dizzy…"

Zibby squeezed Laura-Jane's hand tightly. "I've got a knife in my hand," she whispered.

"What?" Laura-Jane yelped. She stared at Zibby.

"*Shh!*" Zibby stared out at the wedding guests. "It's in my hand. She made me bring it. I can't put it down. She won't let me." Zibby's whisper grew harsh as her feeling of panic increased. "Laura-Jane, what is she going to make me do with this knife?"

Zibby held in the tears she felt building along with the hysteria. Was Miss Honeywell going to try to make Zibby cut off her own mom's head? Was that how the horrible dollhouse game would come true this time? But how could Miss Honeywell take over a body if it had no head? Even Miss Honeywell could not be a headless bride.

The image made her feel faint.

"Fight back," ordered Laura-Jane. "Fight *her*. Remember our plan. Concentrate."

"Right. That's right," murmured Zibby. "Thanks."

Then, as Laura-Jane slumped against Zibby's arm, Zibby had to hiss at her. "Now you fight back, too! Don't let her drain you! *Concentrate!*" She was feeling dizzy and weak, but still her hand held fast to the dagger. She felt that awful heaviness in the air. Was Miss Honeywell going to suck the energy out of every wedding guest?

Zibby and Laura-Jane stared hard at Nell, who was leaning weakly against Ned. They concentrated their thoughts: *You. Will. Not. Win.*

The minister was speaking to Nell and Ned in a low voice. The wedding guests began to murmur among themselves. Zibby's hand twitched. *Use. The. Knife.* The voice was in Zibby's head, loud and insistent. Her hand twitched at her side. "No!" she hissed. And then, "Jude!" she cried. And Jude heard.

Jude jumped right up and walked to the altar. She stood alongside of Zibby and Laura-Jane just as if she were another bridesmaid. The wedding guests murmured in surprise, and Mrs. Jefferson half stood as if planning to come bring Jude back to her seat, but then Penny also slid out of the pew and strode up to stand with the other girls.

Nell collapsed onto her knees, and both Ned and the minister leaned over her. She looked as if she were praying, but Zibby knew better.

All right, young miss. Time for your part. Center stage.

Zibby tossed her head back and forth, trying to dislodge the voice from her head.

Use. The. Knife.

She felt her arm twitch, wanting to move, wanting to strike—but she willed it to stay at her side. *I'll never cut off my mom's head! Never in a million years!*

Not your mother, silly girl. The groom!

Then Miss Honeywell's evil intention became clear to Zibby. The letter opener in her hand was not to stab Nell—no, it was meant for Ned.

Kill him, ordered Miss Honeywell. *I thought Thaddeus would join me here and take over the groom as I will take over the bride, but he has made his stupid choice. So that leaves me on my own.* Her voice was tinged with self-pity. *But I'm used to that.*

Are you surprised? Zibby sent the cutting thought.

They will arrest you for murder, of course, but I shall come to visit you in prison.

"I'll tell them it was you!" Zibby spoke aloud through gritted teeth as she used every ounce of strength to keep her arm holding the knife stiff at her side.

Then, I guess I'll be visiting you in a hospital for the insane instead. Miss Honeywell's cold laughter whispered across Zibby's cheek. *Kill. Him. Now.*

Zibby felt her arm growing numb. She was losing power. She watched the arm—*her* arm—raise up, knife held ready to slice. If her plan was to work, she needed more help. "Now!" cried Zibby as Miss Honeywell forced her to take three steps toward Ned. "Jude—*now!*"

"Charlotte!" Jude's voice rang out boldly, summoning her. Charlotte slipped out of her seat and ran up the aisle to stand next to Penny and Jude.

"Get back here!" Zibby heard Aunt Linnea hiss at Charlotte, and Owen muttered, "Is she crazy, or what?"

Not crazy, thought Zibby. *Just determined. We're all determined you will not win, Miss Honeywell. Old Sourpuss. Repeat after me and believe it: You. Will. Not. Win.*

Charlotte grabbed Penny's hand, and Penny took hold of Jude's hand, and Jude reached for Zibby's hand that wasn't holding Laura-Jane's—and it was with great relief that Zibby felt Jude's thin fingers prying her hand open and tugging the knife away. It dropped to the floor and Jude kicked it swiftly off to one side.

With the dagger out of her hand, Zibby felt some of her strength return, and with it came new determination. She fixed her eyes on Mrs. Howell and nodded. That was the signal that she would also join them: Who cared what the wedding guests thought about these unusual proceedings? With Nell's life on the line, wedding protocol would have to take a backseat.

Six against one, thought Zibby grimly. It was now or never if they were going to try the practical joke. She had not expected the battle with Miss Honeywell over the letter opener. She hoped against hope that her plan still had a chance of working.

"Wait—Miss Honeywell," she whispered in what she hoped was a sincerely resigned voice. "Let's not fight anymore. I've thought of a way to help you without hurting my mom or Ned. You want to be a bride, and so you *should* be a bride. I see you've been right all along. And so now we'll help you. Leave my mom and Ned alone; you won't need them by the time you're tanked up with all our energy instead!"

Miss Honeywell materialized at the altar. Her dark eyes

glittered greedily. *Now you've learned to mind me, my girl. You've learned at last.*

"Yes, yes," agreed Zibby readily. She looked with anguish over at the bride and groom, who were both blank-faced, staring into space. The minister was whispering to them urgently about calling a doctor. He did not seem to see the ghost standing in their midst.

"Come here, Miss Honeywell," continued Zibby in her most sincere voice. "I've got a great plan. You've been trying to suck energy all this time, and it's hard on you. But what if we just *give* you energy, instead? All you need to do is let our energy flow right into you—filling you up to the brim. You'll be so powerful then, you'll still be able to keep your same body. You'll be able to do anything you want!"

Miss Honeywell was nodding. *It's gratifying to see that some children do learn to obey,* she said. *It has taken a long time, but in the end, I have taught you humility and obedience.*

In the end is right, thought Zibby mutinously as the ghost glided to her side. But aloud she said to the ghost, "Oh, yes, Sweet Miss Honeywell. I have learned my lesson. We all have."

Zibby motioned for the other girls and Mrs. Howell. "Focus," whispered Zibby, and the girls and Mrs. Howell all held hands and closed their eyes. Linked to Jude with one hand, Zibby reached out her other and touched the ghost's arm. It was as strong and solid as any real person's arm, but she felt a chill beyond anything she had ever felt seep through her very core. The cold nearly took her breath away, but she fought to stay in control of the moment. This was their only chance. And if it went wrong, they were doomed.

"Relax, Miss Honeywell," Zibby said soothingly. "Relax and let us tank you up with our energy. Just relax and let it flow into you…"

Miss Honeywell smiled with satisfaction and closed her dark eyes.

Immediately Zibby shot a look over at Mrs. Howell and the girls. *"Now!"* she ordered.

"You will not win," they all murmured in one voice. Then they started chanting it under their breath, over and over: "You. Will. Not. Win."

Far from intending to give Miss Honeywell their precious life force, they were hoping to join forces and marshal their energy *against* her. They were a power surge! They were going to short-circuit Miss Honeywell and end her reign of terror.

Zibby felt Miss Honeywell's body jerk, then stiffen. The ghost was aware now of what they planned. She was going to fight back.

Trying to trick me, eh?

The lights flashed. Outside the church, the day grew dark and thunder boomed. *Hadn't it just been sunny and mild?* Zibby kept her eyes closed, holding on as tightly to the ghost as she could—both with her mind and her hand. Even with her eyes closed, she could see the flash of lightning when it split the air of the church. *Lightning—inside?*

Why weren't the wedding guests screaming? Why weren't they running outside to safety? Zibby opened her eyes briefly and saw that the guests were slumping in the pews as if they were asleep. How long had they been that way? And the minister was now collapsed in a faint. Miss Honeywell was draining all of them, Zibby realized. Her grandparents were leaning back in their seats, eyes closed. *Who can we use as reinforcements if all the people fall asleep?* Zibby thought desperately. *Grammy? Gramps?*

The air was growing heavier. Miss Honeywell was winning.

Another burst of lightning, and Zibby closed her eyes. She clung to Jude and Laura-Jane. She knew it would not be long before she, too, grew so weak that Miss Honeywell could make her pick up that knife again—and use it.

Concentrate!

Zibby's eyes flew open at the new voice in her head—and there was Primrose Parson, right in front of her. Primrose pushed into the middle of the group of girls and took hold of Zibby's hand on one side and Jude's on the other. Immediately Zibby felt a new surge of power run through them. "Yes!" she shouted in relief. Primrose had come to help!

"And look—it's Baba," gasped Mrs. Howell, and sure enough, Mr. Pope was striding down the aisle of the church with a young, pretty woman at his side. "Is that—is that my mama?" The Popes reached the altar and held out their hands to Mrs. Howell. "Mama?" cried Mrs. Howell. "Oh, Mama!"

Evelina Pope clutched elderly Mrs. Howell in her arms. "My little Lydia," she said. "When I heard what had been happening, I knew I should come to help. But more than anything, I wanted to see my baby girl." More energy surged into the group as the Popes joined hands with Mrs. Howell and the girls.

Last came Lester, marching down the aisle, a determined look in his dark, glittering eyes. When he reached them and grabbed Zibby's hand, she felt still more energy flow into their midst. She smiled at him in relief.

"Ah, Thaddeus," cajoled Miss Honeywell, ignoring Mrs. Pope, Lester, and Primrose entirely. "You have come to be my groom after all."

"Not at all. But I had to come," said Mr. Pope, "when I realized what you are proposing to do with this bride and groom. I had to come—to stop this evil."

"We should have stopped you years ago," said Lester.

"You wretched boy," Miss Honeywell said, "turning against your own sister this way! I'll teach you a lesson if it's the last thing I do!" and she lifted her hand to slap his face. Before her hand could meet his cheek, he grabbed hold of her shoulders forcefully with both his hands.

"Calliope," he cried, "enough is enough. First I tried to get away. I tried to go to war to escape you. But you were too strong for me, always too strong. Then I wanted to help the little girl, little Primrose, when you were treating her as badly as you'd treated me. I tried to offer comfort when you had locked her in the closet—but in death as in life I was not strong enough. I feared you would kill her as you had killed me. In the end *you* were the one who died, and I saw it as justice! But even after death your power did not abate. You haunted Primrose, you haunted the Popes, you killed Evelina so that you might take Thaddeus as your own— and when he wouldn't have you, you arranged the fire that killed him, too. You thought in death you would have him—but his love for Evelina was too powerful."

When Miss Honeywell tried to speak, he shook her hard, and his hollow voice rang through the church. "There has been no stopping your fury. You sought your revenge against Zibby and her friends, and now you are trying to kill again. But this time, sister, you *will* be stopped! This time I, who have not been strong enough, in neither life nor death, am joining forces with all those who know you to be evil. Calliope, you will not escape justice this time. It is time for you to move on—to wherever it is souls like you belong." His hands gripped his sister's shoulders hard and bore her down onto the floor.

Miss Honeywell fought to rise, opened her mouth to speak, but the other ghosts surged forward. They were all touching one another, and all touching Zibby and the human chain she and her friends had made. The connection formed a current.

Zibby felt a steady pulsing, tingles of electricity flowing through the living and the dead—and all that power, flowing straight into Miss Honeywell, created the power surge that Zibby had hoped for. There was no blood and guts— ghosts don't have blood and guts—but there was a great crash of thunder and a horrible scream. A flare of light... and then a puff of acrid smoke.

Miss Calliope Honeywell had exploded.

"She's gone," Lester said, looking with interest at the spot where his sister had been.

"Thank you, oh thank you!" cried Zibby. "You came at just the right time. We couldn't have overpowered her without you!"

"It was a good plan, though," Mr. Pope said approvingly. "To overload her circuit."

"Zibby came up with the idea," Jude told the ghosts. And Zibby chimed in with the details of how she had thought of her plan the day before, when she saw how the storm gave the ghosts extra power. She'd remembered how the lights in their house often went out when there was a storm. She'd remembered how the computer at the *Gazette* had broken when there was a surge of electricity. She remembered what Mr. Potts had taught his class about how overloaded circuits cut out the power source, and how crossed wires could cause arcing and fire. She'd remembered how four girls had lifted Charlotte up over the back of a kitchen chair using only two fingers—by concentrating their energy.

Primrose's laugh was rueful. "It's the sort of thing I might have thought up myself once," she said. "A very dramatic practical joke—gone wrong."

"Or in this case, right," said Evelina Pope faintly. The ghosts were all starting to fade.

"In any case, it just needed a bit more juice from us," said Lester, "and it worked brilliantly. Hats off to Zibby!" he added, and doffed his helmet, bowing low.

"Hear, hear," cheered the other ghosts, flickering.

"Has Miss Honeywell moved on now?" whispered Penny.

"We all move on, sooner or later, it seems," replied Lester. "Off to...somewhere." He smiled at Zibby. "Calliope was a bitter woman, and she was a bitter girl before that. Maybe our parents were too strict with her—and that taught her to be too strict with those she was meant to care for. But who knows? Then that strictness turned into something else. Greed and a thirst for power. And that sort of thing can so easily turn into evil. Maybe if she'd lived longer, she would have reformed—but who can say? I, for one, doubt it."

For a fraction of a second Zibby felt sorry for Calliope Honeywell, who had led such a short miserable life and who had been thwarted in what she wanted so much—to marry the man she loved. But this sympathy lasted only a fraction of a second. Miss Honeywell's choices, time and again, had been the wrong ones and had led her down an unhappy path to this place, and to this final explosion.

The wedding guests were starting to stir now, sitting up in their seats again and looking confusedly around them. Zibby heard one guest sitting behind Grammy and Gramps comment, outraged, on the fireworks. "What was that? I feel so odd."

And another replied, "Can you imagine? Fireworks inside a church?"

"I thought it was a special touch, dear," chided a third woman. "Something a little different, that's all."

Nell shivered and shook, then rubbed her forehead, looking all around the church. She seemed dazed. But Ned was smiling at her. "Headache better?" he asked. And she nodded.

Jude, Penny, Charlotte, and Mrs. Howell slipped into their seats as before. The minister dusted off his robe, cleared his throat, and began again. "Dearly beloved—"

Zibby bent down to pick up her bouquet. Then she turned to thank the ghosts again—but they were gone.

CHAPTER 43

The service went off without a hitch. Zibby couldn't quite believe it was all over, and she heaved a big sigh of relief as the minister pronounced Ned and her mom "husband and wife." Nell was smiling, her headache having miraculously disappeared after the unexpected fireworks display. Zibby was smiling—her mom had been saved—and she walked back up the aisle after the bride and groom, with a light step.

Much later, when the janitor was cleaning the church, he found the minister's letter opener on the floor in the corner. Baffled, he returned it to the desk in the study.

At Aunt Linnea's grandly elegant reception, the guests piled gifts, wrapped in glittery paper, on top of the grand piano in the large living room. Zibby stood with her family while the photographer snapped shot after shot. Then Aunt Linnea handed the girls vases of fresh flowers for the table in the dining room. The caterers were almost ready for lunch to begin.

Zibby looked around the big dining room with appreciation. The antique mahogany table was polished and gleaming. Silver candlesticks held tall cream-colored candles placed at both ends. The centerpiece was the wedding cake—a three-tiered creation covered in luscious swirls of frosting and strewn with real flower petals. The top layer was decorated with the traditional bride and groom figurines.

"Ooh," breathed Penny. "It's gorgeous!"

There were covered trays of food arrayed on the table. All sorts of dips and breads, little sandwiches and quiches and vegetables, and bowls of steamed rice and rolled sushi. Everything looked delicious. Aunt Linnea's exquisitely furnished dollhouse mansion was displayed on a marble-topped table by the windows.

As the girls set the flowers in strategic spots on the long table, Zibby heard a little noise as if a bead had dropped onto the polished table. She turned—and clutched Jude's arm.

"What is it?" Jude asked urgently.

"The cake! Look—the bride!" was all Zibby could get out. Then Jude looked and saw what Zibby had seen.

The bride doll had tipped over and lay on her belly in the thick frosting. The tiny plastic head had broken off at the neck.

The bride doll had been beheaded.

The girls stared in horror, but then almost immediately there came a ghostly giggle, and Primrose Parson materialized across the room, grinning at them. She wasn't quite solid; Zibby could see the faint outline of the china closet behind her—an unsettling sight. "It was just a joke," Primrose said lightly, gliding over to pluck the tiny plastic head out of the sushi. "You don't have to look like that." She poked her finger into the base of the cake and came up with a smudge of frosting. She dabbed the frosting onto the little neck and pressed the bride's head back onto the doll with another giggle. "There, good as new."

"Primrose," whispered Zibby, glancing at the double doors to the dining room to make sure the guests weren't coming in yet. "I need to thank you. Thank you so much for helping us at the wedding."

"You needed an energy boost, we could all see that," said Primrose. "And we were all happy to help rid the world of Miss Honeywell."

"You saved my mom!" Tears pricked behind Zibby's eyes.

"All in a day's work," said Primrose with her little laugh. "And wasn't Lester wonderful?" Then her expression grew solemn. "Listen—meet me at the dollhouse, and bring Liddie," she ordered—and vanished just as the guests surged into the room.

"Just another of her practical jokes," Zibby murmured in relief. She watched Nell and Ned cut the cake.

"I wish she'd stop," Charlotte said weakly.

The guests reached for plates and glasses of champagne, exclaiming over the beautiful luncheon. They feasted and celebrated, and then everyone waved good-bye as Nell and Ned left for their honeymoon. They weren't going to have a very long honeymoon—just two days—because their work schedules would not allow for much time away. But they were splurging on one night aboard a luxurious riverboat hotel and spa.

As Zibby hugged her mom good-bye, she offered up a prayer of thanks that Nell was safe. Nell gave Zibby a kiss.

"We'll be back tomorrow night," she said. "Thanks again for that amazing fireworks display. I can't imagine how you arranged it without my knowing a thing about it!"

Then she and Ned were heading for the river—rattling merrily down the street in Ned's car, with old boots and tin cans tied on to the back, multicolored streamers flying in the wind, and a big painted sign reading JUST MARRIED taped in the rear window.

ZIBBY, LAURA-JANE, and Brady would all be staying overnight at Charlotte's, so Zibby announced to Aunt Linnea that she needed to get a few things from her house. Mrs. Howell, who had been told about Primrose's summons, quickly offered to drive Zibby over. Then all the girls said they would go for the ride. They hurried up to Zibby's bedroom.

Primrose flickered weakly in front of the dollhouse. Zibby could see the outline of the house right through her. The dollhouse was open as if Primrose had been playing with it. The dolls were arranged in various rooms—seated around the table in the dining room, sitting on the couches in the parlor, lying in the beds. The little girl doll lay on the floor in front of the house. Primrose held out a hand to Zibby. "I want to say good-bye."

Zibby was surprised at the stab of loss she suddenly felt. "Are you moving on?" She tried to touch Primrose's hand, but her fingers passed through air.

"Yes, it's time now," said Primrose faintly. "I can go, and I have you to thank. I never owned up to killing Miss Honeywell before—not even to myself." Then she turned to Mrs. Howell. "And I never owned up to the pain I caused you."

Mrs. Howell stepped toward the little girl ghost, holding out her hand, though it, too, passed through air. "I forgive you, Primrose," she said quietly, "for twice trying to give me a dollhouse you knew was haunted. You weren't trying to hurt me or my family—I understand that now. You were thinking only of yourself." Primrose grew even fainter, and Mrs. Howell spoke quickly to get everything said before Primrose disappeared. "We can part as friends. I'll take your dollhouse to my shop and fix it up to be as beautiful as you'd ever want to see it."

"Electric lights and all?" whispered Primrose in delight.

"Absolutely."

Zibby sensed they were nearing the end of it now, and she was surprised at her mixed feelings of sadness and tremendous satisfaction. "I will never, ever forget you," promised Zibby. She scooped up the little girl doll from the floor and placed it on the dollhouse parlor couch. She reached out one finger to stroke the brown braids, then latched the dollhouse closed. Mrs. Howell put her hands comfortingly on Zibby's shoulders.

Primrose's figure was wavering, growing more transparent. She turned to the window as if someone had called her name. She raised her head as if she were listening. Her dress became wisps of vapor. "Oscar?" she whispered. And then, joyfully: *"Oscar!"*

The vapor swirled around the room. The girls pressed together and linked arms so that none of the travelers on this journey would miss hearing any of Primrose's last words. But though they waited, there was only silence in the bedroom, and a gust of wind rattling the windowpanes.

So that was it. There would be no more ghostly voices in their heads, Zibby knew. No more smoke, no more moving dolls, no nightmare fires. They were moving on, all of them.

It was all over.

Except—not quite over!

The five girls and Mrs. Howell gasped in awe and exhilaration as the entire dollhouse lit up—every little window briefly aglow. Then Primrose Parson, always one to enjoy a good joke and determined as ever to have the last word, moved on in a shower of stars.

EPILOGUE

ZIBBY WALKED INTO her bedroom and put the phone down on her desk. She knew she had a big goofy grin on her face, but she couldn't help it. It was the first time she'd talked to her dad in two years, and he had been so glad to hear from her. She felt giddy with relief at having broken their long silence at last.

Zibby pulled his latest postcard out of her pocket and sailed it onto the bed for the others to read. Jude picked it up first.

Dear Zib,

I'm still thinking about the holidays, still hoping that an invitation to spend Christmas in Venice might tempt you to come to us.

Please say you'll come! I miss you—and Sofia and I are both longing to see you here.

I'll be phoning soon to beg in person—both in English and Italian.

Love, Dad

"But you called him first." Jude looked at Zibby appraisingly. "So—how did it go?"

"It was great." Unexpected tears of happiness pricked behind Zibby's eyes.

"Did he have an Italian accent?" inquired Laura-Jane.

"No, he sounded just the same. He sounded totally great."

"Well, what are you going to do?" asked Jude.

"Hey, stamps like this one would make great pictures for my new dollhouse," was all Penny said, handing the postcard back to Zibby.

Zibby traced her finger over the stamp before answering Jude's question. "I'm going to Venice for the holidays," she said finally.

Jude nodded, smiling. And Charlotte grinned saucily and said, "Probably we'd all better come along to keep you safe."

"Yeah," agreed Penny, tossing her braids so the beads clicked. "In case Venice has ghosts."

"Don't mention that word!" Zibby said with a laugh. It was a relief not to have to worry about ghosts anymore.

It was a relief to have the dollhouse *gone* for a while, too, Zibby thought, looking around her bedroom, where Jude and Penny, Laura-Jane and Charlotte were lounging on her bed, where they'd been waiting while she telephoned Italy. Mrs. Howell had taken the dollhouse away after Primrose moved on, and although the electric lighting was installed a day later, Zibby had given permission for the dollhouse and all the dolls to stay at Lilliput on display for as long as Mrs. Howell wanted it. The governess doll was not among them;

that frown-faced doll in the gray gown had vanished as completely as Miss Honeywell herself.

Mrs. Howell was decorating the dollhouse now for Halloween with tiny jack-o'-lanterns, scarecrows, and little white ghosts dangling from threads in the windows. Zibby wasn't in any particular hurry to have the house back, and she thought she'd let Mrs. Howell keep it to decorate for Christmas as well. Still, as much as she had hated the dollhouse, Zibby suspected she would miss it if it, like the ghosts, disappeared for good.

The only dollhouse she wanted to deal with for now was the one they were building for Penny's trolls. All the girls were working together after school on the farmhouse kit Mrs. Howell had given Penny, constructing it, gluing shingles and bricks, painting, and making miniature furnishings. Zibby enjoyed using her birthday tool set. Laura-Jane was making a chandelier out of a pair of Mrs. Jefferson's old earrings. Laura-Jane had been given a dollhouse kit, too—a Victorian cottage that would be the girls' next project. Nell and Aunt Linnea were thrilled that the girls were taking such an interest in miniatures. Laura-Jane and Brady's mother was returning from her long business trip the next weekend, but Zibby was glad the Shimizu kids would be spending every other week with their dad, plus one month every summer. There would be plenty of time for dollhouse projects—and bike riding and skating.

The girls left Zibby's room and went outside. They ambled through the crackling autumn leaves to the Jeffersons' house and spent the afternoon framing stamps for Penny's dollhouse. As they worked, they talked about Italy, about school, and Charlotte quizzed them on their style quotient from *Fashion Teen* magazine. Then their talk turned to whether they would go trick-or-treating this year, or whether they were too old—and if they *did* go, should they dress as ghosts? They decided they would, escorting Brady as their excuse.

Ghosts again, Zibby thought. *There's still no escaping them!*

Later, as Zibby and Laura-Jane walked down the street toward home, Brady ran to meet them, his cheeks rosy from the autumn cold. He skidded to a stop in front of them. "There's a big box on the porch and it has Zibby's name on it!" he cried. "Hey, can I open it?"

"No!" Zibby darted ahead, leaping up the porch steps eagerly.

Sure enough, the large box was addressed to Isabel Thorne, with no return address and no postage on the box. No one had seen it arrive. No one had heard a delivery truck, or even footsteps on the porch. It was just suddenly there.

"Well, open it!" Brady urged, and ran inside to fetch the scissors. He returned with Nell and Ned right behind him. The opening of a mysterious box was something nobody wanted to miss out on.

As Zibby slit open the tape holding closed the cardboard flaps, she was worrying: *Could it be the governess doll—back again? But no . . .* She broke off with a happy gasp and held up the surprise gift: royal blue and silver Zingers, just her size. "They're perfect!" shouted Zibby. "Thanks, Primrose!"

Laura-Jane laughed.

Nell looked baffled. "Who on earth?"

"Not on earth," said Laura-Jane slowly. "Not exactly."

Zibby exchanged a look with Laura-Jane. There had been ghosts, there had been lost souls and anguish and more than a dash of danger, but now there were just the tangy scent of autumn leaves and a gathering of family in the early dusk.

She reached for her mom's hand. Then for Ned's. The time seemed right. "Come inside," Zibby urged. "Come inside, because Laura-Jane and I have a ghost story to tell you."

"Cool," said Brady. "You mean a real, true one?"

"As true as they come, and guaranteed to make your hair stand on end," promised Zibby, ruffling his spiky black mop. "Even more than it does already."

They all stepped into the house, one after the other, moving on into the rest of their lives.